2FACE

Rise of a Menace

by
Deiverion Mouzon

Order this book online at www.trafford.com
or email orders@trafford.com

Most Trafford titles are also available at major online book retailers.

Note for Librarians: A cataloguing record for this book is available from Library
and Archives Canada at www.collectionscanada.ca/amicus/index-e.html

Printed in Victoria, BC, Canada.

ISBN: 978-1-4269-2126-1 (sc)

*Our mission is to efficiently provide the world's finest, most comprehensive book publishing
service, enabling every author to experience success. To find out how to publish your
book, your way, and have it available worldwide, visit us online at www.trafford.com*

Trafford rev. 11/24/2009

www.trafford.com

North America & international
toll-free: 1 888 232 4444 (USA & Canada)
phone: 250 383 6864 ♦ fax: 812 355 4082

The Prelude

U-r-r-r. Free jumped at the sudden screeching tires of the ford Cedan. The window came down slowly and a voice said ;

Yo. Free what up.

As soon Free recognized the voice he ran to the car.

Yo C.D. what up. The snub nose.38 special took him by surprise , he thought C.D. was his boy, the look in his eyes were cold and death filled the air.

What happened to my bread Free said a angry 2Face.

I, I, I,!

I nothing. You owed me for the last 4yrs.. I put you on when you had nothing remember. Then you duck me like a lame. 2 shots rang off and pierced his brain, the pain free felt was like somebody holding a hot iron over a cut or an open wound. He finally fell to his knees and fell face first on the edge of the sidewalk. Shock was the look on his face when he hit the ground as he died with his eyes open.

2Face and Shorts blew down Fulton , then raced towards Atlantic to East New York from Bed-Stuy. The car was to be burned.

Was that necessary son.

Fuck that nigga. He should've paid me my money. Cats gonna understand it's consequences to fronting on me, believe that.

CHAPTER 1

C.D.. Mommy look its C.D. mommy. He's coming home with us asked lil Kitara.

Yes Kiki , C.D. finally coming home.   Well it's about time said Gina , you've been gone for 3yrs.. I hope you ready now to stay out of jail for good this time.

Just drive the car. But before that Kiki give me a hug and tell mommy give me a kiss.

I love you C.D. , said Kiki.

I love you to Kiki.

Mommy.   What Kiki.

Give C.D. a kiss now , she demanded.

O.K. mooo-ah.

Yeah replied C.D. now I feel welcomed. Lets go home I got a lot that needs to be done.   The drive home was talkative, lots of laughs and reminisces. Everybody enjoying each others company, chilling.

Hey baby, look at that sign Bing, said C.D..You know I can't wait to get in the house, but before we do that stop at the masjid I need to offer salah.

The one in J.C. asked Kiki?

Yeah said C.D.. Then after that I want to go to Buds house and see what up with him 'n the crew ok.

Gina's taxi service as you wish. Laughter filled the car. After praying and riding over to his boy crib C.D. jumped out of the toyota camry, freshly painted and tinted with chrome rims. Hey baby I'll be right back. I'll just wait here baby, hold up I got to run and get cigarettes and Kiki some juice so if we're not back call so I know you're ready. Alright replied C.D..

C.D. walked up the stairs of the 2 story house on seminary ave., the place they made the since coming to Bing a few years ago from N.Y.C. The original crew was Mouse, Hasan,Tone, Reef, Shorts, Rza, Simori and C.D.. Then Bud, Sheen, Low, Munch, Box, Omar, Simeon, Danja, Jubbs and the whole big east. The crew got broke down over the years with Simori becoming a stock broker, Reef in jail for a shooting serving 13yrs., Low in jail for 10yrs. Said he ain't fucking with the click no more Box who had the hood on smash got killed, Omar got killed recently he was once called the war god. Munchy on his own sheen down for 15yrs for stabbing a fiend. Hasan was on his Islam stuck with his wife Danja and Jubbs up in Harlem caking it, Simeon trying to box, Rza he a electrician up in Albany, Mouse Hasan brother think he a pioneer still, Tone stay on the low, Bud on some family shit, Mouse just did 6yrs for a stabbing, but the main cats was Mouse, Tone, shorts, Reef, Bud, his other man Roc a cat he met in jail from around his way years ago that he got tight with and Rza his old stick up partner. Boom, boom, boom, boom, boom. Yo, who that.

It's ya boy. Oh shit screamed Jackie! Hey Bud it's C.D.! Open the fuckin door Jack damn. The door opened, As Salaamu Alaykum.

Wa Laykum Salam Rahmatuallah. The greetings of Muslims. How you been Jack. Jackie was Buds wifey. Good she replied. Where's Bud.

In the room said Jackie playing with jr. I can't believe this fool got a jr. A yo Bud what up youth.

Yo, yo what up son Bud said hugging each other. Yo Bud said C.D. what's good baby boy. Yo let me look at Jr.

Hey Jr. you see ugly. He ugly right said Bud.

Ya big head boy look just like you fool said C.D. smiling. Yo what up with Mouse.

I can't call it said Bud.

I owe son 5 minutes for that sucka shit he pulled Bud, trying to holla wifey. What's wrong with son. Bud said, yo champ breathe easy, karma is a mother fucka.

Where Tone stay at. He still fucking that white bitch. You know he love that bitch said C.D.. A yo how Abu 'n the family.

They good replied Bud. You know Shorts home asked Bud.

Yeah I heard, tell son holla at me later give son my info. After a little more catching up C.D. told Bud a plan to make a quarter mil as Bud sat back and listened, felt the plan even though C.D. never went into detail he just explained the basics. He told Bud he had to talk to 2 more people before the plan was a go. After a couple more minutes of talking 'n shit C.D. called Gina to scoop him up. He gave Bud 5 and broke out. His next stop ma dukes crib, where she had a batch of his favorite chocolate chip cookies, fried chicken and well seasoned rice, with baked mac' n cheese. Yeah! It's going down early yelled C.D. jumping in the car. Hey Cory said his momma.

Hey Ma what's up.

Give me a hug boy. I hope your ass stay out of jail this time. I'll do my best ma.

Hey Gina what's up girl.

I'm chillin Ms. Pat.

Good, good. I got the food on the warmers ya'll sit down and make yourselves comfortable.

After an hour of talking and good eating his ma told him about a construction gig she got hooked up for him. He thanked her for it, walked through the house looking at old pictures of his childhood bringing back fond memories and some dark ones. He and his ma always didn't get along. She made him what he was today in certain aspects and he definitely had a lot of her traits in own, but in his mind the past was the past and you only got one mother, so now he thrived on doing whatever he could for her, if he could just leave the streets alone he'd be the perfect son.

Well momma I gotta go, I got a curfew and I don't want to start off on the wrong foot when I see him so if you'll excuse us.

Ok she said. He gave her a kiss on the cheek and was gone.

CHAPTER 2

Yo Shorts what up. Come in. What's good bee.

Ain't shit Shorts said. Meet my wife Gina, Gina that's my fams Shorts. Now can you exc- use us we have to talk baby.

Alright fine. Probably just men talk any ways.

A yo keep Kiki in the room with you, C.D. said.

Who that asked Shorts.

She my stepdaughter replied C.D.. But anyway my dude lets get to the point. I gotta mean plan to get us rich believe that. Said C.D.. You down with it?

Son I gotta know all the details said Shorts. Shorts was the type of man who played no games he was a thoroughbred , he'll fight ya, stab ya, cut ya, and definitely shoot ya quicker than rattlesnake strikes it's prey. He just did 10yrs., Maxed out too. Him 'n C.D. robbed some kids who tried to retaliate and he blammed 2 of them. Of course in this day 'n age they told. Shorts held it down and C.D. never got bagged. C.D. did his best to hold son down and felt he ow- ed his life to that man, but his run ins with the law himself cost him 10yrs. Of his own in 'n out of prison. He and Shorts knew each other since childhood a bond that can never be broken.   Check it though son. I'm trying to knock off 2 birds in one stone.

How's that asked Shorts.

We get to pop the cat that ratted me out and we gonna use him to get a quarter mill.

A quarter mill. Said Shorts. How you plan on us pulling that off.

Chill son, listen this is what we gonna do. We gonna juxx the bank on Front st. The met bank son.

You wilding replied Shorts.

Nah bee, listen. Yo it's gonna take 5 of us right, I need a trust worthy chick, Bud and I got this I met up top doing my bid. Me and you gonna dress up in all black catch that rat Mike and his wife, kidnap'em drive 'em to the golf course in Ely park and bury 'em. We gonna catch 'em late Sunday night like 1:30a.m. so we got time to dig a hole and bury 'em, then take their car park it down the block from where we do our next kidnaping. Yo Shorts you won't be involved in the other kidnaping that's why I got the white boy. I fitted some ski masks to see how much room my eyes have, so I can put make up around my eyes to make myself look white and go undetected. Me , the white boy gonna creep to the bank manager's house, Billy the white boy is a professional burglar and we'll slip in, kidnap 'em send the husband to work knowing that if he doesn't give the female we sending at 10:00am a quarter mill his family is dead. She will be disguised, wearing gloves. The money will then go from her hands in which she'll walk 2 blocks and switch disguises to meet Bud he'll check to see if the money is real and once he's cleared us, me 'n the white boy will meet everybody at Fitzes for a drink. You'll follow Bud incase he get funny on us. I'm the only one who knows everybody involved in this, I planned this out with the white boy up top. I'm a go check Shanta to see if she want to get down. To me she's trustworthy.

You got it all mapped out huh said Shorts.   When its all said 'n done everybody will have $50,000 a piece. They'll have to sit on it of course, but not us. If you walk with me , we'll buy all drugs with ours make a couple of good flips and we'll have crazy product and our money and be caked up by the age of Legally.

Sounds official said a chuckling Shorts with a sick smile.

Yo I plan to use all my prison resources to flip this money, said C.D..

One question asked Shorts, why kill mike and his wife, then dig a hole? Why not dig a hole first.

Cause son then we won't be riding around for 3hrs. In a stolen vehicle. No sense getting recognized by accident and get knocked, I want this to be smooth 'n quick. We gotta be sober, alert and not leave physical evidence, a dead man can't talk. If we don't catch the wife it could be a problem Shorts. We stay occupied for 3hrs., if everybody play they position and do they jobs we'll be rich and unsuspected whatsoever. How you know so much about this bank? For 1 gotta account there for 2, I'm a mean observer. The only thing getting everybody involved. The reason we'll go undetected is cause cops not gonna look for thugs who it. They know its not our fortay and they don't think we smart enough we the last people they'll look for.

Yo, C.D. asked Shorts you married now huh. How's wifey treating you and why I ain't get invited?

We'll Shorts we got married in jail my next wedding you'll be there believe that! Truthfully son, I don't think she been all that faithful, faithful ain't how we met, she was like me, so I know she ain't right.

Then why marry her asked Shorts.

I just act accordingly like I don't know shit. But I ain't got all the facts yet, but I'll fix her believe that said C.D. Well Shorts not to be rude but I gotta handle a few things, in Sha Allah I'll see you at Juma to let you if everything's a go.

No doubt said Shorts as Salaamu Alaykum,   Wa laykum salaam Wa Ramatullah, a Muslim greeting. C.D. was originally from the Bronx. He grew up in a ghetto environment around lot's of family and friends, he had over 50 cousins male 'n female just on his fathers side of the family, so many he didn't even know half of them. On his mother's side he had lots of family, lots of uncles 'n aunts, cousins scattered all about the country. Most of whom he seen only at family reunions. He was raised by his mother's side his momma didn't take no shit. His late grandmother who meant more to him than anybody kept him in line, kept him working and kept her first grandson out of trouble. His uncles treated him like their own, showering him with gifts and taking him to all types of sporting events. His cousins all they did was scrap and some of them till this day hold notorious reps. His aunts were down to Earth on his fathers side and more like older sisters on his mothers side. C.D. always knew his boundaries with them. Him and his mother while he was growing up had a lot of problems with each other in which he constantly got thrown out the house and to either stay with friends (which was how he took Shahada) or lugging his bags across town to aunts after disputes. It was then C.D. found his life time crew : Bud, Tone, Reef, Shorts, Riza, Mouse and the rest of the east New York crew. He also found Islam with his crew, majority of them were Muslim since birth or took Shahada at At first they were renegade Muslims always tussling, boostin, bagging, the girls, looking fly, then came the drug game that mouse and Reef enforced and they all followed suit.

The life of crime took over C.D. although he's a well liked person he had many beefs in the past over stick ups and the ruthlessness of his boys, he constantly had to watch his back from people who hated his crew. But through the years after lots of shootouts and work being put in by him and his crew the beefs came to an end and now he was grown and about paper.

After running the streets in and out of jail dealing drugs, in and out of different relationships C. D. met his sweetheart 4yrs ago in a night club in a few months they hit it off, found out they had too much in common but their love stuck out like a sore thumb. She was the only woman to stick by him through a bid and he felt compelled to give her an oath, but the trust issues within himself raised doubt about Gina's sincerity and some of his actions didn't exactly help the cause.

Now he was to commit this bank robbery and try to become one of the most powerful African Americans today and blindly change the face of humanity. He had many of talents, many dreams and aspirations, but now it was time to put the thoughts into action.

CHAPTER 3

As C.D. sat in his 2bedroom half of house watching sports center on the flat screen tv his wife bought him as a coming home gift. His furniture was tan leather, carpeted floor and his cat rubbing on his leg to get petted. Gina sat contemplating, she said to herself thinking out loud, I know these 2 are up to something, he's been acting real strange towards me since he came home maybe I should go talk to him.

Gina approached her man in a very seductive way, rocking her daisy dukes perfectly with her hour glassed shaped body and manicured nails, with a fresh pedicure a dark red color. She said to her man: C.D. what's wrong baby?

Ain't nothing just checking sports center out and calling it a night.

Well you're not going to go to sleep yet baby. You don't think I look sexy for you tonight she asked?

Baby you look beautiful replied C.D..

Then why you not showing me no attention demanded Gina?

Come here Gina as he grabbed her by the arm manly and she rested her ass cheeks so that her dripping wet pussy was directly on C.D. hardness. C.D. caressed her hair smoothly and kissed her long and passionately. After the first kiss he grabbed her face and told her: you know I love you to death right? Nothing will ever come between us, believe that!

I believe you baby she said back. They looked in each others eyes searching for any kind of falsehood and neither could find none.

They began to kiss again and juices began to flow, he grabbed her butt cheeks and squeezed as hard as he could, while she massaged his mammoth cock. He used his 3yrs of intense training to muscle her and hold her by the ass in the air. Kissing her and placing her in the plush leather couch while his cock bamboozled through his pants rubbing the wet pussy. As he kissed on her neck massaging her breasts, he used his tongue like he was sliding down a pole smoothly licking until he got to her pink nipple and bit down on it, gently licking it at the same time, making her moan and he licked the other nipple as well and then licked all the way down to her stomach until he got to the crack between the pussy and the thigh for he knew that was her spot. Then he licked her thighs to behind the knees all the way down to her feet, then licked back up her leg till she got to oozing her pussy and licked her clit until she grabbed his head and squeezed him between her legs as she orgasm all over his face and sharp shape up. After she finished, she began to mount her oral sex attacked by giving him head, slow neck taking the mammoth cock as deep as she could go knowing that it excites him. then she began to suck 'n lick his balls until his shit throbbed, then she mounted him and took him deep in her pussy and she rode him long 'n hard bouncing her ass off his thighs screaming until he busted a mean nut, a methodical nut inside her. Both satisfied they went to bed, a little pillow talk and they both fell out from tiredness.

CHAPTER 4

The next morning on the way to holla at Shanta, C.D. cruised through the town in the Camry, stopped at the mobile on main st. it was bright outside, sun shining, the store was packed from people getting gas. His eyes set on a bodacious Spanish mommy with the crazy fat ass, she had on a tailor made to fit business suit, with her pants hovering over her Prada shoes. Her hair was long she had that tan complexion rocking her shades on top of hair. She eyeballed C.D.'s muscularity and his style and dress, his fresh razor sharp line up. Their eyes met as C.D. held the door for her. "Thank you she said".

You welcome replied C.D.. You have a beautiful accent, where you from?

I'm from Puerto Rico she replied.

Word! said C.D.. I'm originally from the Bronx he said as the conversation moved to outside.

Yeah she said, I lived in the Bronx for 10yrs, she said. So how long have you been in bing, she asked?

Off 'n on since the mid 90's.

Wow she said that's a long time, I've been here for 2yrs. She said staring at the ring on his finger. Oh don't sweat that said C.D. I'm getting a divorce soon.

Why she asked? It's a long story she broke my heart truthfully.

I would love to get acquainted with you but I got a lot of work to do and running around and I'm sure you got to get to work yourself, by the way what's your name? Sue she said. C.D. he answered back as he shook her soft hand. He caught an erection instantly he never met a girl who turned him on like that on sight, except that porno chick Lacy in which she was a splitting image of.

You got a number Sue?

Yeah, you don't think your wife would mind?

Fuck her! she done did her share but that's neither here nor there I'm interested in you right now.

You don't care if I'm involved or nothing?

Well are you asked C.D.?

No, she said smiling you can have my number and make sure you call me C.D.!

Oh I will believe that! 15 minutes later C.D. was at Tone and Shantas crib. 2 knocks on the door, who is it asked a soft voice? It's your boy! Oh my God it's C.D.! Tone its C.D. get up!

Son here? Word! Let him in I gotta go hit the gibbs up. After Shanta opens the door she embraced her long time friend. C.D.

Oh my god its been so long, how you been?

Chilling, chilling Shanta what up! where's Tone at?

Getting dressed yo.

Son I'll be right out son.

Take ya time bee, I ain't in no rush. C.D. needed that time to holla at Shanta.

Yo listen Shanta I got a little juxx planned real soon, I know yaw doing eh alright, but I got a plan to put us over the top.

Stop playing C.D. you just came home. Damn you gotta chill, we all miss you out here.

Trust me Shanta, call me tonight don't tell Tone nothing. It's a 4 man operation, 250,000 a 'n better we could get. I need a reliable female ok. I'll call you later but this better be good C.D. Oh it is believe that! Yo son what up you big face bitch you! said Tone.

They embraced, yo son everything everything said C.D.. Son you gotta stay out this time son. Of course said C.D.. Tone was the comedian, C.D. was the trend setter. He was gonna get a kick out of tone running his new line believe that!

Yeah Tone I got a bunch of new sayings and my son in Poughkeepsie act just like you mad loud mad funny and talk cash money shit!

Fuck out of here this nigga always meeting some one. I see you got wild big too! Yo yo money them hot ones will slow you down, believe that! They both laughed that off.

Yo asked C.D. where's mice at?

Who Mouse said Tone I'm a call that nigga right now. Tone dialed Mouse #, it rang 3 times before Samira picked up.

As Salaamu Alaykum. She said

Yo, put that big face bitch on the phone!

Son let me talk to Samira asked C.D.? Salaamu Alaykum said C.D..

Wa Laykum Salaam she replied who this?

C.D. Ricky retardo!

Oh she said what's up boy how you been?

Good, good Hussein the phone! its C.D.! Tell him hold up said Mouse.

Mouse grabbed the phone son what up!

What up Mouse you punk mother fucker! I'm coming to see you son. Ab and Ummie there?

Nah son said Mouse. But who you basing up to?

You bee said C.D.! I'll be there believe that! 20 minutes later the 2 exchanged blows Mouse a little 5 foot midget man had an exceptional knuckle check so C.D. had to be cautious but he could box as welland had quick hands for his size. C.D. bobbed and weaved a wild right hand by Mouse then hit Mouse with a barrage of punches as he curled up in the corner on the ground. Tone stepped in to break it up. Mouse took a broom and viciously cracked C.D. in the back, Tone grabbed the broom from Mouse as C.D. tackled son to the ground when Ummie and Ab walked in the yard from the kitchen.

What the fuck is ya'll doing in my yard fighting? C.D. I'm surprised at you. Hussein get out! Tone you alright? Asked Ummie. C.D. get out! C.D. and Mouse made moves to the car at the speed of lightning before Ummie got the broom and went to work on them. They laughed off the little scuffle and tone followed them to the car lets get some breakfast. Ihop said Mouse.

CHAPTER 5

Tonight's the night baby boy! C.D. said to Shorts after a week of planning and preparing. The plan was a go. All every body gotta do is execute. Shorts you ready?

Ready he replied I was made for this shit! I ain't even worried.

Shanta you ready? Hell yeah! Well lets get it said C.D.!

C.D. and Shorts followed the rat and his wife from club 2000 Thursday night. The night was dry, chilly, the air was thin. Houses seemed empty and deserted by the quietness from the night.

The rat and his wife never saw the ambush coming as they were too drunk and off point to see the derringer as cold steel was pressed real hard, extremely hard against their temples. The state of drunkeness soon wore off as the rat and his wife as flashbacks went through their minds of the people they wronged and ratted out.

Before they could plea C.D. said get in the car and don't make a sound. If you such as move or flinch I'll blow ya fucking head off. It'll look like scrambled eggs covered in ketchup on your windshield. They did as told till they got to the destination secured by duct tape. C.D. used all back streets to get to the back of Ely-park golf course. The night chills didn't help the shivers the rat and his wife were feeling. Curiousity and fear overwhelmed their minds as they were ordered to get out of the car. It was pitch black C.D. turned on the flash light.

Why are you doing this asked the rat? He would never know as the.38 ripped through his skull like a great whites razor sharp teeth as the burning sensation made him fade to unconsciousness a deep sleep that will last forever.

The surprising thing to his wife was muffled sound and the burn she felt pierce through her scalp as she slumped to the ground. Nobody would hear the shots that slumped her to the ground face first into the cold grass.

After 2and a half hours of digging and sweating part 1 of the plan was complete. The rat nor his wife would tell on any body again or be seen again. The phone rang twice before billy picked up. Yo we coming to get you champ, said C.D.. Give me 5 minutes.

Shanta put on so much make up even she had to admire the transition. She had to lie to Tone,   said she was at her grandmother's, well she was till midnight. When she knew everybody was sound as sleep she slipped out the back door and jumped in Buds S.U.V. to go 2 blocks from the stash crib. Dollar signs flashed through her mind. She knew she was taking a mean risk, things could get ugly, but she know C.D. ain't no dummy she thought.

I hope this shit go right Bud she said.

Shit gonna run smooth trust me said Bud.

C.D. always was the wisest and calculates everything said Shanta, but he got that 2face side to him Bud he do do some fowl shit to people.

Yeah but not to the fams said Bud son on some loyal shit with us. She felt secure when Bud said that.

CHAPTER 6

Part 2 of the plan began when Billy and C.D. parked the stolen car behind a churh on a desolate block. The only lights came from the street lights. Stray cats tussled along the side of a closed store front as they creeped to the back of the house, the area was nice as they scoped out for any onlookers but it was 4:30 in the morning most law biding citizens were sleep at this time.

C.D. through his observation knew this type of neighborhood, that people don't lock up they're doors. It was supposed to quote on quote a good community but these people were in for rude awakening.

The back yard was messy from the kids, beach balls lay around, toys and an empty swing which looked frozen and a plastic garbage can filled with empty pizza boxes.   You ready champ? Asked C.D..

Yeah he replied. Yo say no names and creep through the house the kids sleep in one room together, the oldest daughter got her own room, the parents you know already. Every body in the basement.   They crept through house from the kitchen tiptoeing till they reached the stairs. C.D. crept real slow like he was a real pro. Once they made it up the stairs adjacent to them was the parents room, C.D. quickly made his in as the door was slightly open. The door squeaked , the husband John thought the noise was a cat or his kid but soon felt the cold steel pressed hard on his forehead.

Shh! wake your wife up now she better not scream or I'm a make her face look like a bad dish of sloppy joe.

Ok, ok please, said John but his wife heard the noise but she was still a little groggy.

Honey what's wrong you having a nightmare?

Baby said John don't scream or move there's a man in our room with a gun. Panic filled her face as she pleaded, please don't hurt our kids?

Shut the fuck up! replied C.D. your kids are fine as long as you cooperate. Do as we say nobody gets hurt. Now get to duct taping he tossed the tape to John. John was rail thin around 6"ft. struggled to duct tape his wife Lisa who was thick, meaty legs decent face, brown eyes and bodacious tits.

Billy knocked on the door, the glock C.D. had almost went off till he heard billy's voice say   every thing good?

Good replied CD ever thing secure?

Yep! said Billy.

Ok duct tape John every body in the basement. Once every body was in the basement, CD had Billy duct tape they're mouths and taped behind they're backs.

Ya'll hungry asked C.D.? The little ones head nodded yes. What yaw want cereal or cakes? They nodded for the cakes. CD looked at John and his wife to see if they were hungry, they nodded no. Once everybody was calm CD pulled John aside and explained to him the plan, what they wanted him to do. The reason I am here cause I want you to go to work as normal as possible. I understand the situation your in so I sense your nervousness but remember to hold your composure, cause your gonna stuff this bag with a quarter mill out of your bank.

But, but I don't think we carry that kind of money.

Don't beat me in the head with that shit! Ya better find a way.

I'll give you till 10:30 a.m. they'll be a call made to you to meet a friend. You will be instructed to meet my friend outside in a near parking lot. Do as your told and your family walks away. Anything funny anything with the cops, any funny money, any ploys everybody dies. You can do it you're the westside branch manager. Listen John, don't fuck with me do not fuck with me. Once my friend checks the money and everything good you good, you'll get a call from me saying everything is ok.

At 8:30 in the morning Friday John dressed in his black business suit neatly pressed and his face clean shaved. He hopped in his red ford blazer turned on the radio it was business as usual. He listened to the news on the a.m. radio the weather was decent. He fought back tears trying not to lose his composure. He knew if he showed any kind of weakness any kind of danger his family was dead. Police was out of the question until he got his family secure. He wondered if it was more culprits involved in this scheme. He hoped the thugs keep there word. Regardless he had to do this for Jessie, Tony, Mary and Lisa.

John pulled up to the Met bank, the westside branch. The sun beamed through the windshield as he parked the jeep. He hopped out thinking to himself I got to make this happen and save my family.

He entered the bank greeting everybody with a friendly smile. He used his keys to do his rounds in the back area. He had count money out for the tellers in which was his chance to figure out how much and how he was gonna get $250,000 out that bank. He had to adjust the camera somehow, he figured he'd pull the electricity. He would evacuate the whole building and make it look like a fire drill. He'd shut down all the cameras, stuff the knapsack with money and everything will be good.

Chapter 7

Shorts job was easy he thought, keep track of Bud and Shanta. You never know who's gonna flip, plus they were dealing with a lot of cake on the line. He knew Shanta was a street chick even though she act like one. And Bud who had no ties can easily bounce with all that. Shorts thought about CD as well. The plan was foolproof carefully thought out, the make up and all the

disguises was almost movie like even better. He thought about the blood on the they hand as well, the consequences, if they got knocked who will flip? CD was to make sure they didn't get

caught. But he had in mind CD was Muslim 'n all and he had mad love for his man, but if shit wet wrong something had to give and someone had to go.

An angry Gina slammed the door to her house, tears flowing down her eyes. C.D. didn't come home last night, he called and said he would spend the night out at Bud's, but he never picked up the phone. In fact the phone was off. Neither Jackie or Bud picked up the phone or answered the door and a strange red dodge dorango was parked in front of Buds. Her friend said 2 white boys left the crib around 12:30 a.m.. She also said 2 white girls came over earlier then a 3rd white girl in jogging pants and black hoodie creeped over around 1: Her friend Diamond witnessed this from her apartment across the street. Gina wondered what the hell was going on and swore to her self if CD was cheating she'd ruin him. gina needed to get to the bottom of this cause she truly loved him to death.

CD contemplated on the situation. He had every body spread out on the far corners of the basement. He left Billy in the basement while he the duct taped kids something to drink.

Damn! if this shit don't go down as planned I got a whole lot of blood on my hands CD said to himself, Shorts, Bud, Shanta, Billy, not to mention the wife 'n kids and the bank manager.

John kept pacing back 'n forth around the bank doing observations. He tried to look the part but it's hard when his wife and kids are at stake. Wow! said one of the tellers named Mandy. John is acting real strange she whispered to a co worker, Mr. Callahan you ok? Of course, just thank its Friday! replied John.

The clocks ticking John thought to himself. The morning was quiet it was maybe 3 or 4 customers cause the bank was just opening, it was time.

He went to the back of the bank, reached behind the fire extinguisher and pulled the fire alarm. Ee-er! ee-er! ee-er! ee-er! ee-er! The noise was loud and scared the whole spot. Ladies 'n gentlemen, ladies 'n gentlemen,! We are experiencing a fire drill people. Please exit the building once its clear I'll let everybody back inside. This is only a drill, please cooperate thank you.

Once everybody was outside John raced to his office and quickly grabbed the knapsack, went to the vault and typed 38570 a code the door opened. He stuffed the bag with money, 50's, 100's, dubs and tens. The bag was so stuffed he could have put over the amount he was suppose to, but he didn't care as long as his family was safe. He stashed the bag behind his desk. Then before any guards that were doing they're rounds came through for a security check could see him, he found them. Sorry, for the disturbance guys. But I needed to see how fast people react to emergencies.   Sir was this authorized by one of our head branches? Asked the guard. Or was it the Feds?

I'll explain later said John. Lets get everybody back inside.

When Shanta seen the people evacuate the premises of the bank and that cop car pulled up, she thought the guy got scared and blew it up. The nervousness hit her she was ready to tell Bud she was out but greed kept her motivated. She decided to go for a jog until she got the call.

Mr. Secret after seeing the stunt at the bank, called CD immediately. After 2 vibrations CD got the phone. Champ what up!

Yo listen said Mr. Secret ya man pulled the fire alarm! and he evacuated the whole building. A Cop car pulled up to then left when he spoke to security. Ya home girl went for a jog. Hold up people starting to file back in. Yo, if I was you I'd wait about 10 minutes before I make a move.

Bet, replied CD.   CD told Billy to be ready incase the police showed up. He informed about the stunt John pulled.   Ok! everybody back to work! said John. He waited 10 minutes for the call, this whole thing could be over he thought. All he needed to do now was figure out a way to get out of the bank and get the bag off. Once he knew his family was safe he would call the police.   John is acting real strange said Mandy. Very strange. He's pacing, its like he can't sit still she said to her co-worker. On the line there was this light skinned man around 6ft. 195lbs. He was very polite when he asked Mandy; excuse me how can I set up an account here?

You have to have 2 forms of i.d..

Ok Ms Mandy Johnson he said sarcastictly I have all that who do I speak to?

Well our bank manager Mr. Callahan. You got a man who wants to open up an account sir!

Ok Ms. Johnson give me a second.   Fuck! John had to divert this guy so that he can make his move, the call was coming any minute now.   Ms. Mandy you married asked the customer?

Yes happily she said lying. Your husband must be real good to you.

Yes he is she said.

Can I ask why the bank was evacuated? Was it a problem?

No it was just a routine fire drill sir.   Oh. I seen police and all that I thought maybe something happened.

No, no just a routine drill.

Excuse me for one second, my wife is calling he smiling at Mandy.   Ok she replied back smiling.

Yo what up asked CD?

Everything every thing said Mr. Secret.

Good my dude said CD.

Make ya move now said Mr. Secret I'm a keep up my charade,

Be easy said CD.

Ok homie.

Yo! Shanta picked up the phone, lets do it.

John's phone rang twice. Hello said John.

Meet my friend on Oak 'n Leroy in 2 minutes don't fuck with me either!

Johns move was sudden, listen Ms. Johnson I'll be with the customer in like 10 minutes I have to drop my daughter her book bag she left in the car when I dropped her off at school please have him wait.

Ok Mr. Callahan you're the boss. As soon as he walked out she called security. Follow Mr. Callahan. Look something isn't right Kenny she said. What do you mean Mandy?   Ok John has been acting real weird all morning, first the fire drill. I mean come on when do we ever have fire drills? Then check this; his daughter left her bag in the car he has to take it to her. So. So why would she leave her school bag in the car on the way to school? Why was the bag empty when John first came in now its full?

Yeah probably of money Kenny said. So where did he go?

Duh! that's why I'm telling you to follow him dunce cap! Kenny raced toward the door.

Aw shit this could get ugly said Mr. Secret. What's going on Ms. Johnson?

Please be patient sir.

Ms I'll come back another time this bank is crazy. That maybe best sir.

Ok thank you sweety. Mr. Secret made it to the car his blue Saturn. He made sure he pulled out in front of the security guard and cut him off. Err-rrr! The security guard went flying onto the hood and windshield. Oh shit you alright Mr.? What are you fucking blind yelled the guard!

Nah I was reaching for something I didn't see you. John sped up the pace, he spotted the guard get cut off by the blue Saturn. That may have

Saved his family. He turned the corner and bumped into a female jogger, who was finely shaped her tanned looking white skin looked almost golden Barbie doll like. She snatched the bag and kept on moving. John turned around to se where she was going.

Walk around the block don't look back and mind ya business. John walked very fast.

By the time the guard got the corner John was halfway up the block with no bag and to his right a white girl in a joggers suit looked like she was chasing a bus but the driver didn't see her. He didn't see no transaction at all. He continued to followed John.

When Shanta saw the guard keep following John she began to speed walk. She spotted the Bonneville Bud was driving, a dirty looking 4 door piece of shit, but it ran.

The block was full of empty houses people were either at work or at school. She jumped in the car.

You got it asked Bud?

Yes she replied!

Open the bag and make sure the money official. Shanta checked the bag of money ruffling her hands through it carefully and when she saw everything was good joy filled her face. She grabbed the phone to CD's #. Yo what up! you got it?

Yeah we good. Bet he said I'll see you later baby! We out son, back door. Ok people sorry for the inconvenience, your safe now. Peace out said Billy! the head nods from the kids was like they wanted the criminals to get away with this, even though they were left tied up.

The call was made to John as he got back to the bank so were 2 cop cars. Thanks for the donation John don't worry your family is in good hands. Click... the line went dead.

John immediately ran to the cop car and told the police everything. They called in for back up and sent a couple of cars to his house, they found everybody in the basement tied up. By that time CD and Billy were cleaning off their make-up headed in the opposite direction.

CHAPTER 8

Later on that night at Fitze's CD, Billy, Shanta, Bud all toasted it up with a shot of Henny. The pub was shaded green on the outside, tinted windows concealed them from the nosy people. Karrin the bartender came over with Coronas and Heinekens. Karrin was drop dead gorgeous. She had long jet black hair, thick with a shapely ass, the most beautiful personality and most lovely smile. She could also sing her ass off. CD knew her since high school when she used to

cheerlead. He lusted over the mere thought of rubbing her smooth legs. But she was taken at the time by some lame. CD knew she was on some faithful shit, but he still treated her like that was his wife for some reason and he'd let no one violate her.

Thank you Karrin replied CD.

Your welcome sweety she said.

What's this a celebration? Yeah my boy Billy here just opened up a night club in his town out in Michigan. Oh really! that's wonderful said Karrin. I hope your very successful.

Thank you Billy said with lust all in his eyes which almost got him smacked with the bottle but CD had to play it off. As soon as she walked away CD said:

Yo Billy breathe easy with her, she off limits!

alright calm down I seen you grasp that bottle niggas started laughing. Boys, boys said Shanta relax! CD what up when we gonna get our split?

Yeah said Billy cause this town gonna get real hot and I gotta go soon. We'll split everything up tonight I had a couple of extras involved. I got to take care of them too.

What Shanta said!

Hey lower ya fucking voice snapped Bud!

Shanta that car cutting in front of duke was no accident and I had somebody watching ya'll as well. Listen I trying to get over the agreement was 50,000 a piece. Now when we split this up we can either do 2 things. Invest in me and lets cop some pies or sit on it for a minute and spend little bits and pieces at a time, but nobodies gonna be splurging. It draw too much attention. People get suspicious and somebodies always watching. If we work lay low work and stack the job money we'll be able to wash it trust me.

You got a lot of gee said Shanta! You can do what you want but ain't no splurging believe that! He right said Bud. If we start splurging then people will look at us funny, so we lay low. Listen said CD: everybody cough up $20,000 I'll get every one a brick. I'll make us 10 times the amount we have now! we'll flood the small towns. You 2faced motherfucka! this was ya plan all along huh? Said Shanta. I'm a ride with you on this but don't fuck up my money! you lucky I got love for you and I trust you, but for now on I'm calling you 2Face. Hey I might use that name in a rhyme or better yet. I might use the name for now on as my new nickname. I stay invisible that name will fit perfectly. So you in Shanta?

Yeah, I'm in she said.

Bud you in homey?

On some 1 flip shit yeah. Alright cool, said CD. Billy you in?

Nah, I'm a chill, lay low and do me for some time.

Ok cool then Billy I'd rather push drugs and get knocked for that then get nabbed for that bank robbery.

You right said Billy. But I need to chill. Do ya thing 2Face! he said making everyone laugh.

Hey Karrin baby, can we get another round?

Sure she said, why not honey.

Hey 2Face said Bud I think she like you, but she just scared. You've been a thug like ya whole life, look like one, act like one, dress like one. Switch ya style up, ya dress code and become successful, she'll fall for you. You don't need to be rich to bag her I could tell, but you gotta be on some honest shit. She might see the change son. Good advice son, good advice! I will believe that! but first I gotta get us rich, women come later. Besides I'm married anyways, he said with a devilish grin.

See that's the 2Face shit I'm talking about said Shanta!

CHAPTER 9

2Face entered his house as happy as can be. He's got a new wealth, new identity all he had to now was put plan B into motion. The count all together in the bag was $400, 2 He gave everybody $50, 000 a piece, but there was an undisclosed amount of $100, 000 left he had to pay Mr. Secret and he sent a lump sum to the kidnaped family. Hoping they take the money and shut up. He began to like the name 2Face. He stashed the rest of the money incase of emergency. The only 2 people who knew where the money was were he and Bud.

Shanta decided to invest her whole stash so that the money was untraceable. Bud also did the same thing so did shorts. So with $200,000 him and Shorts were headed to New York City this weekend to holla at his fams, and cop 10 bricks of that yehyo. He had a plan to get rid of a lot of product, he had a plan for everything, every scenario, he was becoming a mastermind. This would be his second trip to N.Y.C.. The first he had to get the ratchet and silencers. His man form up top Ghost was a gun seller and put him on to the gun ring he had cause he liked 2Face's style. Now he was gonna holla at his man C to hook him up with a few brawds to transport and do majority of the work.

He was also gonna holla at Damian and Macho his boys from way back he used to cop from them before he went to jail, he blew they're pockets up with crazy cheddar. His man Pudgy was another option he had sweet connects but was a hot boy. His wife's connect was out of the question, he promised her he would chill. She'd flip if she found out about any of this. Gina broke his train of thought as soon as he dropped his coat. Where the fuck where you at last night? Why did it take you all night to get home? And who was all these bitches at Buds house?

What the was you following me for? You don't have any trust in me he snapped back sarcastically?

Who were the bitches CD?

Lower your fucking voice! First of all and what bitches are you talking about?

My friend said there was some chicks that came over and didn't leave like ten minutes after you got there. Then some other girl came over later. You shook for nothing! That was Shanta who came through last night, and the other girls were Jacky's friends. You keep listening to ya bucket head ass friends you gonna be the only one hurt. You know Jacky keep a house full of friends. Half of them scared of black folks anyways.

You better not be lying CD!

Just fall the fuck back Gina said CD!

Fuck you! she snapped at him.

You should of thought of that when I was in jail! Oh what's that suppose to mean?

Lets not go there Gina! Please I'm having a good day please don't ruin my day now go sit the fuck down some where!

Fine! fuck you! she screamed and slammed the door to the bedroom.

CHAPTER 10

Another big risk 2Face had to take. Now he had to travel to the hood to re-up. It was too much money to play with. But Shorts was with him. they vowed to die in the streets before getting bagged again or getting got.   First stop 2Face aunts crib up on Jackson Ave. In the pjs. He had a 3 brick buy with Pudgy lined up then he had to go up the block to Cortland Ave. to see his man Damian and Macho to get the other 7 pies. Then he had to see his man Mr. C in Harlem. He needed them girls to move around. He had a little spot in Brooklyn in the East up on Alabama Ave.. His homies were trying to push forth they're records of hip hop classic so to speak. He was gonna help them out financially and he had another spot in the Bronx right on Fox st.. His cousin Wood would run that show. He was gonna start each spot out with a half a brick in hopes they would blow.

The phone rang twice before 2Face answered. Yo, what up! what's the deal nigga!

What up C. Them hoes ready bee?

Yeah son come through fool said C.

I got some shit to do real quick give me like 2hrs.. Make sure them hoes stay put its big money in this.

Alright I got you my nigga, that bottle waiting to kid, said Mr. C. Alright said 2Face. After handling everything with Pudgy and Damian and going to his Grandmas house. Him and Shorts made the drop off at aunties crib. 2Face grandma was 75yrs.Old, still moving around like she He had all the work he needed now they was on once this flip was complete. They parked on 133rd 'n Lennox across the street from Mcdonalds. Yo C! we down stairs 2Face said in the buzzer.

I'm buzzing ya'll in. The street was crowded, mad thugs had the door surrounded, a little chicken head about 18 eyeballed Shorts. 2Face saw trouble all over these dudes faces, he inform C about these goons. The beige building sat right in the middle of the Ave. so people couldn't help being nosey. Yo Jubbs live 2 houses down son said 2Face.

Word! replied Shorts I ain't seen son in years.

To bad we ain't got time to check him said Shorts. Yeah, yo watch these niggas Shorts you seen how they was looking?

Son I'll blow one of they fucking heads off like a eye lash my dude! said Shorts.

I know said 2Face. I got mad love for you my dude. I got love for all my Niggas as long nobody cross me. Remember we from the same breed, think the same, the same way you shoot I shoot, the loyalty is there I never cross the fams. Nobody else mean nothing to me compared to yaw. But from here on out any body try to stop our flow or cross me click, click 2Faceflashed the hammer, you know the rest.

I feel you son said Shorts with a sick smile.

C what up!

What's the deal son? C and 2Face embraced like 2 brothers.

I ain't seen you since the joint bee said 2Face.

Yeah that punk ass minimum replied C.

Yeah son, this my boy Shorts, Shorts this C. What up what up they said to each other. C was a bald headed light skinned cat, no games being played with him. Shorts tried to peep any larceny but C checked out to be good.

They entered the crib. Yo ladies meet ya new boss said C. Yo this is 2Face, champ this is Monica, Larrel, Shantel, Jamie, LaShay, Monique, and Jessica. Jessica she the brains behind the bullshit C said laughing.

Ok first said 2Face which one of ya'll got kids? Jamie shook her head yes. So you stay in New York said 2Face. Basically, ya'll jobs is to do drop off shit and pick up paper. All you gotta do is follow directions. We gonna be moving shit from the Bronx to Brooklyn to N.C. to Bing and to rough Buff. I got a mean cell phone connect so don't worry about phones. Everybody got a role so which one got the mini-van? Shantel shook her head. You coming with me then. We got a move to Buffalo then we do the drop off in the hood and you gonna go to N.C. with Shorts you and Jessica of course.

I'm just starting so we gonna be stacking. Oh we stopping by your houses so I need I.D.s family info just incase one of yaw get cute. This is big B.I. for me cross me I murder ya whole family. Believe that! Some of ya'll gonna get your hands dirty as well, like Monica and Larell yaw gonna be the stash cribs, Larrel you the accountant which means you hold the majority of the money, Monica you holding the work down so you gonna be bagging up shit. Shay Shay and Monique yaw gonna be doing the drop offs in New York. Shantel you gonna be in bing with me to knock off a little work for a while when you come back with Shorts. I want Jamie to drive the Mini-van if that's cool with you? Its all good said Shantel just don't wreck my shit bitch she said smiling.

Ladies we move low key please and no boy friends please atleast nothing serious until the job gets done.

When we know the Job is done asked Larrel? When ya get hit off real, real lovely answered 2- Face. So ya'll in? Hell yeah we in they said in unison.

Most of the girls were young except Shantel she was young to but a little older than the rest by about 3yrs. C did good all 2Face needed was a come but with these chicks now he can really make it happen. He had Shorts make a couple of calls to find Jubba so they could get like 4lbs. Of smoke that good ole dro.

2Face, Jamie, Shorts, and Shantel drove the mini-van out to the East. Yo this nigga Biz had something to tell us too said Shorts! Yeah I'm already knowing said 2Face we gonna smash these streets its on now! yo we gonna do some shit in 3yrs. My visions is beyond your wildest dreams. All we gotta do is lay low.

Yo as they drove across Brooklyn Bridge and jumped on Atlantic Ave. to get to the East, Shorts reminisced his childhood. When he was running around doing petty crimes. Shorts, Mouse and 2Face used to be boosters running around with low life's. Low life's were a bunch of shoplifters back in the early 90's who Mouse used to run with once in a while with. Thier trade mark was polo. As they pulled up on Alabama and Lavonia the block was crowded, mad niggas stodd infront of Tones Grandma building. His cousin Easy, Tone little brother Vincent, his other little Brother Alex, His older Brother Simeon, Marley, Biz, Popgun, lil Romeo, and Munch and John John. They been hanging in front of the building forever, the hallway smelled like strait haze. 2Face and them used to hang in front with Bop Tone cousin before he killed a few years ago up on Blake 'n Sheffield. Bop was that dude in the East. The block had the elementary school up the block they used to hustle in and play ball. You had Jeff high up the block on Pennsylvania Ave. the Bamas on the next block, Brownsville a few blocks over. The hood was one of the most dangerous in the 5 boroughs. The Bamas buildings were filled with nthing but thugs and bullet holes. The junkyard across the street where they killed Tone and Mouse man Shuabe a young Muslim who was out here trying to make a few dollars was killed by police supposedly by mistake. Shit was definitely real over here. The L train and 3 train ran on the L tracks over here 2Face used to take the long rides daily. Yo, look at Shorts said Biz? Dreads now what up! I see you gained a lil weight to. I ain't see you in like 10 yrs. What up! Niggas was mad hype to see the peeps. What's good yaw said Shorts smiling. Shorts hopped out the mini-van and gave everybody a pound and hug. 2Face jumped out the car as well giving niggas dap. They laughed and joked for a minute. Where Tone and Mouse at asked Simeon?

They chilling doing them. Yo Biz let me holla at you Just then Country pulled up. Yo what's good fools!

Oh shit! Shorts what up!

What up son replied Shorts. Music was blasting from the speakers in country's whip that pulled up.

Yo where yaw gonna be at in minute I'll be back?

We'll be right here son said 2Face make sure you come back. Yeah yeah said Country. Yo Biz we getting ready to hit you with some shit tonight you gonna be ready homey?

Yeah we got this we trying to get our money up so we can push these records said Biz.

Champ I need $40g's back though. I got you replied Biz. This a mean come up son said 2Face lets just stack the money before we move forward feel me? Said 2Face. I'll take care of the label shit. I done came through so far like I promised on my end. I'll be sending my lil brawds to do pick ups next Saturday any drama call Shorts. Oh yo CD 2Face cut him off. Its 2Face now.

Well 2Face remember I had something to tell you? Yeah he replied.

We just seen them niggas porky and his man Kareem on Linden Blvd. Rumor has it they be on Sheffield creping where Bop got killed at. I think duke got a brawd over there but I hear they be outside we gonna do the drive by maneuver.

Nah we got this said 2Face just move the work. Say no more said Biz.

Son keep ya ears to the street ya heard said Shorts. We'll be back in a few said Shorts with the work. Ah right said Biz, ya'll breathe easy. No doubt said Shorts.

Chapter 11

They gave everybody dap and broke out. Once they was back in the car 2Face and Shorts drove   around the corner to Georgia and Riverdale. They parked in front of a Brown stone and it was a bunch of Jamaicans standing on the corner talking shit. It was just getting dark so people were   Trying to see what they was getting into for the night.   Jamie, said 2Face get out the car.

What, she demanded.

Get out the car we going for a walk baby.

Don't ask too many questions please.

Sorry she said. Matter of fact I'm replacing you!   No, no alright! Alright! said Jamie I'm sorry. Ok cool, Shorts sat in the car4 with the ill smile.   Yo we getting ready to do some crazy shit said 2Face, here's the plan. Yo Shorts drive to the corner of Sheffield 'n Sutter in ten minutes. Yo Jamie when we get to the next block walk ahead of me, rock these shades too.

In the dark? She asked.

Yo I told you not to question me! son give me ya ratchet.

Hm son. He passed him the desert eagle.

Lets go Jamie. Jamie and 2Face walked up the block. Press send on the phone if you see a cat named porky out on the corner or a cat named Kareem. Try to draw niggas attention to see if they out there. If not then just keep walking. Your signal lets me know they outside, go head. Jamie walked ahead with a little strut, switching her hips letting her ass bounce drawing dudes attention on the corner in front of the24hrs. Store gawking. Excuse me, said Jamie. Sure baby as she tried to go in the store. They sell dutches here?

Yeah they do said a young kid with a Cincinnati Reds cap on and a red Ken Griffey jersey, blue baggy jeans and a pair of red and white ups. What's ya name cutie?

Ginger she said.

Word I never saw you over here. Yo where you from? I'm from Queens. I'm just visiting my aunt she live up the block by the train station.

So why you ain't go to the store up there?

Because its my business! and I felt like going for a walk. Chill youth! said the older thug. I apologize for my brethren ignorance. Names Porky sweety as he held his hand out to her. Jamie shook it then hit her cell phone simultaneously. Damn said Porky your hands soft as fuck. Why not later if you not doing nothing we go get something to eat my boy right here K. by the car gonna bring his girl too. I know you gonna be hungry after you spark them 2 L's. She smiled and then he heard a voice from behind her. "Thanks but no thanks"!

Who the hell; were the only words that came out of porky's mouth before a hail of bullets hit his lungs.

Boom! Boom! Boom! bitch ass nigga! 3 shots fool! Blough!1 in the dome, Kareem tried to make a move after the initial shock but before he could realize what took place, Jamie had the.38 special to his temple blough! she pulled the trigger no hesitation. The impact from the ratchet almost knocked Jamie to the ground.

Oh my God, she said as she regained her balance. Yo, Cincinnati Red catch! as he stood in shock. No! please. Noo-oo!

blough, blough! as he fell to his knees and hit the ground face first

His eyes wide open. Lets go shorty. Come on! yelled 2Face.

The screams from people out the window who witnessed the gruesome shooting were loud and 2Face knew this neighborhood like his own the code of silence is in full effect here, as Porky, Kareem and they man Cincinnati Red died where Bop did and now his homey can rest in peace, like the sign on his building says.

They walked a fast pace to the car parked on Sheffield "n Sutter, cops were flying to the scene They had just left. When they got to the car 2Face said drop the paper bag in the car. The bag had a hole from the heater. Here son said 2Face, dump this shit in the river bee. I'm a jump on the train. I'll call you in 2hrs. Jamie take a cab home, we'll call you to make sure you good. Don't say a word.

I ain't going down said Jamie. You proved yourself sweety. Here take this bank roll. He handed her a not of money. This is what we do 2Face shouted! You did good said Shorts he said as he drove off. 2Face went toward the A train by Maxwell high and Jamie flagged down a cab. 2Face walked real slow to make sure she got in the cab safely.

Chapter 12

Lil Romeo was on bike coming back from the scene to let the homies it's a done deal and to get off the street. Yeah said Easy, Bops brother! they kept it official. Lets get this paper, but for now we disperse. They all went there separate ways, to await part 2 of get rich. Nobody saw nothing! yelled a detective who was on the scene. That's why murderers keep walking the street like roaches, 'n rats. Fuck you! a bystander yelled.

Frisk him said the detective. The code of silence will be broken, believe you me! Somebody will speak.

The Feds and Binghamton police were still trying to figure out a lead on the bank robbery. With no cooperation from the kidnaped family it was hard. The only description was from John, was 2 masked white males and 1 masked female in a jogging suit.

Martino the ball busting detective banged his hands hard on the desk. Fuck! Nobody ever disrespect us like this!

The Mayor is on my as for this one! said the Captain. Captain Angelino. We must find those perps. We'll get them said Mcgruff.

Martino and Mcgruff had the most busts in the county and

the 2 most dirtiest police in the business from J.C. Raven and Carmitski and the Feds. They were determined for a bust.

federal officer said Run the tape of the customer the guard said ran him over. The secretary went back to the surveillance in the bank. A light skinned man around 6ft. 190lbs. Green eyes. Let me get a close up of that face. No scars, ok said the agent he drove a black maxima 2001 model.

But it doesn't make sense, said Mcgruff. A black man with 2 white boys and a white girl sticking up a bank. Doesn't fit the profile.

Could be crackheads? No said the agent. This was too thought out and carefully planned. Plus adding Martino the guard said it was an accident cause he ran in front of the car.

It could 've been made to look like that as well said Mcgruff. Either way we need to find this guy. Other than that unless they make a mistake which criminals always do, this case is cold. I want a detective to keep an eye on that manager just incase he was in on it. We cannot rule him out. Lets run that face through the computer see what we come up with, right now he's our only lead.

2Face got off the A train at 42nd st. and walked through the terminal to get to the 2 train. Africans were playing drums, Rastafarians selling portraits and t-shirts. It was crazy cause of the crowded, fat asses everywhere, his mind was racing thinking about the scenes unfolding since he got out. They could go from rags to riches quickly. As long as nobody tell they was good money. The phone vibrated in his pocket. When he checked the caller i.d. it was his cuz Wood. Yo! said 2Face.

Yo what up said Wood? Where you at? Coming to the block now. Yo everybody outside bee! Ethel, Ricky, Will, D-boog, Tim, Ali, D-black everybody!

Yo I'm there.

And I got a smut for you too said Wood. Ahright cuz I'll be there believe that! 2 Face stood on the platform till the train pulled up. It was noisy and crowded he bumped his way to a spot to sit down in 11 stops he'd be on Prospect Ave. part 2 of the take over was about to begin.

As soon as he got off the train Shorts was waiting. He rolled down the window, yo son get in. Oh shit! how you know I would be getting off the train.

I'm on point said Shorts. But yo every thing good in the ocean.

Good replied 2Face. Yo Chino next said 2Face here's the address.

It read 1138 Westchester Ave. Apt. 2c. Yo go get Shay Shay and tell her its her time to prove herself. Then take the keys and go to my aunts crib, take the work to Monica and Larrel crib. Pay them and call up Monique and Jessie and tell them to get ready for a trip. Call Shantel and tell her to do the drop offs and give them the prices we want back for the work and tell her to get ready to go with us to Bing.

Shorts don't do no dumb shit! Keep the body quiet so we get away and keep the police out our face and in suspense. Yo check Jamie and make sure she alright. I'll be on the block son.

Yeah replied Shorts.

CHAPTER 13

2Face walked down Longwood to Fox St.. He still missed his old neighborhood the block he was born 'n raised on. His family reputation over here, a few street legends 'n stars came from over here, Fort Apache. The old junkyards were replaced with brand new white town houses, the old burger and pizza shops were still there. 2Face chuckled as he remembered when he almost choked on a extra cheese pizza when he was 7 hanging out with his deceased uncle. The block was crowded on a Friday night. It was around 9:30, the bodegas was bumping that weekend music, 'n that salsa dancing outside. All the teens with the weekend off were standing on the corners of Fox and Longwood. About 6 Puerto Ricans and a couple of mommies were talking shit. 2Face paid them no mind as he walked up to 156St. They was deep about 20 or so heads when he got to the corner, he smelled the aroma of haze 'n hennessy. Heinekens were being passed around as well. What up! a twisted Wood shouted.

Yo what up cuz said 2Face! A nigga finally back in the hood bee said Dboog.

Yo what up family said 2Face!

What's good said Will Woods little brother and D Black

Boogs older brother. They all hugged 'n gave daps to eachother. 2Face ain't see his homies and fams in almost 4yrs.

Yeah Ethel told us you was here said Ali they went to the store to get another bottle of henny. Yo, yo nephew come here bro! yelled Rick. 2Face went to embrace his uncle.

You ready to drop one of them freestyle sessions asked Boog? Cause I know you wrote some shit up top bee. Let me hear something said Black!

Alright said 2Face a quick 16, check it:
Yo when I grab the mic I rap for figures
white chalk, yellow tapes appear when I clap the trigger
ya face rattle like a snake when I smacked you nigga
Yo I'll leave you hanging like a Christmas ornament
get broke down like B-ball tournaments
I roll through the hood with self confidence
leave you stuck in deep subconsciousness
when I spit flames I'm ill to dominant
but peep this son, we used to hop the train
smoke blunts disrespect get popped for ya chain
so high! you can catch me on the top of a plane
plastic gloves, with the ox chopping the cane
a shot caller, don't want nobody mocking my name
and rocking my fame,
then I switched the subject
ya lyrics get squashed in public
catch the mayor put the toast to his stomach
got a class for rap like teen summit
ya lyrics get mopped like vomit
flow from hood to hood like Hailey's comit
I'll leave you zoned like you smoked some chronic
wish I could've went in time and spoke to Prophets
they would've told the logic
but let me go that's the end no comment....
Oh, OOOh! Ok son still got it niggas was screaming! Go D-boog!

CHAPTER 14

Shorts called Jamie to make sure she was alright. She said she was good and couldn't wait for more being sarcastic.

When he hung up he called Shantell so they could meet up in a hour. Then he hit Shay Shay number it rang twice before she picked it. What up she said?

Yo come outside I'm in a blue Camry on 40th and Lenox.

Ah right she said. When she got to the car the automatic locks clicked.

Get in. Shay Shay had on a tight pair of Chanel jeans, manicured nails and long black hair to match her beautiful chocolate skin. Shorts in visioned her naked but knew the rules, leave the brawds alone til its all said 'n done. 2Face warned if you crash and fuck one of the workers you open up doors that don't need to be open. You'll become vulnerable, the money is more important and most of all the freedom, pussy in great lump sums when its all said 'n done any skins they wanted. 2Face made great points, but it took every thing he had to resist if he could. Yo Shay I got a job for you if you up to it? It could get ugly.

But I thought we was only doing the one thing?

Nah replied Shorts, you part of the team love, you gotta put that work in. Plus the pay is worth it. Ahright said Lashay what we gotta do? They pulled up in across the street from the White Castle and the rest in peace sign of Big Pun Graffittied on the building. After looking around for the address Shorts spotted the white 5 story apartment building lined up on the uptown side of the 2 train line on Intervale Ave.

Just knock on the door and start confusion act like ya'll had a relationship going and he flipped on you. When he tries to clarify shit I'm a come through and get to getting.

Ah right got it said Shay Shay. Go D-boog! I ain't gonna front said 2Face my cuz nice bee! Yo when I start this label you gonna be one of my artist cuz. Fuck waiting on a major label we getting ready to real paper to push our music real soon, just be patient.

No doubt, said Boog.

Yo pass that bottle said Wood to Primo!

Yo, Ethel! yelled 2Face my man gonna move that shit as we speak.

He better shit, all that shit fool you done stepped ya game up.

Hm, take this.

What's this she asked? She looked in the bag of 50's and 20's. Don't say nothing Ethel. Yeah yeah said 2Face where Shaniqua?

She out with her little friends on Beck St. Spend some of that on her too!

They had kiss playing in the background listening to D.J. Clue's newest classic. Yo Wood that shit about to be a done deal, I hope you ready?

Hell yeah I'm ready, shit is real homey! I got 4 kids bee. They need to get fed I need real money.

I feel you Cuz, just stay off the streets and don't make no moves let the work move. Nobody will know who the boss is. We got mad workers, thorough niggas any problems holla at Shorts.

Aw shit wifey calling me, hold up said 2Face. Yo where the fuck you at with my car?

Shut the fuck up! The fuck you screaming at yelled 2Face! I'll be back tomorrow.

Tomorrow, replied Gina now I can't get back to work!

Well take a cab Gina, suggested 2Face.

No fuck you! You doing the same shit that got your ass locked up last time! You start your job Monday don't fuck that up. Yo just chill said 2Face. I'll be back tomorrow relax.

Relax! fuck you mean relax! you take my car I don't know where the fuck you at, now I can't get to work, it's cold up here.

What the fuck you want me to do Gina?

Get your black ass home!

I'll be home tomorrow baby. Fine fuck you she said slamming the phone down.

CHAPTER 15

Shay Shay knocked on the door of Apt. 2c. A cute looking Spanish woman answered the door. Hola? She had on a skin tight pair of blue jeans and dress shirt rocking some sandals exposing her pedicured feet. Hola.

The fuck you mean Hola said Shay? Where Chino at, I'm looking for Chino? Is he in here I know he here! the house was nicely decorated, Shay saw a flat screen tv, plush leather couches and love seat, P.S. 3 and 2 little boys playing G.I. Joe. They looked to be from a 5-7 range. Who are you Chino's my husband said the pretty mommy?

Ya husband! He told me he lived by himself. I just fucked him 2wks. ago. We was here and since I ain't hear from him I decided to stop by.

You sure you got the right person asked the Mommy with a strong accent?

Yeah, he short, chubby, with green eyes.

Ok Chino!Chi—ino. Yo what up. he said in Spanish. Chino was in the room rolling up with a bag of dope on the side, it was ready to sniff before he was rudely interrupted. Yo what the fuck is this? Who the fuck is this black bitch?

48

You tell me said the hurt Spanish woman! you tell me she said in Spanish. I-I don't know, know this bitch! Who you calling a black bitch any ways you fat sloppy motherfucka!

A yo why the fuck you got on shades its dark outside said Chino? Yo, who the fuck are you? As Chino ran toward Shay Shay backed up into the hallway, Chino realized he was set up when the knife jammed into his the side of his neck. Then as it was pulled out in one swift motion he was hit again in the kidney, he hurt so much in pain, his scream was drowned in blood, then as he was spun around one more fatal puncture wound as the knife pierced his heart. It was pushed deep into his heart and lungs. All he could manage to say was in front of my kids Bro?

Fuck your kids, you lucky we letting them live said Shorts. Life quickly went out of Chinos body. He fell face first in a pool of blood.

Watch yo step, come on said Shorts. He felt like he was back in Auburn. Chinos wife screamed as she ran to her husband by the time she looked up the assailants were vanished. She was in too much shock to see which way they went, or what car they drove. Another perfect plan another perfect getaway.

CHAPTER 16

Mr. Secret followed Gina's cab to work. He stayed a half a block away from the cab. After a couple of turns on Robinson st.and going up Court st. the cab went strait up the freeway, it stopped right in front of Madamores and Teaser's. 2 exquisite strip clubs. Gina got out the cab rocking a long green trench coat. Her chest was bare and her hair was out.

He thought to himself. Damn! 2Face gonna be tight behind this, he done told this skeezer not to do this no more. You only get one fuck up with son. He wondered what 2Face was gonna do to her once he found out she lied to him. As he made the U-turn to get on the freeway he noticed an S.U.V. pulling out as well. 2 well dressed white men eyed him intriguingly. He stopped the car and got out then walked up to the parked Range Rover. Excuse me gentlemen I noticed you follow me from Bing. What seems to be the problem? You said we were following you replied one of the men? Yeah replied Mr. Secret.

Now why would we do that said the other man in the passenger seat? You tell me said Mr.Secret. I didn't do anything wrong officers so what's the problem? The bank robbery said the passenger. A security guard told us that you cut him off while he was in pursuit of a suspect.

Officer I had no idea about a pursuit. I went there trying to open up an account and the teller had me waiting around. It was a lot of strange movements going on so I decided to take my business elsewhere. The man I was suppose to be speaking to was rushing out the store with a bag, I couldn't wait no more. I didn't really think nothing of it I was in the car looking for a cd not paying attention I admit then I looked up duke on top of the hood. I asked if he was alright he screamed fuck! he kept going so I kept it moving. If he ain't think nothing of it I ain't either cause I was in the wrong so I bounced. I went to HSBC and set up an account there15 minutes

later. I'm a construction worker and my girl spends money on a bunch of dumb shit so I need to save money that's why I was setting up an account.

I also noticed yaw follow me an hour ago, that's why I drove here. I parked on Gaylord st. to see if you would pass me by but then I seen yaw park. I got scared cause of so much shit happening that's why I got out my car to se what was up? The officers were quiet. Well is there anything else officers? No we just want to check out   your alibis if they check out clean you'll never here from us again, we got your info if your not right we'll be there!

Be my guest.

After giving his name and numbers to the agents for his account he headed home to get some sleep for a few hours. Then back to the strip club. The money he payed to the bouncers will help him figure out the rest. He couldn't no longer be seen no more. After setting up all the spots with x amount of drugs and hours of instructions to the girls and peoples, the next time he was trying to be seen was a long time from now. Shantell and Jamie did all the driving as Shorts and 2Face got that much needed rest. 2Face in his Camry with Shantell and Shorts in the other whip with Jamie. They were headed to Buffalo to see 2Face man Gulley. He was another jail connect he had that Boobonic chronic.

CHAPTER 17

When they arrived in Buffalo, Shantell and Jamie were astonished by how big Buffalo was. They rode the highway till they reached the downtown area, they passed Buffalo's eastside sighting the projects and run down areas of the town.

We here yet 2Face said as he yawned? A-aah! As 2Face woke up he called Shorts and asked him was everything good?

Everything good son replied shorts.   Damn said Jamie I didn't know Buffalo was that big.

Yeah said 2Face in the speaker phone you gotta get out the city more. But don't worry you gonna have plenty of time to move around as my Leuitenant.

From here on out ya'll gonna be bosses believe that! I give you a price I expect my change asap when I give you a date he said to Shantell. But right now make this motivated left on Main st. we'll take this to Amherst 'n Main and park.

When they arrived at the destination the block was quiet. Wait right here said 2Face. Shorts jumped out too, wait right here ladies.

What ya'll Muslims asked Jamie?

For your info yeah replied Shorts. Just wait here please. 2Face and Shorts entered the Masjid right foot first. They offered 2 Rakat for entering the Mosque, then Offered DHUR, the noon prayer, lined up side by side.

After feeling somewhat cleansed 2Face looked around and saw his man. Salaamu Alaykum; Wa Laykum Salaam Ramatullah replied Gulley what's good son! What up bee said 2Face what's happening! they embraced and laughed thinking about their times up top. Gulley didn't have the usual Buffalo accent. Lets go outside bee. You straighten out them Bronx cats yet? Remember ya'll had a bad repore from me.

I hope B-lo ain't fall off fool!

Never that snapped Gulley.

Oh yeah! said 2Face, don't worry champ I puts that work in said 2Face, believe that!

Still saying that shit huh?

You know it to the gait nigga! But yo everything is cash money on my end according to plan.

Yo come to the car, oh and by the way this is ya Muslim brother Shorts, Shorts this is Gulley. They shook hands. Good to meet you they both said exchanging Salaams. So you good 'n shit asked Gulley?

Yeah why you think I'm here ricky retardo! Yo meet Jamie and Shantell. You gonna see Jamie a lot believe that! Hi they both said in unison.

Hey ladies said Gulley. Yo you driving son?

Yeah but I'll hop in. They all drove in the van with Gulley navigating to the crib, when they got there only Jamie, 2Face and Gulley got out. Shorts 'n Shantell drove to go get something to eat.

Yo this is the whip you was telling me about asked 2Face?

Yep. You got that paper?

Right in the bag. They went into a room that was small, it had a desk with fluorescent lights you could smell the aroma.

This is how I like business prepared and on point and ready to go. You gotta tell me what you want I got the dro, haze, chocolate regular.

I want 10lbs, 2lbs of dro, 5lbs of that purple, and 3lbs of that chocolate. My purchase is big so I want extra believe that!

Yo that's 28,000 kid said Gulley. Bet, replied 2Face see when we was in the can we planned   this now its happening. This is real life! expect to see a purchase like this on the regular, you do me right I'll do you right.   A yo! snapped Jamie you do me right? That shit sound crazy bee! she said Laughing.

A yo I'm a grown ass man shorty 2Face said. But you got that one he had to laugh that one off.   Ya'll on that Harlem shit huh?

Ain't nothing change bee said 2Face. You know how we do he said.

I'll make sure you right said Gulley that's neither here nor there. But I know you busy but one day we gotta hang out ock. I'll be there believe that!

I gotta place a call to get your order in ya heard! 2Face called up Damian for Gulley and Gulley made sure 2Face stuff got the new hooptie safely. Jamie drove the hooptie with Shorts behind her, Shantell drove with 2Face back to Bing. 2Face kept 2lbs for the town the others went to the hood. With Shorts tailing her she couldn't get funny. He wanted Jamie to believe she was on her own so kept quiet about Shorts tailing her, it was his way of earning trust. You can tell a lot about a person when they alone or behind closed doors, especially when think nobodies watching.

With Shantell in Bing with him he had an additional 500g's. 2Face was the best at protecting himself and he still had his clientele, he already knew the rat and the rat was taken care of.

CHAPTER 18

Check it Shantell, the chocolate you gonna sell for dimes, these size. The haze go for a dub a bag this size. The coke we gonna move in 8balls, halves and ounces. This is 400g's of yea yo all bagged up correctly, this a 100g's of the hard the same shit. I'm a direct all the traffic to you. Don't go out here trying to get ya own clientele, if you get knocked we'll get you out, don't ever snitch. You'll pay with your life believe that! you got nothing to do with me at all. We just know each other from the bar. Don't fuck up my money, party when its all said n' done this is business you fuck when I say fuck, this is real life, real money. You out here with the boss but you deal with Shorts. When you here from me other than the bar we should be enjoying ourselves not me looking for you ok?

Ok she said.

Oh and never get high on your own supply! don't fuck with nobody you don't know. Violate any one of my rules its liable to be punished by death. I don't like giving second chances so don't try me.

Damn. can I atleast get a fucking drink, she asked sarcastically?

Yeah he responded but keep it minimum. You gotta stay on point. You know that I'm a pay you well and safety ain't a issue I won't place you in a situation you can't handle. By me doing that I'm making myself hot, but we family as long as you don't cross me.

You the first dude that ain't try to holla or no other funny shit on the low you serious about this paper?

More serious than a headache said 2Face.

But you know you sexy said Shantell.

See there you go trying to gee.

Please I'm for the money Said 2Face. There's too many of you's out there no disrespect baby. I think you gorgeous but now is not the time. This is business.

The phone went off vibrating in his pocket 2Face picked up on the 3rd ring. Yo, what up?

Yo the feds was following me son, I had to make up that we put together. They was legit said Mr. Secret.

All right well lay low for a few days. I'll have my man Odie and his Chinese connection hold it down. I'll holla, click the line went dead.

Later on that night 2Face went home. His man C drove the Camry up to Bing and parked it by his crib. A furious Gina was waiting.

What the fuck were you doing with my car! you take my shit for the weekend and don't even tell me! you won't tell me where you were at we're fucking married! what the fuck kind of Marriage is this?

Don't ever talk about secrets I know you got a lot of skeletons in your closet! so shut the fuck up!

You shut the fuck up she snapped back! Next time you touch my car I'm reporting it stolen!

Fuck you and your funky ass car bitch! Matter of fact everything is mines, if it wasn't for me your punk ass wouldn't have shit! now I'm a take a shower and get ready for work tomorrow!

Gina stormed into the room and slammed the door. Sleep your fagot ass on the couch she yelled!

Lil Kitara woke up groggy and that's the only thing that stopped 2Face from losing his control for her calling him a fagot.

Did Mommy and I wake you baby?

Y-yes she said all cute and half sleep.

Go back to bed please. Tomorrow we gona have Chucky Cheese.

Yea—aeh! she was hype all of a sudden.

Yeah said 2Face.

Hey Gina I'm sorry said 2Face. I shouldn't have did that, I just wanted to see my family that's all nothing else. He got no response through the door. You want to ignore me fine! I'll be on the couch after my shower watching sportscenter.

Later that night Gina came out the room in some lingerie looking sexy, walking over to 2Face and pulling him to his feet kissing him. he awoke a lil surprised but kissed her back, he was hard instantly. She grabbed him, stood him up and led him to the bedroom by his dick.

CHAPTER 19

Martino and Mcgruff couldn't get in contact with the rat or his wife. They weren't in any bars or at home and their car was no where to be found. That was odd for them 2.

Maybe they went on a family trip, or got tired of snitching said Mcgruff. They weren't supposed to move without our permission.

We'll be patient though, said Martino.

Hey that guy the feds checked out was clean said Mcgruff. Maybe the rat got smart and did this robbery themselves and got recruits, I mean all of a sudden they just vanish?

Did they check the HSBC bank asked Martino?

Yeah, it checked out clean the guy was telling the truth. Something will break trust me said Martino.

The next morning 2Face met up with his man Roc and went to work. Roc helped him along with his moms get the job at Precast construction company. They arrived at the site at 8:00 ready to work.

Let me introduce you to the foreman Bob and Jason the boss said Roc. 2Face knew a few workers from when he used to sell weight to them before his bid.

Hey this is Bill said Roc, Bill this is Cory.

Hey what's happening dude!

Hey what's up Bill, long time no see said 2Face laughing at Roc for introducing him forgetting they knew eachother.

Bob he'll be working with me said Bill, that's my buddy. He had to yell from all the noise from the machines.

That'll be fine said Bob let me brief him first. Bob gave him a run down of the spot and 2Face was eager to learn. Hey Tom show Mr. Jackson around?

Sure said Tom. How are ya? 2Face extended his hand for a shake. Good he responded. Mr. Jackson Tom will show you around and show you the ropes. As they walked Tom gave 2Face another rundown Tom saw a headline on the news paper, suicide bomber kills 21 in Bagdad.

Hey Mark, what's up Tom. Mark this is, hey what do they call you?

C.D..

Ok, uh C.D. this is Mark, he does the checks, the punch out sheets, etc.

I know Mark already. That's good said Tom. Yeah said Mark that's Reggies friend.

Hey Mark you see the fucking Iraqis?

Yeah another fucking suicide bomb. They should just nuke the fucking country, kill all those fucking bastards , fucking Muslims!

Then there would be no oil for us to get said Mark sarcastically. 2Face anger was growing rapidly from Toms comments.

Aw fuck 'em said Tom.

2Face interrupted eh hem! when it comes to enemies you gotta know who you dealing with, especially war. You gotta know the consequences, what your enemy thinks, how he moves and should know the history. That gives you the advantage he may not have. Its idiots like you which is why people like you ain't in charge can't think past go.

Hey watch your; the smack and grab happened to quick for

a reaction, 2Face was on him lightning quick like his old boxing technique.

First off, you don't understand why they fighting or the cause of what they believe in. Mark was stunned. You also couldn't muster up the courage to fight for either side you yellow back coward! disrespect a Muslim they won't find you or your family. 2Face grip was so strong from pumping iron in the yard he almost choked Tom to death. You better not mention this to anyone again either!

After he let him go, Tom tried to regain his breath and came with a weak; I'm sorry. I didn't mean to offend you.

Don't let it happen again, don't ever let it happen again! 2Face walked away, turned and asked where do I start at?

You'll, you'll start at the fork lift shuddering Tom. Tom if I were you I'd never fuck with him again, he's no joke.

Fuck! I think I figured that out now.

Lunch break came, 2Face had a roast beef 'n cheese from Quizno's and a Arizona mystic juice swigging.

Hey Reggie come here he said jokingly.

Yo what up said Roc, how you like it so far?

This shit is fun bee.

I see you got your weight up too said Roc.

Yeah fold you up quick nigga! they both laughed.

Yo bee I choked that cracker Tom the fuck out just now.

Word said Roc, he a piece of shit anyways.

Just watch him bee said 2Face.

He pussy don't sweat him said Roc.

I got Shorts and Jessica going to N.C. to see this nigga Ahm son. You know they gonna have xyz right?

Yeah said Roc.

Follow them make sure shit go right. I may send one of them other hoes to just over see shit too.

I thought Ahm was good peoples said Roc?

He is but this is about paper my dude. When they drop off stay for like a day bee.

Yo Face what you gonna do about shorty?

Who Gina?

Yeah.

Oh we gonna fix her up real nice, believe that!

Oh what's up with billy boy champ?

Oh he alright, somewhere safe bee, under wraps sipping H2O said Roc feel me?

Yeah did you get that paper from him?

Hell yeah! said Roc. Keep that said 2Face that's you.

Good looking.

Go to school with that get that training in. Oh what did you do with the car?

Gave it to some fiends in the Cuse.

Word. they both laughed.

I took it apart so they could sell the parts. Well he out the equation now.

I gotta call this little hottie I bagged, she probably won't even pick up the phone said 2Face. I Bagged shorty last week! Son she bad as hell bee long jet black hair, wild thick and her face is the look of a barbie doll. I'm a try to bring her to Fitze's tonight homey.

Ok back to work said Bob, 2Face and Roc gave eachother pounds I'll holla later.

CHAPTER 20

The phone rang twice before it was answered. Hello said a sweet voice who am I speaking to? This is C.D. may I speak to Sue please?

This is her.

You remember me asked 2Face?

Shoot you remember me she shot back?

I'm sorry he said, I was busy.

Yeah men she said. So why are you calling me now?

To try to get up with you. I got free time tonight he said.

Oh really she said. So nigga you wanna hook up when its convienant for you huh?he was stuck for a moment.

No it ain't like that sweety I'm sorry I didn't mean to offend you or hurt your feelings. If you want I won't call you again he said in an apologetically voice. He sounded so sincere to her.

Ok Mr. I got Gee! call me after work, don't fuck this up either this time.

Believe that I won't, believe that!

Sue went with 2Face to Fitze's at 8:00 p.m. they got the corner table by the bar. Karrin came over to serve them their drinks with that ever gorgeous smile.

Here's your white Russian and here's your shot of Henny.

Thank you said 2Face he handed her a $5.00 tip.

Thank you she said so sweet, hey C.D. she's very pretty.

Thank you said 2Face and Sue at the same time.

So you a heavy tipper huh big baller?

I come here every night. I play pool, drink and Sue cut in fuck with the bartenders!

Naw, he snapped I know most of them from when I first moved up here along time ago. Oh said Sue, I saw the look you 2 gave each other that wasn't no friendly look. She looked like she was jealous or something.

Please leave that alone said 2Face, Sue was laughing.

After a half hour Roc came through. What up boy shouted Roc, R.O.C. nigga! what up! yo Mice and Tone coming through in a minute I saw them at the gas station. Where Shorts at?

I told you stupid he was busy said 2Face.

Oh my bad you big lip fucka he said under his breath.

2Face heard him. oh you want start shooting fool I got jokes for days remember the box nigga?

Yeah I remember Roc frowned up.

Yo who that! damn shorty you pretty as a motherfucka!

This is Sue, Sue this is Roc.

Hi she said.

You got friends baby?

Sorry I role dolo.

Its ok for now but in the future next time have some friends. Sue laughed at him.

A strange chick walked in the bar, she went to Karrin at the bar and ordered an apple Martini. She sat at the bar. Karrin I.D. her she was definitely old enough. 2Face walked over to the pool table and asked Sue if she shot pool? The whole bar stopped and checked out Sue's ass trying to figure out how this guy get her. She had on a Sean John sweat suit, with pink and white Timbs. Her ass jiggled all over them sweats. Roc walked over to him and nudged son: yo I'm feeling that one you hit the jack pot punk!

Wifey find out?

Nope why you plan on telling her 2Face had to ask.

Nah stupid said Roc. She at work anyways.

Yo that's Shantell keep a eye on her too. She got one of my phones. She got the smoke too so pass that around town. Tell Karrin when she here to look out for her Karrin is alright. Shantell said hi to Sue as she put.75 cents on the side of the pool table. As Mouse and Tone walked in Roc slid off to talk to Karrin.

Tone loud ass what up son! look at this bitch ass nigga! their normal greeting when they see each other.

Yo yo what up bitch said 2Face! you bookman from good times in the face ass nigga! Mice what up!

Yeah yeah. son stop that Mice shit too.

Yo who the fuck is that said loud ass Tone?

Oh that's Sue said 2Face Sue this the street fam Mouse and Tone.

Only you sweety said Mouse? Where your friends at?

She role alone her and Roc said simultaneously. They looked at each other and laughed. Roc you's a funny nigga.

Yo said Face too Mouse and Tone. That's a new recruit over there, look out for her for me she off limits. No doubt, no doubt they said.

The night went smooth every call 2Face got he passed to his new protege Shantell.

He drove Sue to Mather and North St.. Did you enjoy yourself?

Of course I did.

Well when are we gonna hang out again?

Whenever you ready she said. He didn't want to impose himself plus he had to pick up Gina in 10 minutes. He kissed her on the cheek and told her he'd see her tomorrow for sure. She agreed.

CHAPTER 21

As he drove he thought to himself everything is place now. Once shit get flowing in N.C. the mission of illegal activity will be complete. All he had to do was collect money and chill. He must keep his job, work mad overtimes and purchase nothing just live normal.

The next day Roc came to pick him up at 7:00 am. What up lets get some breakfast. Danny's or the one on Conklin said Roc you know it be mad hoes up in there. Just as they was leaving 2Faces P.O. pulled up. He jumped out the brown Ford Taurus, 2002 model with tints.

Where ya headed Jackson?

Off to work, first to get some breakfast, why what seems to be the problem?

Oh no problem just doing a routine check he said with his Equadorian accent.

You can stop by the job any time too sir said 2Face.

Is everything alright any police contact or anything I should know?

No sir I'm clean he said 2Face.

Good so can you piss in this cup then?

Sure said 2Face no problem.

Who is your friend?

Oh he's a co-worker. Let me give you this urine.

Please do said Mr. Torres please do.

2Face went inside with his P.O. luckily he didn't do too much drinking or use any drugs. Kitara and Gina were getting dressed, when Kitara said to her mommy; who's that stranger in the house mommy?

That's C.D.'s uncle.

Yeah, she said.

Yeah come on Kitara close the door so they can talk ok.

C.D. went into the bathroom he knew the procedure, leave the door open. One piss coming up you piece of shit he said under his breath. He wanted to shoot this old fucker for disrespecting his honor for him coming here in front of his family like this. Maybe he was just doing his job.

Here you go sir. Mr Torres tested it right there with the stick it was clean.

Ok keep up the good work.

2Face finally got in the car with Roc, that's why I gotta stay on point bee. No chronic and I bag up with gloves. From here on out I can't afford to get my hands dirty. That's why we got the brawds kid.

All you gotta do is observe everything put a lil work in here 'n there. Everybody know they answering to Shorts so he the boss he gonna make sure them hoes on they job. I'm a play chess sit back and direct traffic, collect and advise so relax bee said 2Face.

They got a big fight coming up Damian the Dead Arm Wilson (42-0 39 knockouts) against John the Body Rocker Smith (33-0 with 25 knockouts).

Interesting fight said Roc.

Yeah I want us the whole crew to go see that believe that!

Basically if me, you, or Shorts get involved physically doing anything some one gotta go. In the meantime we work, stack, and

I want you to finish that school thing we gonna enjoy ourselves the right way.

Oh I'm a gut the shit out shorty tonight Roc.

Word! he said, she bad as fuck!

I know, I know I got some treats for my niggas too believe that! we gonna have fun.

The next 6 months ran smoothly. His Cuz Wood 'n them was eating lovely sending back $30,000 a week off the coke 'n pills. That was just in the Bronx.

In Bing once he got Shantell the clientele she was raking in at least $25,000 a week off the coke and crack, plus the chronic.

The homies in Brooklyn was making $15,000 a week and down in N.C. was where the gold mine was they was making $50,000 a week off just weed 'n coke. 2Face and the crew was seeing $120,000 a week grand total and he was loving it just stacking and re-eing up.

Best thing of it all was he didn't have to spend a dime to earn what he had. He put the foundation down, played his part, now everybody getting paid. Niggas was eating good, he re-ed up once a month, which he roughly had $480,000 to play with multiply by 6 you got $2,880,000 wow! Big chips for a drug dealer. And the way 2Face carried himself rocking the same shit every day and working wild overtime at his job you would never know. Shorts and the girls ran things smoothly, they kept it loyal.

CHAPTER 22

With Shanta beefing now about her cut up in Fitze's 2Face thought it was time to piece her off. Shanta please calm down, I got you.

Chill said Shorts you blowing it up!

Nah fuck that! I was suppose to been got my money.

Shh! said 2Face. In his mind she would wash up shore if she wasn't Tone wife, in fact if she didn't shut the fuck up that just might happen. She could get everybody knocked off.

See I had something real nice for you but I'll tell Bud to get that for you alright. Son go to the safe house and get that Shorts.

Shanta if you'd of chilled I would of blessed you real well but greed will always make a person fall short.

2Face I got shit I want to do to.

Ok I understand, but check it: I got a bus taking us to Vegas next weekend to see the big fight. Shantas eyes lit up.

Word!

Yeah but it's a members only thing Once you get paid you ain't considered a active member no more. I got Gina going to Russia. I got a 2week vacation.

You serious you rented a bus? Get the fuck outta here!

Yeah bitch! you still want ya money?

Hell no you been doing something on the low ain't nobody got it to rent no bus trust me. I'll wait she said for mines. Shorts started laughing. She hugged 2Face tightly. Oh thank you, thank you!

Now will you stop screaming at me!

Shantell over heard the conversation on the low. Ok Mr. Vegas can we play some pool now? No doubt, how you though?

I'm chilling everything is good. Good said 2Face, how's school?

Coming along real nice she replied. Karrin was coming over with their drinks. Let me get one for Shantell to please baby. Thank you.

Hey Karrin still singing?

A lil she said.

Well loosen that voice up cause you gonna be the face of my new label.

Really she said, where did you get the money for a label?

See now you asking too many questions just be ready when the time is right.

Where's your lil Spanish girlfriend at she asked so curiously?

Why your always here with her she said.

What the fuck is this the interrogation room? Karrin laughed cause she knew he didn't like to be questioned. Just then Tone and Mouse walked in, oh god she said.

What the fuck is up shouted Tone dumb loud! 5209385and 0 had the serial defaced hoping: son you love my boy Nas huh? Well one day you gonna meet him.

What up Mice! said Shorts.

Yo yo what up fool! shouted Tone. What the fuck you doing here Shanta?

Drinking like your drunk ass is about to be!

Shut the fuck up!

Hey, hey chill my youth said 2Face.

Yo the homies called and said what up too Face said Tone.

Tell the homies next weekend we going to see a fight in Vegas. Yeah I said Vegas fool as Tone looked at 2Face crazy. Son what the fuck we hustle for if we not gonna enjoy ourselves. For years I've sat in jail thinking about all we did was hustle, never really did shit now we gonna live it up.

I knew this nigga was up to something said Mouse you was too quiet! Son, you ain't do all that in no construction to go to no fight?

Son why you always trying to figure out what somebody trying to do? Nigga you ain't that smart bee! you know I do all type of shit floor-covering, roofing, carpentry, masonry, plumbing, dry-wall and framing. You know I work lots of overtime too atleast 2hrs. Extra a day. On the weekends I do side jobs. Why I can't do me?

Son that's some fowl shit kid said Mouse we like family you can't even put niggas on to your moves no more.

2Face whispered; I got too many players we can't have 4 or 5 bosses either so if you get down you gotta take a back seat you hear? I make real moves with real people.

You saying we ain't real asked Mouse?

I'm saying you do you let me do me. Just know my wealth gets shared with my peoples regardless, now I just rented a bus and driver, paid for all our seats at the fight, hotels 'n all. I spent around $400,000 on this trip, he whispered so respect that!

You see the bigger you become the more product you move you gotta become invisible, you must study your opponent to beat him. sometimes you gotta mimic ya opponent to beat him. The more you get the more invisible you and your team should get follow me, the less chance you'll get bagged. The more you treat your peoples to acts of small kindness, the more loyal they become, but at the same time they gotta respect ya gangsta too! I gotta let my peoples enjoy themselves, cause my enjoyment comes from ya'll, I love all my niggas.

Son said Tone that liquor talking again! how long this nigga been here.

Shut the fuck up! Son I'm serious bee! when ya'll happy I'm good and if ya'll not happy I ain't happy then we got a problem Houston! But don't take my kindness for a weakness.

CHAPTER 23

2Face was hype he was going to Vegas finally. He told his P.O. he was driving Gina to the air- port at Kennedy which ha was and that he was staying at his aunts "Ethel", which he wasn't. He didn't plan on taking Sue with him, he had a boat cruise for her planned.

Gina, Kitara and 2Face drove to the City the night before. They all seemed so happy. Kitara had never been to the City before so the tall buildings and millions of people amazed her. She saw the Statue Of Liberty and a few other monument stand it was astonishing to her.

It was early in the morning so they had time to kill. Hey Kitara, you wanna go into the Statue Of Liberty and then Toys 'R Us, then we'll go to the boats 'n stuff and eat lots of ice cream baby! said 2Face.

Yeah, yeah! that's a good idea C.D.

Boy she happy said Gina.

Gina we gonna do some shopping so you can go to Ukraine in style, in some Marc Jacobs, a Marc Bouwer dress, that Versaci perfume you like. The Nanette Lepore and Louis Vitton purses, you going out there looking like a princess.

Baby stuff like that costs a lot of money?

So what, if you happy I'll spend whatever so just let me treat you. Gina gave him a kiss on the lips. I love you baby!

Their day went by lovely they made it to the City so early they had time to every thing. Kitara enjoyed herself they shopped and ate all kinds of food, by the time they made it to the Bronx it was nap time. Leaving all their bags in the trunk parked in Ethel's parking lot, which was right on Westchester Ave. 'n Jackson. Kitara never seen a real live train before. With the noise of the train and the mist of New York air, the filthy streets of the Bronx, all the Puerto Ricans by the store, the drug dealers posted by the basketball courts across the street. The tall project buildings which stood 21 stories high.

A tired Kitara was amazed but she sensed a lot of different vibes than of Mid-town. She was

only a little girl but a smart little girl. Danger was the atmosphere.

This is where I grew up at Kitara.

Yeah C.D.. Yeah.

Come on Kitty, lets hurry upstairs. Gina knew this neighborhood too well traveling with 2Face.

When Ethel buzzed them in Kitara saw the elevator when it opened up and almost puked! Ew! what's that smell she said?

It smells like piss said Gina! all the money you spent you could of took us to a hotel. You bring my daughter and expose her to this?

There was a black lady on the elevator also who looked disgustedly at Gina when she made the comment. 2Face saw the look like this prissy ass white bitch!

A yo this used to be my home don't ever disrespect my hood! I didn't come from a silver spoon in my mouth. I never forget where I come from or my people.

Matter of fact he hit the 8th floor get the fuck out and take the car to a motherfuckin hotel! The elevator stopped, sorry Mam.

That's ok she said with a smile.

Well bye! I don't see you moving yet.

I'm sorry said Gina, I didn't mean to offend you.

Don't do it again said 2Face!

When they got off the elevator on the 19th floor and rang the buzzer Shaniqua answered the door.

What up Cory!

What up Shay! You staying out of trouble?

I should be asking you that. Mommy back in the room. Shaniqua was 19 and well built so he always looked after her like she was his little sister. He was very over protective of her.

You seen Haywood Ethel?

Yeah he outside chill Will with him.

Oh word! I'll be back. Yo Ethel!

What I'm getting dressed, what up with Pat? That was 2Faces mother and Diane was his aunt.

They alright said 2Face.

Oh hey Gina said Ethel.

Hi Ethel.

Yo Shay give this to your mother he handed her an envelope, then gave her $300 shh! this is our secret. She gave him a hug thank you.

Yo give me the keys I'm out for a while. I'm a go holla at Wood for a minute on Fox. He also wanted to observe shit see how the block was running. He was an unsuspecting factor cause he had moved upstate all the people knew him they knew he came around once in a while. Wood was on the block with 2 pretty ass Spanish Mommies. Both of them was bad, with long pretty hair, dark complexions and thicker than a snicker.

Yo—O. said 2Face! what up! everybody was hype to see him, the only ones he didn't know was the 2 chicks with Wood. But even they was happy to see him.

Yo Cor what up bee said Wood.

Slow motion said 2Face, everything good Cuz?

Of course nigga! Got the hammer in the garbage can over there.

Ok said 2Face I got mine on me fool. We out tomorrow for ten days. Be ready for the bus at 9:00 am. I gotta drop off Gina at Kennedy at 6:00 am go get the bus and come get everybody. We going deep believe that!

CHAPTER 24

The bus they was on was packed to the max, with a lounge in the back. The side of the bus was posted The Big East. 2Face brought his Brooklyn crew: Biz, Popgun, Val, Tone, Mouse, Bud, Shorts, Simeon, and his man Chips from the Stuy he was locked up with. His other sons Ghost, Moses, Aaron, 'n Vincent, plus he brought Wood and the family. He stopped in Harlem to pick up C and the Girls then to the Bronx to get the rest of his family Grandma Tina, Ethel, Ricky, Shaniqua, his Moms, Tom Black his other Cuz, Timothy another cousin, his Pops, and his man Roc.

That was all he could fit. The bus was jammed packed. His Moms hated his Pops but came along anyways. Diane didn't want to go cause she had them kids. He did the best he could to bring everyone together, he finally got his cousins to meet his Brooklyn crew. Now he can put together his label and making them the deepest click in the game. He could now assemble his new idea for a nice single called "B-B Boroughs" the Brooklyn Bronx collabo. D-Boog, himself, and The Big East. Once he got the cipher going he could see if the chemistry was there. If it is there he would get the studio time and begin the promotions, with Cool G. Rap already shouting out his homies from Brooklyn this would be easy when you got money to push your shit. D-Boog got the AZ flow and would be a solo artist with a mean team behind him. Chips was signed to the Roc, so he was good he was the ultimate connect that would get them the exposure they needed.

2Face played the "Lean Back" instrumental to get the feel so the homies could get a rhythm.

Yo can kill this beat? Pop gun let me hear something smoke these cowards! Timothy had the camcorder filming the scene as well. Popgun stepped up to the plate, he turned his hat backwards and went in dropping wild metaphors like the late Big Pun. Everybody went crazy! banging the walls screamin'n shit. Then Chips stepped up and went crazy! he was getting at em on that get money shit. Then Biz mania kicked that gutter shit and Val finished on that smooth flow. D-Boog brought it back with no beat flowing for like 3:00 strait. They had fun for 2 ½ days the ride out to Vegas didn't even phase them.

Once they arrived the atmosphere was definitely different, from running around the 5 boroughs to upstate, to palm trees. Prostitution is, gambling and the big fight in a week, everybody was paid to do them and have fun.

The plan was to have fun on your own out here and make the best of this said 2Face. Although everybody got along well they were too deep to stay together, so Wood and the fams stayed together, The Big East and them stayed together. Chips chilled until H.O.V. came through. C chilled with the Girls, and Ethel and his Moms and them hung together. His Grandma and his Pops tagged along with them.

2Face, Bud, Mouse, Tone, Roc and Shorts stayed together. The only time they all seen each other was at the disco club at night. They flooded the strip clubs and casinos in mobs, winning, losing, fucking, partying, just having the time of their lives for the first couple of days.

2Face had paid 2 hookers a day every variety for him, C and Roc, even Chips came through for a good night. All the shit they dreamed of in the pens came true as they hi fived each other in the hotel room sipping bubbly surrounded with hoes.

2Face pulled Chips to the side, see homie you gotta let the crew have a good time feel me just like you would like to have a good time. That makes them feel a part of something special it strengthens the bond. I love all my niggas as long as they don't cross me.

Bud walked up to 2Face in the lobby of the hotel. Damn son, I never thought we'd be chillin like this, I gotta hand it to you Face you did it, you made your dream come true.

Yo its far from over yet, truthfully it hasn't even begun yet. I have to legitimize myself; us. I realize I gotta think for us cause I can't see us stagnate, we put too much work in. Lets go get some drinks and enjoy Birthday Boy said 2Face.

Oh shit you remembered?

Hell yeah!

Where the homies asked Bud? Shorts 'n them layed up with some hookers grinning.

The door knocked twice, Tone, Mouse 'n Shorts was wilding last night. Tone was stretched out sprawled next too him was a bodacious hooker. Mouse was watching Sportscenter getting head on the couch, while Shorts who just woke up with 2 bad white bitches sent one to open the door.

Who is it said shorty with the soft voice.

Its Shanta where is my husband!

Oh shit! Tone jumped out of his sleep and got dressed immediately.

Don't open the fucking door he demanded in a whisper.

Mouse was rolling with his loud laugh as he told shorty to chill on the head. He had a bad ass black sister topping him off.

As shorty stalled on opening the door Shorts got up and opened the door slightly.

Son what the fuck you doing yelled Tone! the anger in Tones eyes was like he wanted to kill Shorts, but when the door opened he saw he saw big headed Bud ugly ass and 2Face.

Son don't play like that word to mother son! said Tone. Everybody including the chicks was laughing. Son I'm a get ya for that, that was some bullshit son! Yo what up said 2Face? Bud couldn't stop laughing. Yo Mouse how them Yanks look last night asked 2Face?

They won son. How them bum ass Mets?

Son they won too son this is what we do son.

Fuck outta here said Tone, them niggas trash! fuck the Mets. Son, son when we play ya'll we smash ya'll, like every time homie.

Son you can't be slipping like that said 2Face what if that was really Shanta you'd of been assed out. Matter of fact pay these hoes and lets role out and get something to eat.

They selected a corner table to eat at for the five of them. The beautiful waitress from the hotel cafeteria had long golden hair, a tan complexion and a beautiful figure.

Now this is what I call beauty, Cindy right said 2Face?

That's my name its on my name tag, may I take your orders please?

Sure as they placed they're orders he and the waitress made eye contact which was all he needed.

Can I share a secret with you cutie? She checked out his pecs through the wife- beater, he was a fit black man in her eyes. All her life she wanted to experiment this it was in her grasp a golden opportunity.

He whispered something sweet in her ear that made her giggle and while she wrote the orders she also wrote her # on the bill to give to 2Face after they finished eat.

Son said Mouse I respect how you came up outta nowhere. I'm still hurt I ain't get put on son!

What you want asked 2Face? You want a brick I got you! yo if I where you I'd fall back cause I'm trying to have enough cake to own multiple businesses. But if you want to do you when we get back I got you. I ain't into buying cars 'n shit, wasting bread, I'm into building money and buying real estate, opening up businesses, creating jobs and giving back to our people we been taking from. Right now I'm making real moves, I'm a even get Reef a good lawyer and try to get son out. I want to provide for the less fortunate.

Do you know how it is to not have or to not be able to take full advantage of an opportunity?

Son I remember being broke, shit I'm still broke said Mouse.

Nah people in Africa is broke, the middle east, the inner city kids in America, who grow up around violence. The shit we gotta do but some sacrifices must be made in order to succeed th plan.

A yo Malcom X said Shorts, when is all this gonna happen? You not even on your dean.

You right but In ShaAllah I will be. Matter of fact lets go the Masjid after we eat. Sounds like a plan said Shorts.

We gonna drop Tony off to Shanta 'n keep it moving Bud said sarcastically, making niggas laugh.

A yo where the fuck is Roc?

He on his batman shit again asked Tone? He better be back before that bus leave his ass!

The food was ready to be served to 5 hungry faces. Enjoy said Cindy as she winked at 2Face.

CHAPTER 25

Around 5 o'clock Cindy got off work and headed to her car, waiting there was 2Face. She was pushing a 2008 Camry, cherry color with chrome rims.

What up Cindy? Looking all sexy wit ya hair out. Cindy smiled all she could think about was the muscles this guy had and his chocolate complexion which fit her mode perfect.

You wanna drive asked Cindy?

Where are we going baby asked 2Face?

Hell yeah! shit this was easier than I thought he said to himself. I guess we'll get to know each other driving he said.

She popped open the car with the automatic lock on the remote, it was a lil breezy but sunny. 2Face got in the drivers side, buckle up!

So where you from Cindy?

Actually I'm from Idaho.

Yeah Idaho he said blankly.

Yeah Idaho you got a problem with that!

No, no, no said 2Face, I'm just in awe a lil cause I never met nobody from there.

So now you have.

Feisty aren't ya he said sounding like a white boy. I like that. I'm from the Bronx, you know where that's at Cindy.

Isn't that New York City?

Yep. I bet you seen a lot of crazy shit huh?

Hell yeah he said.

So what made you settle in Vegas Cindy?

Working trying to build my career.

Career in what?

Well I want to be a dancer.

Why so many young women want to be dancers? What kind of dancing?

Not no exotic shit but like stage performances or video shoots.

You definitely got the body for it and you pretty as hell.

So what about you Mr. 2Face, why the fuck they call you 2Face? You a rapper, you look like one. You look a lil like Fifty Cent, I mean body wise.

Hey I'm my own person and got my own shaped body he said jokingly. She laughed at him. I'm a construction worker, and I do home improvement on the side. That made her laugh harder. What you don't believe me he flashed his I.D.

Are you married she asked?

Yeah but we fidding to get a divorce.

Why?

Because she ain't truthful, it's a long story. We here now, now we chillin.

They checked right into the hotel room at quarter to2Face opened a bottle of Don Perrion.

You drink Cindy?

Sure I'll take a shot.

You smoke weed?

Hell yeah she said. You got budd?

Of course but I don't smoke. You go head, I brought it for

other people to enjoy anyways. Then it won't be fun by myself she said in a seductive voice.

After 2 shots of Don and a hit of the godfather he rolled her she felt tipsy. She grabbed 2Face by the neck and started kissing him on his lips. Her lips were soft and melted right in his mouth. This felt like heaven and he began kissing her neck slow and passionately making her pussy sizzle. He began from the neck to behind her ear using his tongue like a slithering snake. Her tongue was hot 'n wet as she kissed his chest while unbuttoning his Laker Jersey. She pushed him back on the bed then began to suck his stomach licking every crack and every muscle.

Then 2Face pulled her to where they were. 69 position style now. He pulled off her pants as she was unbuckling his belt his shorts dropped.

She was amazed at his size. She was gonna enjoy every bit of this indeed. 2Face like wise was gonna enjoy himself as he admired how pretty her pussy looked and the piercing she had on her clit.

He used his tongue and smothered her pussy with his juicy lips making her moan 'n gasp, while she tried to deep throat him at 3quaters length which was all she could handle while fondling his balls. It was almost enough to make him bust but he held his composure he wanted some of that sweet pussy. He wanted his little man cockron to feel it!

Aaa–aah, aaah! Oh shit she climaxed. You making me cum daddy! yes, yes! She creamed his face as her cum juices squirted out. He kept eating; um, szz um! oh, oh yes oh yeah aaa-aah! Then he flipped her around and said ride me baby!

She mounted him and slid 10 ½ inches inside her. Uh, uh she bounced her fat ass off his thighs she was riding the shit out of him she looked like Coco a lil "Ice T's wife. But the boobs weren't as big. She was grinding son hard he felt her pussy muscles tighten up he almost lost it again but flipped her on her back without exiting the pussy he slammed her now reaming her with deep

strokes; aaah aah. Oh, Oh ah Aah! that's it daddy right there Oh shit! he was smashing the g-spot she was creaming him having a multiple orgasm, baby I'm cumming, I'm cumming! don't stop! please don't stop! the bed rocking and vibrated the room underneath them.

The old travelers downstairs married for 20yrs. Were disturbed by the noise, but flashbacks hit the old white man.

Honey they're loud upstairs his wife said.

Yeah I remember us being that loud some years ago.

What are you saying Teddy bear you got something left in the tank?

Lets do it Martha!

After pummeling her for ten minutes missionary style, she thought this guys gotta be a fucking porn star or something. She knew she had some good pussy she made a lot of guys cum quick, I guess black is beautiful she thought to herself.

2Face now had her where he envisioned her from the get go doggystyle. The backshot was amazing. Her ass smacking off his thighs and stomach he had her face down ass in the air going in deep; uh, uh, aaah aa–aah! that's too deep baby slow, slow aah!

That made 2Face more excited when he knew he had her she couldn't take no more of his meat so he went deeper and deeper. She tried to run; come here szz aah! aah, oh shit oh, oh szz oh! I'm cumming again! he kept on reaming her until her cream was visible on his dick eh was a stroke or two away from his own orgasm, but he slowed down until she recouperated and pounded her again the slapping sounds of her ass and her screams when he spanked her.

Cum in my mouth daddy, she said seductively like a porn star. I want you to cum in mouth! she spun around on him and sucked and jerked his wet dick full of her juices cum daddy cum in my mouth! Aaa–aaah! Oh shit, Aaah I'm cumming said

2Face. Yeah daddy she sucked and swallowed all of his gism every quirt of sperm went into her mouth and she sucked him till his shit tingled he had to tell her to stop. She had homey shaking.

No female ever did that to me. Well I'm special welcome to Idaho.

CHAPTER 26

As he layed in bed and pillow talked she went to get a rag and wash him off. He admired her beauty and didn't ever want to leave that room with her. She was like a Barbie doll to him and she had a sweet personality too. As she was washing his dick;

Cindy I'm putting together a record company within the next year or so if you stay in contact I'll put you on we gonna need dancers.

Really she said.

Yeah he replied.

I really would like to keep in contact with you 2Face. You were the first black guy I was ever with. So I guess once you go Black you never go back.

Yeah, just make sure its only with me please.

Oh, well my services will cost you $5 $500 what! I'm just kidding stupid she said. Shit worth $500,000! you got some good ass pussy and you gorgeous.

Thank you. I wish I could take you back with me, she looked at him curiously. Now is not the time I gotta get situated business wise first so when we meet again we can be in chill mode some where in the Carribean.

You mean that?

All the way to the gate he said. We will meet again believe that!

Yo Bud what up! Son we could hear ya'll from all over the floor as he opened the door. The old couple from downstairs walked up to him and Bud.

Which ever one of you was making all that noise making love, thank you, it rejuvenated our sex life and motivated us a lot. Bud and 2Face was rolling.

Son what up said Tone. Now Shanta was with him every step of the way.

You cheating ass niggas she said to Bud and 2Face. Niggas man!

Shut the fuck up said Tone believe that! 2Face tried to hold the laugh in yeah son tell ya wife to mind her fucking business!

Son it was good said Mouse to Shorts.

What's that son?

That bitch son had Shorts! You ain't here all that screaming. Son was it good asked Mouse?

Hell yeah son believe that!

Look he open said Bud.

Chapter 27

The night of the fight at Ceasar's Palace was crazy! 2Faces whole entourage rocked tuxedos looking like strait V.I.P. status. Stars flooded the worlds largest boxing attraction to see 2 unbeaten fighters. The bets were in the women were out. Everybody was there to see Damian The Dead Arm Wilson at 42-0, 39ko's vs. John The Body Rocker Smith 33-0, 25ko's to unify the MiddleWeight Championship. Wilson held the WBC and Smith held the IBF and WBA.

Yo said Mouse 2Faces sportsman, him and C who you bet on?

I took The Body Rocker said C.

Yeah well I took The Dead Arm said 2Face.

I think Smith is the better boxer said C.

Yeah said Mouse Dead Arm hit hard homey.

Remember I told you Pavlik was gonna knock out Taylor and Taylor was the better boxer in that fight said 2Face.

Yeah well I got a buck on the fight?

I got that said 2Face. Son his power will overwhelm him. Have mine tonight believe that!

Son said Tone how you get all these seats son? He was star struck.

The internet bee. I got the tickets as soon as the fight was signed I been waiting for this. Son I spent some shit for this bee. Over $200,000 on the tickets, $20,000 for the bus, $5,000 for the driver, then $33,000 for the hotel rooms, plus the spending money bee like $50,000 champ.

Son we gotta talk you getting money like a celebrity, Mouse cut in. Son you balling like that! asked Tone?

Just cool it star 2Face said in a Jamaican voice. I couldn't get everybody down here so I had to buy some straggler tickets that's why a few cats is uptop.

When the fighters entered the ring the crowd went crazy trying to touch the fighters. When they stood for the national anthem 2Face saw he was surrounded by stars and legends.

Will and Jada Smith sat to their left, they noticed Bernard Hopkins 'n DeLa Hoya with Sugar Shane to their right. Donald Trump and Jack Nickolaus 2Faces favorite actor cause he was a Laker fan, that amped him up as he pointed in his direction. H.O.V. and N.A.S. sat next too each other Eddie Murphy was behind them.

Son the stars is in the building said Tone! Sandra Bullock, Beyonce, Vida, Janet Jackson, Tom Cruise and Katie Holmes, Alicia Keys and Chris Brown and Rhianna were there representing. They watched the ring side girls all of them Bad, 2Face saw Cindy. He couldn't believe his eyes.

Son you see that bitch said Bud? Shorts was laughing. The bitch lied to ya boy but fuck it I got my shit off believe that! She winked his way, he threw up his fist at her which caught a couple of celebrities attention.

Howard Ledderman, Larry Merchant and Jim Lampley were announcing the fight as they always did. It was a memorable evening for him and everyone else, a dream come true. His Grandma was proud of her boy he had a good heart she thought, despite how he earned his money in the past.

The fight was set to begin after Michael Buffer's "Lets Get Ready To Rumb—le"!They were clearing the ring the fight was set.

Ding, ding, ding! here's the sound of the opening bell. Dead Arm was pressing The Body Rocker both exchanging blows.

Now lets see how The Body Rocker fight backwards, so far he holding it down.

Yeah said C he holding his right now.

Look at this fool Roc said Shorts! Over here he gestured. Roc pardoned his way through the anxious crowd. The action wore on in the ring.

Come on Dead Arm said 2Face! win this money for me! come on keep pressing!

For the next 5 rounds they took turns pressing each other, neither fighter budging. Round 6 though was where everything went wrong as within the exchange of hooks the Dead Arm lived up to his name when they both connected but his was the most effective shot that sent the Body Rocker buckling to the canvas between the ropes. When the Body Rocker got up on the 8 count The Dead Arm hit him with a flurry of punches and the ref jumped in to stop the fight. The Body Rocker was clearly finished.

Its all over! Its all over! Dead Arm stopped him screamed Lampley!

Yeah! screamed 2Face as he jumped up for joy. He hit big time off the bets. Son I just won $250,000 bee! believe that! the fight was a good one though C I'm rich bitch! ha, ha.

When they were leaving there was an after party, he spotted Chips with H.O.V. they walked over to Chips.

Son what up bee! Yo 2Face what's good? Yo this is my new boss. Oh word champ said 2Face! this is H.O.V. this is 2Face. Yo my son trying to get his own label as well.

Yeah said H.O.V. what you gonna name it?

I can't call it homey. Give him some advice on how things go kid asked Chips.

Yeah that would help out a lot I need to know the ins 'n outs most of all your support would be substantial. Yo Popgun! come here son! when Popgun saw H.O.V. he was almost starstruck.

Yo my boy here is a problem child believe that! this is The Big East my man. Biz, Popgun and Val. It's a whole crew of us and my Cuz D-Boog he gonna be a solo artist and I got this white chick who got a voice like Maria Carey she my secret weapon bee!

You got a demo or something asked H.O.V.?

Not with us but here my son out. Give him a quick 16 Pop!

Pop spit the 16 like a vet sounding like a Cool G. Rap/Pun with the metaphors. H.O.V. liked his flow.

I'll help you out son but you want to start your own label you need paper. You want the

mainstream I can help you with that. Its an investment its an expensive industry $50 million will set you strait or you'll be struggling spending money or in debt cause these other labels and distribution companies will rape you. So you want immediate mainstream figure out how you can accumulate atleast $30 mill. That's for your video shoots, studio time, major features and promotional tours.

2Face looked like his world was shot but H.O.V. made sense. Why be in debt if you got it you mine as well spend it to and he was gonna help him wash it by agreeing to front like he loaned the money to him and was collecting off of it the royalties until the money was paid back but the way 2Face explained it the money H.O.V. spent would never be touched. He even broke down how he was gonna franchise another business. He liked 2Faces idea and thought he was a good business man. He gave 2Face his card and told him to call him on Monday.

I'll financially back you think of me as the bank son said H.O.V..

You were gonna do the same thing with the banks anyway so I mine as well get a piece of the action.

I don't want to involve you with my shit H.O.V..

Well as long as you continue doing what you doing you

should be good, you a street nigga I trust you if my boy Chips trust you. Ya'll can sell units cause it's a lot of ya'll. This a big risk but music is a risk you gotta be willing to take. You got insurance and you got me to help promote. We gonna sell records bee. Holla at me Monday, H.O.V. walked off.

CHAPTER 28

He knew they had to hustle hard now which meant expanding more. But better yet he had a plan for that. In the mean time he awaited Sue to come to the X. He told her to jump on the next bus and come to Fox 'n 156st. Asap. They had a flight to catch. He still had that one hotie in mind Cindy from Vegas. She would have to wait though he had to get this money.

Yo Will roll up said Boog.

Shit moving over here I can't front bee said Wood. That's fucked up what happened to Chino. That was my nigga. He poured out some Henny to express his sorrow.

They don't know who did that shit asked 2Face?

Nope said Puerto Rican Willy nobody know who did that shit bee.

Wow said 2Face looking shocked. The cops don't even have a clue Huh?

Nah, bee! they don't even know shit bee. All they know is it was a black chick and a masked man.

Son that's some fowl shit whoever did that we'll get em son believe that! said 2Face. He knew all along he was the culprit.

It was 10:00pm and everybody was outside. It was wild nice

outside bee, the bodegas was bumping they music, there were a few shots up the block and mad chickenheads flocking. They was 20 deep on 156 by the park when a yellow cab pulled up.

The window came down Wood reached for the ratchet in the garbage can when a voice came from the cab.

Can the guy with the Yankee hat and jersey and blue shorts on with the pair of white Air Force Ones come here?

At first 2Face thought she was police he went up to the car. Its me stupid said Sue! come to the cab.

Hey Cassanova you went from Black, to White, now to Spanish nigga! said Puerto Rican Willy. Dudes was rolling.

Yo I'll be back said 2Face.

You ain't coming back said Tim, we won't see you till next December bee!

Hey you right fool holla at me niggas!

They went on the flight to Puerto Rico with 3hrs. Hugging and kissing. Did you miss me asked Sue?

Hell yeah! If this is a mistress then what does your wife get?

You get what you get cause you Suzie I liked you from day one. If wifey wasn't around you'd be my main squeeze.

I don't like being number 2 she said. You got a month to fix that!

Just chill!

No I'm not your sex slave.

You wanna argue right on the plane he said?

Hell yeah! I'm pregnant 2Face she said with sarcasm.

Wow said 2Face. How many months?

3 she said. 3months! how long did you know? I just found out 2 days ago. I didn't want to ruin your trip.

Damn baby! he said. The mood on the ride the rest of the trip was quiet. For the first time he didn't know what to do. When they arrived in Puerto Rico he needed to focus.

Sue I'm sorry alright. Tears rolled down her eyes. He never saw her like that.

I'm keeping it Cory. I don't want to blow you up but be a father to my child please or I will.

You don't have to worry about that, he hugged her and wiped the tears from her eyes, he whispered in her ears, I love you, you in good hands.

When they arrived in the hotel and dropped their bags 2Face was very affectionate. Hey being that you not in the mood to be going out tonight we can just chill our boat trip ain't until the morning. I'll order us something to eat from room service if that's alright with you.

Yeah, baby I want to just be with you. I'm type jetlagged anyways.

I'm sorry for being such a party pooper.

Its alright baby, you got to be you got my little jr. in your stomach.

Yeah well you gotta hurry up and get that divorce.

I just need more damaging evidence on her or I'll make her want to leave me, but don't worry I got a plan, believe that!

Last night they cuddled up and watched horror flicks then fucked.. Today was gonna be fun they were going on their boat trip to jet ski, see the aquarium and cap the night off dancing salsa on the beach. The day was nice and sunny, early in the morning around 8:00am.

Hurry up Sue!

I can't find my earrings.

Fuck them earrings we going swimming anyways. Come on baby we gotta be there by nine.

CHAPTER 29

Shorts got the call from Ahm. Yo what up son!

Niggas is acting up down here said Ahm.

Word! replied Shorts I'm coming down there tonight son! I'll be there in the morning say no more!

You might want to bring some goons with you son these niggas type deep!

Son I am a goon! I don't give a fuck how many them niggas there is, I don't give a fuck about none of that! we gonna handle this.

Shorts was in the East on the low making sure shit was right. He was gonna head to Harlem to check on the stash cribs and tell Shay Shay to collect the $500,000 by Friday. He was gonna check Wood 'n them to make sure they was cash money. He knew shit was cool cause niggas had they own little crews, all of whom was family. He also told Shay Shay to tell 2Face he'd be outta town in N.C. just some bullshit beef. He headed to the car to make his rounds.

He exited the City at like 10:30pm next stop N.C.

Look baby dolphins! there so pretty daddy!

Yes they are said 2Face, a shark need to come by so I can see a good tussle.

Shut up said Sue punching him on the arm he laughed as they cuddled 'n hugged up, walking on the boat. In Puerto Rico people weren't accustomed to seeing a Black man with a Spanish girl but these 2 made a perfect couple.

I'm really glad that you brought me on this trip Cory.

Hey this trip is for you.

Well later me and you are gonna visit my aunt and see some of my family.

You sure that's a good idea?

Why, not? My people ain't on no bullshit, relax!

Later that night 2Face and Sue went to her aunts crib outside the city. 2Face always alert, always thinking had reminded himself that he had homies he met in the pens who got deported back to Puerto Rico. He gave em a call for good measure. His man Oosh, one of his ex work out partners drives cabs so he used that to his advantage.

When they arrived at her aunts crib he smelled some fine herbs and knew it was for them. The aroma even hit his man Oosh.

You enjoy Oosh said with a strong accent.

Yeah I'll have a good time, I'll be back in an hour said Oosh.

Good to see you buddy! said 2Face as he handed him enough money to pay his bills for a month.

2Face and Sue got out of the car. The house was very decent, brown color. The grass was cut, the neighborhood was mostly poor though, with stray cats roaming. A bunch of little kids playing baseball in the twilight hrs. 2Face was observing all this when he heard;

Suzie! Suzie my little sweetie come here! he was surprised by the excellent english.

Auntie Brenda said Sue then the Spanish came in which he didn't understand shit. The gibberish continued for 2 more minutes when finally Sue introduced him to her aunt. They hugged.

So nice to met you said 2Face.

Nice to meet you too.

You know my niece love you a lot you love my niece?

Yes of course I do he responded.

So you both love eachother huh?

Yeah he said.

So how long have you two been together?

Stop it auntie.

Please come inside said aunt Brenda.

We've been together a few months now said Sue.

And you two already in love?

Yes things happen like that sometimes auntie.

Cory said Sue my aunt used to live on Leggett St.

Yeah said 2Face wow get the hell outta here!

I lived there over ten years from the 70's to the 80's.

Shoot you might know my family said 2Face.

Yeah, who ya family she asked?

You know Pat from Fox st.?

Fox and what?

784 on the fifth floor. We lived there in the 70's and 80's when I was a kid. She thought for a second pondering.

Yeah I know Pat! you her lil boy huh? Yep, he replied. I remember you when you was a little baby.

Wow said Sue, it's a small world. Yeah, Pat used to mess with Tyrone the one with all the brothers, Ms. Jackson son.

That's my pops! get the fuck gutta here she said. He was a real playboy back then. Your momma used to mess with Puerto Rican Pete from Southern Blvd.

Yeah said 2Face. You know my family, get out of here.

When your momma moved I moved too. We lost contact. Tell her I said what's up shit we had lots of good times.

They ate wild food while Brenda told lots of stories about

his Moms. She used to be real popular in the hood. Even he remembered when he was little all the parties and wildin out.

Stay the night won't you? My son is in New York visiting, you can take his room.

Yeah Auntie, said Sue. But its up to Cory, come on baby lets chill here. We'll go over our family history, our tree.

Ok we can stay said 2Face I'd be honored he said with a strait face even though he wanted some pussy tonight.

Thank you said Auntie.

Chapter 30

Shorts made it to N.C. early in the morning around 9:30 am. He had a few pit stops on the way he almost got lost in Delaware. He drank a couple of red bulls and some bustello coffee to keep him wired and alert for the drive but he was tired now. Raleigh was a fairly decent sized city, he heard it was wild out here but if you can live in New York City you can live anywhere. Especially in his day and era of the early 90's.

He found the nearest hotel a Howard Johnson and checked in at the desk. A cute little petite darkskinned with a thick southern accent attended him.

Can I help you she said?

Looking for a room sweetheart, something cozy. His New York accent caught her off guard, then she asked the famous question.

Where are you from New York City?

Yeah Brooklyn Shorty.

Word she said, her attitude suddenly became a smile. Your room is 209 sir. If you have any questions holla, the desk# is on the phone.

Thank you miss... Lisa! Ok Lisa, nice to meet you they call me Shortman.

Shortman? Ya'll be having some weird names.

So do ya'll.

Lisa was riding Shorts grinding him good. She was petite but had a nice shape. Her hair came down to her neck as she tried to toss it positioning herself. She was bouncing her ass off his thighs. Shorts had the mean grin as he was getting ready to buss when in one motion she dismounted him, pulled off the condom and sucked Shorts dry into a exasperating orgasm. His orgasm was so crazy his dick was still hard in her warm mouth, then she mounted him again.

The next day 2Face woke up to a good smelling aroma, it just flowed through the house and through his nostrils.

Good morning baby!

Good morning Sue. I went out and bought us tooth brushes for our stinky breath.

Thank you baby. What's for breakfast?

Your favorite steak and eggs, don't worry she know you don't eat pork.

Tell her I said thank you!

You tell her she said.

Come here gorgeous said 2Face. She cuddled up under him. I wish I would've met you a long time ago you deserve a ring instead of this fucking brawd. Trust me she out the picture I got a plan. The sad thing is I love her daughter a lot but her mom is no good behind closed doors.

Look baby I'm here for you just do what you gotta do and do what's best.

Be patient said 2Face baby.

No doubt said Sue.

That's what I like about you, you got a positive attitude and a beautiful personality.

Shorts was on the phone with Ahm. Yo what up I'm in the building homey. Where you at?

At the crib, I'm a give you directions.

Just give me the address, fuck all that directions shit I got a tour guide.

A tour guide said Ahm? Ok said Ahm.

Shortie when you get outta work?

Whenever you want me too she said coming up from his dick as she had a mouthful of penis and spit. Well we out now shortie, who gonna hold the office down?

My lil brother he in the back my parents are out of town.

Shorts thought to himself if he was broke this would be a easy juxx.

They made it over to Ahm crib in 15 minutes across town. Shorts called Ahm on the cell phone 1 ring he picked up, yo I'm in the black Maxima.

Yo I'm coming out from around the housing complex with short building, 10 in exact. Ahm came out building 4 Shorts jumped out the car. Ahm was a Puerto Rican but he was Muslim he was short with braids and had a little build on him as well.

Yo what up son said Shorts!

What up fool said Ahm! As Salaam Alaykum, Wa Laykum Salaam as they embraced.

Lets go inside said Ahm.

Yo son I got this bitch with me.

Man fuck that bitch said Ahm. Where she from?

She from here son. I met her at the hotel I'm staying at.

Here fool! Ahm handed him a envelope. Shorts checked the money, cool.

So you met shorty at the tellie huh he said laughing.

Son she sucked me off and everything son!

Word! well shit tell her come on then fool! she can chill in the living room, wifey in the crib. What up with this nigga Cor?

Son chilling bee! he in P.R. with this hot little Spanish mommy.

Word! said Ahm, but that's neither here nor there homey, yo

these niggas out here frontin son! Shorts whistled to her in the car to come on.

These niggas from the North side. They ran up on some of my workers talking bout our shit too good its slowing down the flow for them this is just a warning. Next time its bullets flying.

Oh word! said Shorts what block they on I'm over there!

CHAPTER 31

Later on that night on Main 'n First st. the block was crowded with fiends lurking through the housing complex. The dealers posted in front of a parked Taurus. Wild empty 40 bottles of St. Ides and weed filled the aroma.

Shorts wanted to make a statement, dressed in all black, black goodie, black Timbs, 'n the ski mask. He crept up to the 2 workers on the corner like a ninja. One of em was headed towards a fiend when 2 shots muffled by a potato hit son in the neck and head he died instantly.

Shorts grabbed the other kid and put the gun to his head.

Yo! where this dude Hank at?

The young kid was terrified after seeing his man get his head blown off. I–I—I don't know!

You got 3 seconds where he at?

3rd and Main 329 Main St.

Thank you my dude said Shorts. A loud blast from the .380 deafened the kid as Shorts stuck the knife through his chest piercing his heart he wiggled it for good measure and violently pulled it out. The kid bled to death slowly. All Shorts knew was

Hank was the Leuitenant causing all the problems and he had to be eliminated.

The fiend kept running to Hank, yo shouted the cracked out fiend. A dirty skinny lightskinned around 5"8 about a buck soak 'n wet.

Yo! Hank said the fiend 2 of ya boys just got popped by some cat in all black on Main st.

What said Hank! he was 6"2 240 an ex college football player gone bad. He already had his goons with him.

Fuck you mean 2 of my boys got popped! you sure the police ain't get em?

Nah, no police they dead son shots in the head. Shot in the head by who? I told you some kid in all black. I heard the shots and stated running. I had just copped from them.

Lets cruise through the hood. You better leave the hammers incase the police get to harassing tonight.

Shorts went back to the hotel. Lisa was waiting for him.

Good evening boo boo.

What up said Shorts. Yo! you know this cat named Hank?

You mean Hank from the North side? Yeah, said Shorts big dude, ex-football player.

Well I heard of him but I don't know him like that.

Oh yeah well you don't know me like that either, I don't exist.

Why you say that Shorts? You in some type of trouble or something?

Nah cutie. I just like to stay on the low, but I'm a take a shower and go for a ride you dig? I'm a go see my boy for a minute.

CHAPTER 32

Yo, said Hank to Jr. then 2 dead niggas! Jr. was the head of the crew the boss calling shots.

Yo nigga said Jr. find them mother fuckas who did this. What about them two cats you pressed the other day? Go check em out. I shouldn't have niggas mustering up courage to go against me in this City!

Shorts drove to the block the scared kid told him Hank was on. No one was outside when he arrived.

Fuck! he said. He wanted to catch this cat, finish him and head back to the hood, but this wasn't gonna be easy.

Ahm had his workers outside like any other normal night. The 2 were young and durable named Ty and Maine. They noticed a car speeding towards them jumping the curb. They both took off!

Catch one of them niggas shouted Hank as they hopped out and split up. The chase was on now! Ty boogied through the alleys at full speed leaving behind nothing, while Maine was moving but Hanks boys was gaining on him. He wasn't a fast runner because he was fifty pounds over weight.

Catch that fat motherfucka! Hank shouted. One of his boys

dived to get one kid by his foot. The nudge was just enough to knock him off balance as he fell to the ground face first. Hands 'n feet met Maine as hard bottoms were stomping the top of his head and ribs. He was dragged to his feet by Hanks men.

You better tell us who your boss is and why ya'll put a hit on my workers said a heavy breathing Hank?

What hit said Main? A right hand landed flush off his temple. He began to see stars.

Don't play with me boy!

I'm his boss shouted Ahm! with like 10 goons behind him including Ty. What up said Ahm?

What up snapped Hank!

Ya'll like killing we gonna get to killing then! 2squad cars pulled up, so did Shorts from a distance. But said Hank them boys here we'll see you around.

Fuck ya'll faggot ass niggas said Ahm!

We'll be back!

We'll be waiting said Ahm.

So-ooo! that's Hank.

Ok, bet said Shorts!

CHAPTER 33

2Face was enjoying a nice afternoon day on the beach with Sue chilling. They laid enjoying the sun in the sand, 2Face displaying his muscles, Sue displaying her smooth beautiful body.

Its definitely gonna be some changes baby! I'm pressing the issue when I get back. I'm gonna

stick to my plans and open up my night club and restaurant and I'm a talk to my cuz and see if he still designing clothes. I got mad ideas to get us rich baby girl. Just chill Sue within a year you won't have to worry about shit! You'll never have to work again. My ultimate goal is that label. Even though the internet is killing the market with the down loading I got a plan for that too. What I'm about to do is causing a divorce, believe that.

Shorts was on the prowl early afternoon. He knew Hanks address and he also peeped Hank had a couple of men out front his building. But Shorts thought if Hank ain't the main guy who is? He would soon find out.

It was early so he couldn't do it masked up but he was dressed in all black. Shorts lived for this the drama. He took the back entrance through the building. Hank lived on the second floor. Shorts got into the building rather easy, he thought it was a set up or was these cats that stupid 'n laid back. Shorts saw the door was wooden he wasted no time kicking down the door making a loud banging noise.

Boom! he was in the crib, 2 little kids were jumping from the sound of the noise, 3 of em on a   pull out couch.

Baby what the fuck was that said Hanks wife! Shorts was behind the wall with the scared little kids looking at the crazed man.

Daddy, daddy said the scared kids, over there! That gave Shorts the chance he needed as Hank came running out the bedroom with a sawed off blough! blough! Shorts popped 2 in his melon and splattered his brains on the tv right in front of the kids. The poor traumatized kids just witnessed their father get murdered.

Being that the job was done Shorts broke out to go handle the 2 cats in the front headed up the stairs with guns out. Hiding behind the stair well they didn't even know they were sitting ducks as the.38 snub nose was pumped into their chest, blough! blough! blough! they didn't even know what hit em. A bloody mess of guts and meat covered the stairwell. Shorts calmly walked past the 2 hit up soldiers and walked out the building and wiped the prints off the gun. He didn't want to get caught with the ratchet and didn't want nobody to find the gun by sight.

Shorts headed back to the hotel to get ready to go back to New York.

Yo, Ahm you should be good now just stay low key ya heard.

I'm always low key champ, hold ya head said Ahm and good looking.

CHAPTER 34

Lisa seen her cousin Jr. for the first time in 6 months. Jr. was a high roller foreal! they was kicking it for a minute.

Yo I met this kid I'm feeling from New York who staying here Jr. His name Shorts he's cute.

Word! said Jr. how long he been here?

2 days she responded.

So why the fuck you telling me for I don't give a fuck about him!

Damn nigga I'm just trying to make conversation! hold on one second I got a call said Jr.. The call Jr. got shook him to the point to where he was frightened. Tears rolled down his eyes as he just found out his long time friend Hank was gunned down. Hank was his man since childhood, they been through it all together now he was gone just like that!

Lisa I'll be back he said all choked up. Hank dead!

What! said Lisa.

He got murdered over an Hour ago. Oh my God she gasped. I gotta find out what happened I'll be back he said with a groggy voice.

Cops were every where in Raleigh. 5 slayings in 2 days this was insane in this city. Detective Marshall a tall skinny black man the color of Wesley Snipes and Detective Shaw a chubby white man balding on the top, his age showed with partial grays on his beard. They were asigned to the case.

The leuitenant is gonna come down on our asses Marshall if we don't find out what the hell is going on here! Things were quiet for a few months now things are outta hand. As they were investigating the potential crime scene Jr. pulled up in a brand new Range Rover with 24's on his rims. He hopped out and casually walked over to the building his friend got killed in he once had.

What happened asked Jr.?

Your boy was gunned down boy just be easy.

Shut the fuck up as he lunged for Shaw after his smart remark. Marshall grabbed him before he could get a good punch off.

Looks like you gonna have to order you some new body guards, some real help before the feds swoop in or you'll be laying there tonight or tomorrow said Shaw.

Come on lets walk and talk said Marshall.

He's drug dealing scum said Shaw. They both ignored him.

He's a piece of shit said Jr..

I know said Marshall. You have any idea who's behind this?

We had some issues with some up 'n comers, as far as them paying homage to us for setting up shop out here, but I don't really know the situation cause Hank was the man out here who handled things.

Maybe these boys ain't playing fair said Marshall. You should have come to me boy. That's what you pay me for right?

You right uncle. But I didn't think it was that serious.

Well it is and if they got to him they'd get to you too. Who ever did this don't give a fuck. Find out some information and get back to me Jr. so we can make an arrest. That keeps my boss happy, then me, then you. Cause shit rolls down hill. He patted Jr. on the back and walked off.

CHAPTER 35

2Face just landed back at Kennedy Airport around 2pm. He was glowing after a terrific trip to Puerto Rico. He had a marvelous time in Vegas treating his people and now all he had to do was put his affirmative action into effect, sit back and relax collect more money and stack. He gonna offer his business proposal to his broker to get his loans he needed to wash his money. If everything went right he'd be rich for the rest of his life.

He dropped Sue off at the bus station, he had to go back to JFK at 9:00 to pick up Gina 'n Kitara. He had time to sleep for a few hours and go check every body before he left.

Jr. drove around every neighborhood to find out any information on who these cats were. None of they're workers really hustled outside so it was hard to find them. Then he remembered his cousin described this New York cat to him. now he was beginning to believe this cat was a hired hit man or something. From New York he thought he was dangerous? Them cats is dangerous period and them up 'n comers definitely had money to play with. He drove strait to the hotel.

Boom, boom, boom, boom! Yo! You knocking like the police!

Open the fucking door said Jr.!

Damn fool! you alright? What they shooting at you too?

Nah, that New York cat still here?

He left earlier. Did you get his number or something? You know what he was driving?

Yeah why? Give it too me! For what she asked?

He grabbed her by the hair. Cuz give me the fucking number now!

Alright let me go nigga! unleashed it. I think did he did this to Hank 'n them Lisa.

Foreal she said concerned?

Yeah Cuz. Tell me what he told you. What you know?

Well he driving a black Maxima with New York plates. He drove me to his friend house on the east side by Sunny Side Projects. He met some cat named Ahm.

Cuz you a life saver. Jr left the crib and called Detective Marshall and gave him the information. He thought to him self this dude is dangerous and with his right hand man and his muscle dead, it would be a better job for the police to handle. He would get the bastard still and not have to get his hands dirty. The kid would have hell in jail.

Shorts had just left Ahms crib an hour ago. He told him to lay low and disappear for a while then come back out when shit die down. He made sure the work would still move though. He also thought to him self he should've took all the work and bounced just incase. He knew he made that city hot as hell. He saw a N.C. State Trooper gaining on him with his lights blaring on him. he thought they was trying to get past him so he pulled over to let them pass.

Turn off the car now and slowly step out with your hands up now! the cop said through a bullhorn. Turn off the ignition now!

Aw shit! what the fuck said Shorts. He knew he was good though, cash money, no guns, no drugs, no kind of physical evidence. The officer walked up behind him as he was getting out of the car.

Get on the ground now!

Hey what's this about officer? Shut up and do as I say! Shorts thought to himself let do what this pig say he looked trigger happy.

Shorts was cuffed and the trooper called for more back up to come.

Officer why am I being cuffed?

Your wanted for multiple homicides. 5 murders in Raliegh. His hearty dropped, even though he knew they had no evidence they could still railroad him.

As Ahm was headed to his car a swarm of troopers from S.W.A.T. tackled him to the ground.

Yo! what the fuck is this! The night stick almost choked spit out his mouth.

Don't fucking resist said Marshall. Cuff him and get him outta here! They cuffed him and got into the paddy wagon.

CHAPTER 36

2Face was at Shay Shay crib chilling with Monique, Monica, Jessica and Jamie. He was checking on his bread collecting when the call came through from Ahms wife. The expression on his face displayed so much anger the girls left the room. He got off the phone and punched Moniques coffee table so hard that the vibration and echoes sent her magazines flying.

Yo Jessy, Monica and Jamie we got a trip to take. We getting a rental have Larrel hook that up. Monique I'm a need you to wire $50,000 to attorney James Buchanon and Rebecca Anderson.

$50,000 a piece.

This fucking idiot Shorts he yelled! He locked up.

What said Monica?

Him and Ahm got bagged for some shit we need to get them outta there now! They being detained and questioned. The lawyers want money for this they said they can get out asap we just need to get the money.

Monique you got the dummy account so we can use it to do the wiring. We out at 11:00 tonight so be ready. Fuck! he said.

Where's this fucking plane at 2Face said to himself? The

116

announcement on the loud speaker was made. Flight 109 from New England has just arrived. Good about time.

10 minutes later lil Kitty was running into his arms. Hey my pretty!

C.D., C.D. what up!

What up he shot back? Who taught you that, mommy?

She shook her head yeah laughing.

Hey Gina he said as he kissed her. How was your trip, good?

Yo! So much is going on in my country its crazy! I mean the suicide bombings the searches now mad police with a.k.'s everywhere.

Yeah. Shit crazy huh? Well baby we need to talk but not now.

Talk about what baby? We'll talk believe that! Being that my boss gave me a extra 2 days off I need you to either stay with Ethel or in a hotel, or shoot to Bing on your own.

Baby I'm tired I want to go home tonight. I know sweetheart, but Shorts got into some trouble I got's to go get him.

Fuck him! What he got to do with us?

That's my boy. I can't leave him down there.

Down where! Down south.

What the fuck is he doing down South? He got no business being down South.

He went to hang out with Ahm and got caught up in some shit.

Wow! well you better not go anywhere before you get caught up.

I'm just going to get him. I'll be back immediately I promise.

What's immediately! You on parole. Shh–!

It's the middle of the airport Gina!

I– don't— give–a–fuck!

Calm down.

No!

Alright bet I'm out, fuck you. When your faggot ass stripper friends need help you stop the world for em. But me no, I gotta listen to you fuck outta here!

C.D. don't walk away from me! C.D.! Cory Jackson. He kept walking through the crowd.

2Face, Monica, Jamie, and Jessica drove down to N.C. the expression on his face was of disgust.

You need to calm down honey said Monica. I'm the same way. I hate arguing. But what do you do why she so mad? She always bitching said Jessica.

When shit don't go her way.

Well any bitch gonna complain said Jamie we females.

You right said 2Face I can't win this argument. She black, Spanish, asked Jessica? She

Russain. Russian! said Jamie.

You married a Russian asked Jessica?

Yeah replied 2Face I don't see color when it comes to human beings.

Well you need to fucking with that bitch! replied Jessica. That's why she always complaining. 2Face started laughing. Easy girls. Nah, fuck that said Jessica cause we from the hood, we understand eachother better, smell me she said?

Yeah I smell pussy said 2Face! everybody started laughing. Don't worry she out the picture real soon, believe that.

CHAPTER 37

They made it to North Carolina early in the morning. Hey Jamie we gonna stay at the tellie in Duram and wait to hear from Ahm's wife. When she say they out then we go get Shorts and Breeze. Monica get Shorts Maxima and Break out Asap, Jessica get the work from Ahm's wife And get their spare car on the westside and bounce immediately. Yaw 2 driving back to New York yourselves. Matter of fact Monica go get Shorts and get him up outta here. Jamie you stay with me. Yaw got that?

Yeah we got that they all said in unison.

They got to Duram 9:00am and got the hotel. They chilled till about 1:30 in the afternoon when Ahm's wife called and said the transfer went through and the lawyers were gonna have em out asap. If they keep they're mouths shut they'd be out cause there's no physical evidence to hold them on. Plus Shorts used his brothers name Rahan. Around 3:00 the call came in, Ahm's wife called 2Face.

They both at my house right now, I just picked them up. Monica and Jessica left asap. 2Face and Jamie stayed in they're room.

Monica and Jessica easily followed they're directions. Monica came to Ahm's crib to get Shorts at 5:00pm. she parked in his Parking lot walked up the stairs Ahm was on point and had the door open as soon as she got to the door.

How you said Shorts grinning. 2Face pist off at you. You need to tell me everything so we can tie up all the loose ends and break out. Shorts and Ahm told her everything.

Ya'll need to pack up and bounce, you and your wife 'n kids. Yaw should leave town it ain't safe out here no more.

Who you telling said Ahm!

Yaw on yaw own from here she said to Ahm. Oh we need the keys to the spare car I got a friend waiting to pick up the rest of the work so we can bounce? I hope everything is there?

Yeah said Ahm everything is there.

Call me when you got the keys.

I got the keys now he said. He went into the room and got em real quick. Ok we out Shorts said Monica sounding like a true boss.

On her way back to N.Y. Jessica stopped at the tellie to let 2Face know the deal. 2Face pondered for a minute.

So he said son was fucking with a hotel chick? He went out did this that 'n the third, last person to see him was that hotel chick. She the only one who knew he was there besides Ahm. Bet!

2Face sat in the car and sent Jamie in a local bar to find out information on this Hank cat and his boss Jr.

Hi said Jamie to the Bartender, how are you?

What do you like he asked her? A shot of Dr. Maggilcutty.

Ok one shot of that coming up. The bar was dark and quiet about 7 people total.

So where are you from sweety? Your accent is a lil different from here.

I'm a student from Buffalo. Buffalo? Yeah I transferred to take computer science.

Wow said the Bartender.

Yeah I just got in town 2 days ago I stay on campus. Shit

I didn't know they give it up out here like that with all these murders. I thought it was peaceful?

Yeah once in a while we get a murder, but we got 2 rival gangs going for the juggler. One from New York the other from here.

Wow! Yeah, there is a cat named Jr.. He owns half the town and the police force. Got a nice little club on Franklin St.

Really said Jamie.

Yeah he lost 5 of his men. Ump, said Jamie. I wonder if his club is open tonight?

On a Monday shit yeah! up until midnight. And he still selling drugs?

Yep replied the bartender. But I gotta attend to more customers I'll be back.

Jamie finished her drink and got up.

Hey said the bartender, where you going?

Oh I got to get some air. As soon as she got outside she went to the van. 2Face rolled down the window.

Get in. She jumped in. What up said 2Face?

He at the club on Franklin St. lets go! They drove down Franklin St. until they saw a night club called: Club Jr.'s. He remembered that Shorts said the cat drove a Green Range Rover. He saw it parked outside.

Now what said Jamie?

We wait said 2Face.

They sat in the car staked out for an hour. the club was emptying out when the last dude came out of another door. Yo! see that flashy nigga right there? He fit the description don't he.

Yeah she said.

Go stall him real quick. Hurry up!

She jumped out the van. Excuse me sir, sir! sir! she screamed!

A tipsy Jr. turned to her can I help you?

Ya'll closed now she asked all sweet? Yeah why he replied reaching for his glock who you? He didn't see 2Face creeping from behind him.

Calm down sweety I just wanted to get a shot I had a long day chill. A drink! A drink! 5 of my boys dead and you want a drink he said slurring his words.

Oh he definitely the right man he was bent too 2Face said to himself. Jr. kept on beefing and didn't see a man in dark behind him. the buck knife punctured his spine and the knife was twisted inside his lungs, his scream was muffled by the sudden choke of blood he coughed up. Plus 2Faces 18 inch biceps were wrapped around his neck. Jr. fell to the ground leaking and

choking on his own blood as the knife was pulled out of him. 2Face placed Jr.'s hat over his face as he layed there to bleed to death. He would bleed to death before anybody would find him.

Your blood thins when you drink he said to Jamie as they walked to the van and drove off. They watched people out front drunk not even paying attention to the van, not aware that a major player in town was stretched out, out back.

You crazy she said to him. you ain't got no blood on at all do you?

Nope! lets pit stop at that hotel. Oh shit I do got blood on these gloves though and blood on my knife.

I just want to say you a crazy motherfucka! 2Face laughed, a sick laugh.

Lisa was at the motel for dolo. Her father trusted her cause she was usually good with money. A strange man with a black Champion hoodie on and black jeans and black timbs appeared at her desk starling her.

Yo! Yo! I need a room sweety.

$50 sir.

Ah right shorty.

You got a accent you from the city? Nah brick city baby!

Where that at?

New Jersey.

Well I need some I.D.

I.D.! come on Shorty. That's the policy fool you ain't never checked in a hotel before?

Nah.

Nah well news flash! you need I.D.

Miss I got I.D. I was just messing with you. I gotta use the bathroom where is located at?

Ok hold on follow me she said. When Lisa opened the door to let the man use the bathroom 2Face asked her if she remembered a lightskinned cat from New York.

No she replied quickly. I thought you had to use the bathroom?

Yeah I do you sure you don't remember him? He was sizing her up for the attack.

Well he told me to tell you good looking for the info you gave up.

What info?

This! The knife was violently forced into her stomach as he shoved it deep into her   then in one motion he pulled out and calmly forced the knife into her temple causing her instant death. Blood dripped off the wall as 2Face calmly walked out of the hotel he rocked gloves so he knew it couldn't be traced to him. he nonchalantly walked to the van and changed his clothes revealing his Rocawear Sweatsuit. The knife would disappear in a lake asap and the clothes burned in an instant. They headed back to New York.

CHAPTER 38

A week later 2Face and Shorts sat up in Fitze's and got 2 drinks and casually chilled in there office.

Son don't do no shit like that ever again!

Son what you wanted me to do?

Think! We can't keep walking around bodying shit homie! Its gonna catch up to us. People get they're deserving that's all. A nigga cross us you get it simple as that, but if we could work shit out first we do that cause its hard to make money and kill at the same time feel me especially on the streets. Always use your first option. I like to kill when I have to not for fun.

You right said Shorts.

I ain't gonna be the clean up man again. And that's coming out your pc, By the way.

What!

Yeah cause of you we lost North Carolina took a major hit from the Lawyers, we had to make Ahm and his wife disappear.

My bad son, fuck it, it is what it is.

I got some other ideas, moreless said 2Face.

Roc what up bee! what's good Face? How was PR. My nigga?

Official my dude.

Word!

Yeah said 2Face.

You ain't fuck no other Mommies out there nigga?

Nah, I just chilled with Shorty.

You like her huh?

Hell yeah she bad ain't she said 2Face? She look and act more better than Gina.

I know said Roc.

Yo Roc! They still following you asked 2Face?

Nah I think they fell back.

Good replied 2Face.

Get back to work break is over gentlemen we got a lot of work to do. I'm sure you guys had enough vacation time to catch up said they're boss. Yes sir replied Roc and the rest of the workers.

A week later 2Face went to his bank. He had a drawn up business plan from scratch. He needed $200,000 to open up a restaurant. He also spoke with Gina and with a percentage of the loan if they got it they would open up a night club. Gina wanted that badly. Being they were married they would split the proceeds of the night club. She had nothing to do with the restaurant. But he needed a white face to draw a specific crowd to his new restaurant and club. He already had the property in mind, the area and the kind of food that would be served. Plus he calculated being on parole he couldn't serve drinks but he had an idea for that too.

Good afternoon Mr. Jackson said Mrs. Kittle a chubby older white lady he used to deal with while locked up doing trans actions for him.

So your interested in receiving a loan from our bank?

Yes he replied.

Please have a seat sir.

I'm sorry I'm a little nervous about this he said.

Oh no need to be I'm sure you'll do just fine. She went over his plan and gave him a stare of question. He wasn't just asking for like $50,000 or no small loan he wanted damn near a quarter mil.

I assume you never had your own business before?

No I haven't.

Have you ever had a loan before?

No.

So what makes you think this plan of yours will work she asked?

Confidence and careful planning Mam. The people that I'm dealing with already are aware of what's needed, deals have been done by handshake until this loan is finalized then I can put things into motion. And I'm not afraid to get my hands dirty Mam so trust me I'll be in the mix. I'll put the necessary ground work in that's needed. Every word he said he was looking dead into her eyes. She seen the success written all over his face and the determination.

I also see you have took care of your debts, your credit is clean, I also see you have saved $40,000.

Yeah $10,000 is from working, $5,000 is from side jobs, the other $25,000 is from a settlement.

I'm willing to give you a chance. I believe in someone willing to take big risks to advance in life. I believe you'll be successful. You do own a car or property right? You know we need some type of collateral.

Yes I own a car and I have my money in the bank plus I got a good job.

I'll go over this with my superiors and we'll see about making this happen within a week tops!

Yes thank you so much for believing in me. If you weren't married I'd kiss you right now said a over joyful 2Face, thank you.

CHAPTER 39

Baby! I got the loan baby!

Wow! she replied. Yes we'll be rich daddy!

Yeah! Said 2Face we'll be rich he said meekly.

So I can open my night club, oh I mean our night club?

Yeah.

Awe baby! lets go get something to eat. I bought back that Russian Vodka you like, we'll pop that at the restaurant.

Whoa! first I need to go to the Masjid and offer congregation Salah, I've been slacking baby. You suppose to be helping me.

Sorry, well come on dick weed, said Gina, cause I want to celebrate now!

Mommy where we going?

Your going to Babistka's house we are going out.

That's not fair Mommy she stomped!

Or you could go hadouche instead.

Fine said Kitara! She had the little cute pout.

Later that night after all the celebrations 'n him fucking with Gina they fucked real good for a hour. while Gina lay sleep he called his man L-Train. That was his man from upstate Poughkeepsie N.Y..

Yo son what up? Its me fool C.D. now known as 2Face.

Oh what it is bee! said L.

Yo you ready for me or what?

Yeah replied L.

Bet said 2Face my son gonna holla at you give you the run down and all. Yo my night club will be opening real soon, I'm throwing a big for all my niggas be there or be square!

Shit you know that, a party I'll be there believe that! said L. he was wild excited.

Alright said 2Face one my dude. One said L.

Now that they had a brand new town to set up in, they would move more units. Now plan 2 was to take in effect, to juxx a major connect get more work for free.

CHAPTER 40

Michelle was getting out of her car infront of Madamore's strip club ready to work. She was tanned around 5"2 very seductive eyes and smooth skin. Tonight she wasn't enthused about working tonight. She wasn't paying attention to the guy in all black creeping behind her either. Suddenly she was grabbed and being choked to sleep. The grip was firm the arms had some size on them also. She was squirming but the arm smothered her neck till she fell unconscious. She was dragged to her car and put her in the trunk, nice 'n easy, nice 'n quietly.

It was 10:00 pm and Gina was headed to work. Everything was fine that night she was in a hell of a good mood. The phone rang suddenly. And when she dropped the receiver she sank in her seat. Tears welled in her eyes.

2Face was coming out of the bathroom from shitting wiping his hands after he washed them ready to offer Salah.

Hey baby what's wrong said 2Face?

They kidnaped Michelle she said sniffling.

What! 2Face said. Who kidnaped her?

I don't fucking know she yelled!

Calm down said 2Face.

Oh God she kept sniffling. 2Face hugged her to condole her, its gonna be alright baby he said calmly. Who was that on the phone? You sure they were kidnapers? This could be a prank Gina.

No! this isn't no fucking prank!

Ah right just chill he said. What did they want? Did they say they wanted anything?

They said it was a letter for me in the mail box. They also said they been watching this house.

What! Yelled 2Face. What the fuck are you involved with the Russian Mafia or something?

No! she said.

Well what did they sound like asked 2Face, Russian, Black, White, Spanish? They had Russian sounding accents she said.

Well is your father or your step brother involved in some shit. You know your momma be into shit too. You sure your sister didn't do no fowl shit?

I don't fucking know she screamed. I just wanna know is doing this to Michelle.

You sure she ain't get into nothing? No baby. Lets get the letter she said. I'll go get it, they might shoot me but at least you'll be able to call the police.

Baby why would they shoot you?

If they kidnaped your friend then why wouldn't they shoot? I don't know she said but they did say something about a sellout like I disgraced my people or something. Man I'm going to get that letter he said. He went outside and looked around for anything suspicious he went into the mailbox and retrieved the letter and quickly closed the door. He handed it to her and she read it.

She filled her eyes with tears again. What the letter say? He grabbed the letter when she hesitated. He started to read it when the phone rang.

Gina answered the phone: You nigger loving scum! I spit in your face bitch! Now here's the thing, you will write a letter the exact name and addresses of your so- called Jamaican posse who has the overseas connections.

What overseas connect?

Don't play games with us bitch! I'll kill your fucking daughter and feed her to the dogs. We'll take your fucking and kill her slowly. She'll die painfully. We'll take scissors and cut through her pussy. We'll cut off her fucking nipples and she'll be duct taped to stop her screams. We'll rip off every one of her nails and cut out her fucking eyes! don't think we can't get your nigger daughter either. We'll tell your nigger husband how your house keeping job at the Holiday Inn is really a cleaning table job at the local strip clubs. You've betrayed our heritage , betrayed our honor. We want the information within the hour. put the letter in the mailbox or the people your close to begin to disappear starting with your friend. Go to the cops we'll kill the entire family including your fake thug nigger man!

2Face had read the letter and had the other receiver he ran in the basement and grabbed the 4, 5ᵗʰ. He came up stairs pointing it Gina.

Listen you listen good. We'll deal with the stripping shit later. But what the fuck you got me into! what the fuck happened in Russia?

I don't know baby, why are you pointing that at me and she started crying.

I'm sorry he said as he had to catch himself. I got a little carried away and panicked, I'm sorry. He tried to grab her to console her. She punched his chest with a flurry, you're a monster you fucking asshole! she ran in the bedroom slamming the door! Here it is our lives are being threatened and you point a gun at me! fuck you!

Gina come here as he followed her to the room. Open the door. He had finally realized he was a monster as he stopped in his tracks. He's killed numerous people times to get what he wanted, even though he spreads love his punishment in the hellfire may not end.

Gina I want to apologize. I would never shoot you, I just lost control. She continued to sob. He could hear her through the door. Stop crying baby. We got an hour to figure out what these guys may do if you don't comply if their foreal or not I don't know if we in a position to find out. Now what connect are they talking about?

You pulled a gun on me you fucking asshole if you ever do that again I'll cut your fucking dick off and feed it to my cat.

A yo chill I ain't gonna pull no gun on you again relax! Yo, yo who's this connect though?

Roland and his Uncle in Queens, they are who they are after. But I don't know how they know about me. Like how am I involved I haven't been around those guys in a while.

Well just give them the information. You don't know what they may try next. If any body comes after us I'll kill em or be killed, believe that!

CHAPTER 41

Michelle was scared out of her wits. Duct taped, blind folded, cold and she didn't know why. She prayed her friend Gina would do what they asked of her so these crazy men would leave her alone. She pissed on herself twice. She never been through no violence she never even had a fight.

Soon my lady this will all be over, soon said the man with the accent. Either you die or you live. We do not want to hurt you or your friend Gina, but she has some valuable information.

Gina put the letter in the mailbox. Now they had ten minutes to wait to find out what happens. 5 minutes later the phone rang. Gina answered the jack on the first ring.

You've done good Gina, our information matches with yours. Drive to your Sugar Daddies and you'll find your friend in the garbage. Be there in ten minutes. If this information is wrong I'll kill you, your whole family, your daughter, your nigger husband and your friends. No one is ever safe! if our information is truthful you'll never hear from us again you know the deal if it isn't.

Your information is correct said Gina. Just let my friend go!

She'll be fine. She'll stink but she'll live, the line went dead!

2Face and Gina drove strait to Sugar Daddies and they found

Michelle behind the garbage bound and gagged and blind folded. She was ass naked also.

2Face untied her while Gina cried watching her ass naked friend in this chilly weather tied behind a garbage dumpster.

As soon as the gag came off Gina asked her if she was alright? Michelle went hysterical, screaming. Aah! aah she screamed! fucking assholes!

Here take my jacket said 2Face, he hit her with the Sean John leather. Cover yourself and calm down, you'll be alright.

Gina was sobbing trying to get her words out, I'm, I'm sorry.

Sorry for what said 2Face this wasn't your fault. We'll get those bastards!

How she snapped we don't even know who they are?

I'm so scared said Michelle. They had me tied up in a basement, it was so cold. They had me stripped the whole time. One of em touched my pussy. It was so humiliating. They taunted me talking about you like it. They said you like to show your body off for scraps so love it! I don't think I'll ever strip again.

Did you recognize any of the voices?

No! I just wanna go home!

We going there said 2Face. What ever you do don't call the cops they threatened our family and yours if you do or any of us do.

You kidding me she said, those bastards!

No cops said Gina. They dropped Michelle off at her place as her boy friend June, June was waiting scared and very upset.

2Face pulled him to the side; not a word of this to anybody ya heard! I'm a deal with this myself nobody threatens me or my family.

CHAPTER 42

This year Halloween fell on a weekend. 2Face told Gina he'd beat his aunt Diane house in which he was. Haywood, Primo, Shorts, Budd and Mouse were set in position. Mouse and Bud watched for the chicks to get off the plane at Laguardia Airport. They knew who was the customs guy that worked for Mr. Biggs, Rolands uncle. They knew the guy from customs stashed the bags and then switches them up. They knew each bag had 50 bricks. They knew who the girls were, they knew it was 2 pick up cars waiting. One to pay the girls and one to snatch the drugs. They knew it was 5 girls coming back from their so called vacation. Their was to murder everybody and take the drugs and splurt.

The airport was crowded wild people trying to get where they got to go. You could barely walk through the crowds in the speedy city of New York. Mouse watched the maneuver as 5 girls got

off the flight from Jamaica. The young girls were around 19 to As the bags were coming of they peeped how they did it, the switching of the bags. Duke is real smooth said Mouse. Bud make the call to Wood.

Yo, yo them brawds is coming is coming through son he said to wood on the chirp.

Good looking said Wood, got you and hung up.

Yo homie Wood said to Shorts they taking them Brawds to the safe house to pay em you heard.

They not my concern said Shorts my concern is getting them bags. I'll deal with them brawds he said just get them bags son.

Got you said Wood my concern to is to get them bags. But my cuz said to kill everybody.

So we should do that said Primo.

Alright said Shorts me and you ride together Wood you good by yourself.

Yeah ya'll ride I got this bee! I'm going to call these 2 niggas and jump in they whip.

Bet said Shorts. They gave each other pounds and departed. Wood called Bud.

Yo! said Bud.

I'm a stick around in the cut bee.

Alright bet!

Shorts and Primo followed Glendall, Trina and the 5 brawds in the Lexus Jeep. Son them cats eating foreal huh? Shit they workers got plexuses 'n shit.

As soon as they get to their destination we going in on them.

In the street asked Primo?

Yeah replied Shorts.

They followed them all the way to Astoria. They made sure they stayed a 2 block distance so they wouldn't be noticed, especially on the side blocks. When the car stopped on a side block the lights went out, Shorts and Primo stopped instantly. Shorts jumped out the car armed with a tech 9 new artillery from the Ghost.

Son wait here son he said to Primo, matter of fact drive up the block around the corner and make a left. Keep the lights off. Shorts was on the move.

Everybody got out the car the girls were ready to get paid. They saw some one headed toward their direction but paid him no mind. They just wanted to get paid and go home. Too bad things didn't go their way. Shorts fired the tech 9 that lit up the block like the 4th of the July.

Dong! dong! dong! dong! dong! dong! the tech was spitting. Flesh was flying everywhere in the chunks.

Shorts got close and fired on the seven people who didn't know why they were dying. Dong! dong! dong! dong! dong! Screams were faded by the noise of the tech and the hail of bullets that sank them into deep sleep they'll never wake up from.

Shorts sprinted around the corner until he saw the ford fusion. He began to walk normally. He did his best to conceal the weapon as possible. He rocked a North Face goose with a goodie. He made it to the car quickly.

Son why you park so far down the block!

I'm saying said Primo I ain't want to look so obvious when they turned the next corner Primo turned back on the lights. Next was Mr. Biggs to go.

Bud and Mouse watched the customs guy get off work and some one they didn't expect to see showed up Roland. They watched him as he was dressed up as a janitor walking with a dust pan and broom outside the airport. They observed the customs guy head nod towards the garbage cans. Roland walked over to the garbage acted like he was picking through it and then struggled with three big duffle bags.

Mouse was looking through his binoculars to make sure they had their man. From the description from the letter said this is our guy and he got some shit in them bags.

So the customs dude is expendable asked Bud?

Yeah I think we follow that Roland cat with the bags headed to the white excursion. Call this nigga cuz and tell him to come on said Mouse.

Bud called him he came jogging to the car. Let me drive said Wood they watched Roland put the bags in the trunk. They followed the second in command.

Roland drove to the east, in Brooklyn. He headed towards Fulton st. he drove up Fulton to New Jersey st..

Damn. we in the East said Mouse this is even better. Mouse was from over here, Bud lived here when he came from Cali in 19 Wood hated Brooklyn but if they knew the area then the getaway would be easier. When they saw Roland stop in the middle of the block they stopped. Wood turned the lights off, him and Mouse jumped out simultaneously. Bud was gonna drive and Mouse little ass was gonna creep low to surprise dude. Wood was still walking towards Roland and Roland noticed him coming he stopped what he was doing and sensed something. Then 2 men came out of no where it was a set up. Roland had felt a set up all the way.

Bud heard a car pull up next to his, then saw the window roll down and the end of a double barrel point at his face. He ducked down as the shot echoed, boom! Bud crawled out through the passenger side door as 3 more shots rang off; boom! boom! boom! luckily son ain't get hit.

Wood heard the shots but his focus was on getting to Roland and them bags. Roland pulled out a 9 beretta and fired at Wood. Blough! blough! Wood dipped behind a parked honda.

Mouse fired 2 shots at the car that tried to kill his home, boom! boom! he knew he had to end this bang out quick.

Wood fired and hit Roland in his shooting hand causing him to drop the gun. Ahh! screamed Roland!

Wood yelled to Mouse: go get the bags hurry up! Shots were fired at Mouse from the car shooting at Bud. Mouse ducked the bullets and ran toward the car where Roland had the drugs.

Wood saw Roland scrambling for his ratchet ran up to Roland and hit him twice in the head splattering his brains all over the pavement. He died instantly with his eyes open. Wood turned and heard Mouse grabbing the bags they fired 2 more shots at a parked Taurus toward Mouse, the shots ricocheting off the car and windshield.

Bud fired 3 shots at the car then Mouse yelled to Bud; Son!

we got what we came for son lets go! All three of them grabbed bags and ran to the train station, fuck the car yelled Wood!

They jumped on the down town train to the Bronx, on the J train. Mad police were blitzing to the scene all you heard was sirens. Another wicked shootout in New York. When they got to the train station they agreed to split up and meet in the Bronx on Wood block. They split up on Broadway Junction and Jumped on the A train to the deuce on different cars. Then switch to the 2 train and get off at Jackson ave. then casually walk to Wood crib on St. Anns.

Chapter 43

Shorts went to the mansion at Mr. Biggs at 7:00 o'clock in the morning. He was riding a peddle bike acting like a delivery boy delivering newspapers. He had paid a kid a couple of hundred for his route. He made sure Mr. Biggs was last.

After hearing the news about the grotesque shooting in Queens and his Nephew who was gunned down in Brooklyn he was terrified. He had called for extra security and waited for them to arrive. He never trusted males, that's why he used all those females to do his dirty work. But some body crossed him. big time! he treated everybody good, he thought to himself who would want to do this? He paced back 'n forth in his mansion. His nephew, and his main players were gone forever. Somebody knew a lot about his organization and spilled their guts. He would have the remaining people killed when he got his new Leuitenant, his cousin from Jamaica. There was a thump at the door. Mr. Biggs ran to the door to open it.

Is everything alright honey? Asked his wife yelling from upstairs. She was white and older and still looked close to Her nails stayed manicured and pedicure, she dressed professional with her long blonde hair.

Everything is fine baby! he opened the door to scream at the newspaper boy for throwing the paper at his door dumb hard!

Hey pussy clod! what the blood clot! Ya not throw a paper at my blood clot door see star!

Yeah me see brethren replied Shorts! a she pointed the gun to his temple. Blough! Blough! the life was taken out of the body of Mr. Biggs. He dropped to his knees and fell face first dead! he heard a scream upstairs he ran in the mansion and saw a pretty white lady he shot her in the chest 4 times, she rolled down the stairs all the way to the bottom. Then Shorts shot her in the head for good measure. 2Face said no witnesses, no feedback! do everything right, leave no loose ends we cash money!

With all the main players dead and the mass confusion, police investigating which would lead to a bunch of dead ends. That's what 2Face meant by no loose ends no feedback, no witnesses. And with all the heads off the body who gonna think for them? Who gonna figure out how to retaliate in any way shape of fashion.

2Face explained that to Mouse, Bud and Shorts when Tone walked in at the office at Fitzes.

What up! he yelled dumb loud.

Ya-O! yelled 2Face! As soon as son sat down Face hit with; son why don't you move back to Brooklyn son? I need you in the East home to watch over Biz and them. I got some shit for you all you gotta do is chill bee! you can make a $100,000 a year.

What! said Tone.

Son you think I'm bullshitting? I'm some real shit homie!

Son this is serious son said Mouse. All you gotta do is get a job, send your son to school get

your crib and watch niggas. Do this for a year you good bee said 2Face. Sign with the Rock bee!

Let me talk to Shanta first.

Fuck that bitch yelled Mouse get this cake!

I said let me holla at wifey first said Tone loud as hell.

She already been hollered at replied 2Face. In fact I even gave

141

her a lump sum of $100, 000 I'll give you a $100,000 tonight if you agree just don't cross me.

You sure said Tone? Yeah my nigga I never shit on my homies, never turn on them none of that. I'm saying if a nigga violate I won't fuck with him no more. I'm loyal to my crew I keep it official, if I got it you got it.

Alright bet said Tone I'm in son.

My nigga said 2Face. Yo Shorts business as usual keep copping them things from Damian and

Gulley we gonna look like nothing changed. No heavy copping of anything. Yo I got everything set up in Poughkeepsie send the girls Thursday bee he said to Shorts.

CHAPTER 44

How Gina taking this son asked Bud?

She sick right now said 2Face, I'll make it up to her. I got the club being prepared and the restaurant right now in renovation.

Word replied Shorts. Yeah, I'm a holla at my cuz Jr. and we gonna set up this clothing line. Some official shit too! If everybody play they position, hold it down and keep quiet,once these business moves fall through our money will be legit washed so to speak. I'm a make sure everybody get paid believe that! remember the code of silence is in effect bee.

Karrin came with they're drinks. What's up guys!

Aah the usual baby how you asked 2Face?

I'm good darling here you go.   Ain't nobody been messing with you or nothing right Karrin if you have any problems let ya boy know, I'm here alright.

I'm good sweetie you stay out of trouble please she replied I know you.

Hmm! Mouse jestured with a curious look to Bud.

You still working on your voice like I told you Karrin asked 2Face?

Yeah I practice a lot. When are we gonna record, soon?

Yeah just be patient, we gonna blow this record label off the roof with you. She blushed and walked off.

Son she white, pretty and got a killer body, plus her voice knock chicks out the box!

Son you heard her sing before asked Mouse?

Yeah stupid!

I'm a have her in night clubs, and local New York bars real soon. Just to get her some attention then when we get under contract we blow her out the frame, she got a voice like Maria Carey and she look like her a little excdept she white with a fatty.

Son you think you real smart with all these visions huh, said Mouse?

Don't hate I used to listen to you when you was the one with all the ideas. I never said nothing I just sat back. But my plans got us rich. Even though we don't spend our money all extravagantly, we able to buy what we need. We spend to get. Don't it feel good to look at and count millions and its yours. Even hundreds of thousands, just to feel secure and its real!

The way L-Train was moving them pies out in Poughkeepsie was absurd. He was moving a pie every three days selling weight, loose rocks and 2Face had Lashay out there maintaining thing with Shorts overseeing it all.

Shantell had things clocking in the town as well she was in her zone. Going back to school, moving a half of brick a week, and selling crazy bud. she even was allowed to call up one of her little homegirls to work for her while she concentrated on her school work. With Tone in the hood overseeing things that allowed Biz and them hit the studio hard. They had the Bamas on smash. Mouse had his second daughter and moved to Brooklyn to be closer to Tone and get paid. They were slowly making a distance from Bing.

Wood and the family was crushing them as well. They had one little problem though with a cat on Cortland ave. this kid named Baby Joe. He was causing a real problem robbing all of the

fiends and workers Wood put out there. He needed to be dealt with but Wood could never catch up to him, he always eluded him some how. But 2Face always had a plan. Once he found out who and where this Baby Joe was he made the call.

Yo Shiesty what up!

What up he said to Face.

Hey man how you been Shiest? Cooling man ya hear. Shiesty was like a old school Shorts 5"1, slim and played no games. He was brown skinned. His era was the 70's and 80's and he was aging but 2Face knew he could get the job done.

Yo Shiest how your pockets?

I'm a little jammed up right now, why what's up?

I got a job for you bro.

Yeah said Shiest! Remember what we talked about in Marcy?

Oh, oh yeah replied Shiest!

Well I got a opening.

You already know I'm down said Shiest.

Bet said 2Face.

I'm a text you some info and holla at my cuz in 10 minutes he gonna plug you in. Yo, I got some tickets to the garden for the Lakers vs Knicks and the Lakers, Nets this weekend. You know the Lakers gonna buss the Knicks ass! Kobe gonna show off at the garden believe that!

You know I'm wit that too said Shiest! and my Knicks gonna show up against them soft ass Lakers!

Yeah alright replied 2Face.

It had been nearly 6 months since the killings and robberies that hit the headlines all over the country. The cops had not a clue as to who was involved all they knew were all types of people were dead. 2Face already had that 50 million for the label cause they were caking it all over the tri- state area. He had his club ready to open in 2wks. and he used Gina as the face. He also had the restaurant ready to his investments were cheap so he was able to set up shop at 2 different sites and recruit his old fiends who he knew were skilled in construction and electricity. Razzac Shorts older Brother was a skilled electrician and helped him for little to nothing cause when they were younger Razzac was his old stick up partner and boosting partner and his conversations helped bring 2Face to Islam. He went and got his boy Kenny a friend he knew for years from Ely-Park. They were real close back in the day almost inseparable. Kenny was gonna run the restaurant like it was his investment. 2Face wanted a certain crowd a white audience that would bring stability and keep his business lasting longer and gain him some man power within the white race. He also got in touch with his cuz Jr. and they were working diligently on his new clothing line Viscario Lemonte. A lemon was gonna be the logo. Jr. hooked him up with a overseas contractor who produces material and mails it off gaining profit. But 2Face had another idea. He knew Jr. was a master drawer and he had Jr. draw out his own designs that 2Face thought of. 2Face wanted his label to be up there with Versaci, Louis Vitton, Gucci, Sean Jean, Polo, etc. he wanted Jean suits, Business Suits, Valour suits, underwear, shorts, lingerie, swimsuits, socks, hats, gloves, baby clothes, cologne, perfumes you name it everything that comes with a clothing label. He was trying to get into shows too like modeling shows ass well. One of Jr.'s gay friends was designer and was pretty nice with it. 2Face hired him and had Jr. set up a couple of wearhouses over in Tibet and had them hire mad workers and payed them double the price they would get anywhere else. He also set up so that he could sell his clothes in other stores as well to gain notoriety. Jr. had his own store which 2Face used as well to sell shit in. He   also set up shop in South America opening up Sweat shops giving opportunity to the people. 2Face was the man behind the men and women the man behind a lot of shit nobody knew about. He never liked to be the center of attention anyway but this type of success it was inevitable.

CHAPTER 45

What up baby 2Face said to Sue?

I ain't see you in like 2 months nigga! where the fuck have you been? She was real big now.

Yo, I've been working real hard trying to establish these businesses baby girl.

What up with Gina asked Sue?

She alright why?

I thought you were getting rid of her replied Sue?

I am just chill baby.

Oh yeah well guess what she said to 2Face?

What?

I'm taking my Shahada she sounded sarcastic at first. But the look in eyes told different.

What! why?

Because I believe in the oneness of God and I think you need to marry me. I'm willing to accept Gina if she is willing to accept me. So either we get married or I tell her everything about your 2Face-ed life you live! What you wanna kill me now she said all snotty? You looking at me like you want to kill me. You got a death look in your eyes she said mocking at him.

This bitch he said to himself. I can't believe you flipping on me.

Well I can't be a mistress anymore. So make a decision or I'll make it for you! She slapped at him but he 52-ed hand blocked it.

Yo! chill what's wrong with you! Look at me she screamed! do I look like somebody's fucking Mistress? I can get any guy I fucking want and you treating me like a fucking mistress?

Listen this is not the time for this baby. Please I'll get rid of her just give me a lil more time!

No! you've had enough time!

Awe man! Don't do this not now Sue.

I have to she said.

We gonna open up the club in a week 'n a half chill! You get everything you want from me why you acting like this?

I ain't no fucking mistress yo! You right but... But nothing nigga! It is what it is. I'm gonna have your seed real soon don't fuck with me!

Tell her then he said sounding convincing.

Oh you want to play games nigga!

I'm serious said 2Face.

Don't call my bluff C.D. I'm calling it he snapped!

She grabbed the phone and dialed Gina's number. 2Face was stunned he didn't think she would do it. Good thing Sue didn't know anything else about his double life. he wasn't a cat who confided his street life with his women a lot of cats did that.

The voice mail came up: Hi you've reached Gina Jackson I'm not available right now please leave a message, beep.

Hi this is click! the line died as 2Face pressed the dial tone before Sue could get a word in. She turned around and said: don't be scared now. I've never known you to have fear C.D.. You better tell her or I will.

Alright relax baby he said trying to touch her she backed away from him swiftly.

Tell her Cory, tell her tonight. She walked to the door opened it and told him again and gestured him out the door. He left without saying a word.

He drove around not knowing what to do. He couldn't risk having Sue ruin his business and knowing Gina she'll make it hot. He had to find a way to get outta this. The stress was wailing on him, he needed one last drink so he headed to Fitze's. It was Tuesday night so the bar was empty. The Dt's usually role around this time hitting spots doing raids. He watched as they looked like they was about to hit something. Karrin was at the bar chilling not working which was unusual. Dave was working and Shantell hadn't arrived yet. Shantell had got a job at Source Corp behind Boscov's and was going to school. She had workers which she paid pc out of her own. That kept her out the street, 2Face knew this he didn't mind. 2Face walked and sat next to Karrin at the bar.

Hi C.D. she said with a weak smile.

How are you Karrin?

I'm fine she said. But she looked depressed. So did he.

You look stressed she said to him. usually you in here hyper, playing pool and talking shit with your boys. Matter of fact where is Tone loud ass? I haven't seen him in a while is he alright? Is he back in New York?

I can't call it replied 2Face.

So what brings you to Fitze's alone?

I had a little baby momma drama you know.

Tell me about it she said. I just had huge fight with my boyfriend. I tell him lets get married we've been together 3 yrs. I'm like gosh what more is there to figure out about a person.

I definitely feel your pain, I can agree said 2Face. I mean me and wifey been together for like 4yrs. I pretty much know her like a book, but the sparks in our relationship have dimmed considerably, so much that what we do is routine and the marriage is less exciting. In a way its good to marry a person once you know the kind of person he or she is and what they feel inside is right for you. But the flip side is everybody ain't for everybody.

That makes a lot of sense she said.

All the excitement is in the first year said 2Face. I don't want to get all Islamic on you in a bar but with Muslims we get married quick its like we go on dates to get to know who you with, but you must be shaparoned because sex is sacred. A womans chastity is very valuable and she shouldn't give it away freely it should be to the man that vows to her for hand in marriage. And the divorce procedure is simple not all the dramatic shit we go through in our society. Yes we sign contracts but ALLAH has already set the rules for the marriage and divorce. So there is nothing to figure out with the procedure.

She looked interested now as leaned closer. Tell me more.

Ok I'll break it down for you. If you and me were feeling eachother and wanted to hook up we'd get a shaparone and go out right. Now if everything go right we would set up a time to get married now say we get married you would ask for dower which is a gift of anything you wanted. I would have to provide it for you. Now we see a Imam have atleast two witnesses or we could

have a big reception what ever. You know we sign a contract not a marriage liscence but similar. Now if things don't work out we would try to reconcile things for a period of time and if it doesn't work we can get divorced. There is another period of time in which we can still reconcile our differences and if it doesn't work we can move on. We are allowed to remarry a couple of times but sometimes things ain't meant to be.

Wow she said. So what does the woman get?

2Face was a little typsy so he didn't want to go to deep in the Islam. I would like to bring you some literature so you can read for yourself if you had any questions holla. I like to protect the honor of a person in a relationship feel me said 2Face. The exciting part is trying to get to know your spouse, see now you can experiment with eachother you know what I'm saying? He said with a smile. That's just my opinion and it keeps you from acts of low morality.

Look who's talking about low morality she shot at him!

Hey look at what un marital sex has done to us; prostitution, rape, fags, lusting, verbal seual abuse, pornication children out of wedlock, kids with no fathers, kids with no parents, drug abuse, greed amongst men and women, men and women fight for power, manipulation and disease. Must I go on? But I can't bore you with this, or preach knowledge tell people to practice it and I ain't. There is an Ayat in the Qur'an; are you one who enjoins right conduct on others and yet to practice it yourself?

No she said I like this kind of talk. I didn't know you had this side in you. I always thought of you as a hardcore gangster, but your very intelligent. I heard a Muslim man can have 4 wives?

Yes we can.

Why?

Well it goes back to over 1400yrs. ago with our Prophet (pbuh) and his companions. There are many reasons why a man can have more than one wife. One was when wars were fought many men were on the road leaving they're wives at home they were allowed to take on other wives, if a woman fears she'll never marry and a man and his wife agrees he can marry her, he would have to make sure he takes care of her equally as his first wife and take of them financially. It's a deep topic. There are other reasons why but I'll bring the literature to you. In some cases there are more woman then men too so we can marry at that cause to. Its hard to have more than one wife it can be a difficult situation. I'll bring the Dalil which means proof in Arabic.

I'd appreciate it she said. Don't go crazy on your boyfriend Karrin he said laughing. She smiled at him. keep working on ya voice too shortly we'll be recording. She shook her head ok. I'm out baby.

Bye she said, see you later.

CHAPTER 46

2Face went to Bud's house for a minute and had a few drinks got some advice and broke out. He headed home as soon as he walked in the door it was on.

So said Gina who the fuck is Sue?

Awe not now Gina! please.

The fuck you mean not now! I want to know who the fuck is Sue!

She's nobody he shouted!

Nobody! Nobody! She's 8 1/2 months pregnant but she's nobody! tears flowed in Gina's eyes.

Oh don't cry said 2Face I cried 3 ½ yrs in prison while you danced your little white ass around

in strip clubs sucking 'n fucking. While you splurged all my paper! While you went on all around the world spending my money. Then you lied in my face on visits and lied in my face while I'm home.

That's not true she said crying.

You still fucking lying Bitch! I got bank statements on how you splurged my cheddar! That's hard earned money regardless how I got it, you had no right to do that! You used to come visit me when you feel like it! This is my house, my car! I got niggas that watch you go to work at your hotel job every night! I know all about your little rendevous.

So all this time you've been holding this in she said. Waiting for this moment you2Faced bastard! that club is in my name and your restaurant I'll fucking ruin all that for you!

2Face grabbed he neck with the grip of death. I put blood, sweat, and tears into what I got! don't fuck with me. Do not fuck with me.

So what you gonna shoot me she said as he let her go? Shoot me you fucking faggot. She knew he didn't like that.

Kitara walked in. Mommy she said with a groggy voice from sleeping what's matter?

Nothing baby go back to sleep Kitty. I want you out of my house tonight she said to 2Face.

Hold up this is my house! I pay all the bills here, you get the fuck out!

I'll call the police and have you violated. This time he lifted her off the ground with his death grip around her neck. Suddenly she saw something in his eyes she never saw before that scared the shit out of her.

I'll murder you and your hole family if ever think about ratting me out. That's a fucked up place I wouldn't send my own worst enemy to jail. I hope we understood? He unleashed her as she fell to the floor.

You're a fucking monster and a piece of shit you violent motherfucker! you have a nice time in Puerto Rico? And where did you get the money for that?

Don't worry about that! don't worry about nothing. Gina slammed the door.2Face woke up at five in the morning with a gun in his face.

You wanna threaten my life bitch! 2Face was shocked.

He calmly told her; put the gun down Gina. You don't know what you're doing.

The fuck I do nigger! I'll fucking kill you she said with tears in her eyes. I do everything for you and this is how you treat me? You get some Spanish bitch pregnant?

Gina put the gun down! Kitty in your room sweetie, said 2Face. Yo! you'll traumatize her for life! Put the fucking gun down.

No! I want to know everything. No more lies, no more games. I wanna know shit. You didn't even get me pregnant but you got her pregnant!

You had a abortion on me four years ago remember?

Fuck you! I fuckin hate you!

Gina he said calmly some body's gonna call the police, its five in the morning people sleep.

No, your gonna sleep permanently! she pulled the gun jammed. 2Face life flashed before his eyes, the second time Allah saved him. he wrestled the gun out of her hands, then flipped her head first off the couch. She layed flat on her back breathing heavy.

You done said 2Face? I don't want to hurt you. I realized I've hurt you enough, I'll leave!

Your not going any fucking place! She got up and walked through the bedroom door and slammed the door.

The next morning 2Face went to work expecting the worst when he got home, not getting much sleep is tiring. Things really got carried away when they both showed up at his job. He was pushing a forklift when Gina and Sue walked in, Roc was rolling.

Yo bee look 2 birds in one stone.

Shut the fuck up nigga 2Face said to Roc.

Son shit could get ugly said Roc. Should I call the boss he said with a smirk.

The boss was already heading to inform him of his visitors. Hey Jackson!

Yes sir.

You've got company.

I see sir.

We got a lot to do today so make this quick. They both look very pist the boss said, even he was laughing.

I'll take over for him said Roc to the boss.

So, 2Face huh said Gina? I'm glad me and her got to talk. You went to Vegas without me? You went to Puerto Rico with her. Now you paying her rent too? So, she said sarcastically where's all this money coming from 2Face? I hope your not dealing drugs again.

Whoa! said Roc to himself.

A yo, said 2Face. Why don't ya'll both go to the crib, relax and catch up a little more. I'll be home in 4 ½ hours.

Fuck you said Sue! then she's pregnant CD oh I mean 2Face! So I was outta the picture?

Son stop fucking laughing Sue said to Roc.

Oh you know Roc too asked Gina? Yeah he's in the bar with him every night. You know I can't even get mad at her she was totally fooled by you. So, not only are you not getting me out of the picture but your gonna take care of this baby too!

Roc couldn't help laughing he was hysterical.

Cause if you treat her unjust I swear to God I'll ruin your life and your stinking friends lives as well! I'll report all of you to the fucking cops. I'll file for divorce and take everything you fucking got.

Ok said 2Face, I gotta get back to work. Seriously we'll discuss this later, please. You got Sue going crazy, Gina's bananas and the both of ya'll gonna get me fired!

When they spun off 2Face was livid at Roc for laughing but even he had to laugh. In fact the whole job site was laughing.

When he went to see his P.O. at his lunch break, he informed him that he would be working 2 jobs one at his new Restaurant called Picante Food Delight. His man Kenny Haur was the supposed owner and had hired him. Once his P.O. approved that would really keep him offf his back. Now he had further distance from him.

CHAPTER 47

Later that night when he went home the 2 women in his life were there every step of the way.

Hi honey said Sue.

Hi honey said Gina how was work?

Work was fine. A yo both of yaw crazy! Ya'll actually see humor in this situation.

No. We see a man who played 2 good women who loved him to death said Gina. So rather than fight each other why not fight the cause of the problem, you! said Gina.

So what yaw want, money? Yaw want me out of ya'll lives? Let me know something. What's good? I would apologize but what good would that do?

You right said Sue why apologize. You meant this but I'm taking my Shahada and were getting married. So now dip shit your gonna support 2 families. Isn't this the Muslim way? Well Gina is willing to accept it.

Wow you can't be serious. Oh really said Gina. Its either this or go to jail and be the reason your murderous crew goes down to. Because quote on quote 2Face can't control his dick!

What crew are you talking about he asked?

Don't play fucking stupid with me I know you like a fucking book. You got your hands in something, something big. How else you take damn near 40 people to Vegas, then turn around and go to Puerto Rico?

2Face laughed. You buggin! I never went to no fucking Vegas crash dummy! you believe what you want fool. But I'm sorry I hurt the both of yaw. He repeatedly apologized and vowed to do right by the both of them from here out.

Gina made him drive Sue home. When he returned home Gina had left out to work. She left a note saying that she'll work where she wants, like it or love it! he crumbled the letter and layed down then fell asleep, he was so tired he didn't even pick up Kitara from Gina's sister house.

CHAPTER 48

Grand opening it said on the sign in front of Picante Restaurant. 2Face had invited his Moms and local family in Bing. to the event to enjoy the food. Kenny the acting owner was nervous calling the shots but had everything set up beautifully.

Hey C.D. your family is here! shouted Kenny.

Get them the best table in the house said 2Face. You also know they're money ain't no good here. Ever!

You got it said Kenny. 2Face left Kenny's office wiping his apron. He was acting like a dish washer making sure the staff Kenny hired was the right personel. Of course he and Kenny were under a hidden contract. He trusted Kenny his old homeboy from Ely-Park.

Kenny short blonde hair, with the same last name as the actor Rutger Haur but no relation was a medium build and very in control of himself. He was smart and fit the face to run a restaurant which was seeking a franchise tag and looking for five star status. They had a ill menu, all kinds of food: seafood, Italian, Chinese, Greek, Soulfood and other American dishes. Tonight's special was seafood, hot and spicy shrimps dipped in a lemon sauce on top of white rice, with fried zucchini and baked cheese flavored bread. With your choice of Martini Dakori.

The people who came to the restaurant entered it and felt so comfortable there Kenny saw the dollar signs right before his eyes. They hired the best cooks in town, so the food would be excellent. The expressions on the customers faces were of satisfaction, a new restaurant with different tastes and the food was excellent. They even had a diet menu. The desert menu had custom made dishes from Kenny himself. He too was a master chef.

Gina and Kitara came in. Kenny went to the kitchen to call 2Face to let him know his wife was here.

Yo, Cor! your wife is here. She brang Kitara too!

No doubt said 2Face seat them next to my family.

The waiter sat Gina next to his moms. Hi, Gina his moms said blank like she wasn't to thrilled

to see her.

Good to see you Misses Pat. Its been a long time said Gina.

This is Cory's wife Gina and his Step Daughter Kitara Aunt Loddie 2Faces oldest Aunt. How are you young lady?

I'm fine replied Gina good to meet you.

I didn't know Cory was married Pat, said Aunt Loddie. Where's Cory?

He's probably in the back doing what he does best cookin up a storm. I'll tell the waiter to send him out. She got up and went to the bar area.

The restaurant blended right in on Old Vestal Road. It had lots of parking space. The inside was a bit spacious 2Face and his workers did a fantastic job building it. Just like the club Gina thought to her self. The restaurant also had a stage for comedy, Jazz music, singing and all types of entertainment. For the most part the place was made for the Jazz and stand up. Tonight they just played Jazz to relax the people. When she reached the bar she saw an arrayment of fine wines and expensive liquor. This is definitely catering to the white audience. 2Face once told her about the Willie Lynch theory and how it worked, how his people need to reverse that theory that has worked to the tee. He was definitely trying to get the white man to spend his money and invest in him and not even realize it.

Excuse me can you tell the owner to come out here, asked Gina?

Why is there a problem asked the skinny white waiter in his fake tuxedo outfit.

I want to see him he's my husband.

Oh, right away mam.

When Kenny came out 2 minutes later the expression on Gina's face was twisted. The waiter looked confused.

Your wife sir.

Where's my wife asked Kenny?

She isn't my wife.

No said the waiter, who are you mam?

Excuse me is this a joke Gina said snappy! My husband is black!

Mam calm down said Kenny I got you alright. I know who you looking for. He went to the back to get 2Face who came out in his apron.

Gina baby what up!

What up she said full of anger and sarcasm. This waiter doesn't even know you own the place! Your Aunt wants to see you.

He pulled her to the side. The reason nobody know I own the place is cause I don't want anybody to. I'm a criminal and I'm black is bad for business. Its not the face I'm trying to put on the face of this franchise. I'm trying to cater to people with money, not the hood. I'll give back to my hood when the time is right. Gina looked like she understood and sat down at the table with the family.

Hi everybody! hey Aunt Loddie, hey Ant unc. What up. Uncle James, Uncle Bob, Momma!

Come give your Momma a hug I'm so proud of you for doing the right thing in life for once.

Damn! said the waiter these people act like being a kitchen worker is something big.

Hey! Kenny shouted get back to work! Matter of fact your fired!

Fired for what?

Cause I don't like your attitude, now get the fuck outta here!

After firing the waiter he had one of the waitresses take over his position. He walked around and asked how the food was and got an excellent review. He knew then they'd be rich within the next 2years cause this was gonna blow up, 2Face was a genius.

CHAPTER 49

The night the club opened catered to the older white crowd with Gina being the face. It didn't do bad at all not as good as his restaurant but it was official, cause so far they didn't have a performance. They did play a lot of classic rock, jazz, rhythm and blues and country. It gave the older crowd a good feeling of 35 and up, they felt at home. He did have live performances from local bands which really set the club right plus a little stand up comedy once in a while. As long as people enjoyed themselves this would be a success as well.

But tonight the Drip set from Harlem was performing. Some actual industry artist in Bing was rare. Then at the same time a wet bikini contest, winner gets $500 cash. The club was $00 a head. 2Face made sure he no where near the door cause of Parole so he had Gina get the money. He had Karrin and Danielle bartend. Danielle used to hustle for him back in the days when he was in the mix.

It was 11:00 o'clock when people started rolling in. Females get in free until 11:30 which brought a huge crowd. Young Santana and Famron. They had a hit single killing the airwaves. Then to

162

top that off the wet bikini contest. There were 20 contestants all hand picked by 2Face.

The whole Fox Family came up Wood brought 5 cars of niggas. They all paid to get in. The homies from the East Biz, Tone and them came up. Shorts was there, lots of college chicks showed up. Bud even showed up and he never goes out. All the locals from the town were there. 2Face also invited L, Mr.C, Chips, Mike Mo, Vinnie, Black, E Money, Mike Mike and a few others that he invited his man from Buff Gulley. Even some Rochester niggas came through. Jah and Kha his old work out partners from uptop.

The place was packed by 12:30 am. They had Styles P. "I Get High on". "I Get High, High, High"! " I Get High, High High"!Hi-----Gh! The strobe lights and disco was illuminating.

Baby said Gina this is big for us, I'm so excited!

Me too sweety you good said 2Face?

Yeah she said, well half the niggas here is from your crew.

Oh yeah we in the building believe that!

2Face walked through the crowd slapping fives and getting the congratulations by everyone in the club. The Drip Set walked in stealing the show everybody got hype.

Welcome the Drip Set said Danja the DJ. Give it up for Drip Set! They came in acting thefool grabbing girls asses, mad loud and they was like 20 deep. The last thing 2Face needed was for a melee to jump off and draw negative attention to the club. He immediately walked over to Famron.

Yo what's up!

What up said Famron who you?

The guy who's paying you tonight.

Oh, oh ok, said Fam. His boys were on guard.

Yo my boy Chips is in the building said 2Face.

I see said Fam.

Yo I don't want no trouble brother said 2Face, please just do the performance, make it good get paid then either chill relax or go your way. Its mad hoes up in here yaw don't got to be so assertive. Enjoy the contest. Your performance starts in ten minutes be ready. A yo Fam! calm ya boys.

What's that my man he said?

I said calm ya boys! I'll see what I can do. 2Face let that one slip. He wasn't gonna talk next time.

As the show started 2Face got with his team. Haywood included. Yo yaw having fun my niggas?

Its mad bitches in here said Dboog.

We chillin said Wood.

Yo next time them faggot ass Harlem niggas act up we gonna smash them niggas in here.

Shorts what up fool! I ain't seen you in eons bee!

Trying to keep ya man L-Train under control. This nigga like to floss to much, we gonna have to relocate son.

I'm a talk with him said 2Face.

Nah fuck talking the nigga hard headed.

Well do you homey you in charge out there. Just make sure our money right.

Oh it will be.

Good once I start this label I'm taking my cut and I'm done with this hustling period. I'm taking things to another level.

What! said Shorts.

Son we got what we need. Niggas is rich we stacked paper beyond our wildest dreams! beyond anybody's wildest dreams. We ain't do no spending I got legit businesses now I got the Label, the restaurant and the clothing line. The club, we got to expand our opportunities. Wash your money Shorts. If not you gonna have a federal indictment with all types of bodies stacked on it. For you son this is a life. You murder for fun, but me I do it for business. Within 6 months to a year I'm shutting down operation street fam. We can't do this forever it wasn't part of the plan. I mean how much money you want to make? Soon you'll have no where to hide it. I've had this planned since day one it can't be fucked with. The performance check it out!

The Drip Set performed and rocked the crowd with the mega

hit "He Crazy". People went crazy. The crowd was estatic. The bar was jumping off and the night was peaceful.

Everybody was enjoying themselves and the wet bikini contest was set to start with Tone being the hype man.

Ladies and gentlemen he said! Is Bing in the house!! say hell yeah!

Hell yeah!

Is Brooklyn in the house! Hell yeah!

Is the Bx in the house! Hell yeah!

Ok introducing first tonight in our wet bikini contest is Charmaine so give it up for her she from Bk!

Charmaine was thick, light skinned with voluptuous breast. Tone had the hose and wet her. You see the nipples through her top. She had on a 2 piece suit made by Viscario Lemonte 2Faces clothing line. It was indeed sexy she had pretty toes a red nail polish and long black hair. Tone had the crowd amp how he was describing her and flaunting her around the stage. Next up a long

blonde hair white girl with curves, then a Asian chick probably Laotion 2Face had the Asain connection as well. Also a bad Spanish mommy, at least 20 dime pieces walked the stage. At the end of the contest the white girl came in second and the light skinned girl charmaine finished first.

The Drip Set niggas stayed behind to enjoy the show. 2Face had a check made out to pay them when they was ready to go until one of them was harassing a group of females, he was grabbing them as they tried to force they're to they're spot.

A yo fam I told you to calm your boys! I don't usually tell someone twice don't push me.

The fuck you mean don't push you shouted Fam! I ain't no punk he said drunk.

Yo! you don't want no trouble said 2Face you out numbered, I got a bunch of ya own homies that'll get ya! Relax enjoy the club. You had a good performance, we chilling don't fuck this up.

A yo you know who you talking to bee said Fam?

Mouse put the dopefiend choke hold of death on Famrod. He choked him strait to the ground. 2Face grabbed a Heineken bottle and crashed one of the Drip Set niggas. He was tackled from behind. Wood saw his cuz in need and tussling by the time he got there 2Face had money pinned pounding him. Tone jumped off stage, biz and them followed suit. 2Faces Laotion connect popped too they had a couple of niggas in a frenzy, Odie and them, his man Mark a white boy had niggas twisted. Shorts was poking niggas, Bud was tossing cats Roc swinging on any body he ain't like in the town. Mr. C, L, Chips and them joined the festivities as well. Karrin looked in horror at the melee. 2Face and Dboog was stomping out young Santana and his man. Bouncers didn't know what to do. They couldn't stop the brawl even other locals 2Face fucked with popped off. By the time the melee was over 2Face was gone before the cops showed up.

The ambulance carried Fam, young Santana and 6 of his homies were being carted off on stretchers with broken ribs, jaws, eye jammies, arms and legs, lacerations, you name it.

The police were there trying to investigate and get the situation sorted out. They wanted some arrests and threatened to shut the club down.

Gina was so embarrassed when the news people came.

Can you describe what took place Mrs. Jackson?

No comment. But those Drip Set guys did cause the problem.

CHAPTER 50

A week went past after the melee. The bank notified 2Face that what took place wasn't good for business. They told him one more outburst like that and the club would be under investigation and possibly shut down. Which meant no more hood parties. From now on it would be a twenty five and up club. He would have a teen night and a disco night but no more hip hop nights, at least for a while.

H.O.V. gave 2Face a call. Yo what up said H.O.V.. Not a good look for business.

I know said 2Face. That won't happen again.

I talked son out of pressing charges said H.O.V.. Now hopefully you'll understand you could lose everything your reputation is on the line. Its cause of shit like this that fuck shit up for the next man.

I know but it was unavoidable though.

Yeah I feel you I've had my run ins with the dumb shit too. But listen yaw ready to get this label started?

Yeah.

Good well I got some people in mind if you looking for experienced management and hard workers?

Yeah I'll need some help, like with promotions and distribution. Everything else is a cake walk believe that!

Oh I can help you out with your clothing line too. I can maybe get you into some fashion shows and even help advertise your materiel.

That would really help said 2Face but how much is this gonna cost me I know this comes with a cost?

We'll chat in my office say a Wednesday.

Bet said 2Face and they both hung up.

2Face knew H.O.V. was after the money, who wouldn't be. Some people take inventory on what you got just by how much they charge you for something. A person can know almost exactly how much you worth off your expenses as well, he thought to him self. But 2Face knew the business, everybody trying to get ahead even the ones who already on top, so they can stay ahead. Even if they help others to do so. 2Face wasn't mad though, he respected the game and learned from it. Shit if I could profit on the next cat shit why not everybody get what they want we all happy. But I must stay a step ahead. He'd been doing this since he came home and started the street fam. He looked at the positive note how he would and already created opportunities to come up for his people. He figured you gotta spend to get, once you get your foot in the door then its up to you to make moves for yourself. The bottomline use H.O.V.'s resources like he wants to use your money he thought to himself all the while driving a Ford Fusion.

Sue had the baby boy. They named him Amin Cory Jackson. The baby looked just like him. Gina accepted would occasionally babysit if necessary. 2Face Moms smacked the shit out of him when she found out about the baby, especially when she found out about the infidelity. She was shocked but happy about the baby. She was happy that he and Gina worked out the situation. She made sure he would take care of that baby. His Momma made him marry Sue Islamically too, to insure her that he would be sincere to her. Other than that weeks done past no more melees at his club so far and the restaurant was doing good.

He called his man Shiest to find out what up with the kid he needed a fixing to.

Son he ain't been around said Sheist.

Just be patient said 2Face.

Suddenly that night on Cortland Ave. and 153st. In the Bronx at the 24hrs. store baby Joe show up. He was back on the block, bragging about how he was in Mass. eating good. Right now he played the block to see what was what, how the flow picked up showing his face.

Sheist peeped that.

Yo! said baby Joe them niggas on Fox still eating to one of his mans?

Yeah replied Action Jackson. Action Jackson was a nut case walking around with mad bodies on his belt. His rep known throughout the hoods of the city.

Sheist knew he was being paid on Joes pay roll to keep him off his shit. Sheist waited for Action to lose focus for one second or just walk off for any amount of time so he could make his move. Finally Action went to the building across the street. Sheist made his move, he didn't use guns because he didn't like noise but what he had was sufficient.

Hey man what you holding asking asked Sheist.

Nothing old man, said Baby Joe. I don't do those bee!

Oh really said Shiest!

Yeah really old man, matter of fact get the fuck outta here! I don't know you. What you the police or something?

Then suddenly he went at Sheist, and lunged at him. the knife stuck right in the heart and deep. The look of shock hit Baby Joe as he looked Shiest dead in the eye. Then in one swift motion the old man turned and spit out a razor and slit Joes throat deep. He pulled the knife out and wild blood gushed forth. Sheist watched him drown in his own blood as he dropped to the ground and died.

Before Action Jackson got back to the corner Baby Joe was dead as he bled to death. All anybody saw was him arguing with a old man and the old man dealt with him. but little did they know the old man came to kill him.

2Face had his cuz Chill Will pay Sheist the rest of the money. Now they could eat on the block peacefully again. Nobody thought that Wood and them set the murder up.

CHAPTER 51

2Face and Shorts was in the Flatbush to check his man Ghost out.

Yo, what up son said 2Face as Ghost came to the car.

Yeah star! what's good family. He looked around hey Brethren come to the club tonight son?

Yeah son said 2Face I'm a definitely come fuck some Jamaican pussy so have 'em lined up.

Not a problem he said star!

And make sure it's a lot of booze too said 2Face.

Star ya not been had problem wit ya drink see Ghost said with his Trinidadian accent. Not in me club do not insult me boy!

Ha, ha, ha! 2Face laughed at him. Yo bee we'll be there tonight at midnight brethren. They slapped fives one son, one my youth.

2Face and Shorts drove around and then went to holla at Chips in the Stuy. He needed him and H.O.V. for some recording time. He called Chips when they got in front of his building on Prospect.

Son we outside!

Ok he replied I'm coming right now. Chips came outside like he was dressed for the Grammy's.

Yo! what up said Chips.

What's good homey.

Yo! niggas is crazy son said Chips! yo ya man Mouse is a beast! But none the less that shit was fun.

Yo Chips we need you for our second single bee. We in the studio tomorrow so be ready. I will said Chips.

Yo said 2Face, why you all dressed up like you bout to go to a show or something? Where the fuck you going bee?

A wedding son said Chips.

Yo! I ain't even gonna hold you up homey, breathe easy my dude. We just driving around to check up on niggas. Right now I'm a head to the East to chill for another hour and then go see the Knicks vs. Lakers at 7: You see I got the L.A. jersey on bee!

Yeah, yeah! said Chips.

Yo I'll holla enjoy this late wedding you going to. One up said 2Face and gave Chips a pound. Yo lets head up Knickerbocker said 2Face as they drove off.

Son stop the car 2Face shouted!

What the fuck said Shorts! Stop the fuckin car bee! he shouted again.

U-rrr-r! Free jumped at the sudden screeching tires, of the whip. Free was 2Face man before he went to do his bid. He still had dreads and still looked the same. But since he been out he had moved to Brooklyn.

The window rolled down slowly and a voice said a yo Free what up! As soon as he recognized the voice he ran to the car.

Yo C.D. what up! what the deal baby boy Free said with a smile. Long time no—. The snub nose.38 special took him by surprise. He thought C.D. was his boy. The look in 2Face eyes were cold and death filled the air.

You tell me the deal. What happen to my bread Free? You told my peeps fuck me duke.

I-I-I-I! I nothing said 2Face! you've owed me for the last

few years and never even attempted to pay me back. I put you on when you had nothing remember! then you duck me like a lame!

Shots rang off and pierced his brain. The pain he felt was like somebody holding a hot iron over an open wound. He finally fell to his knees and fell face first to the edge of the sidewalk. Shock was the look on his face when he hit the ground as he died with his eyes open.

2Face and Shorts made it to Fulton and Blew down Fulton, then raced towards Atlantic to get to the East where they were gonna burn the car.

Was that necessary son said Shorts with a sick smile?

Fuck that nigga! He should of paid me my fuckin money and barked on my girl when she asked for it and said fuck me! Cats gonna understand there's consequences to frontin on me, believe that!

Shorts paid off some young cats on the block to burn the car and get rid of the ratchet. They made sure they wiped the prints off before they gave it up. The block was crowded. Mouse and Tone were back in the hood so it was life.

What up! yelled Tone you could hear his loud mouth from the train on the L-tracks. Yo, what's good in the hood son, son. 2Face and shit! Look gut shot this nigga Mouse slow him down 'n shit! he said laughing.

Ya–O! shouted 2Face as they got out and slapped fives with everybody. Son the game starts in a hour' n half. I got my old timer meeting us he a Knick fan too bum ass niggas! yo biz how that single coming along?

Good homey we think its gonna be a major hit. The hook is catchy.

I'm a have my boy shake a few cats up too. Just to speed up our promotion. I also got a little website selling Big East mix tapes as well. I've already sold $80,000 worth of copies.

Word! said Biz. No doubt homey. You gotta get involved or else we'll lose a lot of sales so lets get a little recognition to boost our revenue. We can't avoid it. Many Face Records is in the building.

Ok said Popgun! but the single done though Vincent laced the track. Now we need the anthem.

Well we recording tomorrow said 2Face.

Son! lets go shouted Tone! he don't want to see the Knicks crack his fuckin team head open.

Homey when Kobe drop 50 in the Garden like Mike did then what and we gonna handle yaw.

Fuck outta here said Tone!

They met up with Shiest at the Garden. What up old man said 2Face!

Hey man good to see you, damn too bad L.A. gonna lose. You know we play our best when we play the Lakers said Shiest. Tone was laughin. Yeah he said Mouse tapping 2Face

Son the Knicks said Mouse.

Son we gonna crack yaw! Kobe gonna show off, Bynum gonna dominate and Gasol gonna do what he do I ain't even worried.

Fuck outta here said Tone. Oh Shiest this is Tone and Mouse yo, yo this is Shiest. What up they all said to each other.

CHAPTER 52

After enjoying the game 2Face was headed to the Bronx to drop off Shiest, then he headed to Midtown to meet with his man Pete Nice one of his Italian friends from up top he did time with. They had to discuss some business. He passed through Fox st. and scoped out the hood. Things looked normal. Primo was on 156 'n Beck in front of the old P.A.L.. He waved at son and kept it moving.

Yo son I ain't even stopping. I just want niggas to know we watching, and I'm around believe that!

When they got to Midtown he parked between 8th and 9th and told Tone to wait in the car while he handled something. He walked into the diner and saw his man Pete short bald headed, around 35yrs. old, 5"6 with a stocky build to him. Pete smiled when he saw his boy from the mess hall where they used to work at every day. They became mad tight from there he stood up and hugged 2Face.

What's up man said Pete with an Italian accent. No more mess hall huh, all that fucking cleaning 'n shit we fucking did with that cock suckin C.O.! Yeah fuck all that shit said 2Face. But how's it going Pete?

I'm alright, the fuckin waiter is takin so fuckin long with the fuckin food its ridiculus!

Same old Pete said 2Face.

But hey I'm chilling though how you said Pete?

I'm good. Pete was connected. He wasn't a made boss but he was in there. Yo, Pete you should of came to the game son!

You know I love that football he replied. But what's up you got some business for me?

Yeah said 2Face I need you to holla at these distributors for me in the entertainment industry for me. You know what we talked about its happening now, believe that! I need to push this label. I got good promotion through my man H.O.V. the greatest. But I need a sweet distibution deal. I want to make sure all our albums sell and our shit is distributed around the world in record stores. Then I need help in the clothing line to Viscario Lemonte. Me and my cuz in bed with that. We hired an Italian designer to design our clothes my way.

Really said Pete those were some smart power moves.

You get a cut for each contract we sign. I'll pay you a mil a piece.

You got money like that! Don't worry about what I got just get the job done my friend. You do remember you trying to get that construction business.

Alright don't sweat it this is what I do. Hey cocksucka! where the fuck is my food prick!

Coming sir, said a scared waiter.

So Pete just give me a call when everything is a go. 2Face handed him a bag. Yo in the bag is an outfit from my new clothing line and here is my cd from or album and the rest of the info you need on the distributors. The clothes are strait Italian so we need to make sure it never get bootlegged. These are the contracts we need signed. He passed Pete a envelope. When the contracts are signed you'll get the other cut. I also got a bonus in this for you too. I'll personally finance you guys a construction business. Pete listened to 2Face with intent. He now really knew he was a man of his word. He knew he didn't play any games.

Oh and Pete don't ever cross me, ever!

You got a deal said Pete. 2Face got up and they shook hands. 2Face walked off. Pete looked in the envelope and counted $500,0 His eyes lit up.

CHAPTER 53

The next day The Big East was in the building. They was pumped up to! Popgun was freestyling in the booth telling a story how he was in Midtown with 2 bad white chicks. Niggas was gigging at son.

Yo! shouted Tone Alchemist is in the building ya heard!

H.O.V. was in the building as well to see how they would perform and look in th booth. This was gonna be fun he said to himself.

Yo what up Alchemist said Biz.

Ya'll ready asked Alchemist?

Yeah we was born ready he replied.

Once Alchemist got set up they listened to the beat to get a rhythm. Chips finally showed up. Now everybody was settled in they listened one more time to the beat the studio was a smoke cloud full of piff. The beat was sick 2Face knew even some gangsta shit on this track would ride the airwaves.

They passed blunts and got bent off Henessey to feel good about themselves. 2Face came up with a hook and said yo play the beat! he caught a rhythm.

Yo said 2Face entering the booth putting on his headset. He

called everybody to the booth. He had Dboog with him to hold it down for the Bronx with him on this track and promote the whole crew as well so when their solo albums drop people will know what they getting a taste of. Yo we gonna call this the collabo! Brooklyn, Bx stand up! matter of fact the whole N.Y.C. stand up! lets go!

The4 whole crew was in the booth now to drop the track: "The Collabo B-B Boroughs". It was gonna be the second track they dropped on their opening album, The Big East. The first of many albums to come. They already dropped " We Gone Eat". They were all over the radio and mix tapes freestyling with Popgun going in. They were ready to shoot the video for "We Gone Eat". All their music was gutter and street. They was trying to bring the hunger back to hip hop through its originality in which artist were creative and had they own style and expressed they're own music their way and not sell out. They wanted to put N.Y.C. back on the map by expressing the streets which would bring back the swagger New York once had. B-B Boroughs stood for Bronx and Brooklyn. The 2 roughest boroughs in The City and maybe 2 of the roughest places in America.

Ya'll ready said Alchemist they was still getting hyped up.
We ready 2Face came on the intro.
Brooklyn — The Bronx — stand up! matter of fact the whole New York City stand up!
Stand up lets go! Biz: I started out a young youth on that Crooklyn shit!
Leave a nigga slumped in a– Brooklyn ditch
Graveyards, bravehearts shoot off roofs like marksmen!
We heartless, I'm roastin niggas up then hang wit my Bronx friend
We done stood on them Brooklyn streets, many homies deceased
Chopped up bodies watch the murders increase
I look for inner peace — to conquer this wealth
So we could all live lavish enjoying our health

But we could all live savage, leave you running for help
They call me ravage, I'm coming for self
Causing mad damage this urge I felt
To kill niggas, bullets fill niggas, my fist drill niggas!
My fifth spill niggas, brains on the pavement
Leave ya memory permanently engraved in
The arrangement, dutches is flaming from project
hallways to Hollywood I'm out of
containment.... Val: I'm the demon who entered ya
brain
I'm the semen in ya girl when I drained
Robbing niggas I'm takin their claims
The most critically acclaimed fuck feelin ashamed!
Its Val killmore, yep I kill whores
Bullets fill 4's and enter ya heart
And pull it out bare handed then put it at the top of the
charts!
East New York is enchanted with criminals 'n murderers
Pimps, shooters, dealers and cat burglars
The mac's servin them, new V's I'm swervin 'em
Gas you like a reverend in a church then I'm burnin 'em
Choke a nigga out till he can't breathe or burp
Stay alert, I love pussy love to flirt
Play with the pussy right till it squirt
Then stick my dick far up her coochie right till it hurt
Then burst, then spurt, you can call me a jerk
Get murdered N.Y.C. I'm driving a hurst! Chorus: The
B-B Boroughs! Niggas is thorough!
Brooklyn 'n The Bronx! Niggas get stomped!
We stay high! We super fly-y!
And its all good, and you know we up to no good!
Chorus repeats: DBoog: I'm a Bx phantom, wit raw
lyrics I wanna kill this anthem
Got my foot pressed on ya neck where I can plant them
Infact, I'm a take it back to hoodies 'n Timbs

Guns like ak's to shoot off ya limbs
What's friends? When you on the block scrambling
Niggas ll snitch, you go to trial gambling
Unless ya team official
Ain't no scrapping we talk with pistols
And we work as one moving the powder crystal
Fiends fryin they brain like crisco, sizzling
Has beens from the 80's fizzling
When I party I like a girl ass jiggling
Wiggle it, a little bit, got mils to get
I'm shaking niggas hoods like a birth contraction
Even the president can't stop this faction
Brooklyn and The Bronx enacting
Bout to take N.Y.C. to rap and re attach it and re-enact it
Take it back to the late 80's 'n early 90's
Fox 'n Longwood puffing boobonic is where you'll find me
Or I'm shooting across town wit my Brooklyn crimes
I'm tryin 'a get this money so the ice can blind me...
Chips: I'm Big Chips and my guns 'll fry big fish
Don't get on my list of beat downs and smacked chips
I pump fist for victory
History, says I'll leave the color of smoked hickory
Its trickery, tryin 'a come from the lowest of all hoods
East New York, Bedford Stuy and Longwood
But I done made it
Rich off entertainment, remember my days at
arraignments
Sitting in a cell complaining
When I was out on them corners
Used to pay lookouts to warn us
When the dee's role and who the informants
Ain't nothing deeper than this hell 'n torment
Till I made my first album studio recording
Now its private jets I'm boarding, fly hoes I'm whoring
All over the world exploring, its metamorphic

B-B Boroughs all the rest get extorted
Done fucked so much exhausted
Buy all my niggas whips 'n chains, don't give a fuck what it costed
Come across the bridge better take caution... Chorus:
2Face: Its 2Face came from the darkest era
Got hearts dismembered, guns in leather, swords to sever
I'm one of the illest, realest
Stray shots, narc cops who try to kill us
My meditation, and deep concentration 84
Is what brings contemplations and street medications
I do this for the ghetto and my niggas in Great Meadow
Who sharpen metal, behind the wall the beef is never settled
The drama, the life, the knife fights excite
Get hype, live trife, deading niggas off spite
Really drama I dislike, I'm peaceful
Had all my niggas in my mind held hostage till this album I'll release you
Check the sequel, Bx finest
All the hoes wanna kiss ya hiness
Talk of the town, walk wit the pound, love the climate
Empty a nigga stomach like gastric acid, its massive
glock plastic, shoot at you bastards!   Popgun: Lets get back across town 2Face: Why so we can shoot at these clowns!   Popgun: Nah, lets call these hoes get some smoke 'n lounge
I don't never scrounge, I ain't a garbage picker
Fuck hoes that's thicker, fillin 'em wit cum 'n liquor
If I was really a demon I'd depict her, inflict her causin much pain
Got's nothin but Brooklyn in my veins
We pops champagnes like stick 'n clutch
Never forget my niggas always keeps in touch
Still quick to blam ya in front the bamas

Bang outs everyday lost mad hammers
Now I got big guns, plays with big cannons
Blow a hole through ya mid section the size of the Grand
Canyon
Popgun; they can't stand 'em, defeat I'll hand 'em
Brooklyn 'n The Bx got a mean tandom
Checking niggas gangstas random
If you pussy so be it, guess I'll have to slam ya
Compared to Popgun ya primitive, lyrics is limited
Drop a verse so deep separate ya body from ya spirit and
I'll rip you, right up in 2 parts we'll split you
One for Biz, one for me we both beast
It takes guns and mad heart just to come from the East.....
2Face: Yeah nigga! Shit is real! Our 2 hoods ain't nothin to fuck
wit! Tone: Realest in America! 2Face: Too my niggas all over!
every hood, keep it real yo! Biz:

East New York, The Bronx, Bamas! Harlem, Q- Borough,
Shaolin stand up!

Niggas in the background talkin shit! Popgun: We out!
After recording that single 2Face headed back to The Bronx.

CHAPTER 54

Tommy Tola was a big distributor in hip hop. He has worked with a lot of major labels. His distribution company was a label itself. Universal Records office was located in Tampa Fla. He looked out his office and viewed a beach from his 7th floor office. He was a C.E.O. so he called the shots. Today he didn't expect company there was a knock on the door.

Mr. Tola!

Yes Maria! You have 3 gentlemen in which would like to talk to you.

Do they have an appointment asked Tola?

No sir they do not have an appointment.

Well tell them to make one damn it!

That's alright I think we'll make one now said Pete Nice. Him and his 2 big ass goons shoved the secretary in the office and one of them locked her in the closet to the left. The office was very spacious. Pete Nice acknowledged that.

You got a good view Mr. Tola!

What do you guys want asked Tola?

We want you to sign these contracts. The 2 big guys grabbed

him out of no where and picked him up off his feet like a piece of paper. Pete Nice opened the slide to the balcony.

Please what ever you want pleaded Tola! I'll give it to you just close the slide please!

Damn said one of Pete's men he's a real coward. This is easy money.

Pete Nice opened a bag and pulled out 2 cd discs. Here listen to this and tell us what you think. Mr. Tola played the cds and was impressed despite the circumstances. He was frightened but knew the song "We Gone Eat" was a hit cause the hook was catchy. The second cd was a bit different it was sounding like a white girl with a voice. She hit notes like Tina Turners "We Don't Need Another Heeer–O"! Now he wished he had heard of this girl and this group himself and signed them.

Oh said Pete Nice dialing a number ya daughter says hi. He passed the phone to Tola.

Baby! Daddy! said the little girl I'm scared.

That's enough! Pete Nice snatched the phone from his face. We don't want to hurt you or your daughter we just want you to know we mean business. Do our people right your family an friends live. No bootlegging, we do that. No one gets copies of the cds! You better not ever call the cops about this. You sign this contract with Many Face Records to sell his and everybody elses albums on that label. All albums will be sold under Many Face Records alone. Don't worry you'll get your normal cut. Read the contract its professional written by authentic Lawyers and Managers. We're sorry we even put you through this, but our boss wanted to be sure that things went well. For a token of our appreciation here open the letter a down payment.

When Tola opened the letter, there was a check signed for $1.5 million by Nathaniel Drakes. The name sounded so professional.

Sign here on the dotted line so we can be on our way said Pete Nice and our daughter can get back to playing in her pool. We already told you if you refuse our offer or go to the police, if any type of word about this gets out lots of family members are expandable. We'll ruin you in so many ways before we kill you you'll kill yourself.

Tola went over the contract again then signed it he knew he would make his off that female alone if they market her right. The goons left without saying a word once he signed the contract. He blitzed to the closet to open it.

You alright Maria?

Yes she responded crying crazily. They even had my daughter said Tola.

You alright sir?

Yes. They had my fuckin daughter!

Should we call the police sir?

Hell no! We don't know who were dealing with. Besides I may have made a good deal in the process. They were thirsty for a record deal without no side tracking.

Sir you don't have any idea who those men were?

No! and not a word of this to a soul Maria.

CHAPTER 55

2Face was holding his new son Amin. Sue, Gina and Kitara were playing PS3. He was showing mad affection to his new son.

There was a knock on the door real loud. Sounds like police said Gina. Who the fuck is it!

Detectives. We would like to ask you some questions.

Questions about what?

Questions about Mike Anderson and his wife.

Open the door said 2Face. Gina opened it.

Sorry to disturb you Mam.

Don't worry about it she said with a disgusting look in her face. Why are you here at my door about Mike Anderson? Who the fuck is Mike Anderson?

My name is detective Martino and this is detective Mcgruff. We're following all possible leads in the disappearance of the couple almost a year and some change ago. I'm sure you know they were the informants in your husbands case you did post flyers announcing that.

Yeah but I never knew they're names I just knew they're street names not they're governments sir.

They disappeared around the time your husband came home

I'd say within a week 'n a half. I'm sure Mr. Jackson can help us with that right?

Wrong! I don't know nothing about no Mike Anderson or his wife.

Well said Mcgruff they disappeared right after you came home ain't that odd?

Hey if they ratted me out they probably ratted others out as well they are informants right? They could of got the wrong person knocked and got dealt with.

What do you mean dealt with asked Martino? If you know something tell us now!

I don't know shit officer! so unless you arresting me I'd suggest you get the fuck out my house so I can chill with my new born son.

Mr. Jackson we're just checking leads. You're right we'll go said Martino.

My husband has been walking a strait line. Even though they should get it for having no honor, my husband is no dummy. He's not that stupid enough to risk his life or his family over 2 people destined to be doomed any way.

Ok said Martino thanks for your time.

Your welcome said Gina.

On the way out Martino said you think he had something to do with their disappearances?

No said Mcgruff this fuckin case is a dead end! he was livid.

Baby I didn't know they vanished like that said Gina?

I didn't know either replied 2Face. But fuck it nobody else will get told on no more, believe that!

CHAPTER 56

3 months had passed Shorts had, had enough of L-Train. They had made enough bread in that town anyways. It was time to relocate.

He thought about his brother Sharif. He's been fighting appeals for the last 6 1/2 years. His case was getting ready to hit the appeals court again. Shorts and the crew got away with so much it would be a matter of time if they kept fuckin with L-Train they'd all end up like Reef. L was a hot boy and he had to go. They were already down to they're last kilo from that juxx. 2Face had told Shorts once that was done he was done. Shorts had his mind made up that he would start his own empire. He piggy banked off the intelligence of 2Face long enough, he was gonna show him he could think. That performance in N.C. was barbaric and stupid he realized. But the matter at hand was L-Train. Shay Shay already picked up money from L-Train $120,000 he was to pick up that next $170,000 tonight. They had the whole town on smash they never had a flow like this one but L ran his mouth too much and boasted all over town causing problems. 2Face said he could deal with him so he was gonna get dealt with.

Shorts knocked on L's door. Yo, who dat?

Its Shatman!

Oh what up said L through the door, then opened it. What's good said L.

What up replied Shorts. He thought to himself this nigga is a spitting image of Tone, loud, a peoples person. But Tone was a smarter hustler he didn't boast about his ones and two's.

Son you all finished so we could bring the next shipment?

Yeah said L I'm good.

Hey baby you want eggs and waffles said a chubby white girl in boy shorts and a white T?

Yeah baby yelled L. that's my lil piece for now said L fronting.

Yeah replied Shorts, but I got's to get going I need that bread son.

I got you said L.

Yo you still be wildin asked Shorts? You know blowing shit up.

Blowin shit up how replied L.

You know how said Shorts bragging, boasting and starting trouble not giving a fuck.

That's what I do though!

Yeah well the homey don't like niggas making it hot. We had good run don't fuck this up.

So you want me to stop being me asked L.

I don't wanna argue just slowdown a lil please. No I need that so I can bounce.

Hold up L went to his room. He came out with a bag. Here he said to Shorts count that up please.

Shorts counted the money, he knew the money was correct. Being it was cold outside he used that as reason to not take off his gloves. He stacked the bread and put it in the bag. Then he pulled out a 9 berreta and shot L-Train between the eyes. He turned the music up in his room to muffle the sound of the second shot he fired into the back of the chubby white girls neck as blood spurted all over the kitchen then he fired into her head to make sure she was dead. He casually walked out and left town he never coming here again.

2Face's highly anticipated moment was here. The best day of his life. He was within seconds of signing his max out papers.

Sign here said his former P.O.. He signed immediately. Your free to go said his former P.O..

He shook his hand and walked out free.

Now I'm Free! Free At Last! God Almighty I'm Free At Last!

Now he could get things going the way he really wanted to. He could come out of his shell now. He was headed to N.Y.C. today as a matter of fact to split the cash up. Everybody was gonna get they're cut tonight. They were gonna meet at the 40,40 Club.

He had all the girls there, Wood and them, The Big East, even Tone 'n them Bud, Mouse and Shorts. Roc even showed his face for this.

Yeah yeah said Bud! my nigga off paper home!

Yeah cuz its over said 2Face sitting with all the girls V.I.P. status, they chilling with him like if he was kingpin or something. He was the kingpin.

Yo pass the Henny and that Moet, yelled Mouse! they was balling all sporting 2Face's Viscario Lemonte suits and Sergio Ferregamo shoes. The girls rocked Viscario Lemonte dresses, bling blinging and rocking Louis Vitton shoes 'n purses. 2Face had told 'em to splurge this one time. Now they were gonna legitimize the street fam. H.O.V. was there with a couple of stragglers at the bar. He admired how loyal 2Face's crew was. He liked how 2Face made everybody feel good about themselves and feel the same enjoyment as he did. He knew they would kill for him in a second. He ain't treat nobody beneath him and none of them was no punks. He knew one of 2Face's rules was no sucka ass niggas in his circle. Show any weakness lights out.

2Face huddled everybody up. Yo,yo I wanna holla at ya'll real quick. I'm glad everybody made it. Tonight we splitting up our remaining ends. We quietly and successfully moved tons of coke 'n weed for 2years. We spent a total of $5 mil to get where we at. Everybody was laughing at the sarcastic comment. But seriously for 2yrs. We quietly bubbled in Brooklyn, The Bronx, Bing N.C. and Poughkeepsie. I tallied up everything we made from all that and we got close to $70 million. Everybody's eyes lit up. This was gonna be a mean pay out. From N.C. to Poughkeepsie we made $20 million, from The Bronx we made $25 million, from Brooklyn we made $23 million and in Bing we made $ 8 Million. Yo my restaurant is getting to be franchised which will generate 100's of millions and my club is doing good but fuck that club. The clothing line is official. Yo Pop and Biz be ready to do that video shoot so we can advertise the single. We shooting the video with Hype W. next week Wednesday. Ya'll doing a good job showing support rocking my labels. I told yaw walk with me, there is no reason to hustle anymore he glanced at Shorts. If we smart we'll all stay millionaires and its always a job with ya boy believe that! so we gonna do it like this: Wood yaw gonna divide up $10 mill, Biz yaw gonna divide up $10mill, Shantell and the girls Yaw gonna divide up $10mill, Shanta you get $2mill, that's for hanging in there with us. Bud you Get $2mill, Tone you get $1mill, Mouse you get $2mill, Shorts you get $15mill, and being im the mastermind I get $18mill. The reason me and Shortman get the most cause we was here from the beginning and we both put wild work in to make your job easier. No complaints I suppose huh? The money yours to do whatever. Don't do nothing crazy with it. Ya'll know who was down who did what to get this cake up so I'm trusting the men and women I gave those bags of money to to do the right thing and portion the cash off to thewell deserving people. If I find out other wise fams or not you will get dealt with. Never shit on your peeps or the little people the pawns. They the ones that make it happen. A jab don't look as effective as it is but it is, it sets the tempo of a fight, just like a pawn in chess. I want everybody paid tonight. Remember we the ones who put it in to get where we at today don't fuck it up. My illegal days are over. The only time you'll hear from me is if work need to be put in or if I'm vacationing and partying. Oh and never give up a documentary on how you got what you got its never over. If you do there's consequences of life 'n death! other than that we balling thanks for your help lets enjoy the night.

See Bud said 2Face after everybody dispersed that's a boss!

I make everybody happy. But I had to keep the money in order to stack it. That's why I held all the pc so niggas would stay focused and not splurge. Now everybody got a lump sum and we living.

That was smart said Bud.

And I invested $20mill in this label under H.O.V.' s name for now. Once I sell all the shares of the restaurant that $20 will turn into hundreds of millions and then th ultimate plan comes.

That was smart investing in your own business.

Yeah homey use a nigga with money to generate your own and now I'm legitimized! Now I'm a live it up, no more parole son.

Yeah, yeah shouted Bud!

CHAPTER 57

2Face was balling now. He copped a estate for Gina and little Kitara and even sent Kitara to Islamic school. He still thought about doing Gina dirty fro all the shit she did behind his back. She lied to him and spent damn near his whole stash while he was locked up. But she played her position and fell back. He guessed she thought she was gonna ride this thing out to the gate. He married Sue Islamic fashion but not legally in the states because he was currently married to Gina. Sue had really took Shahada and changed her name to Aisha. He copped her a pent house in Midtown something she always wanted.

Biz Mania and them dropped their single "We Gone Eat". It was tearing up the radio station. Hot 97 played it atleast 4 times a day, so did Power 1 They was killing the mix tapes as well gaining mad street credibility. Pop gun was featuring on mad tracks so was 2Face and Dboog. They would try to avoid bootlegging by not releasing any songs to the public any Cds. They kept a low profile about the album the only songs from the album heard were the singles like "we Gone Eat" and "The B-B Boroughs".

Pete Nice ran up in Ralph Lauren's office and put a rat in the

C.E.O.'s pants and tied him down until he signed a contract to help promote their clothing line. People like Versaci loved the line of clothing that was produced. 2Face even hand picked his models. He had a variety of clothes, underwear, bikinis, lingerie, hood clothes, business clothes like suits, purses, wallets, and even children's clothes. He even had leather coats and gooses. He had opened up a store in Midtown. He took both his wives on crazy vacations and they shopped like crazy.

Wood 'n them opened up clothing store. Wood chilled out and enjoyed himself and just layed low he never liked to leave New York. Tone, Mouse, and Bud stuck together. They all fucked with Biz 'n them. 2Face left Bud in control of the label making decisions for the most part while delivered tracks. Shanta got real low and just enjoyed her cut raising her and Tone's son. Roc went back to school to complete his degree 2Face had pieced him off lovely and payed fro his schooling.

The girls got their lives strait. Jamie moved to Denver and got married. Jessica went to college, Shantell wanted to finish her school too and went back to college. The others had opened up beauty salons and nail salons and promoted Viscario Lemonte's lingerie.

The only loose end was Shorts. He gathered up some stragglers and went to MiddleTown to bubble.

1yr done passed. His clothing label with Jr. and Fabio the gay designer blew to estatic numbers. He invested a additional $25 mill from the earnings off his labels. His restaurant was killing the stock markets. 2Face kept his money invested in stocks especially his own businesses. The Big East finally landed on 106 'n Park after "We Gone Eat" video landed almost numberThe second video "B-B Boroughs" exposed the homies and the whole arsenal of The Big East. The album titled "The Big East" was set to drop on Tuesday. The beef with Drip Set also brought them out of the gutter along with Drip Set and they hoped it would boost their album sales. The beef wasn't serious to 2Face and his homies.

2Face kept his promise to Karrin and put her on now her

stage name was Miss Elizabeth, Elizabeth being her middle name. Her first album was due in 3 months. She had already featured in mad collabos, with Justin T., Janet, Britney on her comback trail she sang a hook on The Big East album, N.A.S.'s album and Kisses album. She was like a white Maria Carey. She was about to a track with Gwen and P.I.N.K..

Today 2Face was cashing out on his investments. He had to pay back H.O.V. his change for the help he gave even though he didn't need him too much he had Pete Nice. He generated $310 mill of H.O.V.'s resources. Even 50 had to admire him. now just like the drug game when he was knee deep his phone never stopped ringing.

CHAPTER 58

Hello, what's up 2Face said Karrin. I'm in the studio recording my last song, I owe youa celebration! Lets have dinner tonight?

Dinner said 2Face! I got a pool party to go to at 4:

Ok how about 8:30?

I gotta do a few transactions this party at N.A.S.'s crib. Kiss 'n D- block gonna be there, ya know I'm a big fan. H.O.V. is gonna be there.

Well said Karrin I'm free after I finish. Why don't we go together?

Karrin this is a pool party, you know lots of freaks gonna be there, etc.

Ok well your not gonna be freakin off right, aren't you married?

Yeah so.

So! So! If you said something like that to me and I was your wife it'd be all over with you! I probably wouldn't even marry you knowing you don't respect vows, wow!

I respect my vows maybe you need to check my wife's resume. Matter of fact when you finish meet me at my house in Pasiac

New Jersey. Have the limo drop you off. I something I want to show you about vows.

At 3:00 Karrin knocked on his door. His crib was a mansion he had definitely had some acres. She was impressed by his sharply cut bushes and perfectly mown grass. To her left she saw an array of expensive whips, Porches, Bently's and Benzes. 2Face opened the door 10 seconds later.

Hey sexy you look gorgeous Karrin!

Thank you.

Yeah I see you got the open toes showing your pretty ass feet in the middle of July. Them feets looking ump! so good.

She laughed blushing stop playing she said. So why am I here?

Check it out, Karrin my crib official right?

Its nice and cozy she said. Its big as hell though.

These are custom made ceramic tiles said 2Face. Over here is where the kitchen is at. She seen the spacious kitchen in amazement.

Stainless steal state of the art sink. Check out the stove.

Wow she said your living it up Mr. 2Face. Certified real oak counter top. You also like my marble table?

Yes this crib is wonderful.

Now look outside and se all the space. I got the basketball court, tennis a barbecue area and pool. My garage is crazy too! the pool was bigger than the ones in a park.

Lets go upstairs I'll show you the rooms.

Who lives here with you asked Karrin?

My moms. I personally take care of her.

Where is your ma at now?

She in Florida vacationing. The rest of my family is in Texas now. I got them a couple of ranches on some land I bought.

These stairs are nice. So what am I doing here? He took her into his spacious room. I want show you show something.

Cool said Karrin.

I want to show you some photos and a video tape Karrin. One of my boys I sent him to private eye school. You remember Roc? He was mad mysterious right? Well he was getting ready to become a detective but he got caught up in some bullshit, so I sent him to private eye school. He has his own business now. 2Face went inside the closet and pulled out a knapsack.

What's that asked Karrin?

He pulled out the polaroids. Look he said.

Karrin looked at the photos in awe. Oh my god!

Yeah oh my god replied 2Face. There was flicks of Gina in the strip club dancing on a pole, then a second flick with her titties in some older looking white strangers mouth. Gina went into the V.I.P. section with that same man. The next flick showed her hair all frizzled when she was leaving indicating some type of sexual activity took place. Then he went to the tv and popped in a video. It was surveillance.

We're gonna blackmail him for all his money Sue. He wants his cake and eat it too with us and he probably fuckin half these industry bitches. You've seen him in magazines with Vida, Buffy, Kim Kard, Melissa and Ester. He's probably been with all types of mothafuckas. I know he fuckin most of his model bitches anyways. Tears welled in Sues face.

I'll never trust another man again Sue said. I'll sue him for child's support, you sue him for half his fuckin businesses and his earnings. We'll be caked up. Then Sue kissed Gina.

Eew! snickered Karrin!

Yeah said 2Face that is a abomination. Now you call that vows. Like Jay Z told Game "you playing the game I'm playing the game too". Where I'm from you can't trust your family, let alone a bitch. These two bitches is fowl. To me you beat fowlness with foulness, violence with violence. When they move I move first. Until then let them enjoy the ride.

Karrin suddenly felt a warmness for him all of a sudden. She always did like him but she feared his life style would cause their demise. But now she thought to herself he beat the streets and defied all odds. He made everybody rich over night and through all that he never forgot her. He kept his word to her and never fronted on her a second. She knew he liked the shit out of her as well. She stood over him and kissed him on the forehead.

Don't worry Cory, those fowl bitches got what's coming to them. You should see a lawyer and just get a divorce.

Yeah he replied, but what about my kid?

You can raise him, shit hell I'll raise him! It slipped out. I mean I'll help you raise him. if you don't they'll try to blackmail you. You just said strike first not last remember that?

You right he said. Damn you learn fast. Monday I might just do that.

She saw some sadness in his eyes.

I'm very disappointed in Gina. That was my heart a long time ago. Those flicks were when I was incarcerated and the video was a month ago. She was lying while I was in jail I should of known.

Your human Cory your not God. Your not immortal, or a Prophet! Your human and human things happen to you. People make mistakes. Trust me I know your not all right 'n exact so cut it out.

That other grimy bitch Sue she played with the Islam and turned gay.

You play with Islam too! I don't know nothing about it but I know you ain't suppose to be doing half the things you been doing! If not all the shit you do.

You right said 2Face.

I know you probably want to kill her too? That caught him by surprise.

Hey what makes you say that asked 2Face?

Cause you got a look of death in your eyes when you get mad. I've seen that look since we were young.

You seem to know me like a book.

I went to school for psychology remember?

But we better get going Karrin its 3:

How bout we have our own pool party? I like this house.

What shouted 2Face!

You heard me, me and you gonna have our own pool party. You need some alone time Cory. I mean come on.

The look on 2Face was dumbfounded. I'll go and cop you some official swimming trunks and get me a hot 2 piece bathing suit. You down. Karrin had a seductive look in her eyes.

2Face played it off like he was contemplating but not for too long cause he didn't want to lose this moment. It was like a dream come true. Yeah we could do that.

Karrin jumped like a little girl excited. Ok I seen a mall on the way, give me a hour I'll be back.

As soon as she left he called up H.O.V. And N.A.S. and explained the situation and sudden change in plans. They understood and hung up.

His phone rang twice. You have a collect call from; Sharif Abdullah stated the recoring. He pressed 0 to accept the call.

Salaamu Alaykum!

Wa Laykum Salaam said 2Face what up son!

Yo I got good news Face. I'm getting a retrial next week homey. Shoot I might be outta here son.

Word! shouted 2Face. Get the fuck outta here. If you get out fuck with your boy dude.

I have to, you got me the fuck outta here.

Nah my friend Allah got you out of there.

Yo what up with Shorts 'n Razzac?

I ain't seen them in a minute. I ain't seen Shorts since we parted ways and I ain't seen Razzac in eons! Shorts tight at me cause I told him that if he wanna run the streets stay away from me.

Damn said Reef. Yo what up with Mouse punk ass and Bud 'n Tone laughed Reef?

Hey! Hey! Easy that's the street fam bee! But son chillin my dude he just had another seed. Bud had a girl and a little boy.

Everybody chillin though. I be sending ya family ones here and there. You need to talk to Shorts son. He trying to be the both of us combined.

Son this nigga hardheaded said Reef.

I did what I could do like no other cat could do for his crew and he still want more.

Allah said "Those whom Allah guides no one can misguide and those whom Allah leaves to stray no one can guide". Said Reef.

You right said 2Face.

You've been practicing your Islam or enjoying the fruits of life, tv shows, mad hoes, videos, the stars you know the industry life?

I ain't gonna lie I've been dibbing and dabbing. My foot half way in the door. Right now I'm a Juma Muslim.

Son you know better than that! shouted Reef. You was and still is sharp in the dean and in life period, don't die astray!

That shocked 2Face. Reef was the most flamboyant ever! Now he preaching Islam to him.

You the leader said Reef, me and Mouse passed you the torch a long time ago. Niggas follow you and admire you homey. Especially the cats with me behind the wall you a inspiration to a lot of people. We inspired by your success give back to the people. Not just ya family or us butbe a role model. Allah tests us with wealth and family. These are the ayats in the Qur'an brother.

You right said 2Face I've been fucking up out here I gotta get a hold of myself and think.

You have 30 seconds left on this call. Yo said Reef you my boy and a Muslim and I love all my   niggas. Lead the people the right way.

Karrin was walking in right as 2Face was hanging up the phone. What's up you ready?

I was born ready said 2Face.

She went upstairs to the master room to change while

2Face change right in the living room. She came down stairs looking real seductive in her 2 piece, she had gorgeous feet too a maroon nail polish color. Her stomach was flat and her legs look like she could still cheerlead. She still had that killer body said 2Face to himself. Her hair was in a ponytail this was a dream come true.

2Face took her to his open bar and they selected some champagne for the pool side. On the way outside she noticed a library.

I didn't know you like to read she said?

I read a lot when get a chance. Remember I was locked up for almost 4yrs. He forgot the whole lecture reef just gave him. I got 2 champagne glasses for us and a bottle of Don Perrion or we could sip some tequila.

Lets drink a little of both, but first lets get wet she said and pushed 2Face in the pool

Oh shit he shouted laughing! he still had the glasses in his hands. Wo-ooo! This water feel good! Remember I ain't a good swimmer he shouted!

Yeah well you gonna learn today shouted Karrin! She jumped in the water next making abig splash. They had a nice ten minute water fight that led to them wrestling underwater. 2Face was letting her win ofcourse. When they came up for air their eyes met. She made the first move. She always wanted to taste a black mans lips and she liked 2Face's juicy ones. He kissed her passionately. They liplocked tongue kissing for five minutes strait. She had him pinned against the side of the pool. She began to kiss his neck, squeezing his muscular chest. She felt his hardness and it wetted her right up. Her juices were flowing. His dream come true was really happening. As soon as her smooth hands grabbed a hold of his penis a car horn beeped.

Yo, who the fuck! 2Face was livid foreal. The phone rang.

Yo, its Hovie baby! We in the building my nigga! Niggas

want to see the face behind the face. They was laughing in the background.

Awe man said 2Face to Karrin, its H.O.V. and N.A.S. 'N them.

Get out she replied!

Don't get all star struck you done did songs with Justin T. 'n them.

I know but all this is out of nowhere.

Karrin said 2Face as he was getting out of the pool, I like you cause of your personality, you're a sweetheart foreal. You also very pretty too.

You mean that she said blushing.

Yeah he said, that's why I never forgot you. When I think of all the females I had a crush on you on the top of the list. Even the celebrities.

Wow why do you like me so much?

Cause I just told you I like your personality. You're a beautiful person with a very good heart. He walked to open the door but grabbed his snubnose incase a nigga got stupid.

Yo, yo what up shouted H.O.V.!

What up fellas,ladies. N.A.S.! What's good! D-Blizzle! J-Kiss, homies the P what up! Wow said Face all sarcastic. Come in. They had 2 Maybach's parked outside and a Porche in which 4 broads hopped out of. 2Face mouth watered but he couldn't blow his chance with Karrin, this was gonna be hard.

H.O.V. and them came with their own drinks. Karrin stayed close to 2Face as he introduced his

artist to them.

My number one fan said N.A.S. to 2Face.

Yeah I used to look in your music for a answer to my problems.

No doubt said N.A.S. atleast somebody got something positive out my music he gestured to H.O.V.. J-Kiss I needed yaw niggas when I was in the pens bee. Yaw got me through all the bullshit plus kept me away from the ring tone music. Yaw murdered the mix tapes. H.O.V. you a cat I needed when I was on the grind bee!

Yo said J-Kiss I want to hear The Big East album I know its fire with you and them niggas. I can't wait till you and D-Boog drop a album too. And I want to do a track with Miss Elizabeth.

Dboog like the Az of The Bronx, said The P.

Yeah son nice said J-Kiss. We gonna do some collabo's with him too. Set that up Face!

Yo everybody standing here I want on my album. With J-Kiss and The P going back 'n forth.

The 4 chicks asses were so fat you couldn't see the thongs they had on as they jumped in the pool.

H.O.V. said so the new Maria, you getting ready to blow, would you like to feature on my album?

Yeah, why not, can I Mr. Face she said sarcastically.

Sure she can. She elbowed him in the ribs.

You look at that girls ass one more time I'm leaving she said. Alright he said.

H.O.V. Pulled 2Face to the side. I had to bring these guys to you I know you love these niggas and they the liveliest artist in New York. If we gonna bring it back we need cats like this in our corner. We is keeping it New York right?

Yeah replied 2Face.

I see you ain't shake them snow bizzles yet! 2Face laughed. Chappter

An hour later after some good booty shaking by them hoes and mingling about ideas on music, H.O.V. and N.A.S. Broke out.

Karrin you can shower 'n get ready to head to dinner. Then he had a idea.

Hey Karrin why don't you let me cook for you?

You know how to cook?

Hell yeah this is what I do believe that!

Ok she said but don't blow this meal buddy!

Son kitchen was state of the art. He was an exceptional cook, perfect with the seasonings, knowing the herbs 'n spices to put in each meal. She watched him for the next hour 'n some change hook up some Halal lamb with gravy, 'n onions with peppers and fine seasoned pilaf rice with some spinach.

2Face set the table forShe was even impressed how he cleaned up after himself and didn't leave a mess.

Wow she said after he pulled out her chair for her to sit down. You cook fast but the food loks good 'n shit.

Old jail habits taught me how to cook fast. If they left the stove dirty we suffered we got shut down for a week.

Seriously she said?

Yeah you got some dirty motherfuckas out here in prison!

Well you don't have to worry about that no more, you living legal and you rich.

Lets eat he said and took off his apron.

Her first bite she was impressed. Umm she said you nice huh? He was winning her heaert by the second. This is, this is pretty good she said with a mouthful.

Oh shit I forgot juice. What do you want? Some water.

That'll be just fine she said.

Cool here you go thank you. They ate and kicked it for a while. After they finished they washed dishes but smoking. Then after they washed their plates. She didn't want desert, she just wanted to chill for now.

So she said as she sat seductively on the couch crossing her left leg can we toast one more time sweety? I'm not really much of a drinker but I feel safe with you for some reason.

You do said 2Face?

Yeah she replied, I never seen nobody back you down and you always stood up for me. 2Face was touched.

How bout some scotch on the rocks Karrin?

You trying to get me bent huh? He poured the drinks and sat across from her on his personal love seat.

Karrin I got some dark secrets, I don't want to scare you away and I don't want you to a part of my madness. They call me 2Face for a reason.

You don't scare me I think your sweet. But if you got some dark secrets you should keep it between you and God and ask for his forgiveness. Do you ever pray for forgiveness?

Once in a while he said.

Well you need to pray more. You damn right about that!

Ok she said so after today we gonna work on your repentance to God. Tonights my night though come here she said seducingly.

2Face got up and sat next to her on the couch. He never seen her so aggressive, but it turned him on. She pulled him close to her and whispered in his ear; baby I want you to fuck the shit out of me right now!

She kissed him slow 'n seductively on his neck, unbuttoning his shirt. 2Face lifted her by the chin gently and french kissed her passionately. Her pussy was streaming from the touch of his lips. He had his hand fondling her mouthful of breast. She kissed his diesel chest using her tongue to lick his nipple with one hand on his penis massaging it with her smooth hands. He was definitely bigger than any of her previous.

They took it to the Persian rug next, rolling to the floor. 2Face took charge trying to please her as much as possible. He used his tongue to lick her from the chin all the way down to her left breast. Then his warm tongue licked her right side until he smothered he nipple with his juicy lips sending a chill through her spine. Then he passionately licked her belly button making her moan like a purring cat massaging her breast with both hands. She continuously squirmed and moaned from the licking.

2Face unbuttoned her pants slid her out of them. He started licking the soles of her feet to the heel, then all the way up to her toes, smothering his mouth over her pretty pedicured soft toes. He licked the back of her leg all the way up to her thigh then up the crack by her pussy finding that soft spot between the pelvis and hip that almost made her jump. He licked that spot a few seconds then found his way to her sweet tasting pussy. She had a nice shaped clitoris in which

his tongue attacked. He felt her hot juices flowing in his mouth as she climaxed. She moaned and shaked for a minute in a half. 2Face smothered her pussy with his lips.

Daddy come fuck your pussy! Come fuck me!

She pulled him close to her and kissed him. his cock was playing around with her clit, then feeling the juices flowing his dick throbbed. She grabbed his cock and slid him inside her, very deep inside her she gasped at his penetration, she never felt a rod this deep.

He wasted no time stroking her tight wet pussy. She screamed off the first stroke.

You alright baby he asked her?

Yes. He took it slow on her, he gripped her ass to pick her up carrying her from wall to wall fucking the shit out of her.

Uh, uh, uh, uh,!she moaned, fuck me daddy! Uh, uh, uh, uh, aah! I'm cumming she yelled. She squirmed all over him.2Face spun her around with her facing the wall and re-entered her from the back. Her ass was so soft it was bouncing like waves all over the place with every stroke. Her   screams excited 2Face as he pounded her from the back making her cum again. I want to get on top she said. This was her show now. She dug her nails in his chest marking her territory her ass was bouncing off his thighs smacking. She was grinding him now feeling all that cock in her.

Its in my stomach daddy aah! Your dick is in my stomach!

Face was ready to explode, she was grinding him and bouncing off him for 10 minutes. Her pussy was so good he thought to himself. She was roaring with every pump, her pussy was so tight, she felt him throbbing.

Cum in me daddy! Cum in your pussy! Cum in me daddy! he couldn't hold it no more.

I'm cumming baby, I'm cumming! Aaaah! He squeezed in her and shot off a humongous load in her.

Yes she screamed as he screamed again aaaah! She bent and kissed him in the lips. I love you Cory.

I love you too he said back at the same time didn't realize what he just bought himself with those lines.

CHAPTER 59

Shorts was wilding without 2Face being the brains. He watched his boy blow up into a hip hop icon in less than 2 ½ years. But he was his own man and caked up, fucking mad bitches now. His way of the law was violence and he'd been sloppy at it. He shot a cat at a night club in front of a crowd of spectators, he ordered a hit on a rival drug dealer one of his workers shot a old lady during the drive by. He shot a little girl by accident in Middletown chasing down a cat who owed a couple of hundred. That really brought the heat on the whole town now the Feds were watching him. his arrogance and pride would cause his demise. He didn't have the resources he had with 2Face, he also didn't have a thinker in his crew as well. People feared him more than they respected him.

He waited at court for his brother's new trial. He knew 2Face would be there too. 2Face had been avoiding his calls for the last year 'n a half. Shorts felt the phone vibrate off his hip, he stepped out the court room to receive the call.

A strange voice picked up; The Feds is watching you they on you, they want you bad, they might even try to get you in the court room. Yo, yo your team is a bunch of rats by the way.

Yo who the fuck is this? The line went dead. He saw his brother being escorted to the

courtroom in shackles. He contemplated staying about 30 seconds before leaving. He didn't even get in his ummies crib to lay low. That call and then the chill in his spine scared him.

Sharif was in the building. Today was the first of the re-trial. Roc and 2Face showed up first, then Mouse and Tone 'n Bud. They slapped 5's, and sat in separate rows.

All rise said the judge. Sharif looked back and grinned. He seen the success all over their faces. He was proud. He hadn't seen his boys in years. He was 8 yrs into his 15yr bid. The first went well for Sharif with 2Face getting all the press. Reef showed sadness in his eyes when his homies left the building.

One my brother said 2Face, all iced out in mad jewelry. He had a free Sharif t-shirt on, so did Mouse, Roc, Tone and Bud. the C.O.'s walked Reef out.

Fox 40 news was outside trying to interview 2Face. Gabrielle one of the anchors had the mic.

Can you tell us what happened in there.

No comment he kept it moving.

Dboog album dropped today he was Midtown signing autographs, getting ready for 106 'n Park tomorrow. His single sold millions on the U-Tube, which made the album release crazy. His video was one that featured the Big East, N.A.S. D-block, and they squashed the beef with Drip Set. 2Face didn't show because of the trial. H.O.V. didn't show up either, but none the less today he sold so far $350,000 records, not bad for his highly anticipated album release the new coming of AZ.

Miss Elizabeth aka Karrin album sold like crazy. She appealed to the white audiences and black because she had a voice. She didn't need American Idol, or Star Search, Pussy Cat dolls which made her sell more, she came out of no where. The white teens loved her and she appeared on MTV for her album release. She repeatedly thanked 2Face for this opportunity of a lifetime. She went platinum that day.

CHAPTER 60

A yo hanging out in project hallways 'n buildings
knife fights, thick hoes, drugs 'n mad killings and
I can make it out only if god willing, spend a few million
trickin, gettin my dick sucked fuck feelings
tryin a get this loot drug dealing, swindling life dwindling
 smoking on blunts 'n drinking liquor
The cops lurkin they funny faces
police chases is the basis of a cop racist, basic
doing maneuvers concentration
the sewers be a street plantation where we plant seeds
the dirty slums where the heads breed
but they call this N.Y.C., but back to me
blowing on trees in a jungle concrete
my whole team elite, victorious up in defeat
glorious when we touch the mic, get hype 'n speak
walkin by squeezing on cheeks, bad bitches
mad riches, giving niggas wired up jaws, 'n hundred stitches
We polly in tailor made suits regularly
mentally build empires, lounge in the hills of Beverly
But I still take it back to the Bronx

ain't no comp, niggas get stomped, that's the penalty
lyrics perspectively, I'm coming intellectually blazing
all you dumb ass niggas who ain't amazing
and when I buss guns they ain't grazing
can't walk, can't talk, South Bronx, nigga shots get launched

N.A.S. sang the hook one more time. This was the completion of 2Faces album. The fourth of many more atleast 10 he needed to make him and his crew. Popgun was next to drop his album, he was one of the nicest out of The Big East with that Big L type flow. 2Face hit single was called "Bow Down To The Face" in which he went off like he was Big Daddy Kane. They was gonna start shooting for the video in a month. The good thing about this is people know about 2Face but nobody didn't really know him, he didn't put himself out there like that, but now that he was promoting his own album people would know now. He usually refused interviews and didn't talk to the magazines cause he didn't want to take away the spot light.

Yo Kiss, N.A.S. I appreciate ya'll showing your support. I tried to keep it New York for the hood and for hip hop. Oh and holla at Fat J. for me too so he could be at the shoot.

Ahright said Kiss. Yo Miss Elizabeth what up you good Ma? We still gonna make that song together right?

Yes she said smiling later guys!

So 2Face what do you have planned for the night she asked?

I gotta do some paper work and finalize this divorce and I'm selling clothing line.

Why asked Karrin?

You see how busy we are. We barely have time to sit down. I ain't never been this busy. I got too much going on why be so greedy, I'll sell my majority shares and then reinvest and enjoy myself.

I understand said Karrin. But you worked so hard to obtain what you have Cory.

Yeah I know but check it I got Bud on the other end running things, like the label, and maintaining Jr. and the clothing line. Kenny controls the restaurant but he getting ready to be a politician. But the restaurant ain't really a problem it's the chance of one going bankrupt. Let some body else control the majority shares. This label is a problem cause I put too much work in. I gotta concentrate on making my artist sell records sellout shows and be caked up. I also got this divorce to handle I haven't seen them in months and they ain't losing no sleep on it. They don't care they having fun feel me. I got Roc dropping the bombshell on them tomorrow. As soon as we get divorced, 2Face dropped on one knee, he pulled out a jewelry box out his front right pocket. He placed a brollic diamond ring on Karrin's ring finger.

Will you Marry me Karrin? He looked directly at her eyes with conviction. She stared in his eyes for a moment simultaneously they passionately looked at eachother. Then happy tears welled in her eyes and she whispered, Yes!

2Face hugged her and kissed. I love you Karrin with all my heart.

I love you too baby!

CHAPTER 61

When the lawyers dropped the divorce papers on Gina she was stunned. Sue couldn't believe it either.

So the bastard wants a divorce huh said Gina? Well we'll break his fucking pockets to death!

What's this video tape attached to the letter about asked Sue?

Well lets find out will we.

Gina read the letter. It stated if you do this willingly we won't push prosecution for conspiracy. What! said Gina.

What does it say asked Sue?

It says: If you do this willingly we won't push for prosecution for conspiracy. It says I can have the club and you can have five million and go. But he wants the kid. He wants Amin in custody or this tape gets played nationally and we both go to jail.

They were filled with curiosity so Gina popped in the tape. It immediately showed them conspiring on his wealth. It showed naked pictures of Gina in the strip club, going and coming from the V.I.P. room with frizzy hair. The most embarrassing flick of all or video tape was when 1 the Muslim sister kissed Gina and they stripped down going down on eachother. The evidence was over whelming.

That fucker! yelled Gina. This 2Faced bastard knew all along about us and about me in the strip club. He was a step ahead of us.

We have no choice Gina atleast the bastard gave us something said Sue with tears in. She was full of betrayal.

Why did you do it? A females voice said didn't we deserve our lives? We should of got a second chance asshole! 2Face was tied up. They poured boiling hot water on him the water didn't seem like it was from this Earth.

Aah! Aaaah! you fuckas!

What are you gonna do kill us, said another familiar voice?

We're already dead! your dead! you took lives that didn't need to be taken!

You played God said another familiar voice. Voices were coming from all angles.

We was boys said a Dread! sure I owed you but you didn't give me a chance to explain. I could of worked it off. Allah gave you plenty of chances and you still didn't take advantage, yeah you got money but is it halal?

Are you doing what you promised? Rebuilding your communities said his Grandma, you hear me Cory!

Aaah! Aaaah!

What the fuck 2Face said as he jumped out of bed!

Lay back down baby, you alright asked Karrin?

Nah I can't lay back down, I ain't going back to sleep.

Awe poor baby! you had a nightmare Karrin said Laughing.

Its not funny! If I tell you the things that I've done you'd think I'm a monster and hate me.

Baby I told you I'm not afraid of you, I'm not scared of you no more. I think your sweet, sexy and kindhearted. Everybody got a dark side to them.

Oh yeah he said what's your darkside?

You don't want to know my darkside bitch! She started

laughing. I'm just kidding I don't think I have a darkside. I didn't grow up the way you did. Maybe mines ain't that bad as yours.

Karrin you don't have a bad bone in your body. You probably would do certain things if you have to. But Karrin I can't get into detail but what we got comes from my mind and the work I put in, in the streets. Me and my crew put a lot of work in. A lot of violence took place. I'm telling you this cause I believe I can trust you. But baby I masterminded a lot of violence with many lives at stake.

So you telling me you a murderer?

I'll keep that between me and Allah.

I'm not gonna look at you no different baby. You did what you had to do to get where you at. You didn't do no crazy shit like kill old ladies or some innocent people.

Anybody I ever did something to either did something to me first or deserved it or was a stepping stone. But I don't kill for nothing though. I know cats who kill for nothing, for fun and most of em 6ft. under.

Well I think you need to return back to your lord sweety and repent. You should repent a lot. Give back, become a man of God, maybe you'll feel better.

You know Karrin when you believe medicine will heal you when you got a cold and you take 1 that medicine believing that the medicine its gonna be worth it. Your cold suddenly doesn't bother you. Its physiologically proven. The cold didn't go away you just believed it did. All the medicine did was contain it.

I read that in one of your natural cures books she said.

You right 2Face said to Karrin. Our deeds do impact how we feel on the inside. You know what made idol worshipping so popular? They believed if this statue in my house is praised good things will happen, because ever since I got the statue nothing but good has come. So you get my point?

Yeah I get your point said Karrin.

But Allah is real, he tells us through signs. Do you believe in God?

Yes I believe in God she said. I just don't know what path to follow Cory. Like its so many different beliefs in which they all say theirs is the truth.

Well one day we'll go through The Qu'ran and ancient history. I'll show you some confirmations. I'll show you some proofs of how we living in the last days as well. Even Nastradamas predicted but he was no Prophet. Our Prophet (p.b.u.h.) Told us things about the life of the present outer space the creation of life in the womb, the spliting of the moon the plots of empires conspiring to kill him, I mean I can go on. These things were predicted over 1400yrs. ago. He told us of the world wide violence of our time the disobedience of our children and the dressing of women.

You got a deal said Karrin. I want you to show me.

Alright bet said 2Face!

CHAPTER 62

The defense attorney said his final piece to the closing arguments. Now the jury had to deliberate. The prosecution really had no solid evidence. Bullets didn't match the casings, witnesses statements didn't consist or were credible. Reef had a good chance at beating trial and walking right out of the court room.

After a couple of hours of deliberating the jury came back and the people stood, all the Reef supporters and 2Face stood rocking free Sharif t-shirts.

2Face had hired a bunch of attorneys on Reefs behalf. 1 law firm in each state he offered for students in college to oversee the state facilities backed by NAACP. The lawyers would once a month speak with ILC reps of each facility in each state to make sure the inmates were treated fairly. Any resistant of cooperation by staff would result in a full scale investigation. 2Face knew the brutality and how the CO's over step their boundaries. The officers constantly abuse their authority so does staff. Something had to be done about that. It was a $10 million tax right off.

Once all the papers were finalized within 6 months inmates would have a sense of security and this method would avoid future rioting.

You like my video Karrin?

Yeah its real ghetto she said sarcastically. Baby your album drops in 2 weeks.

I know.

You ready to do more shows, sign more autographs than ever! It gets crazy. You should already know watching me, your cuz, and The Big East. Now you sweety.

Well I 've toured with Biz 'n them before. I've been on tour with you.

At times she said. You didn't do no performances on your own and didn't become star feature either.

I'll be alright baby. I got a cross country tour coming up to promote my album. We starting in Philly and ending in Tennessee. We stopping in Florida, Texas, Arizona, Vegas, Seattle, Detroit, Minnesota, and Chi-town and Cali. I might even be at Summer Jam. I hope this Reef mess ends soon and I hope I get this divorce settled soon like tomorrow.

Well I got a world tour from England to Germany. I even got a concert in China. Oh and I get to go to Austrailia! And I get to perform at the Grammies she said all excited. You better be there too!

Hell yeah we got nominations, shit you definitely getting one. Dboog performing at the MTV and BET awards. We nominated for group of the year. So yes Karrin we gonna show up mob deep.

So who's touring with you she asked?

A couple of singers, some south cats, the MOBB, Kiesha, we gonna have fun baby.

Well I'm going on tour with Kelly Clacker, Maria C and T.P. and Led Z. that should be a lot of fun she said. We got legends performing a bunch of varieties. Hopefully Britney be ready as well. Me and her have a collaboration together that's fire said Karrin.

Damn said 2Face we gonna be apart for a long time.

I'll miss you she said.

I'm a miss you too he said. Our secret wedding in Finland is set for my birthday he said. That's where your family from right Karrin?

Yeah she said surprised by what 2Face said. Awe baby! your so sweet! we gonna enjoy today.

Promise me you'll stay on your dean Cory. Start praying more and stop the drinking. We've done a lot of studying a lot of research I might have a surprise for you. I would like to see you change Cory after this tour and our Marriage. Me I'm a drop one more album then I'm done. We'll enjoy our life together baby!

Sounds like a plan said 2Face.

The phone vibrated on 2Face's hip he saw a strange number.

As Salaamu Alaykum baby boy!

Wa Laykum Salaam who this?

Me dummy! said Sharif.

Son where you calling from?

My house said Reef I'm home son! I got acquitted son!

Yes! shouted 2Face he pumped his fist in the air. We coming right there now to get you it was too many reporters for me to stay there.

What happened baby?

Sharif beat trial!

Oh my God that's great baby congradulations!

Thank you baby. He hugged her. We going to crib now son!

Well I'm at ma dukes crib holla!

Yo Mouse snatch Tone and call bud up son we going to Reefs crib son gto acquitted. The nigga won his appeal.

Oh word said Mouse. He was excited. Yo we coming right now son. We'll meet you and go together.

Bet said 2Face.

Reef was sitting on his porch at his moms crib. He was reciting Qu'ran. Reef was serious about changing. He knew Allah let him out to do deeds of right conduct not to run the streets.

His mother came out.

Hey Ummie said Reef where you going?

To pick up Amina, I'll be back.

A black Maybach pulled up with 24 inch chrome rims spinning. The suv pulled up infront of Reef's moms crib. Reef jumped out his spot to see who these cats were. 4 cats jumped out.

A yo what up son! a loud voice said.

A yo Tone you big face bitch you Reef said!

Mouse, Tone, 'n 2Face Salaamed Reef's Ummie. She hadn't seen them in years. She gave Mouse and Bud a dirty look.

Sharif she said let me have a word with you inside.

Hold on ya'll I'll be right back he said.

When they went inside 2Face asked them, Yo son why she looked at yaw like that?

She don't like us said Mouse remember when all the bullshit was going on? Some people don't let shit go son. But I can't blame her one bit.

You better not get yourself involved in no shit boy! Sharif you just got a major blessing from Allah don't do nothing to deserve his wrath.

Ma he said, I'm staying on the dean. I want to find Ramal, he need to chill and get on the strait path. Nobody knows his where abouts maybe they can find him for me.

Look I don't care about their money I know that boy 2Face got you out but you be grateful to Allah first. You done did a lot of time you a grown man just don't do it to your self. And don't look for your brother he got himself in all kinds of bullshit. He dug his own hole, but its your decision. I'm gone.

She walked out and didn't even much look at 2Face 'n them. Reef came back out.

So what up son! you home now baby boy said 2Face. Yo! remember my moms used to say the same thing about yaw. Now you know Reef! Yo, my moms would say you and them boys leave them boys alone. They trouble! niggas was laughing at 2Face cause they remember.

Yo, none of yaw heard from Shorts asked Reef?

Nope they all said. When he came to your first hearing I sent him a text message nobody heard from him since. He probably laying low said 2Face. He'll pop up. Yo Reef we in the hood, I got court tomorrow so these 2 can sign these papers and I can move on. Really its just gina who need to sign them papers. Its Gina who needs to sign the papers cause Aisha or Sue is only a Islamic marriage. You can't be legally married like that in the states. But I agreed to give them $5 mill a piece and she has to give up custody of Amin.

But yo Reef you still into boxing son asked Mouse?

Yeah I still feel I can knock you out he responded as niggas was rolling.

CHAPTER 63

Damn son you got a nice crib home. You living good, that industry life.

Nah, said 2Face but yo remember Karrin? The white girl who used to cheerlead for high school son?

Reef looked puzzled. I'm trying to think son. Little short chick right?

Yeah with the curly brunette hair.

Oh yeah, yeah son I knew she looked familiar that's uh Miss Elizabeth! word said Reef you signed her ass too. Wow! I ain't know that was her.

Yeah son well me and her about to get married cuz.

Get the fuck outta here!

Yeah after our tour we tying the knot.

Yo not for nothing said Tone I think she right for you son! She got a little sense and carry herself respectfully.

Yo, Reef you staying with Mouse, Tone and Bud in the East. Or you want to fuck with ya boy? I got some nice toys to play with remember you like beamers. But just relax and go on this tour with us.

We all going on tour said Bud.

I ain't know yaw wanted to go said 2Face?

Hell yeah I want to taste some of this industry life. I'll be your head of security money said Reef!

No doubt said Bud.

But true story I'm a hang with the Face he put the paper work in to get me out.

Truthfully Allah got you out brother believe that! Tomorrow we gonna set up a account for you and get you some clothes. Tonight its too late. You could stay in the crib, I damn near got a Masjid in there. I got mad literature, you could just chill.

No doubt said Reef.

Good right hand said 2Face to Reef. They was in the ring. 2Face hit him with a sharp combo. Good said Reef.

That's instinct said 2Face, I gotta get back in shape.

Yeah son you mad rusty said Reef as they took their gloves off and head gear.

Yo, tomorrow I got my release party too I'm mad busy tomorrow 2Face said breathing heavy. Son you don't know the drama and hurt I been through ock. Lets go offer Salah.

With Reef in the crib 2Face could concentrate on perfecting his dean. Son I gotta go sign these papers you rolling?

Hell yeah. You spoke with Razzac yet?

He working and chilling said 2Face. Lets get ready.

Gina saw 2Face for the first time in almost a year.

How's my 2 dike doing? Reef was laughing.

Fuck you said Sue!

You know the Prophet (P.B.U.H.) Said if he could throw all the faggots 'n lesbians off a highest cliff he would. You people are a abomination!

Whatever said Gina!

Eh hem! the lawyer stepped in to speak before things got out of hand. Mr. And Mrs. Jackson you both agree to have hearing right?

Yes they both said.

Read over this contract and sign here please. You'll receive a document allowing you to keep the club and receive $5 million and you Ms. Rodriguez agree to sign over custody of your son to Mr. Jackson, in addition you'll receive $5 million. So whatever is exposed in this agreement you all know you'll be prosecuted, the judge said to Sue and Gina.

Once everything was finalized 2Face was overjoyed. Yeah now yaw can go live your lesbian lives said 2Face. Reef was rolling.

Fuck you and ya mascot said Sue!

Hey, hey! Easy now said Reef.

2Face called Karrin. Its over baby girl now we can get married for sure now!

Awe baby she said all sweet on the phone. Baby I'm so happy.

You'll be at my party tomorrow night right Karrin?

Yes of course I will baby you stay out of trouble.

2Face was in Midtown signing autographs with Sharif posted as bodyguard. Mouse and Loud mouthed Tone was hollering at young smuts. Today 2Face releases War Stories his first album.

Son all this pussy around and you not tempted home said Reef?

Nah son I'm having fun right now my nigra. 2Face we love you shouted fans!

2Face pulled out a glad garbage bag and dumped wild money picking it up and tossing it in th air. There were stacks of $20's, $50's and $100's.

All come get some! this is a token of my appreciation to my fans! yaw supported me and The Big East since day one! New York City is you with me!

The young crowd was blitzing trying to get that money. Some were less fortunate than others but they all would never forget this day, as the frenzy continued.

Mouse stepped right to 2Face. Son why you do that for?

Son it's a publicity stunt fool chill!

Son you should've told us before hand so we be on point.

That night Karrin showed up decked out in a Dulce 'n Gabana

dress and top rocking Versaci shades, with her famous Prada shoes. She loved showing her feet cause they were so small and perfectly pedicured. 2Face's album did surprisingly good today selling 250,000 units the first day. She was extremely happy for her fiance. Now she didn't care who saw them together, but 2Face did he didn't want to ruin her fan base any.

Baby I'm so happy for you she kissed him on the lips before he could get out thank you. He saw the camera shot.

Yo pardon me Karrin! Yo! 2Face grabbed the reporter and snatched his camera from him. don't ever take no flicks of me again ya heard!

Sorry said the camera man, after he saw 2Face's entourage behind him.

Diddy Bop and H.O.V. rushed over to Face immediately.

You alright asked Diddy Bop?

I'm good money just keep these camera men away from me!

He work for BET said H.O.V. relax. 2Face loosened his grip.

Can I have my camera back please? 2Face took them film out the camera and gave it back to the camera man. The camera man was tight and walked off.

Diddy Bop crib was laced. He had custom made chandeliers, a giant pool room, a big ass swimming pool with tennis courts and a basketball court. His garage was like a parking lot.

All kinds of celebrities were there, N.A.S., showed his support too! Jr. and his designer was there. Mad singers were there, movie producers and actors and actresses. Diddy Bop really knew how to draw a nice crowd.

Hey Face said H.O.V. your album sold 400,000 so far I just got another tally 10 minutes ago. Yo people like your album, but you gotta show ya face more. You gotta start going public bee! You just do a video or 2 people will see you but they won't know you.

But H.O.V. we got like 10 videos out already bee. I've featured in 2 of them. I got Karrin on 'n 1 got her grammies. What more publicity do I need.

For you to be seen as a public figure.

I've made hundreds of millions off clothes and my restaurants. People don't know that I'm responsible for those great successes. That's why I can walk without security.

Well you on 106 'n park with sexy ass Rocsi and Terrence, handle that well, said H.O.V. Right now its some nice pieces of women up in here. You still with that snow bunny Miss Elizabeth huh? I seen you was getting ready to pop for that just now!

That's cause I ain't want her spot blown. If people see us it'll start controversy.

See if you was a major public figure you wouldn't have to worry about that! they'd want her with someone like you.

Yo, we getting married.

Get the fuck outta here! Homie you dead serious huh? H.O.V. started laughing, you's a funny nigga!

Karrin walked over to them. Cory!

Hey baby what's good! H.O.V. was dying laughing, Oh shit he said you a funny nigga!

Lets sit down said Karrin. There are a lot of nice women in here.

Yeah tell me about it said 2Face.

Listen she said don't feel stuck with me alright. If you want I'll... he cut her off. Listen baby you was always my dream girl since you were in high school. I was a knuckleheaded kid just coming to Bing trying to make it. I always said to my self if I had you I don't need anybody else. These other girls mean nothing to me. Besides they ain't got nothing on Miss Elizabeth he said with a smile. They looking for a way to the top, they need people like me. These hoes is gold diggers. He noticed H.O.V. pointing to him with Mouse and Bud laughing. He tossed him the finger. You all that matters to me Karrin.

Awe that's so sweet. That is the sweetest thing you ever said to me. That's why I love you Cory. I want you inside me right now! his eyes lit up like the Forth of July.

Lets blow this joint said 2Face!

You want to leave your own party?

Fuck it he said. As soon as H.O.V. turned his back they slid off without nobody noticing them except Bud. they head nodded. He alerted sharif he was out by phone when he was gone. Homey vanished at his own party.

They were in his Benz making out passionately. She mounted him and sat on his cock until it was deeply inside her. They rocked the car with her bouncing them thick thighs 'n ass off legs. She was taking every stroke deep too.

Umm, Uh! Uh! Ummmm! Ah! I'm cumming daddy! oh shit! She squeezed his dick mad tight. Then grinded 2Face like a porn star, he pumped her setting those juices to flow again. Ummm! Uh! Aah! AH! Aaaah! daddy im cumming again! she was shaking from having a orgasm. She grinded and bounced off her ass off him a few more stokes before he blasted an enormous load in her screaming aaaaah! he nutted so good even he was shaking. She bent over to kiss him. his dick was still rock hard inside of her.

Chapter 64

2Face was so nervous he was about to do his first stage performance where he was the main attraction. The spotlight was solely on him tonight. He was good cause he had his homies with him. but he wanted to face the world alone tonight. He Dhikred to Allah to help him through this. His new support crutch Karrin had went on her own tour for over seas. She was promoting her second album.

Hold ya head baby bro said Mouse they just announced your name big home and the crowd went nuts!

He came out on 106 'n Park with the mic by his mouth amped screaming at the crowd of youngsters, yaw ready!

He performed "Bow Down To The Face" his hit single. He had Mouse, Bud, Loud Mouth Tone and Reef with him as Hype Men. Biz 'n them ain't show cause they were preparing for the tour.

Yes, yes said Rocsi, 2Face is in the building people! the crowd was still roaring and clapping. Lets go to the number 8 video two of ya own artist. Its been in the top ten for 9 weeks now! Miss Elizabeth in " Lovers Diary" featuring Dboog!

Damn said 2Face to Rocsi that song still on the countdown?

Son that joint sold records said Mouse.

You did good said Tone patting 2Face on the back.

2Face was strait gutter rocking his legendary Champion Hoodie with Construction Timbs, and Blue Viscario Lemonte Jeans. He did however sport a $40,000 rolex and brolic ass Bx chain, with about a thousand diamonds in it. The piece was similar to the one Big Pun had.

After the commercial Terrence introduced him one more time and gave him a pound. 2Face waved to the crowd. Rocsi gave him a big hug as he sat on the famous couch that so many successful artist sat on.

What up fans yelled 2Face! the roars got loud again. Wow this is great thank you he said to everyone.

So said Rocsi your obviously enjoying this moment, how life been treating you?

Shoot life treating me good believe that! Terrence started laughing.

First of all, all praise is due to Allah, first 'n foremost. He allowed me to make it this far and to have the success I've had.

I mean said Terrence you had the audacity to start your own label making underground music and made it mainstream, being that mainstream is predominantly Southern rap or R&B. Like what gave you the idea to bring it back.

To me we was losing hip hop said 2Face. Its like this I used to watch videos like these fans and I'm like its so watered down man. It was only a few cats left holding it down the real pioneers and New York fell off the map badly. Why cause we lost the originality. Artist aren't allowed to be they self. The sad thing is there are some real mc's in these ghettos that if I name em we'll be here all episode and they get no recognition they deserve. Some are vets, some are up 'n comers.

Yeah said Rocsi one specific artist did say hip hop is dead! do you think you can ressurect it?

Well said 2Face we gotta get creative. We gotta stop the beefing on wax and settle it in the booth, like the 90's when cats used to collabo. Dudes used to go they hardest back then. Half these cats would've never made it with these silly ass songs they make up. For example you get a track like " John Blaze" Nas, Kiss, Big Pun, Reakwon The Chef and Fat Joe. These dudes knew they had to come they're hardest. Look at the competition, all great ones. Was they beefing after that? No. So that beefing stuff is whack. The shit is corny. They couldn't bleep out the curse in time.

Yeah said Rocsi everybody beefs 'n bickers.

Right said 2Face that separates the creativity of our music and stops a lot people from getting on too! Like we built hip hop on collabo's and competing on wax in the same song and made money off it. Even when dudes were beefing names never got mentioned, but you knew it was competition. That's how you battle. If you really want to beef and battle on the street they got places and people who promote shit like that like Smack dvd's. Shit we can even put up our wages and battle on Freestyle Friday. If you really want beef see me in the ring or something win lose or draw or just keep it off wax. Its too much money out there for the drama. Other than that we need that NYC gutter stuff back in Hip Hop.

I really like what your doing said Rocsi.

I believe that we gotta do things ourselves to get it right. Even police ourselves. Open up our own businesses so we can run things the way we want to. I love that gutter music. I was raised on the underground. I liked NWA, BDP, Big Daddy Kane, Cool G. Rap, Nas, Big, Jay Z, D- block, Wu- Tang I can keep going on bee Big Pun, Big L. This is music you couldn't get out of nobody ears back then even today, classic hip hop. So why not bring hip hop to its originality. That's how we got to 106 'n Park in the first place, the commercials and what not. Them cats made music from the heart, not some ole dance hall garbage or love songs. I mean its alright but not all day in America, hell no! The only love rappers back then was LL Cool J. even he can get gutter. We been taken out of our own music and our comfort zone. Now you got artist trying to be something they not. They careers are going wood, one hit wonders. The ones who try to keep it hood don't get the recognition so I'm signing cats and producing records so these cats can be themselves and shine, make respectable music for the public ears and I got the money to do it.

Wow said Rocsi that's deep. I respect that. But we must go to our next video 2Face would you like to introduce our next video?

Sure Rocsi! hmm. My very own 2Face "Bow Down To The Face"! The crowd cheered as his next video played.

Ok back to 2Face said Terrence, a very generous 2Face. We heard that you gave away a bag full of money?

Yep help those who help me feel me. For some of you that know, I've organized a system that evaluates correctional officers in order to help protect inmates rights. I'm also working on building more community centers and gyms for after school activities, providing courses for those who can't afford to pay. I'm also trying to buy more property to expand opportunities for us and create more jobs.

Wow said Rocsi, that's wonderful.

But said 2Face I can't do it alone. I need your support people to achieve this and take advantage. I need my big pocket celebrities and stars to support as well. Believe in your boy. We together can clean up our neighborhoods. Shoot I came from nothing to something. I used to watch this behind walls and fences in state greens. I even used to say watch Rocsi sexy ass blow up! Nobody believed me.

Rocsi blushed from that comment it was so visible, Terrence had to laugh it off.

I watched my boy Terrence keep it live in here. He brought humor and personality to 1 Big up to them said 2Face! the crowd went bizzerk.

Thank you 2Face said Rocsi with all smiles. So when does your tour start?

This Saturday in Philly. Its called "Save The Hip Hop Tour".

I'll have Beans 'n Free with me that night. We'll be on the road buggin believe that!

2Face thanks for stopping by and much success to you said Terrence.

Thank you said 2Face.

Lets go to the next video said Rocsi. A world premiere folks!

Oh it's a surprise shouted 2Face! This is called "Pledge Allegiance"! Featuring Me, H.O.V., N.A.S., Kiss, Cool G. and Chips. Oh and last thing crowd be on the look out for The Big East new album, "Hip Hops Rejects"!

Thanks for stopping by said Rocsi.

Any time said 2Face, this music thing is my rec, and for the people. The crowd cheered as they went to the next video. The video was classic material.

CHAPTER 65

Tone was driving a black Expedition with 24 inch rims. They was headed to the Bronx 2Face was riding shotgun. They had to pick up Wood 'n Dboog for the tour.

Ever since 106 'n Park people all over bigged up 2Face. He was being shouted out everywhere. They drove through Kelly to 156 st. they parked across the street from the old P.A.L.

Yo son it all started here and right down the block for me. Now we all famous home.

Son this is what we do son! we did too much not to enjoy success and yo money! yo! you masterminded all this.

Homie said 2Face you know the crazy thing son? Everybody thinks I'm just a Ceo and that's it. Now they don't know that I own a franchise restaurant and clothing line. I built those companies from scratch. I'm getting ready to start my own radio station next.

Word son! Hell yeah said 2Face.

Yo nobody still ain't heard from Shorts yet huh?

Nope said Tone. I hope son still alive 'n shit.

Son probably on the low bee said 2Face.

A yo what up bitch! Tone said to Wood dumb loud so the whole block could hear it.

Ya–O! shout Wood, what up cuz?

What up shouted 2Face! everyone was giving dap and hugs. Dboog jumped out a brand new red Mercedes Benz.

We still got the block on smash bee said Wood.

Wood I know you not still pitching nigga asked 2Face?

Nah bee, we got the barber shop 'n the store front relax fool I ain't stupid.

Yo Boog! You ready for this tour bee?

You know it fam, what's good though?

Chillin, we out now bee. The bus waiting for us as we speak.

It was too late cause the whole block saw the 2 mega stars back in the hood. Little kids 'n teens ran up on them begging for autographs. They was in front of the bodega signing autographs on footballs, t-shirts, baseballs, basketballs, even ripped up paperbags.

Damn, said Boog I forgot to tell you we heros out here now bee! I can't never chill out here with out peace.

Fuck it said 2Face I like making the people feel good and proud. This is probably the best days of some of these kids lives. Last night I chilled up in Sue's last night with Fat J.. Son a alright dude but they was showing me more love than him.   1

Hey ya'll check it out! Yo kids! 2Face screamed. I'm a do something real special right now, just wait here.

Yo Wood lets go to the store. An hour later2Face and Wood came back to the block and bags of clothes and hundred dollar money orders in each bag. The first 20 kids got the bags, everybody else was short. But atleast the kids had something to go home to talk about. It was getting late 2Face signaled to Dboog so they could get out of there.

Yo, we gonna get twisted tonight bee shouted Wood!

Yes sir said Tone crack that bottle fool!

I'll smoke but no booze bee. I gotta stay focused said 2Face.

No booze said Wood! Not the alkie 2Face.

Yo I ain't trying to drink no more bee.

You freestyling nigga! said Wood.

You made that all the way up said Popgun.

That brawd got you all fucked up bee said Wood.

Word pussy whipped! shouted Tone! white bitch got homie gassed up huh? Mouse was rolling!

Is this what yaw gonna do said 2Face? Is this what it is he said laughing? Son I ain't drinking no more.

You a funny nigga bee said Wood. So chronic no more booze?

Son I'm done for now kid.

For now said Bud you'll be back.

Now I know you freestyling bee said D-Black! that bitch got you in the matrix!

Ya—oo! shouted Biz, yaw dudes is crazy.

The next night they was up in Philly chilling with Bean and Free. They was gonna perform at his show tonight. They were the opening to the show. Then the Big East, Dboog and then 2Face himself. That night beans 'n them rocked the house.

When 2Face hit the stage the crowd went bananas!

Philly is you with me! Hell Yeah! they shouted. Him and Tone jumped around the stage. 2Face dropped his hit single and then dropped 2 more tracks. He finished with a sneak preview track off his album "Don't Snitch"! That song put the crowd in a frenzy. after that they were done everybody was satisfied. They went to a hotel party with Bean and Free. A bunch of chicks with fatties.

Reef got weak fuckin with Mouse 'n Tone. They slid off with 4 chicks into 2 separate rooms. One of them was all over Reef, she was redboned too. She took Reef in the closet while Tone was getting topped off by a darkskinned freak. Reef made mad noise knocking things all over the closet. He might of needed the seclusion as he came out with that infamous grin that mad ehim so dangerous.

The next stop was Detroit. They were greeted by M. and

performed after D- Dboogie rocked a couple of his jams and hyped up the crowd with a freestyle. 2Face capped it off with a song called "Motivated To Rap" an a unleashed track.

Detroit had some nice pieces of women out there. The hoes loved 2Face and his entourage. 2Face found a nice red boned and a big booty Spanish girl to his liking, he took them to his jacuzi and gutted both of them out.

Sharif was open now. He was fucking everything moving. Mouse 'n Tone had jokes.

From there they went to Minneapolis, to Seattle, to Portland all the way to Cali. Cali was where 1 its at said Reef.

Son he said to 2Face. Damn my nigga I'm fuckin up Ock.

I know me too home, said 2Face. This tour is crazy. We done ran through so many bad bitches said 2Face, from Detroit, Philly, Portland, Canada, Seattle, Minneapolis and now we in Cali.

Yo I stashed $350, 000 so far off this tour. I should've brought D-Block with us bee!

Oakland is sweet said Tone I'm feeling this. Then we headed to Sacramento, then last stop Hollywood and then the BET awards shouted Tone we living dude!

Yo said Mouse Hollywood is porn city son! Yo! Word to mother son we gonna fuck like rabbits money!

Porn city this shit is porn heaven said Wood!

Yo Dboog we going to a shoot to said 2Face believe that! We gonna be in Cali at least a month fucking.

Yo Biz yaw perform at the BET awards to so I know yaw hype for that asked 2Face?

Hell yeah said Popgun. Damn son look at that ass son!

Mam excuse me mam! chocolate!

Excuse me she said with a strong western accent?

You want to hang back stage with us tonight at Club Sugar's sweety we performing?

Do I look like a groupie to you! she snapped at him.

Damn ma just chill, I just trying to be friendly.

Well I don't do those she shot at Pop.

Yeah you only do dicks shouted Biz Mania! Mouse was rolling.

Reef stepped in chill yaw what's wrong with yaw niggas.

I know he just ain't disrespect me? You motherfucka I'll have ya'll rolled on out here fools!

Ma said Reef.

Don't ma nothing she said.

Mrs. Please we ain't looking for no trouble said Reef. A couple of stragglers rolled up out of no where and saw the harassment saw her beefing and went to her aide.

Mrs. You alright?

Nah the motherfucka disrespect me! Ya'll wanna talk shit motherfuckas!

This bitch tripping home said Reef. Chill shorty let me just talk to you and diffuse the situation please!

Homeboy she don't want to talk to you back off!

Reef caught duke with a mean over hand right dead arm that sent him sprawling into a building window. He was out on his feet.

Mouse fiend the other one out till he was sleep.

Tone bottled one of the other guys with a Arizona Iced Tea bottle.

The 4th kid try to help his man but Reef finished him off with a strait right to the chin, putting him strait out.

Mrs. I told you I ain't want no problems. I apologize for this incident and my boy sweety. Pop, Biz and Val was stomping the third kid out.

2Face came running him 'n Bud. Yo what the fuck is yaw doing! We came all the way out here for this? Yaw fucking stupid! He pulled Pop 'n them off homeboy. Mouse and Tone kept going until Bud grabbed them up Wood and Dboog stood in amazement.

Oh my God 2Face! Dboog! I thought I recognized yaw motherfukas! Yaw The Big East! 1

Miss what happened asked 2Face?

Your boy Biz Mania is very disrespectful.

I apologize for him Miss.

Reef told Biz to apologize to her for his comment.

I'm sorry he said to her. We was only messing with you.

Baby girl said 2Face he signed off a check. Yo here's a thousand dollars please don't blow this up. Then he wrote out $5000 checks to the men that were beat up. He also asked them not blow it up. They agreed and they all had free backstage tickets the concert.

All of this is courtesy of Biz Mania said 2Face. Please come to the concert asked 2Face to chocolate?

I'll think about it she said.

Bring your friends too said 2Face laughing. Sorry for the inconvenience. Shorty walked off, yo lets get up off this corner before somebody else blow us up.

Later that night after the concert Reef was backshotting chocolate. She had ass like the porn star Beauty. All Mouse heard from Reef room was oh, ahh, aah! oooh, szzz! Son that nigga gutting that right said Mouse. My son been on a rampage this tour.

Let him enjoy him self said 2Face the man been locked up almost 10yrs. But true story what up with Ab 'n Ummie? One started laughing.

They chilling said Mouse. Everything, everything son. I was just on the phone with them and my daughter.

Yo you know what porn star I wanna fuck bee said Dboog?

Who asked Wood?

That white bitch Alexis Texas! she thick as a motherfucker bee!

Hey, hey! Easy said 2Face. That's my bitch there home team. I can't front I want to fuck Tiffany Mynx, Gina Lynn and Katja Kassin. Shit I really I could have Lisa Raye or Megan Good, or Christina Millian. Matter of fact said 2Face I'm a make a few calls to put that together. I got a hook up at a porn shoot out here. I'll treat and spend some bread on that so we can wild out he said to Boog. Son we gonna bug out in Hollywood.

CHAPTER 66

Palm trees it is said Reef. Damn son a few months ago I was in 5 Points Correctional Facility, now I'm in Cali living a hood niggas dream, wilding! Son that bitch with the fat ass in Oakland Renee son aw' man!

2Face laughed at his boy so did Dboog. Well said 2Face we going to the Porn studio. And later I got tickets to the Lakers game sitting right next to Jack.

Fuck outta here said Tone! you ain't get no tickets for the homies though.

Yeah fool I never forget my homies. I got us all tickets to the All-Star game bee. That's in a month bee. Trust me I plan things out precisely.

While Reef 'n the homies checked in the Hilton, 2Face and Dboog went on a 2 man trip to Hollywood. They saw the Hollywood sign, then the palm trees and all the signs and studios. They drove a rented BMW through the illuminated streets of Hollywood. They made it to the studio on Sunset Blvd. They parked and got out. 2Face knocked on a back door behind the building.

I think this is the address he said to Boog.

Knock again said Boog. He did a big bald head white guy weighing in at atleast 350 answered. 1 He had tattoes all over his body a scary looking dude.

Who are you guys he said in a deep baritone voice?

Were looking for John and Justin. I'm 2Face and this is Dboog.

Oh shit said the guard all excited! Come in, come in.

Face and Boog looked at eachother grinning. All they heard was Uh, uh, uh, uh! Oooh, ahh! Ah ah, fuck! Shit! Oh, oh oh!

Mad skin smackin said 2Face. They walked right into a Sophie Dee scene. She was getting plowed from the back by Mandingo. She was taking deep plunges into her small tight pussy.

Ok cum said the producer filming the scene. Give it to her all in her face!

Aaah! Mandingo let off as he creamed her face with his gism. Aah, aaah! She sucked the remains of his juices out of him.

Hot damn shouted 2Face! this is crazy cuz he said to Boog.

Hey said John! What's up Face?

How are you said 2Face in response.

Dboog how you, you look different in person I didn't realize you were so big.

A yo! pause said Boog. What do you mean so big?

John looked at him confused. 2Face laughed.

It's a joke said 2Face.

Ok but anyway check it said John. Dboog you' re gonna do a track on one of my cd's and a song for one of my movies?

Yep. Boog replied.

And Mr. Face you've bought the best pussy money can buy. Come this way.

A yo! Dboog caught John again talking reckless.

2Face was led into a room with just a bed and a mirror in it. Hey said John I got 2 out of 3 for you Tiffany Mynx couldn't make it. But the replacement is off the hook.

Who said 2Face?

Hey it's a surprise guy. Trust me she's out of this world hotter than Tif to me. Which one you want first?

The surprise said 2Face.

A redboned beauty walked in the room seductively. She looked Spanish she was wearing a mask, but she had long black hair, perfect toes, nice perky tits and when she turned around she sported a pair of lips on her right cheek. She paraded around him enticing him very sexy, leaning over him taking off her bra and placing it around his chest as she massaged his muscles. Lacey Lipps was in the building.

Dboog wasted no time. He had Alexis Texas bent over throwing her ass back off everyone of his strokes back at him. Dboog gave it to her though she was taking him deep inside her.

Uh! oh! oh! oh! ahh! screamed Alexis Texas.

2Face was laying on the bed Lacey was riding bouncing up 'n down screaming yes! yes daddy! her ass was so soft it bounced like waves all over the place. He squeezed that ass now then he flipped her on her knees and punished her from the back, Uh! Uuh, Ohh! he had her face in the pillow thrusting and guttin the shit out of her as she grunted, urrrg–urgggg!

Sunny Lane walked into the room next with Alexis she immediately kissed all over Boog. Then she kissed Alexis and pushed her away as Boog tried to sit up Sunny pushed him back on the bed and gave him the top of his life.

Alexis sucked all over Sunny's ass and pussy from the back as Sunny creamed her face.

2Face thrusted hard then pulled out and blasted Lacey in her mouth as she sucked him clean. She sucked every bit of cum out of him.

You should of been a porn star the way you fuck she said in low whisper. You big enough with stamina, I would enjoy lots of scenes with you.

But your nights just beginning said a gorgeous blonde walking in the room next, Gina Lynn was so sexy she looked like a Barbie doll. I heard I was your favorite Porn Star she said.

No said a next chick with a accent, I should be his favorite. They both was holding the German one with accent had a slightly bigger butt.

So why don't you compete suggested Lacey. Then you'll know for sure who's the best by who can get him to bust his nut. 2Face gave the Reef grin.

Alexis was sitting on Sunny's face while Dboog had Sunny missionary style. Then the roles reversed when Boog flipped Sunny on her knees as Alexis bent doggystyle so Sunny can eat her out. Boog was having his way with Sunny.

2Face put it right in Katja's ass just as she likes it. He had no mercy on her either his strokes were deep she couldn't even eat out Gina Lynn. Aaah, aaah! Slow, slow she whispered.

2Face had to control himself cause her ass was so soft. Katja came so hard she backed 2Face all the way to the wall. Oooh! she sighed she pressed her ass 'n thighs all over 2Face and creamed his balls with her juices. He pulled out to stop the momentum then put it in her pussy and pounded her from the back, he was having the time of his life. He pulled out and blasted all over the tattoes on her ass and back.

Dboog was wilding on Sunny Lane from the side now, the new angle had her estatic.

Oh, ohh! fuck me daddy! yes!

Alexis Texas was licking his balls at the same time, he barely pulled out but Sunny was a pro at this and spun to catch his hot sperm while Alexis sucked his balls.

Aaah he grunted! he was shaking from a orgasm. He squeezed all in Sunny's mouth.

2Face was fucking Gina Lynn from the back now, she was indeed a Barbie doll in his grasp now. All he thought of was when he used to flip through the pages of Buttman in prison wishing for this day.

She spun around and pushed him to the bed and mounted him, looking him in the eye.

You like this? You like fucking me she said? She bent down not even waiting for a response grabbing his muscular chest and licking his neck bouncing off his dick.

Oh shit! I'm cumming daddy! yes! ooh, ohh! She squeezed his penis so hard he didn't know a pussy could get that tight.

He couldn't hold it no more I'm cumming he screamed! Aaah! she jumped off him and caught the remaining nut swallowing it hole.

Thanks John for the good time. I got a Laker game to catch. He left John a check for $300,0 Those were some of the best fucks of my life John. Wew! John just laughed as 2Face and a speechless Dboog left.

CHAPTER 67

The Grammy's were full of mega stars. All of hip hop best were there, P-Diddy, Dre, Jay-Z, Nas, Alicia Keys, 50, M&M, Britney, Pink, Billy Joel, wild Celebrities there. Evrybody dressed they're best for the red carpet entrance.

2Face had the whole team dressed in his Viscario Lemonte suits, 'n dresses. $10,000 Gators on they're feet, everybody iced out. Reef, Mouse, Tone, Bud, Wood, and the rest of the crew shining. The Big East was rehearsing so was Dboog. Lots of rock stars showed love to 2Face and them.

Damn big Homie I never thought we'd make it like this son! said Reef all star struck. Son keep it real I know you get star struck too he said to 2Face?

2Face just laughed but he knew he was star struck as well. He had mad butter flies in his stomach.

They enjoyed Monique's jokes and some good performances. 2Face sat in the crowd with his entourage while Dboog was getting ready to perform. Wood was with Dboog all the way. D-Black his brother flew on a plane to help his brother out it was a surprise.

Oh shit what up Bro said Dboog when he saw Black.

Yeah I'm in the building bee just relax bro, you got this bee!

Son I ain't never perform at no shit like this in front of all these crackers!

You gonna be good said Wood! the rest of the family here too bee said Black.

Word said Boog and Wood at the same time.

Dboog came out and rocked the crowd with a mixture of songs in a 5 minute performance. 2Face and the entourage were on they're feet when he performed hype. He had the crowd rocking bouncing around the stage yelling and waving.

30 minutes later 2Face and The Big East were gonna do they're performance. Dboog was apart of this too so was Chips.

Dboog, Dboog! Popgun was teasing Boog.

Shit ain't funny nigga yaw next bee!

You gonna be up there right with us fool replied Popgun.

Yeah said Val lose the stage fright you did good just now.

Christine Millian announced the best female performer of the year and Miss Elizabeth won. 2Face was surprised but he had to make a victory speech for her in her behalf. So he amde his way to the stage with the entourage.

Ehem! Miss Elizabeth could not be here tonight unfortunately. But she is currently touring over seas she did leave this message she gave me if she won.

He pulled out a piece of paper. Thank you god, thank you fans, you supported me from day one this wouldn't be possible without you. Thank you 2Face and Many Face records for not giving up on me and helping me achieve this living dream, thank you all the artist that I 've worked with. I accept this award for you fans!

The crowd applauded. If Puff believe in you, you good money said 2Face before he left the stage.

The Big East performed "We Gone Eat" then out of now where the stage got full of Celebrity rappers when the beat dropped for "B-B Boroughs". The crowd stood up especially the New York artist. The whole crowd was hype Loud Mouth Tone was one of the illest hype man ever. He jumped around the stage with each performer's verse. The NYC part of hip hop was ignited again. Nobody knew how to get a crowd hype like New York City.

15 minutes later Megan Good announced the best group of the year and it was with no surprise The Big East. They came up on stage mob deep. 2Face stood in the back. He went from dress suit to jeans 'n hoodies.

Biz the spokes man spoke on the mic. We dedicate this to the ghetto! Thank you God for blessing us with this talent. We thank 2Face for masterminding all this and giving us opportunity.

Brooklyn shouted Tone!

The East, yelled Pop and Mouse!

We ain't forget our homies in the pens either, you fans for your support, hold it down baby! thank you people.

Next Bboog got the best lyricist award. Miss Elizabeth she won 2 more awards for collabo's and best single of the year.

2Face saw the market of his label rise with each award. They celebrated with a party full of call girls for The Big East. Boog and 2Face were drained from the experience earlier. But those wee some of the most exotic girls on Earth.

L.A. was wild and a great experience nobody wanted to leave, but the show must go on to Phoenix, Vegas, Houston, New Orleans, Atl, to Florida and back to hood for Summer Jam.

Son I can't fuck with all these awards son 2Face said to Bud. You got the Soul Train, Vibe, MTV, and Source Awards. Karrin will be back for maybe 2 of them and they'll probably want her to perform as well. I'll send The Big East to represent us fuck it.

And you got a wedding to attend son said Reef.

Yep we'll be on the first thing smoking you fisher price in the face ass nigga! Tone was rolling at the insult to Reef from 2Face.

You Grape Ape in the face ass nigga yelled Tone!

They was up in 2Face's Mansion in Jersey cracking jokes when a hard knock like banging came from the door.

A yo! who the fuck is that he screamed at the door! boom, boom, boom,.

It's the FBI!

The FBI! 2Face said puzzled. What the fuck they want with me?

We're Agent Gibson and Special Agent Moss. We'd like to speak with you about Jamal Abdullah.

What about him asked 2Face?

We need to know his whereabouts said Agent Moss.

Damn Agents I don't know what to tell you. I just got back from a long tour I've been relaxing.

Sir your in no trouble we would like to ask you a few questions?

I don't talk to police! I don't know shit about Jamal Abdullah or his whereabouts and that's the truth! But tell you what I'll contact my Attorney and he'll talk to you and straiten this all out believe that! any other questions.

Thank you for your cooperation said Moss. Say do you happen to know his brothers whereabouts?

I'm right here shouted Reef!

This is even better. We would like to speak with you Abdullah.

2Face never opened the door. No! yelled Reef.

Mr. Abdullah do you know that your brother killed a Binghamton Police Officer last night. He'll be shot on sight if we don't find him or turn himself in.

I haven't seen him since my case was overturned. Matter of fact none of have saw or heard from him in a very long time.

Thank you for being somewhat cooperative said Gibson.

Officer you said he killed an officer in Binghamton last night.

Yes a officer named Mcgruff.

Wow! sighed Reef.

He's also wanted in connection with 4 other shootings and 5posible shootings in North Carolina 5 years ago. we want him for drug racketeering which will land him with life in prison.

Your best bet is to call us if you see him or tell him to turn himself in.

Thank you for your information Agents said Reef.

I'm not never opening the door for them pigs. 2Face looked worried he made Ahm vanish so there was no link to N.C., but Shorts had got bagged there. All they had to do was match his face to other photos in the precinct sown there. He also thought to himself how the fuck he let himself get all jammed up like this.

Son ya brother is crazy! That's why I cut him off. If I'd of let him stay around niggas while he was still in the grind for nothing he'd get all locked up with his fucked up way of doing things.

2Face had Roc stop by and check his entire place for bugging and electric monitoring.

Yo Roc you ain't tell me that man did that?

Son I ain't know it was him son. But somebody ratted him out home.

Can't fool you stupid! said 2Face. We gotta find him and get him out of the country. If we don't find him first the pigs gonna kill him or finish him for sure.

Son you got a wedding to attend said Roc.

My niggas come first.

But son said Reef! the man is my brother but he put himself out there for that. He caused his own demise. Don't jam yourself up over another man's mistakes. Now if we can help him then we'll do that but if not fall back and do what you been doing. You cut him off for a reason to distance yourself from exactly what he doing now. Atleast he realize to keep away and let you live without involving you. Son know what he doing.

CHAPTER 68

2Face his Moms, Grandma, Pops, his homies, aunts and uncles rode private planes to Finland. Karrin had her family already there. Finland was beautiful decked out with wild green mountains.

Damn homie this is dream land said Bud. we came from nothing to a fortune in less than five years.

Son we living life's dream son word to mother son said Tone.

Cory this is beautiful, give your mother a hug! Hmmm! I'm so proud of you. I appreciate this said Ethel to Cory. To get away for a while. The whole hood ask about you all day long.

Yo, yo Ethel you got this boy started young said Rick his uncle.

Yeah Ethel you started me! Running around with you as a kid cursing I picked up quick. You too Momma. All those house parties you used to throw. We got a lot of memories.

A nervous Karrin sat in her room. Ma I can't believe I'm doing this.

Do you love him asked her mother?

Yes!

Well then you have my support. I think he's a nice guy. He

made you a star. He kept it real with you is how they say. He believed in you. Look at you your so beautiful.

Momma its not about money or none of that, it's the fact that I know he's got a darkside to him and I'm afraid of it I don't want to lose him cause he does things I don't like. I'm more scared for 1 him than anything. I know he'll protect me and I know he wouldn't hurt me but anybody else I can't speak for.

Well atleast he ain't no punk said her Mom. I'd rather have a guy who would look after you with his life than a guy who will let you down or let some one harm you. I think you should continue to be his crutch and advise him wisely toward right.

Ok Ma.

The reception was set, the Imam was ready, the women were crying when they saw Karrin in her white Georgio Armani dress. She was stunning in her dress.

2Face hadn't seen her in almost 6 months. Even he almost cried. She looked so innocent and so damn gorgeous, better than any chick he'd ever been with.

As they looked in each others eyes for the first time in a long time. The connection was there. The ceremony was quick and they partied, singing and dancing from stars on the low that were there, like Bon Jovi, Johnny Gill and Cheryl Crow. The rice throwing and Karrin finally got to meet 2Face's family and he met hers. His Mom and her Mom clicked from the rip so did Karrin and his Mom. 2Face and Karrin were lead off by limo to the airport strait to France.

Baby I missed you so much, I love you to death she said.

I love you to he responded.

I needed this vacation badly to spend it with the man I love she snuggled under his arms.

They stayed in France for a month he took Reefs advice and didn't contact anybody. He just enjoyed the beautiful moment. When they got back to New York she informed him that this was her last album.

Baby I'm done Karrin said.

Done! You sure baby?

Yeah she said. I want to have a family and raise kids. I mean we both have everything we need. We have each other, money, family and friends.

I'm saying you right. I always used to say if you got hundreds of millions what more do you need. Why still chase the money. But its like a rush baby

Baby that's greed she said. I also want you on top of four dean again too. You've been slipping without me haven't you? You do a lot of things against your religion you shouldn't be. But with your status who can blame you.

I do need to slow down.

Yeah baby we can sit back collect royalty checks 'n stuff, give back to the community and help people. Isn't that what you wanted?

Yeah he said.

Ok so think about it sweety she said. I'm jetlagged.

Let me carry you up the stairs.

Ooh I get to feel those strong muscles. Baby she said one day real soon I'll surprise you. Just wait 'n see.

CHAPTER 69

Shorts hid out in Elmira with one of 2Face's distant cousins Petey. He used Petey to get money and shelter. He took a page from 2Face's chapter and layed low and spent no money. He tried to let other people be the leader. He thought who gives a fuck as long as your pockets is right. You 'n your workers know who is really boss. 1

Shorts wanted to see his brother. He saw him in videos and at the awards, he saw 2Face and his boys having the time of they're lives. He wish he could be there with them balling but he didn't think they would make it. It took everything he had not to contact them, if he did now he would jeopardize their careers. He understood the choice he made when he chose to stay in the street, but the paper chase was too calling. He had Petey contact Sharif and Sharif contacted Petey when he was there in Elmira.

Yo, fam I'm here in Petey town, said Sharif.

Yo, I got the call from your bro just now he said he in town Shorts.

Send him over said Shorts.

Yo, said Petey come to 357 Main St. apt. 2.

Alright bet said Reef I'll be there.

The FEDS had the call recorded. They been on to Petey for 6 months. They wanted to wait till they were for sure he was coming to see Shorts.

Hey Moss said one of the agents. Were getting the warrant signed now. Should we go in now?

We actually heard Petey say Shorts as he was trying to muff the receiver. I think we got for sure this time the fucker has ben alluding us for the longest.

We can't fuck this up said Moss. I wonder can we tie 2Face into any of this? Maybe we can tie Sharif in too!

No sir said a white female agent. She had blonde hair and the FBI field jacket on. 2Face hasn't contacted Sharif so we don't know if he knows anything about this. He hasn't spoken a word to Shorts in years. And according to the phone calls Sharif doesn't know who wants to see him.

He may have an idea.

Yes but is it a crime we can charge him with for being around a fugitive you didn't know was gonna be at a place you've never been? I think sir we should see what happens.

Yo son what up said Roc to 2Face? Yo ya man going down today!

How you know son asked 2Face?

Where's ya boy Reef at?

I can't call it why?

He in the EL with your cuz Petey and Shorts been on the low out there for 6 months. They got your phones tapped in the crib in case one of them contact you so they can tie you into this bee. Petey told Reef that someone wanted to see him badly in Elmira.

And this motherfucka went huh?

Yep said Roc.

Call his dumb ass and tell him to fall back now bee!

Got you home.

Reef talked to Roc and got up outta dodge immediately. Roc told him it was a set up. Having Roc on the inside was a key to the success they al got now. Roc blended in well and moved like Batman. 2Face called him the David Copperfield of the street.

Shorts sensed something wrong the minute Reef didn't show up on time.

Yo where the fuck is your brother at son asked Petey.

I don't know son been out here with that white bitch before. He love that bitch! he probably think she called for him. I know he know the town the bitch took him through the whole shit.

Shorts looked out the window and saw 2 FBI agents in they're field jackets swarming around the perimeter. They blitzed toward the building. He backed out 2 4,4 magnums. 1

Son you set me up you coward ass nigga! that's why Face don't fuck with you!

Petey looked confused, set you up! You calling me a rat fams? Me and my cuz had a fall out that's why I don't fuck with him.

So why the FEDS swarming the building said Shorts? You the only nigga who knows I'm here! the 4,4 blast echoed through as he shot Petey in the chest. The shock on his face said it all as he tried to muster out his last words.

2 officers heard the blast, Shorts heard the microphones.

Come out with your hands up! was a loud call from the bullhorn.

Fuck you cowards! You fucking pigs! he shot the 4,4 out the window and it barely missed one of the cops.

As the FEDS swarmed the building Shorts made moves himself. He headed to the roof and climbed down the fire escape. The FEDS were back there too and they shot at Shorts as he tried to get down twice. He fired back echoing, boom! boom! the loud echo of the 4, 4 was deafening. He continued to climb down using the steps as a shield.

There was a sniper set up but he couldn't get good position. Shorts shot one of the agents in the head and when one of his partners turned to check the agents status Shorts vanished from his sights.

Shit! yelled one of the agents. Toms down! get a ambulance now!

Shorts made his way to a fence with vines all over it as pedestrians got far away from scene as possible as directed by police and agents. Behind the fence was a parking lot on Main St. if he could get to the side block he was good he thought to himself, he ha da getaway car parked hust incase over there.

A few bullets whizzed by his head, but he kept low. La Ilaha Illalah Wa Ashadu Anla Mohammadan Rasullulah! he said to himself. Shorts was hoping those words would save his life from the fire. He spun and fired ducking behind a car. He hit four shots and hit 2 more officers.

Ah shit! shit! yelled one of the officers. This fucka hit Gino.

Almost home Shorts said to himself. His lights suddenly went out. The pain was almost non-existent in his head as he fell strait to the gravel. The loud echo was the last thing he heard as blood spurred everywhere. Shorts run was over as officers walked over him and came from out of the alleys.

You thought you were gonna get away bitch! the officer walked off into the alley and vanished.

Hey Moss the suspect is down! yelled one of the officers at the immediate scene. I repeat suspect is down!

After things settled agent Moss wanted to know which officer took the shot.

So who took the lucky shot to stop this cop killing bastard? They all looked confused.

Sir we thought a sniper took him out said one of the field agents?

My snipers say they couldn't get a clean shot through the trees so he held fire.

Sharif banged the cell phone off the dash board as tears formed in his eyes.

2Face sat in silence when Roc told him the news. A tear rolled down his eyes as he made Dua for Shorts asking Allah for forgiveness to spare his soul.

What's wrong baby asked Karrin? I never seen you cry. What happened?

They killed my boy! 2Face sniffled. Shot my son right in the back of the head. I should've never started this shit!

Started what baby asked Karrin? Look I know you were just as murderous as he was I can see it in your eyes, you changed and got smart. I mean you were always smart but I mean you wised up and become a better man. He made a choice to keep running the street and killing, you did the right thing. I know that was your boy, your heart but don't beat yourself up over his mistakes.

I'll pay for the Janazal (funeral). I'm so close to his family, Mouse, Tone's family. They know mines too. I grew up with my crew since we was 12 yrs old. I damn near lived in Mouse crib. Me and my Moms didn't always get along, so I lived in the streets. That's why I was the way I was when you met me. Fucking with them is how I'm today. I gotta face his family now.

Well said Karrin you need to re-create your friendship with God and keep it. Pray to him baby. You can even dedicate a song to this. She hugged him tight. He smiled.

You my inspiration Karrin, you don't know how much you mean to me.

Awwe! she said. Wait till Paparazzi knows of us. But like I said this is my last album. Cheer up I'll make you a snack.

CHAPTER 70

The Janazal was deep. Shorts whole family was there from all over. He had 18 sisters and his 3 brothers. Rza his brother wasn't all that sad surprisingly. 2Face hadn't seen Rza in years either. When the family washed the body the whole crew was together for the first time in years minus Shorts. Reef and Rza's Pops was there he wasn't all that sad either. Shorts Ummie was crying her eyes out. The Big East was there too shedding tears. Tone was teary eyed, Jubbs, Mouse, Bud and Danger, George Jubbs and Dangers brother was there, so was Tone's older brother Simeon. The girls showed up to pay their respects, they brought flowers to show support. Lashay was extremely teary eyed 2Face was even surprised. Shorts baby Moms was there with his young daughter. 2Face and Karrin stood side by side watching with Karrin holding on to him with no regards for cameras.

After the Janazal prayer a few words were said and Reef's Pops ha da few words that he wanted to get off his chest. He admonished the brothers something fierce.

All praise is due to Allah he said with his opening to the Khutbah he getting ready to give, as he proceeded: Brothers, brothers! Another one of our youth fallen! was he fallen for the cause of Allah or for the dunia? We as Muslims forget we here on Earth to serve Allah and worship him. part of our worship is to obey Allah and his Messenger. Doing acts of charity, kindness, defending good and right conduct opposing evil and fighting evil. You know its kinda hard to do that when you are evil. Allah is the best of all planners. There's no excuse brothers. Allah and mankind already made the covenant before the creation of Adam, why you think all of humanity is born pure. We stray from that by the things we're taught growing up by our parents and our surroundings. But Inshallah we get it back. Some take Shahada, some don't. Your actions and deeds are the cause of your own demise. Allah will guide you according to your deeds and intentions. We need to straighten up brothers 'n sisters! So much of our youth end up like this its got to stop! We as Muslims should take a stand! and if we can't make a stand here then Allah has made the Earth spacious for us and a dwelling place! we have no excuse our women shouldn't be whores degrading themselves! Our kids shouldn't grow up worshipping man and his creation and becoming unshameful of how they earn they're money! the power of a dollar is crazy brothers! we selfish! chasing illusions! these wordy things can't enter the grave with us! you enter the grave with good deeds or bad deeds! we should respect one another and we shouldn't live in fear or have hatred or far fetched dreams. Those whom Allah has blessed should give to the poor. Help those without and stop being selfish and maybe we can avoid other young brothers to turn this route!

Damn that was deep son said Rza aka Razzac to 2Face. As Salaamu Alaikum rich guy!

Wa Laykum Salaam. Sorry about your brother.

Hey he got what his hand called for said Razzac.

Yeah I heard it was some funny shit in his shooting too. I got lawyers on that now bee.

You should let that go and don't involve yourself and jeopardize your career with this mess.

Shorts was always crazy and bloodthirsty. He told me he was a bad man and wasn't gonna change.

I know said 2Face but when it comes to family and my street fam I got to get in it. But I need you to talk to your Pops I got some major plans if he is serious about making a stand.

Alright bet said Razzac.

Pardon me Razzac, Yo Biz! come here son! yo let me talk to you!

Yo what up!

I'm a drop a solo track called "Stories Untold" and we gonna drop the video "Lost Boys" fro the single, dedicated to all the deceased crew, Box, O, Shorts and Uthie.

Good idea home said Biz.

Get the studio tonight said 2Face.

Got ya replied Biz.

2Face had another funeral to go to Petey he apologized to the family and to his oldest cuousin Jerry who was Petey's Moms. He saw family he hadn't seen in years.

After the second funeral and recording tracks with The Big East and Karrin he had a long night him and Karrin had coffee on 42 street and 6ᵗʰ ave. when Paparazzi showed up and started flicking them up together. One of 'em yelled: rumor has you two are marred! 2Face and karrin laughed.

Baby this is the first time I seen you smile in days said Karrin. I can't keep our marriage in secret like this too much longer.

Ok lets get up outta here said 2Face. We doing this secret thing for your album sales. We know we love eachother fuck the press.

Jay-Z and Beyonce went public!

They ain't a mixed couple and she don't got hillbillies listening to her music like you.

What do you mean she got fans all over the world! yelled karrin. Ok so what about Seal and Mrs. Klum?

He not a thug or proclaimed animal the cops hate!

Fuck the cops and fuck my album she snapped! I wanna express my love for my husband when I feel like it!

Can you just have patients please!

They jumped in his Jaguar and drove to the Bronx weaving in 'n out of traffic away from any Paparazzi. They made it to his old neighborhood and hung around with Wood for a while.

You'd never been to the Bronx before huh Karrin?

No.

Well this used to be my home said 2Face. They left Wood and drove through The Bronx and stopped at all his old neighborhoods. She was amazed at how many people he knew personally in each hood.

Wow! I know it was rough growing up here?

Yep.

My poppa moved to Brooklyn when my mother and him eloped from Finland to the states. They stayed and made enough money to buy them a house, so they searched the states looking for a good community and sought Binghamton as the most suitable, then they had me, my sister and stupid brother. My father always wanted the best for me and protected me from bad guys like you she laughed. Then he got sick from cancer.

Sorry to hear that he said to her as they drove across the Brooklyn Bridge. When they got to   Alabama Ave. 'n Lavonia, he didn't see Popgun or the rest of the homies out there. He saw Lil Romeo chilling up the block.

Yo son come here! Let me talk to you shouted 2Face!

Oh shit yelled Romeo 2Face!

Shhh! keep it on the low said 2Face rolling down the window. And why you out here looking like you bout to do a juxx?

Shit rough he said walking to the car. This the hood not Hollywood my nigra.

Shit could be a lot worse duke said 2Face. Why the peoples ain't put you on bee?

Cause Biz said I'm a fuck up! I don't bring nothing to the table.

I'm saying what he want you to do?

Help with shows, pass out flyers, clean shit up, etc.

And you can't do that? What's wrong with that bee.

Not for no table scraps. I want big dollars too! I want to drive a Lexus. I can't do that with no gee a week.

Lil homie niggas would kill for a gee a week. What are crazy or something? And check it right the shit we got we earned that on the street, put that work in you seen us. Then we put that hard work in with this music. So don't think money is handed to us free. You got to earn it bee. See what he meant to tell you was your mind ain't right yet. 2Face got out of the car. When you get your mind right call me. I'll help you feel me. We chase the material things in life ruthlessly. Too bad you can't ask Shorts, Box, and many others who chased the glory if they cars, jewels and other things came with them in the grave. Get your inner self together so when you get it you do what's right with it. Yo, here's a check 2Face pulled out a check book and signed a check. Son this is a check for a gee.

Yo mad little niggas is coming home said Romeo.

2Face! 2Face! 2Face! can I have your autograph, yelled one lil Black kid?

I got something for yaw! he wrote another check. He counted ten kids. A couple of Spanish and West Indians and a couple of black kids.

Yo Rome! when you cash the check I gave you make sure you cash this one too. Its $2000 make sure each one of these kids get $200 a piece.

Now yaw know Lil Romeo right?

Yeah they all said.

Tomorrow when yaw get out of school Romeo gonna meet yaw here and he gonna be here till 3:45 pm waiting for you. He gave Romeo the pen copy they're names son. Make sure they go to school and meet you here. Hey kids don't go to school and act crazy. Go to school to learn and be good kids. We will be checking. 1

He turned to Romeo, that's your job, you just earned that gee. But nothing is free. What they might learn in school tomorrow can help them in they future. Instead of running the streets learning how to get shot or shot for no cause.

What do you guys say he said to the kids.

Thank you 2Face!

Oh Romeo if you ever cross me or the street fam the crime is and could be punishable by death understood?

I got you said Romeo. I'll do exactly what you say.

Good.

Hey 2Face thank you!

You welcome replied 2Face.

You got a good heart said Karrin as he got back in the car.

I had to get outta there before everybody starts coming out. I'm surprised that they ain't recognized you.

Lets go to a park asked Karrin?

I must offer Salah inside a Masjid. They went to famous Masjid Taqwa. Imam Miraji was present. They immediately recognized 2Face. Salaams went around the board as the Muslims greeted each other. 2Face's surprise was to see Razzac and his pops there.

Brother Abdullah said 2Face. Yaw alright?

Yes brother replied Reef and Razzac's pops.

He had left Karrin in the car. She was just chilling.

You had wanted to talk to me about doing some things in the community?

Let offer Salah first then we'll talk.

After he prayed they formed a Tasleem circle and sat amongst each other.

Miraji opened up the discussion with Dua, supplication.

So this brother gave you Shahada? He pointed to Abdullah.

Yes I grew up around them said 2Face.

A brother had came in and told 2Face that he had left Miss Elizabeth in the car.

Thank you brother replied 2Face. I didn't expect to stay long.

Well I won't hold up too long. If she is properly dressed she can sit with the women in the other room. Truthfully you shouldn't be riding around alone with her Ock said Miraji.

That's his wife replied Razzac.

Oh get outta here Miraji said shocked!

Yeah we've been married like 6 months.

I sent a sister to invite her in while you brothers have your discussion said one of the security of the Masjid.

Thank you said Miraji. Miraji was aging but still had the fire and determination. The drive in him to carry a movement. 2 celebs in our Masjid wow!

2Face was reciting the opening to the Khutbah Miraji was surprised at how well the brother was reciting. Plus 2Face had it memorized.

I was an Amir up north said 2Face. I used to study a lot up top. You know we got nothing but time up there.

That's good replied Miraji but we must put our study to use in the real world.

Ok said 2Face from my studies if we want to change our communities become more self based 1   opening up our own businesses and providing opportunity we gotta change the economy. But we must first change the out look of ourselves. Then we need to change the outlook of our people as well. We must give hope and create trust. Sometimes you gotta think like your enemy. Study your enemy! For us to gain respect you first gotta earn it. People respect violence. You gotta use violence to prevent it. That's how you gain respect. We get the respect we get the trust. But we don't want people to feel afraid we want them to feel safe and to turn to the Muslims for help. We want people to believe in us. We gotta fix our own communities first. We as Muslims are the best example to mankind. Allah gave us the book, the guidance of Prophet Mohammed (p.b.u.h.) And once we attain the knowledge we turn it into Hikma (wisdom). Now to make this work its gonna take more than us, we need each other. We need the leaders of the majors cities involved.

We can show these crackers we ain't monsters or terrorist. I also have ideas to form a Muslim government in Africa. Miraji and Abdullah I'll need your assistance in these tasks. We need some connections to some outside help from different countries. We need the help of those who ain't scared of the U.S. we keep our selves secret. Our reward comes from Allah remember that. This plan is gonna take our lives and dedication. Lives are gonna be lost at any given time but this for the cause of Allah. Brothers lose they're lives everyday over seas while we sit and talk. These people rape us of our way of life, they put their hands in all kinds of affairs they got no business in. Lets throw a monkey wrench in their program. Believe in me we can do this. It takes patients and time you ever heard of Willy Lynch Razzac?

No he answered.

Well he had a theory I suggest you read it son its deep. Look at all the ancient civilizations. Slaves built these empires, while the rich got the credit. We built this country and they disrespect us, but we disrespect our selves. Look how we live and view eachother. This ain't a black 'n white thing no more it's a less fortunate and fortunate thing. The powerful vs the less powerful. So lets give hope to the people and spread the fruits of Islam.

That little speech opened the eyes of the brothers. He told them also don't worry about the money. He had ideas on raising plenty of money. Once he gained the trust of certain people and the loyalty his financial issue wouldn't be a problem. They all agreed and also knew any resistance would get dealt with violently. But he didn't want people to fear them he wanted the enemies to, and respect them. He broke out.

Karrin 2Face said driving back to his house in Jersey across the G-dubb. I'm a show you how if we stick together how much change will come about. I also want to show you how drugs effect our communities and economy.

How she asked?

Don't be naive! Think!

I do think she yelled! 2Face laughed.

Baby I want to tell you something I hope you don't get mad.

Get mad at what sweety.

Your gonna be upset if I tell you that I know you robbed that bank, and I know you had an operation going on. I know that girl Shantell worked for you.

He was rolling now driving. You serious!

Yes this isn't funny!

What the fuck are you a FED? I knew it was to good to be true. So you gonna arrest me?

I'm no fucking FED! If I was a FED you'd of been locked up! 1

So how the fuck do you know then?

I went to school for Pyscology remember! One thing I was taught was body language, I watch your expressions, your eyes. How do you think I see death in your eyes?

So what now?

I love you baby it changes nothing she said if it did I wouldn't have married you baby. I just couldn't hold it in no more.

Do you trust me asked Karrin?

Yeah I trust you, just don't cross me.

I'm loyal to you baby, she said. I got another surprise for you, after I drop my next album I'll show you. You'll be so relieved when this happens and you'll be wild happy. You'll see. This is something I want to do from the heart. That's why I want to wait till I'm out of the lime light.

CHAPTER 71

Miraji got the head of all Imams in each major city in the US to agree to a private meeting. Abdullah went over seas to handle and organize project escape.

2Face organized a meeting with certain people who donated to charities and those other folks who want to help. He had some of hip hops legends as well with their support. He brought N.A.S., Puff, H.O.V., Russ, Kiss, Run, Billy G. Oprah couldn't attend. He had the support of many actors and actresses. He was donating money himself some big bucks. He wanted to fuck with Bill Gates, but he had his own charity funds. Maybe some where down the line they would link up. He was about to give a speech. He had a auditorium full of celebrities chilling, eating refreshments and getting entertained by comedians Saturday Night Lives crew.

He stepped up to the podium mad nervous he had never spoken to this many important people in his life. But this was needed to gain the trust of Americans.

Ladies 'n gentlemen! ehem! Ladies 'n gentlemen! we are here today because we want to help an ailing economy, we want to set the example for the people that support us in our success in life. while this country goes through the trials 'n tribulations, we are living extravagant lives am I correct? We need to stand up for the same people who buy our music, watch our programs, go to the movies to see they're favorite actors, debate about who's the best Pac, Nas, 'n Big! pay they're hard earned money to see they're idols in sports and while this county is in need of our help we need to atleast show some type of support and give back. We need to make our communities safe from crime as 2Face looked to hip hop artist while making that statement.

The auditorium was packed as he had the attention of the people. Most of the people were dressed down and looked bummy to disguise themselves from attention as they met up in the Bronx, Bx Community College.

We need to police ourselves, instead of always sending people to jail, lets help people and give them a chance. Instead of calling the cops lets stand together. We can avoid the drama if open up more community centers for kids to keep them off the streets. We can open up more gyms and fields and give these kids more chances of success. In he future we'll have more athletes and keep the great sports going on and keep producing the great actresses and actors. Look at boxing for instance the talent level is at its low cause most of the talent is in jail or on street corners. Baseball too lacks the black athlete. But we not here to talk about that, that's just part of the solution, but the Rucker did produce a lot talent and gave our people hope. We can help our youth achieve a better education and make it fun and rewarding we want our children to be the 1 smartest in the world, right now our education level is down. The youth is our future we should interact with it. This can happen people with your help and support. I have the backing of other charities as well we need to help our government fix this economy. There are lots of charities with money ready to pitch in. We can build new parks, 'n stadiums, we can build playgrounds, buy land and build malls, create more stores, and eventually more jobs to help the people. Everybody will benefit. We can open up new gas stations, I was even thinking of building new colleges to expand the opportunities of the less fortunate. We'll push the drug dealers out of the streets we walk on and make our streets safe. We'll open up rehab centers for drug abusers, get these people help. But my biggest concern is pushing the drugs out the neighborhoods if there are no drugs people can't get high. If we get these people help when they return to their streets the craving to get high won't be as great cause its not in their face, makes sense? The more we put our little donations in the more money we'll get to help fix our country. We as Americans must stick together. Ladies 'n gentlemen we need to gain the trust of our government and the people. This is serious what I'm trying to do. I don't care if your white, black, green, or whatever if a person needs help the people of fortune should be there! events like Hurricane Katrina should never effect us the way it did. We should never just look for our government to bail us out. Why blame the President when its millions of millionaires in our country. We got hundreds of billionaires, it should be no reason for poverty in our country! Not the land of opportunity.

CHAPTER 72

Abdullah contacted his son Razzac. Tell Abdul that we got that and it will be there shortly. Shortly was coded for 2 weeks. 2Face had wanted help from overseas so he sent for their best military trainers so that he could first build his army up for what he was about to do. He had already had the support of several Vets and Military officials. He needed their experience from Pakistan, Turkey, Iran, Beruit and Iraq. Men would be stationed all over nothing could interfere with his project. He would be able to pay more for the troops once he got the trust of the investors. But truthfully the brothers he had working for him couldn't ask for more their reward was paradise. No suicide bombing though if things get hectic, he didn't believe in that. He opposed that cause Muslims don't believe in suicide. Innocent people shouldn't die.

After 2Face dropped his speech he ended up with 231 signatures to join his trust fund. A lot of others said they'd think about it. He gained $11 billion in charity. Eventually i twould become a tax free write off once Red Cross n' Blue Shields got involved. Some celebs wanted to forward what they had in charity already into the 2Face Trust Fund.

Roc called 2Face while he was in the studio.

Yo, said Roc you ain't gonna believe this but I know the pig you after! you'll find a letter in the garbage holla.

2Face quietly stepped off, he went to a specific dressing room, looked to the right of him and found a garbage can. There was a letter pertruding from the garbage bag. He opened it and after he turned on a light he read the letter. It read: Baby boy Martino held a vendetta for the homie popping his partner. Its more, the police and the Mayor trying to cover it up. None of the pigs shell casings match the bullets that hit Son! nor the gun that was used. They did however match Martino's with it. They knew he did it but they feeling sympathy so they covering it up. Also so they don't make the Bureau and the cops look bad.

There was nothing else to talk about. 3 days later him 'n Reef creeped out to Bing. they staked 1 out Martino's crib. He was on the field till 1 am. With Reefs pops the weaponsry master noise wasn't a problem. They borrowed a couple of his guns for this mission, he was gonna use karrin as they're alibi. The key was mad time had passed and Martino had lots of enemies out there. Lots of people wanted him dead. Then if they unveil his plot and the cover up a lot of people are going to jail. They would expose the Binghamton Police and FBI.

Son said 2Face we walk to him no talking and pop him you do the rest alright. They were in a black Galant, nobody noticed the car.

When Martino pulled he noticed the Galant. He figured some one would come fro his head soon. He got out and walked to the black Galant but nobody was in there. The block was type quiet 1 in the morning.

2Face hit Martino in the voice box with the silencer knocking the breath right out of a stunned Martino, he couldn't scream if he wanted to. He fell to the ground he was on one knee Reef came with the long machete in one motion severing Martino's head clean off his shoulders. Blood splurted everywhere as his head bounced off the ground like a dead basketball. Reef Picked up the head looking at him in disbelief. He threw the head in a bag and jumped in the car.

They tapped home wrecker on his forehead and dropped it off right infront of the Bing Police station.

Aa–aaah! Yelled a police secretary who discovered the bag with Martino's head in it. Police and pedestrians were in a frenzy. nobody knew what happened or who did this. Sirens were everywhere! the news crews arrived immediately every one of them trying to get the big story first, so they could be credited for breaking news. The field anchors hounded the stunned Mayor as he arrived on the scene. Crying police men and women watched in horror. Cnn was on it asap they had received word through a source and it made Headline News.

Mayor can you tell us where the head was found asked a reporter from Fox 40 Bing?

He was a good cop replied the Mayor. All we know is his body led a blood trail and was found in a dumpster at the electric plant on Clinton St.

Commissioner Jones yelled a reporter a police secretary found his head in a bag early this morning. They say his car was found by his house in his garage, telling by the trail of blood I assume that's where he was killed?

We found a great amount of blood in front of his home but nobody saw a thing according to sources.

So your saying there were no witnesses asked a female reporter?

Nope nobody saw nothing we'll know after we conduct a full investigation said the commissioner. Was there a bullet hole in his when he was decapitated? We never found a bullet hole. According to what we know from our CSI members the whole crime happened there. Make no mistakes we will find the culprit! we will investigate every lead! the Commissioner said firm.

Another reporter asked do you have any idea who could of done this?

The Commissioner and Mayor started to become agitated.

Mam said the Mayor he was a detective and had a lot of arrests and enemies!

Rumors had it he killed Jamal Abdullah,. And he was dirty shouted another female reporter from CBS News?

That's ridiculous stated the Commissioner. I said we'll investigate every lead possible!

2Face sat in his house and had his feet kicked up laughing at the horror filled faces on tv. Fuck that pig! he was ready for the harassment from the police and the FBI. He had bigger fish to fry though.

Hey baby did you see the news in Bing?

Yeah Karrin, he yelled to her while she was in the kitchen cooking.

That's fowl whoever did that she commented. Whoever did that is fucking crazy! They're fucking sick in the fucking head.

2Face was thinking if she only knew, he wanted to tell her he did it, but it really didn't matter. As long as she held up on his alibi he was good. Sharif was covered he was with Jamie and was scene at her house playing black jack until 2am with Shay, Shay and Monica.

Boom! boom! boom! boom! It's the police open up w swan to have a word with you!

2Face jumped up and ran to the door but didn't open it. Why ya'll banging on my door like that! Am I under arrest or something? What the fuck is going on! yaw got no reason to be banging on my door! he was flipping.

If you were under arrest we'd of kicked your door down! we just wanna ask you some questions.

Questions about what?

About a grizzly murder of a Binghamton Police officer!

Baby open the door you didn't do anything wrong said Karrin being nosey.

She opened the door. Hi officers what seems to be the problem?

Miss Elizabeth our home town hero asked a stage fright officer?

Yes its me.

You 2 are?

Yes!

So the tabloids are true then, wow!

Miss Elizabeth we would like to question Mr. Jackson if you would step aside please.

I'm right here officers, now what grizzly murder do you want to question me about. 2Face went back to the black plush leather couch he offered the officers something to drink they refused.

So we see you watch the news Mr. Jackson?

All the time, cut the fucking small talk I don't like police around me and definitely not in my house.

I'm officer Davis and this is officer Smith. Where were you last night?

Here with my wife in my bedroom. Before that Biz Mania one of my artist stopped by around 11pm to drop off a new demo he dropped last night in the studio. If you want I can give you his number and you can call him to verify that?

The officer took down the number. The officers were looking for any sign of guilt in 2Face they really saw none.

Do you know anybody who would want to kill officer Martino?

Sure drug dealers, criminals, half the people he crookedly arrested and the court system did them filthy. It was so sarcastic that officer Smith had to sigh.

Did he ever arrest you?

No but he was at the scene of one of my cases for a drug sale. But he never personally did any investigating of any of my cases.

Now I was watching the news just before you guys came here and one of the reporters made a statement about Martino being the one responsible for murdering an ex street buddy of mine. What's the deal with that? 1

Who knows Mr. Jackson we don't have any recollection of Martino being anywhere near a crime scene let alone killing a suspect.

So why are you here then asked 2Face?

Hmmm! said detective Smith. Were just following leads.

Ok but what leads you here? Listen said 2Face I'm trying to do a lot for our communities and this country as far as keeping drugs off the streets, keeping our kids out of trouble and help our economic system. I'm pushing to make our streets safe and your jobs easier. I got a lot of good people backing me. So unless you ready to expose the FBI and Bing police for covering up a homicide by a detective of a fugitive, a fugitive he killed out of emotion and had nothing to do with the FBI case, then fall back from me cause I got nothing to do with what just happened. I definitely don't have any knowledge on it either so please get out of my house I've answered any questions that I could.

The detectives were dumbfounded, your absolutely right sir! we're sorry we even disturbed you.

When the police left Karrin was shocked at how he handled the detectives.

They can never prove a case against me, even if they tried I'll expose their own crookedness. See now I have the money and resources to keep them away believe that! they ever fuck with me again they only gonna expose they're selves and get a lot of good men fired Karrin.

2Face was having one of those nights again. You still killing huh? Said his Grandma. Cory I didn't raise you to be like a monster!

Grandma he shot my friend from behind!

He killed my partner in cold blood too said Mcgruff!

You tried to kill me first pig!

Hey fuck you man!

You was my boy 2Face, you let your homie kill me.

I was your cuz, ya homie shot me for no reason and called me a snitch!

276

You pussy to how bout that Petey yelled Shorts!

2Face you caused all this shit said Chino! We're still waiting for you to join us!

In hell screamed Hank! in fucking he–llll!

Baby wake up your having a nightmare!

Huh! what the fuck! another one of those dreams again Karrin.

You need a vacation, get up get dressed we're going to Hawaii honey! we need to talk! Look we finished our sophomore album and my video will drop next Tuesday. I'm finished with all my filming, plus I did a couple of guest appearances on shows too, they want me to film a movie for kids. I'm exhausted lets go now! Baby get up.

CHAPTER 73

Hawaii was beautiful, nice coconut trees, clear water, and a very humid climate. The beaches were gorgeous so were the hotels which were high priced.

Baby this is so beautiful I'd never dream I would come like this. She snuggled under his arm.

Yeah this spot is nice I got to admit replied 2Face. More cameras were flashing at the 2 as people stared in amazement. They checked into the Hilton hotel. They got the most expensive room with the biggest bed 2Face had some nice plans in mind for this. They had a great view of the Pacific Ocean.

Baby lets go the beach? Alright let me get dressed sexy. They even got a gym, I can watch you workout she said smiling.

You know they always flashing shots in the news paper following celebrity couples. The paparazzi always follows people.

They set up shop in the sand damn near touching the ocean. Karrin jumped in the water immediately admiring the clearness and observing the ocean floor.

2Face had on his shorts and no shirt, rocking his custom made Viscario Lemonte flip flops. He rocked Versaci shades cooling out looking like a star. The Sombrero Hat covered him from the sun. son just sat in the beach chair and sipped Dasani water.

Karrin came back to him in her 2piece bathing suit made by Chanel. She still had the killer cheerleader body. Her muscular legs and scrumptous toes.

Let me lotion you baby asked 2Face? She went into her Dulce 'n Gabana purse and pulled out tanning lotion.

I want this all over. 2Face began rubbing lotion on her back and massaging her ass and back legs at the same time. Umm! that feels so good she said exasperating. Daddy your touch feels so good. So tell me about the murders.

Shock hit 2Face as she stunned him with the sudden question. What are you talking about?

Don't play stupid with me. The dreams you know people don't dream for nothing and they definitely don't run and talk all crazy in their dreams either. Now you done did some serious shit you need to get off your chest. I'm your wife I promise I would never turn on you. I wanna know what kind of man I married. Your gonna tell me everything you did when you got out of jail.

You tripping shorty!

Listen she said either you tell me or I'll file for divorce! I can easily find a husband that trusts his wife. So no sugar coating or half ass stories! talk you got 30 seconds.

You crazy said 2Face.

29, 28, 27, 26, 25, 24–.

Alright, alright! You sure you not a FED or working with the police?

No stupid! You you've known me way too long for me to be that. Talk!

It all started behind the fence, this idea I had. He started about the Khutbah he gave about unity and taking care of our own, to the bank robbery plan, to how he was gonna flip the money, he told her about the snitch, about down south, the expedition and clean up job he had to do after Shorts screwed up. He told her about the mass murders in The Bronx, and Brooklyn, he broke down how he always had shit covered, he even told her about the kidnaping of Gina's friend for the connect, he told her about the trip to Vegas and about how he had Mafia dudes shaking people up in the industry, he told her how he washed his money. He told her how he keeps the loyalty of the hood, how him 'n Reef planned to do that cop in for Shorts and how he covered his tracks in that. He even told her his future plans he had for overseas already in progress. When he finished it was dark outside.

So there you have it. Now you understand my nightmares Mrs. Pyschiatrist. So what now. I bet you want a Divorce?

No! Hell no!

Do you think I'm crazy?

No I think Shorts was crazy. I think you're a street genius.

A genius?

Yeah. Shorts was bananas how yaw say it she smiled. You are a thinker, you carefully plan out all your movements and you cover your tracks as good as the government. If they knew about you and what goes on in your mind they'd kill you because you're a threat. But believe it or not I think you got a good heart. I think God wants you to change and make a difference in peoples lives to make up for those you destroyed.

I really didn't want to tell you cause I love you and want to protect you said 2Face. Now in too deep. You do realize that if you expose me I'll be forced to kill you, I tell everybody that rule.

Oh please she sighed I don't think you would kill me but I would never expose you I'm no rat! you're my husband dummy. Did you plan our marriage?

To be honest yes I did. I didn't actually plan it like this. A lot of stuff just happened I did hope though. She kissed him on the forehead.

If you threaten me again or cross me or ever break my heart Cory I'll fucking kill you first. He looked into her eyes she was dead serious. He grinned cause he liked that she understood him and his cause.

Its time for Salah he told her.

Go pray I'll be right here.

Karrin's sophomore album was even better than the first. She had good collaborations with big named stars. Plus her overseas tour made her world wide and the record would sell like Michael Jackson. She had H.O.V.'s wifey on a track they were in he midst of making a video to. She also featured on her track. She pushed 3 videos from her album. She stayed on talk shows, she even had a commercial, mad guest appearances, photos had her 'n 2Face together on the beach at dinner parties damn near everywhere they were together. She finally admitted on MTV that her and 2Face were married then People Magazine published it showing them to together. She won 16 awards, over 25 nominees and went diamond, she was definitely the face of Many Face Records.

2Face was watching the success of Dboogs second album none of them could match Karrin she had a wonderful personality and just fit in everywhere. But just going one time platinum was good. The Big East took a break and Biz dropped a solo joint and Popgun did the same. They didn't do too great they combined to sell $1.6 million records. 9 albums on the Many Face Records brought more success to his label. He was quickly becoming a great black entrepreneur. If they only knew of his other investments. He even signed other veteran artist to his label especially after they dropped "Hip Hops Rejects" where they let the outside vets shine. His label allowed the artist to be themselves and make the music the way they wanted to if they fail they only fail themselves. His clothing line took its self to new heights as well, new designs had him in a class with all the 5th Ave clothing and Apparel makers. He even bought a store on 5th Ave ust to finally have his line next to the great ones wild expensive as well. He now sold shoes, perfumes, watches, cologne, kids clothing you name it purses etc. His restaurant was so public and nation wide he just let the investors have they're way. Kenny held it down for him for real. Now that Karrin 'n him were exposed they kind of became the public face of hip hop culture and entertainment. They stayed in magazines and talk shows especially Karrin she enjoyed the fruits of the celebrity life. she especially like to talk about what they were doing in the community. While 2Face was starting his new operation she was his anchor in the media.

2Face was in a meeting in his high rise office on 5th Ave. he was having a discussion with a greedy lawyer. 1

Sir you sure you want to do this. Sir this is millions of dollars you're throwing away!

Shut the fuck up! I know what the fuck I'm doing! Mary are the transfers in?

Yes Mr. Jackson.

Good. I've only restarted my account in Africa where all the treasures originate. I also sold Many Face Records to my buddy Nathaniel Drakes.

Sir for $1million.

Yes fuck that record label. Trust me the company will run the same every one will still get they're royalty checks, you'll still get paid greedy man! everybody already involved will get paid and they're good for life. I also have accounts in Finland and Switzerland. Hey Bud sign here the label is yours bee! you still owe me $20, 000,0 Cuz you have 2yrs to pay, but if I was you I'd sell the company after 2yrs.

Jr. the clothing line is officially yours, same rules apply. Sign here. Kenny the Franchise is officially you so sign here.

Now Mr. Manchetti I'm trying to buy a radio station so help me out said 2Face.

Sure said Manchetti.

Miraji called 2Face. How's everthing in the field asked 2Face?

We making very little progress said Miraji.

Ok where are you having trouble Ockee?

The major cities with the drug dealing. As far as buying up property we're doing well. We've been renovating and building so things in that department are moving good. We do have a lot of kids going to school and doing good. We implemented prizes for the kids as rewards for their academic efforts.

Good replied 2Face, I want teams stationed in every major city we gonna play fire with fire we tried to be nice but people respect violence. I want them to find the major leaders in control of these hoods and start making examples and make the block hot so nobody will want to play the block. We'll talk later when I see you.

CHAPTER 74

Still no leads in the investigation said Davis to the Captain.

Ok its been a year 'n some change since Martino's murder and your telling me we got no leads.

Sir with all due respect we're doing our best. We got no witnesses no real motives nothing.

The Mayor will have my job said the Captain.

He may know more than us said the Detective. I believe he'll provide you with the best information. When you heard what I heard you'll just let it go sir.

There was a knock on the Mayors door. Come in!

Sir I got a few questions I would like to ask you asked captain Hardy. With all do respect sir there something I don't know about in the Martino case?

Something you don't about what Captain?

About the Martino case.

Captain sit down please. Close the door too. What I say doesn't leave this office.

Tell it sir. I promise this will not leave this office.

Ok we believe that 2Face aka Cory Jackson is behind a string of crimes. First the disappearance of our informants, he may have been smart enough to pull the bank robbery off. We also believe he's been involved in several homicides a few in the Bronx and multiple homicides in Brooklyn. 1 We believe he dealt kilos of drugs going all the way to North Carolina, we also think he was behind a mass murder in N.C.. We couldn't find 2 suspects a married couple who just vanished we think he had them executed as well. We believe he washed his money within the music industry his accounts just vanished out of US.

So this Jamal Abdullah where does he fit in? He's had no contact with 2Face in like 4yrs.

He was the dirty man while 2Face masterminded everything, but somewhere they didn't see eye to eye. We believe 2Face gave up the street life while Jamal couldn't let go.

So if know all of this why not take the bastard down?

The problem is its all circumstantial evidence and we can't place 2Face at any crime scene or do we have witnesses. Our theories come from the actions of Jamal Abdullah. We do know for sure is that 2Face worked construction and successfully completed Parole. Nobody we questioned knows anything about him. We know he took a $250,000 loans from his bank. He has millions floating around somewhere. He pays taxes, now he's a public figure a favorite especially amongst celebs for his new efforts to help fix our economy and clean up our streets. They're all backing him.

You keep saying we and they who are we?

The information we got from the Government. He's being watched severely. But he has information that can bring our judicial system down.

So we really can't touch him then sir?

We need him to make a mistake. Now he has no reason to. His poison pill Shorts is dead now, he was our only link through his actions and him running his mouth bragging to certain femals about his boy and they're come up. But all we have is circumstantial evidence. We can't link him to anything.

So what about the retaliation on Martino?

Jamal and Mcgruff got into a verbal confrontation and he tried to kill Mr. Abdullah but only Abdullah shot him first when they both reached. The verbal dispute took place cause Mcgruff vowed to put Jamal away forever. Jamal said over his dead body. Mcgruff told him to watch himself that he's plays dirty. When Abdullah tried to walk off he grabbed causing a tussle. Abdullah carried a concealed weapon and there was a struggle, Martino happened to be there while they were tussling and pulled out and fired trying to hit Jamal but he was cunning and pushed Mcgruff in the cross fire. Mcgruff was hit in the side and Jamal finally pulled his piece. Mcgruff tried to draw Abdullah shot him in the head. When we found Abdullah's location Martino went to finish the job in Elmira without permission and wasn't involved with the case, which is homicide. None of the FBI or the Elmira police guns matched the bullet found in Jamal Abdullah's head. We covered it up. Some how we believe 2Face knew of this and had a retaliation done. So if we pursue this case which we have no solid evidence, his lawyers would chew us apart and expose us. We lose our jobs possibly jail time, the FBI gets a black eye and they all risk jail time. It will become another OJ scandal that will uncover lots of criminal activities within our precinct and the FEDS. Then he will walk scot free suing the shit out of the government.

How did we lat a nigger get that smart said an angry Captain.

It had nothing to do with color asshole said the Mayor. The young man is very smart. Until he slips like I said its pretty much nothing we can do to him. However we can find a culprit for the crime to please the public so that nobody thinks they can get away with murder.

CHAPTER 75

2Face and Roc met up on 42st at the late night movie theater.

Yo what up they said to eachother as they took they're seats in the back row.

Got some info on ya boy?

The FEDs is thirsty to bag you, but they got nothing just speculation.

Shit home team that's all they need bee.

Yeah but it would expose a lot of crookedness they've been involved in, covering up prior cases. They'd rather pin it on someone else than fuck with you and make public fools out of themselves.

They still don't know a lot of shit Son said 2Face. You know why big homey? Cause I play it cool. I wasn't in the streets spending and splurging, I wasn't partying. I didn't broadcast to bitches 'n shit. Whatever I did in the street I did far away from home. See when you move low key and then explode when the time is right, onlookers get confused. They can't figure out a clue of how you got what you got but they gotta respect it. I'm in the process now of anchoring my own radio station. I'm a have Mouse run the sports segments, I got him studying getting prepared. Tone will be hosting the hip hop segment from 8pm to 3am. I'm trying to rock from 4 toI got Lashay and Monique and Monica hosting a afternoon segment from noon toWe got rock 'n roll, country music, R&B and classic rock. I kept Monique and Jessica on the low cause they used to handle that bread. On the weekends we got a religious segments which we got Bible studies and Qur'anic studies.

Son I'm impressed said Roc.

Yo, always keep people on the inside said 2Face. He handed Roc an envelope full of money. Enjoy the flick he said as he broke out.

Roc mysteriously vanished as an onlooker watching a movie looked over and was astonished how swift the guy just vanished.

Louie was a big time coke dealer up in Washington Heights. He was responsible for a major supply of kilos in the hood. The Cuban born 5"6 185lbs man made of money lived up in Jimmies Café in the Bronx. They were having a very important meeting about a turf war up in Harlem. Some cats from Wagner were pumping on 123rd 'n Lex, while Lou's people were pumping some dope in the same area but the crack made it hot. His men and they 're men got into it but Lou wanted to resolve this peacefully. They didn't pay attention to the groups of men who were stationed on both ends of the dance floor. They had came in a hour apart. Suddenly the 2 groups formed together as 6 men pulled out machine guns and started firing at the drug dealers. Semi automatics were spitting rapidly wetting up their little round table, as guest were screaming and running out of the club.

Aah! Aah! they shooting! yelled a running female.

Dong! dong! dong! dong! the tech was spitting.

Which one of ya'll is Louie yelled a gunman?

Dong! dong! dong! The gunman hit 2 of the men sitting at the table. They didn't answer fast enough! Spread the word! we murdering all drug dealers! Please don't be scared this is operation take over the hood! everybody at the table was hit with bullets.

Up in Queens Big John was pushin crazy weight. He sold as much as up to 15 ki's a week. He sat up in his high rise apartment in Astoria counting money. He had mad stash cribs, and this was 1 one of them. He also had 8 different coke and crack houses. There was a knock on his door. The sudden knock startled him. Nobody knew he was there. He tried to ignore it but theknock got louder.

Boom! boom! boom! Who is it?

Its me Crissy from next door. I got to talk to you its important!

Hold on! he put up his money, then walked to the door and opened it feeling funny.

Hi, John she said then out of no where a baseball bat to the knees came. The pain was excruciating. Then the bat hit him in the shins, he anguished in pain, aaawe! then he absorbed a strait right that pierced his skin leaving abrasions under his eyes and he saw stars as he was being dragged through his living room to the window and on the balcony. A voice said:

Spread the word. He was picked up over the balcony and was being hung off the balcony now.   Promise me you won't sell another drug again fool said the big man towering over another big man in big John holding his life. I'll drop you the fuck off this balcony!

I don't know what I did but I'm sorry please don't drop me sir please!

You got to promise me you will never sell drugs again! Its better me than the police!

I promise I'll never sell drugs again!

Good now tell all your workers how good you can fly! he let go of John then suddenly caught him by the leg.

John was in severe pain both his legs were broken as he was pulled back on the balcony.

Next time I see you and you still hustling drugs you'll be laying with the maggots taking a dirty nap! got it!

Yes John said as he passed out.

They were already in Ponchos house in Brooklyn. He was a major dope pusher. The fat Puerto Rican spit at one of the men that had him tied up along with his 2 daughters and wife.

Fuck you he said puneto! One of the men slapped the shit out of Poncho.

Where is the money and the drugs?

I don't have any drugs replied Poncho!

Baby just tell them where the stuff is said his wife!

You better listen to her said one of the goons!

Hey said one of the assailants he lied to us. You know what that means right? Cut off his fucking fingers! another assailant pulled out some metal cutters he had in his pocket he gripped the right middle finger and squeezed.

Aaaah! he clipped off the finger and mad blood squirted all over the floor. The assailant then tossed the finger in his wife's lap.

Aaaah! oh my God get it off me!

Tell us what we want to know! we don't want to do this!

I ain't telling you shit yelled Poncho!

Ok this nigga want to play games for real. Lay him on his stomach on the ground. Open his shirt. One of the men pulled out a scalpel.

Yo! yo, cut him open just a little bit!

Oh God please said his wife!

A yo gag her and blind fold her and them kids. Once they did it they reached into a duffle bag that one of the men brought and pulled out a cage. A New York City sewer rat was inside the cage. Blood dripped down Poncho's pants.

Yo open his zipper. You keep it official but I hate rats and I don't like them around me. But I guess you like them. He opened the cage dropping the rat in his pants, the dirty rotten germ infested and squirmy rodent crawling all over him picking at him made him cry.

This is what we do to drug dealers. Your organization will never sell drugs again, kappeesh!

Yes said a whimpering Poncho. they left Poncho and his family with the rat tied up.

I think he'll try to retaliate said one of the assailants.

You sure? Lets be certain. One of the men went back to the room and slit Poncho's throat he died with his eyes open.

2Face was at the Mosque praying Fajr in the morning. As soon as he was finished.

As Salamu Alaykum warriors.

Wa Laykum Salam the Muslims replied.

How was our first night of terror?

Very successful answered Rahim.

We must offer Salah and ask Allah for forgiveness. We should offer lots of Sunnahs. I wonder how the brothers are doing in the other cities? I guess when we turn on the news we'll find out. Today after we get some rest we'll shoot up some blocks. Our job is toscare drug dealers and   \make it extremely hard to hustle. We'll keep after the big timers though. Once we get police out on the street, we can go public with my ideas. But right now these thugs only respect violence. The sad thing is I used to be one of them.

Him 'n Karrin watched the news at 11pm. They were in one of his down low high rises in Midtown.

Baby why are you gonna go and shoot up blocks, that's gonna make things extremely difficult.

Listen, listen he said! The New York City Mayor was on the air.

We are not I repeat not gonna have vigilantes terrorizing the streets of New York. They will not run all over the city. We will apprehend them soon and bring them into custody. We got cops for this for Christ sake!

Well obviously you ain't doing a good job we got guns, drugs and vigilantes filling our streets and impregnating our youth said an onlooker!

Hey arrest this man yelled the Mayor!

Arrest mem for what? I have a right to freedom of speech said the black old man. That's all ya'll do is arrest us! he was quickly escorted.

Mayor this is happening allover the US said a reporter, Chicago, Miami, LA and DC. They had huge shootouts in Baltimore, Detroit, Boston, Houston and the violence is against all drug dealers.

Is there a statement being made behind this? What are your thoughts Mr. Mayor asked a female reporter?

This is obviously an organization of a lot of men. The Mayor of New York looked into the camera, we appreciate your efforts but it is criminal and if it doesn't stop you will be prosecuted to the fullest. We do not deal with crime in a violent manner. It's a hard struggle dealing with these drug dealers as it is. This secludes them more if you ask me.

There so confused baby said 2Face. The violence is only a mere statement and a theme to buy time to allow our projects to work. We gonna start with helping the youth in our schools and working with them to open up after school programs. We will also open up free food programs and rehabs for fiends and to help them shake their habits. Sorry about the violence.

For the next 4 ½ months big time drug dealers were being forced out of every major city. Drug dealers were losing money and their spots were being either shot up or shut down. The violence continued they even tried to fight back but with no avail. Old folks felt safe now to come out in peace without worry of being robbed or seeing transactions in their hallways or in front of their stores. Police now patrolled and did lots of routine pat frisks. Rappers like N.A.S., Kiss, and label owners were now beginning to speak out. There was lots of construction was being done in the hoods, lots of renovating, schools were being fixed, new gyms, they opened up community centers. More jobs opened up with the construction as the neighborhoods were being cleaned up. With the opening of new buildings mini malls and stores in the mist of being built the economy would recover quickly. Dealers and pimps who used to post on blocks and in front of building now lived in the same fear they once portrayed. 2Face plan was working he helped people lose habits and helped keep kids of the streets and brought unity to black folks.

He held a charity meeting in public. He wanted to address the people. They were lined up by the hundreds.

Can I have your attention please! 2Face stood on the podium confident. A year ago I stood here and addressed you people ideas I had on helping our ailing government and our people restore their lives. Now we've rebuilt tenement houses and bought tenement buildings and rented at a reasonable rate. We've bought land and have built shopping centers and have created more jobs, we've cleaned up our streets some what by doing our best to rid the neighborhoods of drugs, we've opened up more youth centers for our children to be successful. But as far as the violence me and my staff have nothing to do with anything we just do best to protect the people. I believe people get fed up and act on their own. I don't want the people to think that I condone violent tactics that would make me as bad as the people I'm trying to rid of in our neighborhoods. But we do have the help of the Muslim community in which they provide extra protection against street thugs that don't want to get off the street. Along with the police the Muslim will be a factor in cleaning up the hoods. Why lots of our thugs listen to the Muslim cause a lot of Muslims been there where they are and have risen up and plus we know how to deal with them. We have rehabs and we need bodies to fill them, we have youth centers and jobs that need to be filled. We also can now provide after school jobs for our youth, programs and employment for ex offenders trying to get right, which will keep them from going back to jail. We are assisting with helping out our education system in which we can provide rewards for our youngsters who do good which should make a kid want to do good in school. We will open up more sporting events and tournaments in which we will provide scholarships, we can also pay for more vocational training so that people can acquire skills in which they will need in order to succeed in getting hired. We are also providing housing for the homeless lets help them get off the streets as well and get back on track. Just think we put our money into all these charities but where does the money go? With all the money we celebs, politicians and big corporate men and corporations have why are so many people on the streets homeless or drug dealing and people with less opportunities then others. We should be pouring money into helping our fellow people. I mean there were always programs for the poor but they weren't taken advantage of because most of us don't know. Most of us don't give a fuck! that caught everyones attention. But I'm here letting everyone know that we here for the very people that support us. Something like Hurricane Katrina will never effect us again. We should not point the finger just at our government. What about our rappers, actors and actresses and successful people why aren't they helping out! I mean we got more than 1 enough cake so lets show people all over the world we can stick together!

Lots of applauds and cheering after 2Face gave that speech.

This will also neutralize the gang violence in our country. We today are gonna take a stand and clean up our country! Lets restore the ethnic and values God planned for us since the beginning. Thank you people!

2Face got lots of personal congratulations that day. Senators and Congressmen and even a few Police and government officials had a new respect for 2Face now. He definitely did a 360 in life from criminal to head of the justice league.

CHAPTER 76

My radio station starts today you wanna come with me baby?

I need to run some errands replied Karrin, but I will come there sweety I'm so proud of you. I got that surprise I've been telling you about too baby! I'll meet you at the station later ok baby. Give me a kiss!

They kissed each other goodbye then 2Face sat back and reflected on his life. he acomplished   so much in a short time. Allah allowed him to get away with so much now he has the support of the people, the whole country. He had athletes and stars holding him down. He went from selling drugs and robberies to opposing and defending the same people he terrorized. Only few know of his dark secrets and one of them is in the grave. It was time to move his family out of the country immediately. But first he had to appear at the biggest moment of his life. the radio station his dream come true. He also knew now that he was a public figure and hero he was the governments enemy. Anybody that can gather crowds that's black and gain followers that are willing to sacrifice whatever is a threat to their way of life and opposes their control.

Mouse hosted the sports talk show early in the morning and

he had some very interesting topics to talk about. 2Face observed him and Mouse loved to talk sports, the Yankees, Mets, Lakers, Knicks, Giants, Broncos, Jets, Hockey, Track 'n Field, Volleyball, college sports, Olympics, whatever you name it he will discuss it. Everything was in writing as well so that he can catch the freestylers. 2Face was official with the sports as well probably better than Mouse. 2Face didn't want to join in Mouses session because he didn't want the focus off sports. Right before 11:30 am before 2Face was going on the air Karrin came in wearing Hijab.

As Salaamu Alaykum baby! she said all excited.

Wa Laykum Salaam Wa Rahmatullah, replied 2Face, what did you take ya Shahada?

Yes baby I did it today.

2Face frowned. Did you do it for me or for the sake of Allah?

I did it for me and us. I really do believe there is no God but Allah and Mohammed is his slave servant and Messenger. I believe I should pray to God 5 times a day to protect myself from sin and to protect myself from the hellfire. I believe women should walk with dignity and cover themselves from impurities of the sick minded men and women. I even did as you taught me and I studied history and I found truths in everything the Qur'an speaks of, plus I want you to feel totally secure with me by your side.

His frown turned to a huge smile, come here baby girl. You look even sexier in a Hijab. She hugged 2Face.

Oh and baby she said I'm pregnant!

2Face dropped his headset. What!

Baby I'm three months pregnant. I just got my pregnancy result today. I went and gota routine check up, I just wanted to tell you at the right time.

He kissed her this is the happiest moment of my life. You are a blessing to me and you are my inspiration. Damn without you I'd be still running crazy! I love you he said hugging her.

I love you too baby she replied.

His first few callers were mostly praising him and applauding his efforts to straighten out the country.

I believe in this country and it's a great country because it allows the freedoms other countries don't. It allows a human being to be whoever he wants to be and he can live however he wants to live, practice whatever religion he wants and it brings all the ethnic races together. To live in peace under a body of laws and as long as we abide by them rules we all have equal opportunity. But there are short comings. Gangs and street violence, drugs and alcohol weaken a good country but they are the least of our problems, there are bigger problems ahead. The street life stunts the growth of our people and the human mind gets subject to one lifestyle. We as people need to change these horrific lifestyles that prevent our youth from growing, keeping us in prisons and on drugs. One caller asked him about athletes and steroid use.

Caller: I want your opinion on athletes that use steroids?

2Face: What do you mean?

Caller: I mean like you think the government should get involved and if so are they too hard on it. Also how do you feel about athletes who receive gifts and money in college?

2Face: I don't think that; first of all that the government should get involved nor does it need to get involved.

Caller: Why?

2Face: Because we dealing with athletes not criminals. I mean how many people in the government cheat and lie to us every day? If I had a quarter for every politician that lied to us I'd be a millionaire with out working for it!

Caller: But that's not the point!

2Face: Not the point! ok, check it: Do you think this is fair? Hear me out now, a rich politician or cop gets caught speeding 10 miles over the limit, once the traffic officer sees his credentials he tells him, hey don't do it again, go on. You think that's fair caller? While we regular citizens and don't be black for crying out loud they'll put one of us through the system!

Caller: But... 2Face: But hold up wait it gets worse! They're citizens just like us, human beings like us, how they get above the law. If they go that extra 10 miles they pushing it could be the difference in a pedestrians life especially a child. It could get crucial. I got hit by a car cause a lady did 35 mph in a 30 mph zone and she was pushing to catch a yellow light that turned red, she paid for her crimes. But the point is we look at everything the way the media does and its wrong. The government and media should mind they business in certain matters. They should be organized with facts atleast before putting men on the stand and ruining a great career. Some of these rats like company in their misery. But the government should let baseball or whatever sport handle the penalty for cheating in baseball. All Pete Rose did was gamble on his team he can't even get in the Hall Of Fame and he was one of the best to ever play the game and manage it. But the mob can gamble in Vegas and us? I mean come on what did he do so wrong? If the drugs are illegal in the courts then its nothing I can say. As far as college kids taking gifts I mean, what's the big 1 deal? Does it enhance their performance on the field. I mean we stress the rules so much, these schools make millions of dollars off these kids from tv, advertisements and fans. Some of our families pay tuition. They get money when they win bowl games and get to the tournaments and you got kids coming from poverty, hell yeah they gonna take it! But caller I gotta break thanks for calling.

CHAPTER 77

The music in the background playing was "Why" from Jadakiss.

Caller: Hi, I'm Bob.

2Face: How you doing Bob?

Caller: Fine, fine!

2Face: Well thanks for calling Wiz Radio Station. How can I help you?

Caller: Ok you say you a Muslim right?

2Face: Right, what's up?

Caller: I don't like the fact that Muslims are terrorist and what they did on 9/ They're a bunch of animals who live in deserts!

2Face: Wow! Yo!

Caller: Yeah, that's how I feel!

2Face: Yo, yo listen! Yo Muslims are animals right, what about what white men did to blacks in the slavery days! Hey were they animals too?

Caller: No, I don't agree with that!

2Face: So why would you make that comment on Muslims? You

just stereotyped a whole religion you know nothing about. What if every black man took they ancestors frustration out on people like you?

Caller: Well...

2Face: Well nothing! Then blacks should go around hurting and disrespecting whites for something that they had nothing to do with or happened a century 'n a half ago. let alone the stuff your ancestors did after, the lynching, banning us from schools, sit on the back of the bus, can't go to the same schools or drink out of the same water fountains you name it being called a nigger! Should we go around blaming every white person on Earth? Especially the people teat never lived through that or believe in that mess! that goes for Italian, Black, White, Christian and Muslim! look at the Christians don't go there! God made us different to get to know each other. Every one has a unique quality. Its not our jobs to be judgemental to the people, especially when we just freestyle images and don't study or understand a people or religion, what they about and why they even going through what they going through. Your comments were very ignorant! Next caller.

2Face: Caller please no ignorance on my radio show!

Caller: No! no my name is Jacob. My question is what's your take on rap music and its influentialality?

2Face: I love rap music, like people love The Beatles. Its our culture, it also got us where we at today. Its so watered down that people don't respect it no more. It became a business. A business of bragging and exploiting our women instead of a black mans expression. We so worried about money than we is making good music! That's why its so whack now and dudes got disappointing 1 albums.

Caller: Thank you I feel the same way.

2Face: Thanks for your call, next man!

The success of 2Face put a voice behind the name of a very brilliant mind. After 3 months of excellent ratings, his talk show became the talk of many in the media. He now had guest appearances from N.A.S., D-Block, Russ, Diddy, and now Opral wanted him on her show as a guest. Next week he had Kiss, N.A.S., and Russ. As they entered the booth 2Face and J-Kiss gave eachother dap and friendly hug giving their congratulations of the success they formed giving back to the community.

Ok now we on the air today with J-Kiss, N.A.S. and Russ is in the building again! What's happening brothers! All three responded what up.

We here to talk about what has been going on in our community, not just talking but we doing it! I'll let the brothers explain it, Kiss you go first!

J-Kiss: well first off the brother 2Face came up with the ideas to buy land and apartment buildings. We bought land in order to build up store fronts to create more jobs especially in the hoods. We trying to help the less fortunate in our communities, and this is nation wide! this is for the low income and we taking public assistance for 6months after that there's a grace period, but you gotta show us that you putting that work in after that grace period you on your own that way people don't get caught up in thinking that we just gonna provide cause we rich or whatever. It's a 2 way street you know. Show us you willing to get your self together so we can show these pigs we about something! This should help people and give a person an opportunity get right, feel me. N.A.S.: Also those community centers will be opening up by the hundreds for our youth said N.A.S. cutting in. We gonna do more for the kids educationally, and vocationally, and recreationally. This is based on the kids age, needs and career choices we can make.

2Face: Russ tell them how pushed the drug dealers off the street if they are not willing to participate and how we kept down the crime rate the last year 'n a half. Russ: Yes and hopefully we'll be able to help our ex- offenders. Ladies 'n gentlemen this is a one shot deal! but you gotta be able to be willing to get your life together first! millions need help, we can't play games its time for the black man to step up and be leaders by action! 2Face made a lot of people realize this now, including celebrities. We spend millions on nothing and there are so many less fortunate, which drives us to hate and crime and other things. This isn't a black or white thing, this is for the struggling American citizens who need help. Why sit around complaining about what the government ain't doing and won't do and we got the means to do it ourselves. If majority of celebs and rich people pitch in whatever they can afford along with what the government already provides that should be enough.

After airing that show 2Face knew the success was to come for his radio show. But the interview on Opral was crucial, lots of big people were siding with him now. The e-mails were rolling in. He already got his family out of the country. The record label was good, the clothing line was good and his restaurants were in good hands, never could he let what he built from just go that was his bread 'n butter his stock in his creations would last a zillion lifetimes. His money wasn't even accounted for even though he had plenty of it to go around, he knew pretty soon he would need to vanish. He beefed up his security for he knew the attempts on his life were coming.

He jumped off his private jet in Chi- Town and hopped into his own custom made limo. He had 1 the Machine with him and his man Rahim his boys from uptop a few cats he could trust for security reasons he never walked with any security he didn't know.

The thing I like about this Machine is we got brothers in every major city ready for war on the low and we not bound for money, we bound by Allah! Our abode is paradise. We also got plenty of help over seas plus our mission is in effect already. Its gonna get ugly but this country is blind to the fact that our rights are being stripped away slowly. The world will belong to the government 100% if someone don't start the revolution. We'll be like robots, the New World Order!

They arrived at the Opral show just in time for 2Face to freshen up. They had a under ground route he took to avoid paparazzi, he went back stage and it seemed to him all type of weirdos were in his face. 2Face hated this with a passion. He didn't want weirdos touching him or in his face. The lights illuminated from the back stage to the front stage as Opral was excitedly introduced.

She waved at the crowd for about 5 minutes and then sat down to talk a little bit to her fans about her own personal issues and cracked a couple of jokes. After a commercial break she addressed the crowd one more time before introducing the man.

Ladies 'n gentlemen I would like to introduce to you 2Face people! Give a round of applause!

The crowd went bananas! People cheered like crazy! 2Face always liked Opral and respected her, she wasn't a snobby rich lady billionaire, but a caring and loving person and always willing to contribute. The embraced eachother very tightly.

Cory sit down said Opral.

Yes. Yes replied 2Face. He was cheesing and very excited.

So how was your flight I hear you scared of planes she joked?

Yes I do but I fear Allah more and when you on a mission with a belief and faith in who you trying to please, nothing can harm you in the least bit, not even death cause if I die in the way of Allah on my mind to please him then its all worth it. But other than that I had no choice. Shoot how else I'm a get here.

Aah ha ha! people laughed at the sarcasm.

This country is twisted Opr. You know the poverty the less fortunate, the prison system, the system itself. You know we trying to bring the people together. We need that American bond in this country that this place was quote on quote founded upon! This is serious, these people try to control us, we gotta realize this is not a race about power and control. They look for ways to take away our rights we have by any means.

9/11, look at Iraq. How we go from fighting terrorism to invading a country and destroying it that had nothing to do with anything, then turn around and want to take away our rights of privacy and stricken laws. Plus not only that when the government needs the support of the people something tragic must happen to instill fear in the people. You ever notice they'll do anything to discredit a leader who gains the support of the people in which opposes they rule. The media is down with it scandals 'n all they puppets. If you try to stand up watch what happens. I mean its for the American citizen to decide. Pretty soon only I mean only police and government officials will carry guns, they probably won't even allow hunting unless you some type of worker or something. Look they even control how we raise our kids that's why so many kids are disrespectful. They take a incident and blow it way out of proportion in order to rewrite something. They allow disasters in order to find a reason to go to war. Ladies 'n gentlemen don't 1 think these attacks go on with out knowledge the intelligence knows damn near everything on Earth, if not they behind the scenes. Pay attention how after every disaster rules are enforced. They can't just go Hitler and do them cause they know the people ain't going for that. We'd be in outrage.

2Face watched the amazement of the eyes of the people in the audience.

All the elections and rigged campaigns and then only a percentage of our votes count! Wake up American citizens we need to take back our country!

Wow! Said Opral. That's deep! We'll go to a commercial break and be back with more of Mr. Jackson! the crowd clapped.

The mics cut off instantly on stage.

You know you need to slow down said Opral! You gonna get yourself into a lot of shit!

I realize what I'm doing but it has to be done.

We're going on the air in 5,4,3,2,1....

The clapping began lots of applauds.

So you teamed up with a few politicians and celebrities and a few hip hop legends in a quest to clean up our streets and help fix an ailing economy and I hear you having a lil success.

Yeah said 2Face we actually made the streets safe without sending people to jail and we   providing jobs for the people cause I believe if we the very people that gain the support of the fans and citizens who are less fortunate don't lend a hand in with the government then what good are we. We are a lot of kids and grown ups heros you know so why not give back together. You know if we give back as one look at what success we have. Look at what can get done. Even prisoners and ex-cons need our help in order to maintain a clean society. Don't get me wrong some people need to be locked up. But the youth need our help the most, I don't want them growing up twisted like me. These kids need the proper education in order to succeed. Other countries are advancing while worrying about getting high, getting fat, kids dropping out, hanging out, who got more money than who, who the best rapper, who dress the best. Pretty soon we ain't gonna have nothing if we don't start paying attention to what the real deal is, we need to do something to get these kids interested in education. Our government doesn't help enough. The way sting are set up you gotta be damn near perfect. But we gonna make it happen and the thing about it is, put the camera in my face; this world is a hell for the believers and a heaven for the non-believers. You can knock me off it won't matter try to discredit me with bad media or whatever you ain't stopping the movement. Trust me its millions ready to step up, believe that! We reproduce like flies. We can barely spank our kids! can't even defend your self, police do what they want. Can barely talk on the phone privately, they injecting our food. They gotr natural remedies to cure all types of diseases but the FDA won't allow this to take place cause they'll lose trillions, but we in a recession. I ain't doing this for profit or personal gain or for glory, mine comes from Allah, this is real folks.

Well our little interview slash speech was very interesting, we want to thank Mr. Jackson for stopping by. Hopefully you'll come back and we can get into your personal life with your loving wife Miss Elizabeth. He smiled. Thank you Mr. Jackson.

Thank you Ms. Opral. I apologize to you and your audience for my speech, I'm just frustrated sorry.

Its not a problem said Opral. The audience applauded one last time as exited the stage.

CHAPTER 78

The phone rang, 2Face picked up on the second ring. He decided not to have much security just Reef, if he was gonna go out he would go out with his homies, fuck security.

Hello this is the President of the United States. Is this Mr. Jackson a.k.a 2Face?

Yes he replied sounding shocked.

Well I would like to meet with you in Washington in private.

Mr. President that would be an honor sir. When would you like to meet sir?

Whenever your schedule is free.

For you Mr. President how bout tomorrow?

That would be excellent!

Baby I don't want to go to Finland!

You going and that's that! You gonna have that baby safely!

But why? I want to stay here with you, she had the sad puppy face.

Listen I got you a private jet for you, your moms and your family. Yaw need to get going things can get ugly baby. I want you safe. If something happens to you I'll lose control Karrin, but I promise we'll be alright I just want you out of the country for now.

But baby she said crying, I'm not leaving you!

I don't want to leave you either, but we have to be apart to just weather the storm for a bit and shit settles down. I promise I'll be alright. Now please the car is waiting, Machine will make sure you get there. Machine is a beast believe that! I had all military training for all my personal goons and I got plenty.

I love you Cory!

I love you too!

I'll see you in Finland he said wiping the tears from her eyes. She blew him a kiss. He held back his own tears. His heart 'n soul was leaving him even he wondered if he'll see her again.

2Face was met at the airport in DC by armed US C.I.A. members in black suits. They drove him to Maryland into a mountain region until they landed upon a small cottage. 2Face was escorted to the cabin. He was let inside by one of the men.

The President was sitting at a wooden table with the Vice President. Mr. Jackson nice to finally meet you, said the President. This you know is our Vice President.

Nice to meet you gentlemen, replied 2Face.

Please sit down sir.

It is an honor to even sit with you sir in your presence.

Are you hungry asked the President? We have clean juicy Deer meat, with biscuits.

No thanks sir. I'm interested in what the President has to speak to me about sir he said to the Vice President.

In that case said the President I applaud the fact that you have rallied a group of radicals and celebrities and put forth an effort to bettering America. Your violent tactics have actually worked we would do that but the backlash is crazy. But any way crime is down and drugs have not been a factor except some angry Mexicans and South Americans ready to go to war with you and stuff. You even have gang bangers calling police on your people, everybody in the room laughed at that one. You people have engaged in after school programing and have helped add jobs by your buying of land and construction work. In a short period of time you have raised billions in charity to help an ailing economy. Your doing better than me. But first off who gave you the permission to take it upon your self and try to fix a country its my job to do that! he said as he got loud. 1 You've challenged us like we're the enemies! we won't tolerate that! I am the President here not you! You need to start making us look good!

Hey Mr. President did you know I created 1000's of jobs before I started the charity fund thing?

We know you mercilessly sold drugs up and down the eastcoast. We know you issued a lot of murders. We know you washed your money through that hip hop mess! We know your behind the vigilante violence which has the streets scared to death we are doing our best to keep cartels from starting a war in our streets! You have slowed our pockets down with your antics! People don't know drugs make the world go round because it turns into money. People buy drugs use em, buy em sell em, when they sell them they become consumers, when we bust them we take they stuff 'n money and reproduce it and still make money off it. Our prison systems will shorten. People will lose jobs! this keeps the market afloat a bit until we come with a solution. Without the markets there will be no stock exchange.

So Mr. President you know all this about me why aren't I in jail?

Good question said the Vice President. Truth is we have no evidence. You've slipped through the cracks for so long before you know it you're a public figure. We never thought you had this much influence.

And you want drugs on the street asked 2Face?

We want you to stop the vigilante stuff and stop calling us out please. We would like to work with you and gain some credit in this. We will give you the proper assistance for the operation. We can work together asked the President.

What if I refuse asked 2Face?

Well you refuse your in for a lot of trouble. You don't want to have trouble with us. Right now you are getting on our bad side if we wanted you could've been dealt with! But we admire your intelligence despite the fact we know you live up to your name 2Face! We're inviting to work with us.

Like Bin Laden 'n Saddam Hussein huh? Look I respect your antics and I know Ya'll know mostly everything but ya'll don't know shit!

They looked shocked at the remark.

Yaw don't know half the shit I pulled! All I did was open the publics eyes to a lot of bullshit. Now ya'll want to threaten me fuck you. We'll have a Holy Jihad right in this country! I'm sure you don't want that Mr. President. So I guess you can have me dropped off at the airport, for a minute I thought we was getting somewhere in this meeting.

Is that why you closed your accounts and moved your family out of the country? Why do you have all those private investments?

I always invest my money into my own companies, the restaurants, the label, the clothing line and the radio station. I used bank loans and did contracts like roofing and shit do help earn money. I haven't sold a thing since I 've been home.

We don't believe you said the President.

Then prove your case!

No! we'll prove nothing you watch yourself and friends.

Is that a threat asked 2Face/

No it's a promise.

I've said what I to say, you know the consequences if you touch me or my people. I'm holding you personally responsible.
1

It's a shame we couldn't unite said the Vice president you'd have elite power. We'll give you time to think about it.

See you a little more reasonable in that case I'll think about it. Thank you gentlemen it was a pleasure.

Nice sit said the Vice President.

Its Armani replied 2Face.

2Face was escorted back to the airport. He slept his flight and then went to his secret hideout and slept all night.

The next day he was fresh and took a nice shower, got dressed rocking a Sean John sweat suit and he had his little Betsy with him. Betsy was his 21 shot Glock he carried when he was alone. He called Karrin and she picked up first ring.

Hi baby! she was wild happy to hear his voice. As Salaamu Alaykum. He greeted her back.

Hey I was calling to make sure you alright, 'n if you made it safely?

We're fine Cory. So how did your meeting go? It went sour but we both know where eachother stand, believe that! I'll be there to see you soon baby alright. I love you and I miss you.

Baby don't get off the phone yet.

I have to get to the station cutie pie.

Fine she said back I love you be safe. She hung up.

CHAPTER 79

2Face was taking calls. He commented with his co-host Angie Stone. She was a former jockey from Hot They briefly talked about homosexuality and its acceptance. 2Face had brawd views but kept it minimum. His first caller was a female.

2Face: Good morning how are you?

Caller: Fine how are you?

2Face: Couldn't be better. I'm sure plenty of people are listing, so get ya ears wet for this one.

Caller: My question is first are there rumors you control an Islamic extremist group right here in this country?

2Face: What's your name?

Caller: Janet.

2Face: Well Janet let me ask you something? Does Muslim and extremist go hand in hand?

Caller: I don't know what you mean? 2Face: Let me break it down for you. A Muslim is one who submits his will to Allah so he follows the guidance of Prophet Mohammed (pbuh). No where does he tell a Muslim to take his own life. in the Qur'an Allah tells us that it is a sin to commit suicide. A Muslim cannot be fanatical. A Christian shouldn't be fanatical either. But unfortunately we do have extremist in every religion. I don't believe in extremism. I believe that we should obey God's command. But I am aware of the rumors. I'm not killing nobody or none of that. I don't attack women and pedestrians and I damn sure ain't committing suicide. Them extremist attack women 'n children in real life Islam Allah tells us leave the women 'n children out of attack. It's a major sin. Some Muslims believe its Jihad butt isn't. They take the Qur'an and run with it. Oh I'm sacrificing my life for the sake of Allah. This is a grave sin.

Janet: Thank you for clarifying that. The reason I asked you is because you've done so much for our country and your bringing unity to the people and yet they still or some people want to hate 1 and call you a monster.

2Face: I can't change people's opinion, tell me though what I've done to people all my life I get hated on people hate to see me do anything family 'n all. Why? Maybe I got a perception of myself that everybody thinks I'm doing something wrong. It comes from lack of trust. So basically they never trusted or had faith in me from the get go. Its like we waiting for me to do something wrong so they can run they fat mouths! That's what you call a true hater.
Janet: I hear you baby! you keep on going strong honey.

2Face: Oh yeah! cause no matter what you do when you got strikes on you from there on no matter what you do from there on out in life especially good they gonna look for a fault in you. They'll even go to your past to dig up something to gossip about. These people will even go to your childhood and hold you accountable for that. Society don't forget. God forbid you make a mistake. We human we all make mistakes. They'll be on you white on rice if you slip. Whether rich or poor, middle class. So I don't do things to be seen of men or care what they think. I do what I do for the blessing of God. The Prophet said if you see a wrong change it with your hands, if you can't change it with your hands then use your tongue, if you can't change it with your   tongue then change it with your heart and that is the weakest of faith. Janet: Thank you for the insight.

2Face: You welcome. Ok next caller.

Caller: Hey I don't think gays was a creation of God, I think those people are sick!

2Face: Ha, ha, ha! 2Face was rolling. Yo you didn't even introduce yourself yet man damn! But I like that topic even though I can't comment on it to tough. I might get sued. But F– it! Caller what's your name?

Caller: Tom.

2Face: Tom, I personally think its an abomination. God made us as men 'n women to be companions of one another and to reproduce how can we do that if we messing with the same sex? There's a morsel of flesh in the body if it becomes good then the whole body is good. If it becomes rotten the whole body becomes rotten just to keep the hadith short. That morsel is the heart. The reason I gave you that is because in my belief homosexuality is a disease and it spreads. Now they want to raise kids and that will influence a child's life cause children pick up what they see. 9 out of ten children won't grow up normal when they see abnormal things in they're childhood. That is a proven fact. Things like 2 men kissing or 2 women kissing in their household and this is mommy and daddy? Kids might think that's the way to go. Not to mention the drama they'll get from school kids if they find out.

Caller: I definitely agree with that.

2Face: Well do your history read the Bible and the Qur'an with an open mind and heart. Then read encyclopedias about the destruction of great cities especially Sodom 'n Gammora. That's your example for homosexuality. The Prophet said in Hadith to throw them off the highest cliff. No believer in God truly would go for that mess. Its excepted in this country for economical reasons not morally.

Caller: Thank you.

2Face: You welcome.

A few weeks went by 2Face was gonna celebrate his Birthday turning He kept himself in shape and looked like he was He had most of the homies stay out of sight for a while. Mean while the community centers were blossoming. The land that was bought now was now all 1 renovated with stores and parking lots they were now shopping areas he had created more jobs than people could imagine. They built gas stations, fast food restaurants, restaurants, his to, shopping malls, apartment buildings and rehab centers and shelters to get the homeless off the streets the ones that wanted to come. The community centers provided activities like basketball football and baseball and boxing, soccer, ping pong and education, vocations and even anything religious. He even bought out some of the grocery stores in New York City so the blacks had their own businesses in the neighborhoods and not all the foreigners just coming buying shit up while we hustle in front of their stores and spend our money supporting families who ain't even from our hoods, when we built the hoods. Things were looking positive for the commmnuties blacks and other minorities.

He had planned on celebrating his birthday at the Manhattan Center. The Rev and Miraji was there along with mad celebrities. Miraji and Rev had pushed for a bill to help out those involved in Hurricane Katrina. The government agreed in addition that the charity would be provided in fixing up Louisiana.

Karrin called and wished him a happy birthday. She had wished he could be there. He told her not to worry cause Muslims don't celebrate birthdays this was just for publicity. He was sharp in a Viscario Lemonte 2 piece suit. With a pair of Gucci Gators and platnium cufflinks. Reef, Mouse, Bud and Tone was sharp as well rocking tuxedos. The Big East was there all fresh. His boy Kiss and H.O.V. was there wild celebs were there. There was plenty of entertainment, good music stand up comedians.

Reef 'n them was rounding on 2Face on how his Moms used to throw him out for like 2 or three days and then come looking for him at the basketball court yelling Cory! get ya ass in this house! niggas was laughing at son. The big surprise cake was rolled out by the waiter all of hip hops finest sang happy birthday to him. 2Face was smiling and cheesing.

The Rev damn near came to tears in is eyes. Right after the birthday song the Rev came up to 2Face. Son a young boy was shot 'n killed in Brooklyn by police.

Get the fuck outta here! how old was he?

17yrs old.

You serious huh?

I just got the call 2Face.

We need to find out what going on first. Ladies 'n gentlemen! I'm sorry but I have to depart my own birthday party. A situation has occurred where a young boy was shot 'n killed by police officers and beaten. I want to get to the bottom of this now! if you'll excuse me.

People's faces were shocked as they watched 2Face and his entourage left some of them left behind him like an angry mob they rode strait to Brooklyn right in the back yard of The Big East and the homies where they grew up on Riverdale 'n Williams.

The incident happened right in front of the corner store on Williams 'n Riverdale where the yellow tape was at. It was another angry mob of youngsters and parents ready to riot as they wheeled the young dead boy on the gourney into the ambulance covered by a white sheet with blood spreading over his head. Yellow tape barricaded the scene on both sides as cops tried to calm the on goers down. But people were forming in mobs once 2Face 'n them showed up.

Ain't this where Shuaib was killed son 2Face asked Mouse?

Police killed him right over there!

He was They stay pulling the trigger over here on some kids. Since then niggas be trying to 1 kill police over here bee.

They had just killed 2 patrolmen on Alabama 11/2 ago said Tone.

The 78th precinct was run by Chief Ganji. He was on the scene talking to reporters. Police were really trying to keep this angry mob back as the shouts were coming.

Fucking pigs! Kid killers! Yaw just thugs! Fuck the police!

The Rev took position as the spokesman and talked to the reporters but he didn't know anything yet. He pushed his way to the Chief.

Who's in charge here?

I am this is my precinct said the Chief!

We just want to know what happened asked Miraji?

We had a situation where an officer ad a young boy got into a dispute while the officer's partner was getting coffee.

What kind of dispute asked 2Face? The officer told the young man to get off the corner and not to loiter in front the store. The boy told the officer f–you! I ain't moving no where! and then he got into the officers face and I'll do what I want! You don't run the streets! The officer went to grab him, the boy reached for his waist like he had a gun the officer in the store witnessed this and pulled his firearm in defense of his partner. The officer and the boy struggled then, he grabbed hold of the officers gun and the witnessing officer had no choice but to fire to protect his partner.

So the officer fired on him asked 2Face?

That's bullshit shouted a girl from the angry mob!

You seen the size of that boy he was mad frail Chief. You can't possibly expect me to believe that? You not gonna tell me a 17 yr old boy with no fight experience is gonna give a trained cop problems! Get the fuck outta here!

Do you know officer that this is they neighborhood Miraji said.

Tone was talking to the peoples trying find out what happened. A young girl said she witnessed the whole shit son yelled Tone! these cops is fucking lying!

Come here Sheena! She was a12yrs old black girl and a long pony tail.

Yo, shouted Tone! She saw the whole thing! she said that cop told him to get from in front of the store, but lil homey ain't move fast enough so he grabbed shorty up and started tossing the kid around, then the other officer came out when he turned to his partner the kid tried to run and that's when they shot him cold blood!

Hold up you said they! replied 2Face.

Son she said both of them opened fire son word to mother son!

What color was these cops asked Rev?

Where are these cops at sir asked Miraji? How did they get away so fast!

Why did you lie to us asked Rev? They were blitzing the Chief with questions.

This was the story they told me!

So you were gonna go with that Chief? No investigation nothing huh replied Miraji?

That sounds like a cover up to me said the Rev. now your word is no longer credible. Where is the boys family asked Rev?

I do said the girl who blew the cops lie up. He was my cousin Jaquel.

Lil Jaquel yelled Tone!

Oh shit said Biz and Pop that's Keso lil brother.

Awe man said Tone as he put his hands on his head.

You haven't answered our question said Miraji, where are those officers?

Unless you're a lawyer you have no right questioning a superior officer!

Your right said Miraji, hey Rev call up the Mayor. We're launching a full investigation I'll have your badge for this one you lying bastard!

I'll make sure they get prosecuted to the fullest and so will you for lying to us said the Rev.

Can we calm this angry mob down please shouted the Chief!

Why should we said 2Face? They have a right to be angry. Hey lil Sheena where did you witness this from? She pointed to a third floor apartment right above the scene.

I'm her mother shouted a skinny black lady 30 looking like That was my nephew oh my god! she was balling tears hysterically.

Where is his mother asked 2Face?

She on her way right now she work at Brookdale Hospital replied the Aunt.

I'm so sorry Miss he said to her! he hugged her to show his support as she cried like a angry new born. Something will be done about this believe that! he whispered that into her ear.

The mother finally arrived wilding! she had to be restrained screaming where's my baby! oh my God my baby! Where's my baby! bring me back my baby! she was flowing tears like a waterfall. She found out he had been pronounced dead at the scene. She really went bizzerk!

We'll get you the best lawyer money can buy said Miraji. We will file for an autopsy report and we'll see how he died!

The news was all over it. They even exposed the polices masquerade asap on eyewitness news.

That night 2Face watched the news as the names of the cops were revealed. So sad he said to himself, he was dressed to go to the Masjid until some tragic shit happened.

This is Lisa Collagessi reporting from Eyewitness News down in South Carolina. A viscous killing took place today in which a newly wedded inter racial couple and their infant son was savagely killed. Sources say the crime was a bias and a hate crime. The Husband 22 yrs old African American Sean Davis was visciously beaten and burned while Wife Courtney Jenkins Davis was assuredly raped and manually strangled! The baby 3 month old Jamal was found floating face down in a lake when the crime took place. She had to refrain from tears. They were all pronounced dead at the scene. Sources say that someone smelled the bodies and the fire. Then uncovered the heinous and grisly savage attack. Police are searching for a who some sources said they witnessed fleeing the sceen a 33yr old white male name John Diggins along with three other hooded suspects. They are looking for him for questioning.

This is Lisa Collegessi Eye Witness News.

Tears formed in 2Faces eyes. He said to himself they drowned a baby. We gone fix that town take my word for it!

CHAPTER 80

Gary Florence an old friend of 2Face was a tough hard nosed white guy that 2Face fucked with hard when they was young. But he was actually Gary's brother's friend Mark and was one of the rare black guys that they hung with. People used to think that Gary was a racist because he like and got a kick out of beating up tough black kids that other white kids were scared of. He had some information that was very alluring to 2Face. The small town of Bailey. 2Face found out the victims were high school sweethearts and John Diggins hated it. He even once said that he'd kill 1 that nigger baby! It sent him over the top that a white woman would lay in bed with a black man and have a baby. He came to a local bar boasting he did it for white power. Gary over him and caught him outside and socked him one blackening his eye. 2Face sent him some money for his troubles along with a carload of Muslims who were gonna burn that town to the ground. Majority of the town opposed of the victims and refused to cooperate with the authorities except the young girl who found them.

Machine and Rahim were upstate with 2Face while they did they're bids in some of roughest parts of the state of New York.

319

He trusted them cause they popped off several times in their together.

Gulley was down for it too. He had a white wifey and didn't tolerate racism.

Razzac was a weapons technitian trained by his Pops his Son A victim of racism, he was ready to lynch this hick town. They drove in 2 separate cars to be well rested and were fully equipped for war and specific instructions. They met Gary in a Charleston Railroad station. Rahim was strong as a ox powering 665lbs on the flat bench. Machine was a martial arts expert, Gulley was a strait street nigga. Gary directed them to the small town Bailey. They parked the car inside a parking lot outside a mini plaza with some convenient stores and a McDonalds 'n Taco Bell. Gary, Machine, Rahim and Razzac were on foot hooded. They cut through some woods that led to a back road, the back road led to small little farm. A house in the middle of the woods a pigpen with 5 hogs a couple of grazing cattle and some chickens in a coup. Ock this look like some Texas Chainsaw Massacre shit said Machine. Lets do what we gotta do and get outta here! Is this the house whispered Razzac? Yes replied Gary.

They crept to the door moving like wind. Razzac had the desert eagle cocked the element of surprise was gonna over take them because it was 6 in the morning. The front door was locked as Machine tried to open it. Fuck it said Rahim boom! He kicked the door down startling two kids a boy and a girl around the ages of 6 to ten in pajamas. Aah they screamed! Shh. Where's your daddy asked Rahim? Is he upstairs?

Yes they shook their heads scared out of their minds at the masked men.

Gary noticed John Diggins with a shotgun at the top of the staircase. Duck dude! He shoved Rah out of the way as the shotgun blast boomed! Machine was on the side of the staircase he fired 3 times hitting Diggins in the right shoulder. Aww! yelled John as he dropped the gun. Rah charged up the stairs as John grabbed his cousin's wife from out of the room, he reached in his pocket and pulled a knife holding it to her throat. Hey John let her go what the fuck you doing! yelled his cousin.

Shoot this fuck yelled John!

Let the girl go you redneck coward! yelled Rah from the middle of the stairs. No! I don't think so, said John. Rahim ducked as the loud blast took a chunk out of the rail. Gary didn't have a gun so he took a picture frame and threw it at John to drive his attention. 1

Let her go yell Gary. Tell ya nigger friend to drop his gun! Pick that shotgun up yelled Machine! To hell with this said Rah may Allah forgive me. He shot the girl in the shoulder. Aaah! She screamed in pain. John was shocked as he lost his grip of her as she slipped into unconsciousness leaving a wide open face shot. Rah instead shot John in the side. John was agonizing in pain. The scared cousin was blown into the bathroom by the desert eagle in Machines hands. Hold him down said Rah to Gary. John rolled in pain.

Machine shot 8 shots into the cousin's head.

Razzac after tying up the 2 kids and scanning the whole house down stairs came upstairs to join the action. He shot out both of John's knee caps. John anguished in pain. Gary unzipped his pants, Razzac pulled out the big Rambo knife and began to cut into the penis of John Diggins. John was in so much pain he passed out. Razzac continued to cut like he was cutting the leg off a turkey. When he finally cut through clean, they dragged John the half dead girl and the kids outside tied them to a tree. They hung John to another tree and poured gasoline on him stuffed his penis in his mouth and lit him on fire. Then they spray painted on the grass black power. Once they made it back to mini plaza they bricked the Mcdonald's and threw a fire bomb in it. The fire bomb were filled with liquor easily igniting as people blitzed out the fast food chain. They ran into the supermarket and started shooting at the ceilings and the glass allowing pedestrians a way out. Razzac and Gulley ran through all the isles pouring the gasoline all over the foods and everything they could see, then Razzac lit the match as fire quickly raced through the supermarket. As they made they're way out Rahim threw another fire bomb causing a huge explosion. They drove through the small downtown while police and firefighters were responding to fires and screams of innocent citizens. With all the distractions they stopped in front of the courthouse poured gasoline in front of it on the lawn as Rahim threw another fire bomb through a glass window of the courthouse they lit the fire and drove off. Then they hit the racist bar Gary had told them about in which where Gary punched John outside and they refused to cooperate with authorities. They fire bombed the place causing fierce blazes and a huge explosion from all the liquor once the fire hit some of the broken bottles. Then they drove outta Town leaving a shaken and confused police force and town.

CHAPTER 81

Richard Mckosky was headed home from the gas station. He'd been on suspension for the shooting death of Jaquel Johnson. He'd been laying low since the shooting. He had a court appearance tomorrow. His involvement in the incident was the choking of the young boy. He jumped into his Mazda 6 and headed for the highway. He had reflected on the situation and wished he'd of left that nigger alone he thought to himself. Then he thought of the riots fucking young punks he cursed to himself. He looked to left as a dodge intrepid pulled up beside him, before he knew it 16 shots were fired in his car all 16 hitting him as he slumped on his steering wheel. His car slowly rolled forward into traffic. Trial was being held here in the streets of Amityville Long Island. Further in Nassau County Orlando Schinsky was on his way for a morning jog as he stepped into the street. He saw another jogger approach him wearing a mask it didn't look good for Schinsky. The jogger shot him dead square in the forehead as he slumped in front of his car the sound was muffled so no one could hear it as the jogger kept on jogging leaving him in a pool of blood. At the radio station 2Face was taking in all the calls about the recent tragic events.

2Face: Its so sad. Why would a human being want to kill a child and his parents because of racial preference? What drives people to hate like this? Lets take it back, I got a theory but its dealing with religious beliefs. See the first thing we need to understand is that this is something that is created in us. Then comes faith we can't have faith without trust and knowledge, so what I'm getting at is this. Now folks what I'm about to say is a lil far fetched but these are not my words, these words come from our beloved Prophet Mohammed (p.b.u.h.). When Allah created Adam, Adam was like a statue for some time around 40yrs. Now what makes mankind unique is that Allah created Man and fashioned him with his own hands. He illustrated to us our oaths to him which is why we cry out Oh God when we think we gone die he said laughing. But on the real though mankind testified there is no God but Allah long before we were created. Now you have the Jinn a creature which is created out of smokeless fire in which the so-called fallen angel but his name is Iblis was a Jinn the devil some may call him but any way Angels are created from light. Now Angels do what ever Allah commands, while Jinns and Man have choices. The difference between us and Jinns is our descriptions and we can't see them and they can fly. They usually eat out of garbage or drink from unhygienic water or fluids. But some are good and some are bad. Some sense they can sense a Jinn. This is a major reason why we may think a house is possessed but it could actually be a Jinn. Muslims usually call the Adhan when moving into a new home. 2000 yrs before the creation of Man, Jinn ruled the Earth. They had a war and Allah sent the Angels to destroy them so they split to remote Islands of the good Jinns was Iblis he was infact leader of Jinn. He was sent to the Heavens to dwell their in. it was until the creation of Man when the Angels had some questions Allah shut them down by revealing to them he know what they know not. Angels questioned why would you create something that will cause mischief in the land? But after that Iblis would go through Man's body and said he could overwhelm him that Man is weak and hollow. When Allah finally breathed life into Man and asked the Angels to bow down all did but Iblis because he was too proud and felt superior. When Allah asked Iblis Why don't you bow? His response was I am created of fire he is of clay I am better. Allah told him get down from here to hell you will dwell forever. But Iblis now a Shaitan asked for respite and vowed to bring Mankind with him to the fire. Allah granted him his respite and told him that he could never control his followers. So if you pay attention you'll get the moral to the story. Shaitan or Satan only wants to mislead us. He will allure us with all the fine things in life even our woman. The arrogance was and will be always there. The stereotypes will always be there and the racial profiling as well. Allah sent us Prophets and Messengers and pious people to guide those who want to be guided we all need guidance but don't want to follow that's our choice. Whom so ever Allah guides no one can misguide and whom so ever Allah leaves to stray no one can guide. So as we know Shaitan misled Adam and Eve so now we have to earn our way back to the paradise. We must realize Satan has no authority over us but his whispers. But understand we can repent as long as we alive. A co worker handed him a paper. This just in ladies 'n gentlemen.

The 2 officers that shot Jaquel Johnson were both gunned down this morning. Mr. Mckosky was gunned down at a local gas station in Long Island. The other Officer Schinsky was gunned down while preparing for a morning jog right in front of his crib. Both Officers were pronounced dead at the scene. A co worker handed him another sheet.

Oh wow he said as he read the paper. My God. Hey Angel check this out. A dodge intrepid with 5 unidentified assailants just burned an entire small town down. And guess what they did it in the same town as the slayings of the small family that were brutally murdered in a cowardly bias attack. They sprayed Black Power on the grass of the hideout where John Diggins was found hamstrung with his penis lodged in his mouth and severely burned. His cousin was found shot dead in the bathroom in their home. While the wife 'n kids found tied up and gagged watching the horrific events take place. Several stores were burned down, at least 50 people were hospitalized with severe burns, a proclaimed racial bar was firebombed along with the courthouse. Wow! Said 2Face. You see how the actions of 1 can cause a domino effect? This needs to stop. Something should be done about this before this country is in a race war. We're going on commercial folks holla back! 2Face's cell phone rang the call was restricted. He had a feeling about the call already. I'm glad to catch you at work. I asked you to stop the vigilante mess and to calm down your efforts. I know you are behind these grizzly attacks to send a message, now you got this whole country scared and in a uproar! Who the fuck is this and how I get the blame of something I have no knowledge of replied 2Face? You know who this is you bastard! You or someone close to you will pay dearly for this, take my word for it! Shh. 2Face jestured to Angel you recording this? She shook her head yes. So you threatening me asked 2Face? You sound like our current President, is this our President? The line went dead. The motherfucker hung up Angel. You got that though right? Yes she replied. Ok give me the tape. Matter of fact make a copy of it and mail it to this address don't use your Don't use your name. Hold that copy down until further notice. Angel please be careful. He wrote down a address and gave it to her. Matter of fact when you finish recording those tapes give me the original I'll hold it. When tonight's over we'll leave together for our own safety. 2Face what's going on she asked? The Government thinks I had something to do with the attacks in the small town I just read about. Shit she said. We back on the air.

Caller: How are you Mr. Face. Your right if we don't stop this it'll be a race war in our county said an Irish sounding fellow. Nobody is gonna stand behind and let their people get butchered and the cops aren't capable of stopping it.

2Face: You're absolutely right sir. Those were all hate crimes and horrific and idiotic and nobody should stand for it.

Caller: But there has to be a better way?

2Face: Sir you said something like nobodies gonna stand around and watch their people get butchered for no reason Right? Now me personally I don't agree with these attacks but when you start something heinous like that people do have a right to stand up for them selves. Maybe those butchers went to far but believe me there was a message sent and that is blacks have been the target of butchering by white supremacist for centuries, some people feel its time to stand up and fight back. Its sad that after all this country been through we still judge by the color of a man's skin. The sad thing is people respect violence. I got a bad rap in my days but people only respect that to slow em down, but I definitely don't condone these actions hell no! Caller: I definitely agree. People called in all day with their opinions commenting on the recent events that would go down in American history. People were definitely scared.

2Face scanned outside very carefully before him and Angel jumped in a cab she had called. They left the Manhattan studio and drove to the Bronx dropping her off first. Then 2Face had the cab drop him off on 222nd street 'n White Plains rd his old neighborhood. He chilled in the bodega right on that very corner with a old time Dominican named Ricardo. He used to look out for 2Face in his broke years right before his beloved Grandmother passed away. Poppy what up! 2Face screamed as he entered the store.

Oh my God C.D. how are ya bud shouted the old man? Just wanted to stop by and see what's up I never forget my people. Si, si said Poppy. 2Face rocked a black Champion hoodie under a Pelle leather with some blue Polo jeans. He looked like an average thug. He pulled out his check book, Poppy this should help you out after all you used to do for me.

Senior I can't take ya money you earn it pi. Hey don't be like that I just wanna give back it don't matter what you do with it ya family may need it please take it.

After he wrote the check he grabbed a soda and a bag of chips to grub on and walked around the corner. Mad cats was posted outside looking ready to start something. Normally this area would have been shut down but the riots brought a new look to the hood again. Nobody noticed 2Face walk up 223rd st. He walked to the bodega on 223rd 'n Barnes calling Tone. Yo son what's good ask 2Face? Yo son what up! Yelled Tone loud ass. We in the hood in front of Grandma house nigga come through! Nah homie, that's why I'm calling you listen bee get off the streets now. Son them boys gonna try something, right now I'm on the low my nigga. I want you, Mouse, Reef, 'n Budd off the streets. Tell Reef I said to call ock I got something special for ya'll too. Yo son niggas is wildin out here son! It's a no police zone out here! Niggas is bottling cop cars, shooting at em and it's happening up the South Bronx too, Chi-town, L.A., Philly and Detroit said Tone. Son we worked hard to get these streets cleaned up now niggas is wilding in our own neighborhoods get off the streets now! Do it Tone or I'm a have the brothers do it for me. What was done was done already people gotta fall back! Fuck that shit son! Fuck them crackers too! We here with it in the hood! Tone hung up. 2Face called Miraji, they Salaam each other. Yo what the fuck is going on yelled 2Face!

I'll tell you what is going on whoever ordered that hit and stunt in that small town created an uproar. Then someone ordered the hit on them 2 cops in retaliation that got the ghetto riled up. Then the protests in front of the precinct turned violent then the looting started. Have you been watching the news the last couple of hours? No but I will fire my reporter for not informing me of anything new. Listen said Miraji we gonna have to talk to the press tomorrow get with some leaders and work this out to squash this, this is crazy. They Salaam and both hung up, 2Face laughed it off.

CHAPTER 82

Hi Gloria!

Oh my God! Hey C.D.. How are you? I'm doing fine, and you? Oh I'm doing fine she replied. Ya know my daughter had a boy his name is Miguel, n he's seven. I'm still sorry about ya Grandma. Thanks for your support she lived a glorious life you know. Yeah so are you Mr. I'm rich 'n famous she snapped. What brings you back to the ghetto? Never left the ghetto, believe that! You watch the news she asked him?

No but I got the radio station so I know pretty much everything that goes on. I know it's a lot of riots. How's ya son doing?

Who Francis she replied? He in the house. I close in five minutes. Good I need a place to stay for the remainder of the night. Maybe we can hang out and catch up you can hear some of my wild stories, huh? You know you always welcome C.D. always welcome. Did you eat yet? Put them chips down, come. They caught up for about 2 hours eating and listening to 2Face tell Francis all his amazing and wild experiences. 2Face called his lawyer to inform him that he wanted to sell all his estates and cars he had registered. He knew his run in America was up.

Gloria had no idea she was harboring the most dangerous man in the world in her living room. 2Face placed a call to his main man Pete Nice. What up son, son! You need to stop this shit its getting bad real bad for our business. Hey thanks bud replied 2Face. Hey, hey this is what we do damn it! You're my boy I love ya but this is bad bud its gotta stop. You the only one who can stop it dude, please! I got you boy ya hear me? Yeah said Pete. Alright I'll holla said 2Face. 2Face slept gun in his grips. The time was 4:00 am when a phone call woke him up. 2Face was groggy answering the call. Yo son its me Mouse son. Tone dead son he whisper in the phone. He got killed in a drive by an hour ago. 2Face jumped up, what! The fuck you just say! Mouse was sniffling on the phone in a low voice, they killed homie. 1 You sure he dead? Yeah son.

It didn't sink in yet for 2Face memories of his boy flashed through his mind of everything they done together growing up together, he fell silent on the phone. Nah son, stop playing bee! Son I ain't fucking playing yelled Mouse! Where you at asked 2Face? The hospital son Brookdale son. Stay there son. 2Face hung up the phone sank in the couch and cried. He cried for ten minutes strait before he mustered up the courage to take Gloria's keys to her Volvo and leave her a $100,000 check then bounce. Oh he was hot now, somebody a lot of people he called Mouse back. Yo ya'll seen who did it? All we saw was a black limo out no where pull up open fire at us and skid off. Hit son twice in the face. 2Face hung up, still crying. Once he heard limo he already knew the Government was making a statement. Now it was his turn. He wanted to call Pete Nice but Pete was the one who shot the cop who was about to take his morning jog. He didn't want to over burden him. He knocked on Pete's door. It took Pete a minute to come to the door he was pissed and fuming. Bro what the fuck! How the fuck do you know where I live and why the fuck you at my doorstep? Calm down Pete I need a favor. Bro its almost 5 in the morning, my kids are sleep are you mad?

Pete I need some plastic explosives. What! You gotta be

fucking kidding me. I just bought this house a couple of months ago. I wanna be a free man better yet alive to enjoy it. You're my boy but ya fucking bugging! Listen Pete these pigs killed my boy! I want the fuckin explosives! Ok said Pete. Have a seat said Pete. He made a few phone calls and told 2Face to drive to Burnside'n Jerome ave in the Bronx and look inside the garbage on the downtown side. There will be a garbage bag full. Bro you got money? Can I get paid?

Pete I got you just relax! I can't give you a check right now but I can give you a nice payment just bare with me. I need $500,000 for the inconvenience! Got you bro. 2Face went and got the bag out of the garbage and drove a long ride contemplating to 100 Centre St. this was a daring act by him. He opened the bag which contained five explosive devices with instructions on how to use them. He casually crept to the garbage cans out front of 100 Centre St. and placed 2 explosives in one in each can. He then crept into the garage and placed 2 explosives underneath 2 squad cars. Most officers were either going through shift change or out in the field trying to contain the riots in the streets. To top it off it was early in the morning. The focus wasn't on downtown for that particular moment. He placed the final one in the car he drove directly in front of a parking meter rocking gloves and a face mask with shades his identity was sealed for the most part.

The explosives were well hidden it was around 7:00 am, lawyers and judges and D.A.'s were starting to file in. 2Face was late offering Fajr prayer, he offered it in the park next to the train station. He was careful not to touch anything he masked back up and gloved up he had one extra explosive that he went to place in the back off the building Pete Nice hooked him up. He had a remote control to detonate every single one of them at the same time he was gonna make a big statement. He hoped the $100,000 would keep Gloria's mouth shut. He had cleaned out the car for all identification ahead of time so nothing could trace him. Masked up he cause of the weather he hoped people would think he took off the license plate numbers and switched them in the Bronx no ties at all. Somehow unnoticed ha walked right to the train station, people were so busy filing in rushing they didn't noticed anything in particular. It was show time now they want to play he said to himself lets play ball. He made it to Chambers St. once the train came and he found a seat in the corner of the crowded train people reading their Wall Street Journals and newspapers nobody paid attention to man in the corner. The train was headed to downtown Brooklyn as soon as they made it to Borough Hall he hit the detonator on the remote. Boom! Boom, Boom, Boom, Boom! Huge explosions took place. Burning flesh and screams were heard from across the Brooklyn Bridge. The building shook and was rattling, the impact or the explosion almost crumbled the building. The C-4 broke every window and blazes of fire spread rapidly, it was shades of 9 The people inside were trapped. 2Face had also leaked a couple of gas tanks to further ignite things. People trapped inside were choking from smoke they inhaled and burning from the hot fire torching their skins. 2Face overheard a businessman who somehow got frequency; Oh God no somebody just attacked our Courthouse.

CHAPTER 83

2Face took the 2 train to Flatbush Ave. then jumped in a cab to the hospital. Did you hear the news asked the cabbie? Nah what happened? The Courthouse on 100 Centre St. just got bombed. You didn't hear the huge explosion sir? Nah get the fuck outta here! Yeah it blew up with people inside burning. Wow! Damn, could you drop me off right in the emergency exit. He paid the cab and went in through the emergency entrance. Excuse me nurse? Yes, may I help you? She had a African accent that was deep. Wild people filled it up with all types of injuries, Brooklyn was way out of control.

My friend Anthony Gaines was shot tonight. He said in a low voice he passed away. I'm here to see his family.

You must be a friend of the family then? Yes I am Miss.

Well he was brought in around 3:30 am. He died at the scene, I'm sorry.

I accept that, but where are they located? The 3rd floor in the coroners department. She looked up he was gone. He was on the 3rd floor moving fast he seen Tone's Mother and sister first. Then he spotted Mouse and Tone's brothers Alec and Vince,

Bud, and Reef. They all sat on benches across the 1 main office of the nurses, this is where the family comes to identify the body.

Awe man! 2Face shouted as he peered through the glass to see his boy stretched out bloody and naked like a slab of meat to be butchered and processed.

I'm sorry he said to Mommy with tears in his eyes. I'm so sorry. Mouse broke down again and in unison Bud and Reef broke down as well shedding. Tone was the coolest nigga ever bee said 2Face! Son I just talked to son on the phone before I fell asleep. I told him to tell yaw to get the fuck off the streets. Son ain't listen he whispered. Yo I believe the Government did it. They out to get me and they said they'll get someone close to me. They trying to stop the movement, but the movement can't stop take my word for it! Their focus shifted to NY1 news. This just in about ½ hour ago 100 Centre St. was attacked by a series explosions sources say it could of been one bomb or 2 but forensics are just going through the rubble to search for clues. The blast killed 6 and injured 25 severely. Luckily a lot of the force were out in the field and a lot of civilians weren't in the building yet but citizens are wondering if Al Qaida is in our very streets. The Mayor is issuing a statement in just a few minutes, there are no suspects to this point. Also the race riots are getting more intense all staring with the killing of a young boy in Brooklyn and then the bias crime in South Carolina, then the retaliation by blacks since. The K.K.K. issued this statement; "you people don't want to start something you can't finish." The President is going to talk to some civil rights leaders in ordered to bring these riots to the end and be peaceful. Carolina Tatalini Eyewitness news. The KKK is the least of our worries, they stay in them little ass towns they don't have the guts to come and hit our big city. Son it don't matter this situation is way outta of control way outta hand. I'll have a fill in for you today, so don't work said 2Face, matter of fact lets go. Son family here his, wifey here let them get some quality time. This place is crawling with police anyways. They gave their condolences to son family and began to get on elevator and caught it to the first floor.

Son call a cab Reef said 2Face. Sharif was dialing the number, 2Face noticed 2 black vans had pulled up in front of the hospital entrance with their blinking lights on. Reef hang the phone up said 2Face and use the pay phone to call Miraji so he can pick ya'll up.

Reef called Miraji, once he got him on the phone he passed it to 2Face.

Miraji want to holla at you. Yo the government is trying to get at us they shot and killed one of my peoples said 2Face! I heard replied Miraji. I'm a send my homies through the back door of the emergency exit come get em now! This is operation escape! Got you Ock. He hung up the phone. Yo yaw I want ya'll to go through the emergency exit there is gonna be a car waiting for yaw in 5 minutes so hurry up. Yo where you going asked Reef?

I'm a catch up with yaw believe that! Just make moves. When they started to head to the emergency exit 2Face walked out the front door. As soon as he touched the pavement 3 huge muscle bound men jumped out in business suits reaching. A deep voice yelled the President would like to speak to you asap.

Over my dead body I answer to no one said 2Face and kept walking. So be it said one of the men and pulled out a 40 caliber and let off a shot. Luckily 2Face used his periphial vision and dipped behind a car. 3 more shots rang out whizzing off the ground. 2Face was creping low trying to escape when the second van pulled up. 2Face moved quick jumping over a ford escorts hood as more shots rang out from the second van. 2Face fired shots at the vans window in vain. A huge man was creeping 3 cars down from 2Face behind a range rover. 2Face saw him and fired before he did hitting him in the neck. Man down 2Face heard one of the men on a radio. Then all of a sudden 2 more men were creeping. Now 2Face was stuck behind the last car and a 10 foot wall. There was no escape the other 2 men open fire as they let off at least 18 shots a piece turning the car into Swiss cheese. 2Face waiting patiently spotted one of the men to his left and fired 4 shots at him hitting him in the shoulder. Awe the man screamed in pain from the burning sensation in his shoulder. 3 more shots were fire at 2Face all missing. 2Face thought to him self either these men underestimated him or they weren't professional. Now the van was coming at him with speed now at 40mph. He peeped it and made a daring jump for the wall hoping the third man couldn't get off a good shot he was halfway over the wall when the escort was crushed. The third man loaded a rocket launcher aimed at 2Face's back he clicked back as 2Face near the end of his reign looked back thinking to himself its over La Ilaha Illalah 6shots rang out then there was an explosion.

CHAPTER 84

Karrin was safely in Finland holding 2Face mother's hand both crying at the horrific events over the last week. This just in as breaking news said the eyewitness anchor. Hip Hop icon and entrepreneur 2Face was reported to involved in a massive shootout and explosion at Brookdale Hospital with unidentified men involving 2 black vans. One caucasion man is pronounced dead at the scene. A bullet ridden black van which reamed a ford escort where the explosion took place is where police found a driver dead. No other bodies were recovered. Sources don't know why or what were the motives behind this and don't have a clue if 2Face aka Cory Jackson is alive or dead at this point. 2Face head of one of the richest charity funds in history was very controversial in his efforts to clean up the streets did provide more safety and a bright future for young Americans and also provided millions of jobs for a once reeling economy. Police and fire men are still digging through rubbage but so far no bodies were found. We will be back with more details Carloina Tatalini Channel 7 Eyewitness News. Karrin was crying and sobbing hard now. 2Face mother surprisingly smile with no worries at all. Calm and collective she told Karrin. Calm down baby. Rubbing her back I know my son he is a survivor and he is always a step ahead even in defeat he finds a way out, I know he is still alive I can feel it. A mother can feel her child's presence and my boy he is on the run. He'll be alright, I know my son. You'll soon see he is a survivor.